The Gopher &
The Erstwhile Wizard

J.L. Rallios

BLACK ROSE
writing™

To Juliett,
J.L. Rallios
11/5/16

ISBN: 978-1-61296-493-5

PUBLISHED BY BLACK ROSE WRITING

www.blackrosewriting.com

Printed in the United States of America

Suggested retail price $17.95

The Gopher & The Erstwhile Wizard is printed in Cambria

Dedicated to Laura, the love of my life.

Acknowledgments

Whether directly or indirectly, it took many people to help me write this book, and for whom I am forever grateful. My father, Richard, first instilled in me a love of stories by simply reading the first page of Tarzan to me when I was young. (He never did finish it, but I did many years later.) My mother, Carol, fostered my imagination through making a loving home, by providing great encouragement, and by living a life that is an example to my own faith. They both instilled a sense of commitment that helped see me through the completion of this story. My wife, Laura, and our son, Josh, spent many hours editing this story as well as putting up with me. Most importantly, she almost literally made this book possible with the few words "to either write it or quit talking about it." My mother-in-law, Raylene Morris, also spent many hours in invaluable editing, and who has also been a great encourager. My pastor, Kenneth Priest, challenged my thinking and inspired my imagination almost as much as the writings of C.S. Lewis did, which he had introduced me to when I was a teen. (It is this influence that I credit my love for fantasy.) There have been many others to whom I owe a debt of thanks: Reagan Rothe, creator of Black Rose Writing; Teri Tiner Ridlon, a fellow author who helped edit the back cover; and the other authors on the Black Rose Writing Facebook page for their encouragement and suggestions. I know that I'm leaving someone out, and for that I apologize, but this acknowledgment would not be complete if I did not include thanking my Lord and Savior who has taught me that the greatest achievement is not the writing of a book or even having a great family (such as I have), but in knowing Him who gives life true meaning and purpose.

The Gopher &
The Erstwhile Wizard

Chapter One

In days long ago, when stories of wonder and magic were turning into legends, but had not yet become fairy tales, something happened that did not seem so wonderful, nor did it seem so spectacularly magical. Some thought that it was because it had happened to a gopher, one of those pesky, thieving rodents that farmers and gardeners hate and will go to great extents to eliminate. Little did they know that, if they had done so to this particular gopher, a great evil would not have been averted and an even greater good would have been missed.

If you had seen him, however, you would not have blamed them for their ignorance. He did not look different from any other gopher. He measured 8 inches long – or 10 if one counted his short stubby tail – and three inches wide, except in the middle where his paunchy stomach gained half an inch. His cheeks, when filled with extra food, nearly matched his stomach. He looked at the world through almond-shaped black eyes, heard it through ears that were almost completely set within the sides of his narrow furry head, and sniffed at it through a nose, the tip of which was shaped like a small inverted black triangle. Besides his curved claws and two long front teeth, they were the only parts of him that were not covered in grayish brown fur.

He did not look special simply because he wasn't special. Seldom is anyone born special, but it's what happens by the choices they make along the way. For this gopher it began when he ate a carrot from a garden. There was magic in it, though it looked no different from any other carrot just as he looked no different from any other gopher. The tip of the carrot, which was like an orange stalactite sticking down out of the roof of his tunnel, certainly did not smell as if it held any magical qualities. Even when he bit into it, it did not taste better than any other carrot he had ever eaten; although the moment he swallowed it, something indescribably wonderful entered into him that was greater than anything that he had ever experienced before. Yet the feeling that it gave him wasn't a taste at all, because with taste, one always wants more (that is, if it is delicious), and with this, he needed nothing more. It could be called a peaceful feeling, which nothing could disturb, though it was not like the peacefulness of slumber. In fact, he never felt more awake and alive. It was better than any feeling no matter how big or grand or satisfying or rapturous or thrilling or awesome. It was more than all of those feelings rolled into one, for it was even better than life itself.

The Wondrous Feeling seemed to overflow into everything around him which definitely set it apart from taste since he forgot about the carrot altogether as he took in his surroundings. The dimness of the tunnel seemed suddenly comforting, and the loam of the earth smelled rich and sweet, the coolness in the air felt pleasant, and even the silence was peaceful.

Comfort... rich... sweet... pleasant... peaceful... these were the kinds of things that gophers cannot comprehend, much less appreciate – that is, for gophers who haven't eaten a magic carrot. This new comprehension did not stop with the awareness of his surroundings, for suddenly he also became sharply conscious of his own furry body. Nobody ever thinks of a gopher's body as being anything special, but at that moment he felt towards it a sense of wonderfulness that made him marvel to think that it belonged to him. All of these discoveries to him would be like to us discovering a new color or the taste of chocolate for the first time. Actually, it was like both all at once. His surroundings had not changed, nor was his body any different than it had been before. The difference was that he really saw them more truly for what they were.

Suddenly, however, the peacefulness of silence was intruded upon by sounds coming from above. At first he thought they came from a wolf because he had bitten one on the nose once and it had made whimpering noises, but these particular sounds were different than any animals that he could think of. Many creatures are born curious, and sometimes in their curiosity (and foolishness) they even forget their animal fear. Normally, however, this particular gopher was so far from being the curious type that anything that was unusual would often send him retreating into the security and sameness of his dark tunnels. In fact, it had taken a week of hiding to get over the wolf incident. After eating the magic carrot, though, for the first time in his life he became curious. He sensed in those sounds an emotion that was like pain but still different, a deeper pain. Since the world was so wonderful, it struck him odd that something in it could sound that painful.

It was his curiosity, though, that almost got him killed, because he forgot his natural animal caution as he dug upwards to those sounds, which happened to be near the spot that the magic carrot had occupied. When he poked his head out, however, what he saw did little to satisfy his curiosity, even though the source of those sounds was right before him. It was that of an old man with a frowning mouth framed by a short, scruffy beard that was as gray as his head, upon which sat a brown, short-brimmed hat. Tears flowed from his brown eyes that were set in a mass of wrinkles and overhung by bushy gray eyebrows. He was on his knees, his shoulders shaking up and down as both of his hands seemed to be choking the handle of a spade in front of him. Yet this was not how the gopher saw him, for he had never seen a man before, and his eyesight was so poor, being used to darkness, that what he perceived was a gigantic, blurry figure with a strange scent.

The gopher almost stared for too long, because suddenly the man exclaimed, "You filthy thief!" Of course, the gopher did not need to understand what the words meant (or that they were even words at all) to know that he was in danger. His instinct came alive lightning-fast, which was equaled in speed by his quick reaction, with which all healthy young rodents are gifted. He ducked in time before the spade could take off his head. Swiftly he scurried backwards almost as fast as he could go forwards.

When he reached the tunnel below, it was still not far enough away to suit him. He sped as fast as his four short legs could take him through the darkness. The tunnel was part of a maze of passages and burrows, most of them intersecting and looping each other, while others were dead-ends or led to entrances to the forest above. The gopher knew every inch and he unerringly and without thought threaded his way speedily through them. He stopped at last when he reached the deepest warren, which was about three feet underground. It was the same one in which he had hid for a week from that wolf. Like that last time, when he came to a stop, his breathing and the pounding in his ears and chest seemed in time with the uncontrollable trembling of his entire body. And, like before, the pounding gradually slowed as the trembling became more manageable and less frequent and his breathing shallower. Finally, as his energy was expended, exhaustion overcame him, but, instead of dreaming of packs of wolves (or angry, screaming giants), he had a wonderful dream that danced tantalizingly on the edge of his consciousness, but which faded away upon waking. Try as he might, he could not recall it.

He discovered something else to preoccupy him after he awoke. It was a newfound restlessness. There was no way that he could hole up in his tunnels for a week like he had done before. It wasn't exactly because he was braver or because his fear was less real. It was quite the opposite of the Wondrous Feeling; it was called Emptiness. Some may call it boredom or restlessness or discontentment, but perhaps they are just descriptions of what Emptiness does to a person, like the symptoms of a disease rather than the disease itself. How this came about was that the Wondrous Feeling had created a place in his heart, which now felt like a vacuum. Even more than that, those delightful things seemed to be calling him from the outside world, inciting him to discover them anew, even in the face of the risks involved. Hiding in the darkness of the burrow began to feel as if he were hiding as much from the delights as he was from the dangers. The rodent-side of him, however, continued to resist this new feeling.

Two days later that side lost. He was no longer able endure the Emptiness or ignore the lure of the outside world. As soon as he started through the tunnels, though, he didn't feel quite so empty inside. And when that happened, the fear returned. He also became aware of another more familiar emptiness. It was called hunger. In no time he found roots not far from where he had been hiding. They were dry and old but his famished state made them taste like the best he'd ever had; so delicious, in fact, that he took it for the Wondrous Feeling itself. The food also served to distract him from that Empty feeling as well as to forget about the outside world. When he had finished eating, though, the Emptiness returned, but this time he mistook it for hunger, which he thought could only be fixed by eating more. He dug high and low for more roots and found himself eating more than usual that day, long after his hunger had been sated. In fact, the more he ate the less wondrous he felt – and, ironically, the less he was able to stop himself from eating. He even reached the point of absolute misery, which comes from stuffing oneself. Thankfully, he simply was not *able* to look for more food, even if he could bring himself to wanting to.

Not surprisingly, he found it difficult to sleep, but, as he tried to think of a way to escape his misery, he remembered the Wondrous Feeling and more than half doubted that it had been real after all. He actually felt that he had been "let down." This made him even more miserable, so much so that the Emptiness – which was definitely real – was unbearable to the point that he didn't want to live. Then he remembered the beauties of the outside world and he determined with iron resolve that tomorrow he'd go have a look. Oddly, it was that resolution, and not the cessation of his stomach pains, that gave him peace and enabled him at last drift off.

By the time he awoke in the morning, it was close to midday. He immediately remembered the misery of the day before and, subsequently, of the promise to himself. He set out at once to keep it. He did not take the shortest route, however, for that way brought him close to where he had eaten that carrot and where, most importantly, he had found danger. Instead, he took another route and, after a little digging to clear the way, he poked his nose through a little used hole.

It opened into the deep shadows of the forest, but what he saw of it delighted his dim-sighted eyes and reaffirmed the existence of that Wondrous Feeling. Light falling through the canopy of tangled limbs overhead splashed the surroundings in swatches of colors – browns, greens, yellows, and reds –which he had never paid attention to before, and now he wondered why he hadn't. More than just the colors, he delighted in the variety and strangeness of everything from the low-sweeping pine branches just above the hole, to the unique shapes, sizes, and looks of each tree. Even the scattered patches of thick prickly undergrowth held more undiscovered beauties and delights than they did of danger, at least to his mind. Sweetest of all, an unseen bird somewhere above twilled a piercing flow of sounds that made him forget about himself. The notes, sweet and lively, seemed to promise him even greater beauties and joys, though he wondered if anything could be as beautiful as that song. By comparison, he felt small and insignificant and vulnerable, but that hardly mattered. He was overwhelmed with something greater than himself. Somehow that just made it that much sweeter and more piercing. Without thinking, he came out of his hole, drawn by both music and beauty. Craning his neck, he searched the branches above for its source with his eyes and then, unconsciously, he moved out from the shelter of the branches for a better view.

This was to be the second nearly fatal time in which he ignored his natural animal caution. A twig snapped somewhere to his left where also a trace of a scent reached him, contrasting against the fragrance of the pines and elms like a sour note in a symphony. Instantly the spell of enchantment burst like a bubble and he knew three things all at the same time. One, it was the smell of a bobcat. Two, he was now too far from his barrow's entrance to reach it safely in time, and, three, he had very little hope of surviving. These realizations led him to do something that was almost instantaneous: He scurried as fast as his little four legs could take him in the opposite direction.

A cattish yowl went up behind him and the crunching, cracking, and snapping spurred him even faster. Only the rodent's small size saved him for the moment, because it enabled him to dodge quickly in and out, over and under, the thickly tangled undergrowth and low-lying branches of the forest, while the much larger size of his pursuer did not. He knew that he'd be killed by a single branch tripping him up, or stumbling in a hole, or if he took one wrong dead-end turn. He had no choice, but to dart this way and that in moments of split decision, because any hesitation would be just as fatal.

Just behind him, much closer than he hoped, the cat yowled again, this time in a shrill of frustration as it wrestled and wended its ways through the forest's wild growth. Twice he felt the brush of a paw touch his tail or the scrape of a claw on his back. This did not inspire much confidence in his speed or in his hope of living for more than a few moments longer - if even that long.

Then he really knew that he didn't have a chance when suddenly he dashed unexpectedly into a large clearing. Any moment the cat would also be free from the forest, so he ran as fast as his four legs could take him towards a huge odd-shaped thing at the other side of the clearing. It was wide and peaked on top with a flat ridge. It was unlike any tree, boulder, or hill that he had ever seen. Normally he would not have run toward such a thing, not knowing what it was, for his animal caution would have highly suspected anything different as being dangerous. Yet, when he saw it, something beyond his rodent instincts told him that safety lay in its direction. If only he could reach it –

His thought was interrupted when the bobcat emerged. The gopher did not dare to see how close it was behind him as he gave it one last all-out effort, shooting across the level ground. It was not enough, nor did he make it farther than another foot when a dark shadow suddenly blocked out the waning sunlight above him. It was the bobcat springing for the kill. Suddenly he froze as terror held him in a vise of dread expectation. He did not have enough time to start to tremor much less to curl his legs defensively under him before the bobcat's sharp teeth pierced his back, sending fire-hot streaks of pain through him. Vaguely he felt himself being flung about helplessly in its jaws and its sharp claws digging into his neck and shoulders. Then he entered into blackness where thankfully the pain could not touch him.

Chapter Two

It was his flight towards that odd-shaped structure that helped save the gopher's life. What he saw was really a cottage, but what he didn't see was its owner outside of it. He was a hermit and the very same old man who had tried to remove the gopher's head with his spade. Oddly, though, this time it was the man and his spade that came to his rescue. He had thrown many things in his long life, but nothing as ordinary as a spade. Its design for digging would seem to make it an awkward implement for hurling through the air, but somehow he threw it like one who was an expert and the spade flew so smoothly and straight that it was as if it had been meant for nothing else. With one blow, the bobcat was knocked lifeless and the body of the gopher dropped from its jaws and plopped on the ground.

The hermit did not react as surprised at the success of his throw as most would have. Rather, after jumping about almost like a young man would, he said with a grin, "Who would have thought that I'd feel this way at saving a rodent?" But he sobered when he saw the gopher's motionless body. He stroked and plucked at his short, scruffy beard as if he were trying to stretch length into it. "If it *is* dead, maybe it's not the same one anyway," he murmured to himself.

Then the gopher's tubby stomach rose and his left eyelid quivered, which was followed by his back leg stretching;

movements so faint that he would not have seen them if the hermit had not been closely looking. Carefully he scooped up the gopher and, as if carrying a great but delicate treasure, he disappeared into the cottage.

•   •   •

For the next three days, the old man tended the unconscious gopher by applying a foul smelling concoction to his wounds and carefully pouring tiny amounts of water down his throat through a funnel. The rodent was kept snug in a little bed, strapped to it by two strips of cloth. Constructing the bed from odds and ends in the little work shed behind the cottage had been the last bit of real work he'd done, for most of his chores around the cottage had gone neglected so that he could tend to the rodent.

When the gopher finally gained consciousness and his eyes opened, the creature discovered that he could not move, though the two strips would not have kept him there if he hadn't been so weak and pain-ridden in the first place. Instead he could only just lie there, shivering and looking wild-eyed around him.

It was the strangest sort of place. It seemed too confining to be above ground but yet too spacious and airy to be under it, especially since sunlight filtered through the chinks around the door, the boarded up window, and down the unlit fireplace. It illuminated enough for him to see an interior that was far too roomy to be comfortable. The smell of the ointment on his back made it seem even stranger and, therefore, more menacing.

Above him a voice spoke: "Don't worry. That cat won't return."

As reassuring as the words were obviously intended to be, however, to the gopher they were just strange sounds – strange because they weren't the typical noises of hissing, mewing, barking, growling, but yet they weren't altogether unfamiliar. Where or when had he heard something like them before? Then he recognized the face belonging to the same large blurry giant that had threatened him. Weakness and pain had numbed most of his senses already, except for fear. It welled up within, all the more because he felt so vulnerable.

"My name is Menlow," the giant said and offered his finger, which the gopher managed to bite in return despite his bonds, proving that fear was stronger than pain and weakness put together.

He closed his eyes, instinctively expecting the same kind of violence in return. Instead, however, he heard something new: laughter. Not knowing what it meant, except that it could not be good, he kept his eyes closed.

"I forgot," Menlow said, nursing his finger, "I, too , am the enemy, but my gopher-killing days are over. I promise...Here, my little friend, from now on you don't have to steal."

The gopher smelled something besides the pungent ointment that his fur was slathered with that was familiar and reminded him of... Opening his eyes, he saw that the giant was proffering a turnip within less than an inch from his nose (this time with his fingers safely distant). He was too confused and frightened to be hungry, though. The old hermit ended up just laying it there, and then he stood up slowly, unfolding stiff limbs with grunts, which unsettled the rodent even more.

"Well, Gopher, maybe you'll want it for later," he said. "It's high time for me to be about tending to my own needs."

It was the first time he was called Gopher and, as plain as it was, it stuck and became his name thereafter. Of course, Gopher was unaware of being named, but at the time he became aware of something else. It occurred to him that when the giant had offered the turnip, he had not meant it for harm. This dawning fact eventually allowed his appetite to return, but only by slow degrees. In fact, by the time he began to nibble at the turnip, Menlow had already started a fire, had cooked his porridge over it, and was now eating it at the table. The more Gopher ate, the less he became afraid, and when he had finished the root, he actually found himself more concerned about getting something else to eat than about his own danger.

Over the course of the next two days this lessening of fear

continued to the point that when at last he was well enough to escape his bonds, he did not flee the cottage or even try to hide, though he had the opportunity. Menlow's back was turned. He was placing some wood on the fire, talking away to himself like all hermits do. All Gopher had to do was to scramble up on the hermit's bed, move quietly over to its foot, hop on the stool nearby, then on to the table and out the window. It was not the lack of fear, though, that kept him from attempting it, but rather it was the man's talking that stayed him, for suddenly he realized that they weren't *just* sounds. He had no idea what else could they have been, but there was something tantalizing about them that drew his curiosity. This time his curiosity did not get him in trouble.

The moment for complete stealth and escape was lost when the hermit turned and looked at him with raised eyebrows. Then, scratching at his smooth jaw as if he expected to find a beard (having shaved just that morning), he smiled and went on talking: "Good to see your strength returning, Gopher. And that you are still here. Good, good; maybe there is some hope after all. If you don't scurry away, how about a bowl of stew?"

Gopher stayed, but he kept both his distance from, and his eyes on, the hermit while the old man cut up the vegetables and meat and put them in a pot. He also kept trying to decipher the man's ongoing one-way conversation. He was tempted to change his mind about staying when the old man left the door open as he carried a large pail outside. Menlow, upon returning with water, looked at him with surprise and then smiled broadly.

"Good! Yes, very good! Still here. Now for a real test: if my cooking won't drive you away, nothing will!"

Laughter followed, but this time Gopher recognized it as something positive and the recognition felt like the exuberance of a miner striking gold. It certainly lessened his fear all the more – and, eventually, so did the stew, which wasn't great for those who have tasted good stew before. For Gopher, though, it was delicious and unlike anything he had ever eaten. On that first bite he forgot his fear – that is, until Menlow bent down to pour half a ladle more into Gopher's bowl. Even so, the rodent only backed up far enough to feel safe.

Such careful boundaries he maintained the rest of the week; Gopher watching and listening from a distance, always ready to flee at any unsettling event, but never getting more than a few feet away. It occurred to him at one point that he did not have anywhere to flee *to*. Unlike any gopher that had lived before or would live after him, he found that dark tunnels no longer appealed to him and that companionship was better than the security that the underground provided. Even at night, when the cottage was at its most frightening with the mysterious noises and shifting shadows, Menlow's snores and tossing about comforted him with its unique sense of security.

Yet there was another type of discomfort at night that Menlow could not help. It was the hard wood floor that Gopher slept on. He avoided his little bed. He did not know why, but whenever he looked at it, a shiver would threaten to course through him like an earthquake. For some reason it was worse when Menlow tried to encourage him to lay on it. Gopher would hide under the hermit's own bed for hours until the shivers went away.

Then one night Menlow solved the sleeping problem. He simply removed the restraining straps from the bed while trying to make it look more attractive for the rodent. It was then Gopher realized that all along he had been afraid of being tied up again! The self-discovery – and the thought of being able to sleep comfortably – gave him such joy and relief that, as he settled into his little bed, he started laughing, which sounded like a series of high-pitched coughs.

"Are you all right?" Menlow said, but his consternation, as he watched and rubbed his chin, slowly faded as his eyes brightened with understanding. "So you didn't like those straps, eh? Now you can forget all about them, okay?"

Menlow threw them out the window with a dramatic flourish,

and then he chuckled, which was soon followed up with another and then anther until it was full-fledged laughter. Gopher, who was still laughing, thought that he had never felt happier. (Of course, that was only because he had forgotten about the Wondrous Feeling.) It was the beginning of a mutual friendship, which also meant that it was the beginning of a great many other things.

Chapter Three

"Now you might not want to do that, Gopher," Menlow warned, almost two weeks later. The tone in his voice, however, did not convey enough of a warning, so the rodent went ahead, unknowingly, and reached for the edge of the plate over his head.

Crash!

Gopher managed to dodge in time as the wooden plate fell off the table, all the vegetables on it scattering nearly to the farthest regions of the wooden-planked floor; it was not a large cottage so that was not saying much. Nevertheless, it was amazing the places the peas and diced carrots could find to hide in. It took Menlow some time to find and gather them all back on the plate, though the potatoes and turnips were not so difficult.

"It's a good thing you're not particular about dirt on your food – and that this plate is of wood. You know I don't have too many of them, but then you probably don't know that." he said. "Now let's try again, Gopher. I'll put it back where it was... Try to find a better way to get to the food."

The rodent understood without knowing the words. Leaning back on his hind paws, Gopher raised up to where his nose nearly reached the plate that was overhanging the edge of the wood-planked table. A week ago he could not have reached so far; he had grown to nearly twice the size and weight of most gophers.

And he was more than twice as intelligent. As he studied the edge of the plate, he cocked his head and studied Menlow who had retreated to his stool near the fireplace. Then he also considered carefully his immediate surroundings. After a moment, he made his move in a most deliberate fashion: Leaning with all his weight, he shoved one of the legs of the stool away from the table, and then he did the same to the other. Going back and forth to each leg, he managed to move the chair a little at a time. After about six inches, the legs slid against a slightly raised floor plank, and he could not budge it any farther. He did some more studying and made up his mind that it was enough. He leapt on to the seat of the chair and in the same motion sprang from it to the wall, against which he pushed off and upward with his hind legs, twisting as he did so. He landed with more than half of his body on the edge of the table, which was a good thing since his fat stomach would have dragged him down. With quick scurrying motions, using his upper body and front paws, he wiggled the rest of the way on to the table and then shook himself as if he had just come out of a bath. Using his claws and also his teeth clamping on its edge, he carefully worked the plate until it was no longer overhanging the edge. Then he ate.

Menlow's mouth had fallen open from the very first of the performance, but still nothing came out at first as he watched the gopher eating like any other rodent, with a combination of voraciousness and cautiousness. Gopher paused from time to time to peer around him, though he did not look at Menlow as somebody he ought to be cautious about. At last the hermit said, "Well done! You learned from your mistake. Very clever," and then muttered to himself, "and how rare."

If the hermit had known the full truth, though, he would have felt even more pleasure and pride. Gopher had not only moved the plate in fear of knocking the food to the floor, but he had done it also in consideration of Menlow himself, for he remembered how much work the man went to in cleaning it up the first time.

Yet there were other accomplishments by which Gopher showed his consideration (as well as talents and intelligence) that were more obvious. Every morning Gopher made his bed and throughout the day would do some housekeeping. The former he did so by using his teeth to pull at the edges of his blanket (a small square of fur) and tucking its edges in at the sides with his claws. For housekeeping, he swept as much of the floor as he could with a "broom," which Menlow had made by tying a bundle of straws together with a string in the middle. He also retrieved small objects like forks and buttons that Menlow accidentally dropped from time to time. In the garden he was the most helpful by digging trenches and eating weeds (which he found were not as tasty as they had once been).

Unfortunately, that was almost all that his paws would enable him to do. Mostly he just watched the hermit and tried to copy him whenever his size, shape, and his claws allowed him to. He even began walking upright on his hind legs and found after a while that the discomfort disappeared altogether, especially since his body changed to accommodate the new posture. Walking on all four, though, still proved the easiest and fastest.

It was this busyness that helped Gopher become increasingly accustomed to his new life above ground. Although he continued to keep a distance from Menlow, now it had gone from being a safe distance to a comfortable one. It was not because the hermit still worried him, but rather it was his size that made Gopher feel so small and vulnerable. Over all, though, he felt quite contented.

One morning, however, a change happened that set his contentment on edge – and which ultimately changed everything for Gopher. There had been no clue that forewarned the change just as there had been no clouds in the pale blue sky. Leaves innocently rustled in a pleasantly cool breeze and the birds were melodically chirping in the branches of the trees that edged the clearing. Gopher idly enjoyed them from the windowsill that Menlow had built for him.

It began when the hermit returned from the stream, carrying two water jars instead of one. Gopher only vaguely wondered about it. One jar he set on the stool next to the fire; the other he took back outside. The rodent knew that he would use it for the regular watering of the furrowed rows of vegetables (which Gopher had dug) in the garden. As usual, the rodent watched, and when

Menlow returned, the rodent turned on the windowsill to watch the hermit.

"Top of the morning to you, too," Menlow said. "I've got a surprise for you, but you'll have to wait. I'll be back before you know it. I could just tell you, of course; you probably won't understand me anyway, but why take the chance and ruin the surprise?" He laughed.

Then he went to the wood pile in the corner of the room and drew out a stout branch and did a very strange thing with it. He plunged half of the stick into the water jar on the stool and immediately stuck the dripping end into the flames long enough so that when he pulled it out, the stick was a smoldering torch. He left soon after, but not soon enough, for almost instantly it filled the cottage with noxious smoke that burned Gopher's lungs, stung his eyes, and made him sneeze. He turned and saw, through tears, that Menlow was already out of sight, though leaving a smoky trail that led in the opposite direction of the stream and up the slope where the woods seemed thickest. He was sure that it was the same area where the bobcat had chased him.

He might have shivered at the memory if he wasn't so puzzled. Gopher watched for his imminent return, while wondering what the smoldering torch was for. After watching a few clouds coming into view, he realized that the morning was approaching noon and decided to keep himself busy until his friend's return. Tending to his bed first, he decided to make a perfect job of it. With meticulous care, he tucked in, and smoothed out, the fur patch, but upon surveying his work, his pleasure diminished when he realized that Menlow still hadn't returned.

His friend's absence, casting a shadow of concern over him, got him pondering the hermit's parting words while he set to sweeping the floor. It had been almost a week since he had given up on wondering what the strange sounds meant since trying to figure them out was difficult and gave him such a headache. Giving up on deciphering those sounds had resulted in instant relief and a new sense of freedom. Furthermore, Menlow's talk became like music without the lyrics, which he was perfectly happy to live with – until now. Some instinct told him that what he had been told before the hermit had left had been important.

As he thought and thought to try to remember and understand what Menlow had said before leaving, he also swept and swept. Around the bed and table, and then under them, he herded dust and breakfast crumbs down through the gaps between the floor boards. He usually avoided the vicinity of the fire where he could never feel safe from the unexpected little cinders popping out. Now, however, he thought about risking it because he saw some cold ashes on the floor in front of it that needed to be cleaned up and, besides, it did not seem risky since the fire seemed to be dying out...

The fire.

Something about the fire bothered him. It was smoldering much like Menlow's stick had been, and he stared at the dying embers, thinking... and then he got it! Menlow should have been back by now to tend it.

The hermit *never* would have let it die out – especially on a day like this, he thought, when he noticed for the first time that the wind was whistling outside and there was a pattering of rain on the roof. Quickly scampering up to the windowsill, he saw with surprise that the idyllic morning had turned into a stormy one. Thick dark clouds and a chill wind promised more than just a splattering of rain drops. He tried to reassure himself by remembering that whenever it had rained, Menlow always came in from whatever he was doing – and, given the look of this storm, he would come in quickly. He waited expectantly like before, but, unlike before, as the minutes ticked away Menlow did not appear.

The final convincing proof that something was wrong came when Gopher's stomach rumbled. Menlow never would be gone so long to let that happen! Yet it was more than just proof; hunger gave him an awful glimpse of what life would be like if the hermit *never* returned. Finding his own food was the least of his fears, however. The thought of being lonely, of never seeing his friend again, was intolerable. Although chiefly imaginary, it was his first taste of grief.

Suddenly, when it was unlooked for, the hermit's parting words

25

popped up in his memory, and they came complete with perfect understanding. Instead of rejoicing, though, or appreciating the breakthrough, he felt deeply troubled because of Menlow's phrase, "I'll be back before you know it." It meant he hadn't intended to have gone for long, and it confirmed, too late, what Gopher already knew: Something had happened to his friend. Understandably, a panic swept over him: He must do something, anything, to help him!

Gopher left the cottage by jumping out of the window. It was the first time he had gone out by himself since the day he nearly died in the jaws of the bobcat. But he had no thoughts for bobcats or for the prickly rose bush in which he landed. It hardly proved an impediment to him, nor did he notice their piercing thorns as he brushed past them. He was heedless of even the puddles, the increasing rainfall, and the wind gusts in the clearing as he rushed in the same direction that Menlow had gone. The only thing that got his attention was the sudden realization that, upon entering the woods, he did not know where to go next. Then he saw a path to his left that led into deeper shadows but not to any surety that Menlow would be found anywhere along it. Yet, because he saw no other path, he took it, though with very little hope. That deep sense of loss quickly seemed to becoming an unavoidable reality – a reality that he was more afraid of than the thunder and lightning that erupted overhead.

The sudden intensity of the storm threatened to erode what hope he had left. How could Menlow survive this? Still, he fiercely pressed on, against despair as much as against the wind and the rain. He didn't care if he died trying. It would be better than to live alone again, he thought, but just then sounds reached him, even though it was impeded by the far-off thunder, the whooshing of the wind in his ears, and the torrential pattering of rainfall. It came from down the path and it sounded like definite splashes of something large and heavy. For a moment he thought that it might be predator, but such was the desperation of his failing hope that fears of the unknown were impossible. He rushed headlong down the muddy, puddle-strewn path.

He might have been stomped on by the hermit, for his friend was at the moment distracted with his single-minded pursuit to reach the cottage. Gopher swerved in time, but, instead of realizing how near to death he had been, the rodent's hope blossomed into full blown joy, such as when the magic had first coursed through his veins.

"Menlow!"

Although it sounded a little like a squeak, it was his first word, and he didn't even know he'd said it. Menlow heard it, however, for he stopped and, gave out a cry that was drowned out by thunder, as he scooped up the little rodent. The booming in the sky stopped a moment later, and Menlow could be heard exclaiming, "You can talk! You can talk!"

Chapter Four

The enthusiasm and joy of their first conversation during this joyous reunion were not dampened by the downpour and thunder that were on top of them, though they had to yell into each other's ear to be heard.

"I can talk, I can really talk! Can you hear me, Menlow, or am I dreaming?" he said fluidly. For someone who had just learned the language, he had done it with the adroitness of an expert. The truth was that, of course, Gopher hadn't learned everything in a moment as it seemed. It had begun ever since eating the magic carrot. Every word that Gopher had heard, everything that he saw Menlow do, and all that he observed in the cottage, or while peering out the window at the world outside, had amassed within the rodent like a deep well of knowledge, from which he was now able to withdraw.

The hermit replied, laughing: "Yes, I hear you! Do you understand me? Amazing! Ha! Ha! It's been in you all this time! I just knew it! I would have gone looking for honey long before this if I had known this would happen! There was more to that carrot than making you clever! The Traveling Merchant was right!"

"But why now?" Gopher asked, and he wanted to also ask "What Traveling Merchant?" and "What carrot?" but the blinding flashes of lightning, which were too close for comfort, banished the questions from his mind. They rushed back to the cottage with the hermit holding Gopher close to him. The rodent remembered his old fear at being touched and wondered at it, for right now nothing else could make him feel safer.

Coming in out of the storm and being dried off rigorously by a cloth added to that feeling of safety with a sense of being cared for. It felt good, the peaceful kind of good, in which the rodent could just let himself being take care of, but Gopher was too excited. Everything felt good, especially talking, of which he did the most. It was as if he could not hold back the floodgate of words (which competed against the downpour of rain that could be heard thudding on the roof). It was like a man who had been dying of thirst being given a full flask of water – only Gopher had not known until now just how "thirsty" to communicate he had been.

He could never remember what he said that afternoon, but it went something like this: "I saw you leave and I got tired of waiting so I swept and swept – but first I made my bed –and I noticed the fire – when I was sweeping, that is – and it made me think of that smoking stick and I remember what you said, but I didn't know what it meant. Then I got hungry and I knew something was wrong..."

The retelling of his whole morning went on in a single continuing sentence, like everything else he said. Thankfully, however, he was interrupted by Menlow sneezing just when he was getting into a grand storytelling mode. That sneeze did more than interrupt his story; it made him aware of his surroundings and particularly of Menlow's condition. The hermit's face was covered in bruises and little red welts, and his beard was snarled up with twigs and leaves. The old man's clothing did not look any better. His soaked robe was muddy and torn with a right sleeve that was missing and with the other one torn and splattered by a little blood. Closer inspection proved that Menlow was even worse than the condition of his hair and clothing. His nose was red, and his eyes watery and puffy, and Gopher recalled how Menlow had walked, while carrying him; he had been limping.

All this made him realize that he had forgotten about why he had gone out in the storm in the first place – that he had been desperate over Menlow's welfare. It had been an innocent forgetting, what with all the excitement and joy, but he felt guilty nonetheless. It was as if his breakthrough in being able to speak had become so important to him that it overshadowed his concern for his friend completely. Now, however, his speech ability didn't mean so much, which showed that deep down he had the makings of a true friend, though at the moment he felt far from being one.

"I'm sorry! Are you all right?" Gopher said.

Menlow sneezed again, which was followed by a laugh.

"Of course. Don't be a silly gopher. I probably caught a little cold. I've been through worse."

Yet the hermit already sounded different – like he was talking through his nose. It was enough for Gopher to know that he wasn't being silly; something wasn't right with his friend, even though the hermit was so caught up in sharing his joy that it didn't matter to him. But it mattered to Gopher. Although still happy, his joy was tempered with consideration for his friend and a desire to find out more about what had happened to him.

That did not turn out to be easy since Menlow constantly barraged him with questions. Finally, by asking his own, Gopher got out what had happened to the hermit that morning. The surprise had been honey to go with their supper, which Menlow had planned to retrieve from a hive that was nestled in a hollow knothole of an oak, but "the bees were being terribly selfish," and they had not been driven away by the smoking branch, as he had hoped. Then, to top it all off, a bear had come along who had wanted the sweet stuff, too – except it had changed its menu choice when the hermit had been spotted.

"It was good I brought the stick after all or I would not have made it to the tree," Menlow said. He was sounding more and more nasally, his nose now a constant drain, so that what he said sounded like "Id wath good ah brought da stick afder aw or ah wad not have made id to da twee." In similar nasal tones that were hard to interpret, he added that that was where he had spent the remainder of the morning until the bear had finally decided that honey was less of a bother to get.

"But how did you hurt your foot?" Gopher asked after

deciphering what Menlow had said.

Menlow laughed and replied, "By lawnding wong when I jumt owt uf de twee!"

The cut on his arm, however, had come from climbing out of the bear's reach in the first place. Menlow thought it was funny that the tree did more damage than the bear. No longer bleeding, the hermit cleaned it with the remaining water in the jug and then bandaged it using the same strips of cloth that had held Gopher to his bed during his time of healing. (The hermit had retrieved them the next day after he had thrown them out the window.) Meanwhile, Menlow's sneezing and coughing increased in frequency, but they did not daunt his high spirits. He even laughed when he announced that he had a fever. His broad grin did not make him look sick, but his glassy, watery eyes did.

Instead of dampening his joy, the rodent focused his energies on tending to the hermit's needs. When he urged Menlow to lay down, his friend hesitated for a moment but then patted Gopher on the head and complied, sniffing and wiping his eyes. It did not occur to the rodent that the tears might be something other than a cold. Besides, he was too busy to notice them or the other signs on Menlow's face that showed he was touched by Gopher's kindly ministrations.

Of good intention he had plenty, but he quickly found that wasn't enough, for he could do very little in actuality. Not only was he limited by his physical strength that matched his smallness, but also by the awkwardness of his claws, which were meant for digging and not for carrying cups of water or plates of food to the bedside. Even dampening a cloth in the water bucket to put on Menlow's forehead had proven a difficult and messy job.

The hermit offered directions in how to do things, like hugging the cup to his chest with his front claws and letting the moistened cloth drip longer into the bucket before going across the floor with it. Mostly, all he could do was give general encouragement whenever the rodent struggled with the simplest of chores. Simplest, that is, for the hermit; Gopher had never worked so hard.

Yet the rodent did not need much encouragement and his joy

provided him a bounty of energy. Instead of being discouraged whenever he made a mistake, often they would both laugh and Gopher would try again. After one such incident of shared laughter (when Gopher had fallen into the bucket of water while dipping a cup into it), it dawned on the rodent why laughing felt so delightful. It turned something that could be taken seriously (after all, the water was cold and he had barely dried off) into something joyful; the seriousness felt like a heavy burden that he hadn't known was there until the laughter came to both reveal and dispel it all in the same action.

The day seemed to pass faster than Gopher had ever known it to. That was because he never had been about such a purposeful business of taking care of someone before, while filled to overflowing with a steady stream of joyful exhilaration. It was a rare combination, which people rarely find in their work, but when they do, there are few experiences in life more satisfying and that make time go so swiftly.

They ate a dinner of raw vegetables, which Gopher had retrieved from the "pantry" (the vegetable bin between the table and the fire wood stack). The dinner, like the rest of the day, was just as satisfying, though it had more to do with the feeling of pleasant exhaustion and the coziness of the setting than it had to do with the food. Menlow ate in bed, while Gopher sat at its foot, quite comfortable in the folds of the rumpled blanket, eating and listening to the hermit who told of a similar hunting accident. Gopher learned that it wasn't the first time a bear had chased him up the very same tree. In fact, the first bear to have done it (about three years ago) had similar markings around the eyes and made the same whiny noises as the most recent bear did, though was much older: "Prawbly the fawder." He laughed (and coughed), adding that it was a good thing its son wasn't a good climber either – or at least that's what Gopher understood him to say. It was not surprising that Menlow's voice finally gave out. After saying their good nights, Gopher went to his own bed and even fell asleep before the hermit started snoring.

The next morning Menlow's sickness worsened and his

elevated mood from yesterday had slipped down a few notches. He sneezed twice as much and did not smile or talk as often. Gopher noticed more wrinkles around his eyes, too, which, the hermit said, with a moan, was due to a headache. It occurred to Gopher how much his happiness had always depended on Menlow's happiness, now that there was less of it. Yet he learned to depend more on another source of joy; it was that of helping.

And he had plenty of helping to do. He hadn't realized until he got started how much of a mess the cottage was in. A film of dust now covered the floor – and just after a day of over-sweeping it! And dishes were unwashed. To him that was a lot, but then Menlow listed a few more: the water needed changing (especially after Gopher accidentally fell into it while soaking a rag), the fire had to be relit, the garden was in need of tending, and the chickens in the small pen next to the wood shop out back had to be looked over and fed; and then there was the preparation for the meals. The hermit tried to tell him not to worry about it, though his nearly unintelligible speech gave no such assurance, nor did a fit of sneezes that interrupted him.

Unable to do most of these things himself, Gopher did what he could, which was the usual: make his bed and sweep the floor when he was not going to and fro from Menlow's bedside with wet rags, water, and food. It was these last items, which were getting scarce. The pantry was already running low, and the rodent could not carry a bucket that matched his height to the stream, though it would not have been safe, even if he could.

By the late afternoon, just when exhaustion and frustration had eroded his "joy of helping," Menlow announced that he felt better. Gopher was so relieved that he did not notice that he did not sound or look better. Before the rodent could catch on, the hermit was up and about, retrieving water and gathering produce from the garden for their supper. He also did the rest of those things on his list, and by the time the sun's dying rays glistened on the leaves outside the window, a pot of vegetable stew was simmering over a roaring fire.

It turned out to be excellent, though Menlow said that it needed more salt or something to add flavor, "bud nod bawd." He didn't eat much of it, though, saying that he wanted to save the rest for breakfast. Gopher was no longer fooled; Menlow still looked miserable and sick.

They talked for a while, but it was not like last night. The enthusiasm had been dampened, and there just did not seem to be as much to talk about. Helping, he decided, was a poor substitute for laughter. It still made time seem to go fast, but only up to a point – which was the point of exhaustion and then a time for rest couldn't come soon enough.

When they said their good nights, Gopher, despite his exhaustion, found sleep elusive, for he had made the mistake of looking around. After all his work, everything was a mess again. Menlow's half-full bowl lay on the floor next to the bed. The uncovered pot with the leftover stew on the table beckoned him to be cleaned and put away. Logs, which had tumbled down from the stack earlier, lay precariously close to the fire, though the flames were dying down, which meant that it would have to re-started in the morning.

Gopher restrained himself from trying to tidy up because he was dreadfully exhausted. Yet as he lay there, the solitude that was invoked by the darkness and the sounds of Menlow's congested snores brought to the forefront a frustration that he had been battling all day. He was either too small or too weak, and his claws were just too awkward to be able to *really* help at all. If he had not been so tired, he might have laid there awake for hours, fretting about his inabilities and wishing that he were human, with human hands and stature and strength. But consciousness, like his limbs, had limitations. He dropped off to sleep before he knew it.

When the rodent woke the next morning, he doubted his senses, though the smells of fried eggs and potatoes that greeted him were not totally unexpected. It was as if he had smelled them in a dream that he could not quite remember. He let out a breath of contentment and satisfaction that he could not account for either, especially since he knew that he should be confounded. He could almost make himself believe that he had feasted in his sleep and was waking up to the memory of its smells – only these smells seemed all too real.

At last he raised himself up and saw Menlow looking down on him with an odd look in his eyes. His brows were furrowed and the corners of his mouth were turned down, perhaps from tugging on his beard, which had grown an inch these last two days. It was a mixture of bewilderment and... something else. Could it be repressed merriment?

"Gopher, get up. Take a look," he said.

The rodent couldn't believe his eyes. A fire blazed in the fireplace. The wood was neatly stacked; the water bucket full; the floor appeared to be without a speck of dust; the pot of stew was gone; and the dishes were cleaned and put away – except for two plates that were on the table, which Menlow lifted Gopher up to see. On them were fried eggs and red potatoes, steaming as if they had been freshly taken off the frying pan.

Gopher was speechless, but not from surprise. Like the smell, the sight of it all was vaguely familiar.

"Do you know who did this?" the hermit said.

"You?" Gopher said, but somehow he knew better.

Menlow chuckled. "No, not me... I think you did it."

"But how?" he said incredulously, though he felt the truth of the hermit's words. That didn't mean he understood it, however.

"By the magic that is in you, that's how," he replied.

Chapter Five

Unlike the cleaned-up cottage and the prepared breakfast, Menlow's answer was completely unexpected. Ironically that was because, of all the words Gopher had learned since eating the carrot, not once had he heard the word "magic," though something inside Gopher seemed to tingle in response.

"What is magic?"

"I don't know how to – excuse me," Menlow sneezed. (It was then that Gopher noticed that the hermit sounded much less nasally.) He went on, "Actually I don't know *where* to begin. There's a lot to tell – but first it would be a shame to waste this breakfast now that I feel like eating."

Gopher was too intrigued to have any appetite. He ate anyway to make his friend happy – and it would have been perhaps the finest breakfast ever if he had had the capacity to enjoy it. As it was, it was a long time (to Gopher, at least) before Menlow finished his meal. The hermit remained in his seat, leaning forward with his elbows on the table. He gazed at his empty plate as if he were seeing something else. Finally, he looked up at Gopher.

"I cannot tell all, for I have lived a long time. Wizards do – you see, I was one. What is a wizard? He is simply one who possesses magic..." A look came over Menlow as if he wasn't really there, but in the next moment his cheerful countenance returned.

"But I am ahead of myself," Menlow resumed. "You asked 'what is magic?' It is a connection to what is around us. Many think it's a power, like wind or fire. That's only thinking of it from a practical point of view, since this connection allows us to do things... magical things, good or bad, depending on who uses it. Originally, though, magic belonged only to the fairies in the First Age of Magic, but then the Fallen Ones came and deceived them. The Fallen Ones? They are those who were not of this world originally but who came to conquer it. The fairies had their magic to stand against them, but then some became deceived and gave away their powers. This, in turn, allowed the Fallen Ones to intermarry with the daughters of men. That was how the men of renown, the heroes of old, came into being, the Nephillim. Many appointed themselves as kings and were much like the Fallen Ones. They ruled with violence and cruelty. A great flood, however, destroyed them and ended the First Age of Magic. The Second Age came about because many of the fairies had survived.

"What had also survived," Menlow continued, "was the change in mankind that the Fallen Ones had wrought through the Nephillim. 'A door, once opened, cannot be easily shut.' We now had the gift of magic, except it only popped up in a few here and ther. Obviously, I was one of the very few... but I am a wizard no longer. I gave it up – well, I gave up most of it. The carrot you ate, you see, held the last of my magic, but I am getting ahead of myself again. Let me tell you why I gave it up..."

.   .   .

Menlow went on to tell that, like everything else in life, the magic eventually began to wane in the land, though it did not weaken as age weakens a body. Instead, it became more unmanageable, even to the point of becoming dangerous. Once a flood wiped out a village with a flash flood after a great wizard had summoned rain to alleviate a drought. Another time a woman disappeared by a blast of magic that was supposed to be a charm spell. Menlow knew of a deathly sick boy who was turned into a puppy by a common healing spell ("and to think I had used that spell many a time!" he added).

His first magical mishap occurred when he was trying to enchant an evil sorceress; his spell ended up nearly ensnaring himself into a deep sleep instead. Many believed that it was the sorceress who had ensnared him instead and that it had turned out to be his ultimate fate, but Menlow, who was steeped in the magical arts, managed to escape his own spell. That was when he decided to retire and go into seclusion as a hermit, for he knew these magical mishaps to be omens that the Age of Magic was coming to a close. When the close actually came, it had been sudden, unmistakable, and tragic. The hermit said even now it was too painful to talk about. At any rate, it decided him once and for all against using his magic anymore.

Of course, that was not the end of using his magic. Magic could not be laid down easily if one still possessed it. It helped the wizard incognito to build his cottage, to do chores, and to provide for himself. It wasn't simply because it made doing those things so much easier; rather, it was because he was not accustomed to using his hands – and because the magical power held an almost irresistible lure to him.

But one morning when he tried to start a fire with a simple incantation, his second magical mishap occurred: An explosion shot out from his wizard staff in all directions. It was only his survival instinct that kept him alive. By simultaneously countering the blast with a magic shield, he got out in time before the intense flames could break through it. He dared not use magic, though, to stop the fire, not knowing what new catastrophe *that* might incur! He could do nothing but watch the fire destroy his cottage, workshop, and garden, nearly everything he had. A downpour, though too late, halted the flames from spreading any farther than a few trees.

Two hours later he still had not moved from the edge of the clearing nor was his mood any less black than that burned-out clearing when an old man came sauntering through the forest. He was whistling and humming as merry as a lark and greeted the hermit with a broad smile, wishing him a grand day as if they were old friends and there were no smoldering ruins.

Although that may not have been true, Menlow recognized him at once. He was called the Traveling Merchant, a funny old man who went around selling things that he claimed to be magical. For many years Menlow had heard about him and might have met him a time or two, but he had never been quite certain. Most people said he dealt in tricks and lies and would even cheat a man out of his livelihood. Others said he was just crazy in the head, but harmless. It was also said (but only by those who thought good of him) that he would be recognized by those who needed him most – and at that moment, as low as the hermit felt, he needed something. He thought, when he recognized the Merchant, that maybe they were right, though at the moment he was speechless with surprise and indignation.

'A good day, this is!' The funny old man repeated himself.

'What do you mean?' the hermit said, nearly spluttering, 'You do not appear blind; look around you – here is where my cottage used to lie, and I am to blame.'

'Ah, but I see better than you do! I have eyes and so do you, which prove that it takes more than those to really see. You're alive! Do you not see that?'

'I know you mean well, old man,' Menlow sighed, 'but I have nothing left.'

'But you do have something, don't you?' he replied, pointing. 'Isn't that your staff over there, or do I miss my guess?'

The staff was where he had dropped it in the midst of the ruins when the fire had exploded from it. It was undamaged. He was not surprised; it had survived much more in the past, but at the moment he did not have the slightest desire for it, except to get rid of it. In fact, he stated that to the Merchant.

'What?' the Merchant responded outraged. 'Don't just give it away! Nothing that has worth should be given away as if it didn't. That would be for the wrong reason. Giving something of value away like *that* would be one of the most foolish things one can do!'

Menlow replied, 'But it has no worth to me, when I don't dare trust it. What better reason do I need?'

'Ah!' he replied, 'but it does have worth to you... Surely, trading it for something even better would be a good reason, wouldn't you think? What about this?' He pulled a bag from a pocket in his baggy trousers.

The hermit shrugged. 'Fine – even if it is a bag of dust, I would gladly part with my staff.'

The old man grinned. 'That's what it is!'

And indeed, after the old man opened the bag, he saw that it was full of dust!

'You must be jesting, sir! That pile of dirt for my staff?'

'Ah, but I do not jest,' he replied. 'I mean what I say, but it seems that you do not. You said that it was not worth anything to you anymore. The truth is my dust is more than equal to your staff because it can do what your magic staff no longer can. In a short time, it can restore the trees, the garden, and the cottage.'

'Then how can I refuse? Here, take it!'

It did not matter whether or not the ex-wizard believed him; he knew that he would be at least safer with a bag of worthless dust than with a staff that could not be controlled.

The Traveling Merchant took the staff and gave one word of caution before he left: 'Make sure you spread it carefully when there is no wind whatsoever– or you may reap something other than what you intend.'

'But how do I know I can trust its magic?'

'Firstly, by trusting what I tell you; and secondly, by finding it out for yourself; but follow my advice: beware the wind!' He cautioned and went on his way whistling and twirling the staff in the air as if it were a toy.

Remembering the Traveling Merchant's warning and knowing the nature of magic as well, he waited to use the dust. Two days passed before there was not the slightest breeze to stir some of the grass around the clearing that had survived the fire. By that time Menlow was cold and hungry and had almost given up, but he forced himself to act merely because he had waited that long already. He spread some of the dust around where the garden used to be without the faintest hope that it would do any good. Nothing happened, but when he awoke the next morning, the garden was restored with an overabundance of fruits, vegetables, and herbs. His spirits and hopes were especially restored after his first good meal in days. He was so excited that, as soon as he had eaten enough, he began spreading the dust around the clearing. He stopped suddenly when he had felt the slightest breeze. The Traveling Merchant's warning! It was too late. Some of the dust had floated into the air and disappeared. Nothing happened, but Menlow was not so sure nothing *would* happen. To be safe, he waited that entire day and night in a cave. Early next morning a fierce windstorm swept the valley and uprooted some of the small trees and broke the limbs of the older ones. Glad at least that there had only been a slight breeze, he could not have imagined what it would have been like if the wind had been any stronger. It took two whole days before it calmed down and another before the wind died altogether. The garden had been destroyed, of course, and the chimney – the only remnant of the cottage – had toppled, but Menlow went back to spreading the dust around, being careful of the slightest air movement.

It took nearly a week to empty that bag, but the results were well worth the constant, painstaking vigilance. The dust not only restored the garden and burned-out trees but had also restored the cottage and workshop as if they had never burned down. The only thing left for him to do was to remake the furnishings, which he did this time from tools that he bought from the village rather than with his magic. When the furnishings were completed, Menlow surveyed it with some pride and satisfaction at having done it with his own two hands. He felt so satisfied that he swore to himself that he was done with magic forever, even for fulfilling the most trivial of his needs. It was at that very moment the Traveling Merchant came sauntering through the woods again. He was as cheery as before, and Menlow, being very appreciative, made him welcome. They talked of his wizardry days over two bowls of rabbit stew as if they were old friends, but the hermit deduced that his visit carried a purpose. At last the Merchant came to it as they warmed their feet in front of the fire.

'Do you miss being a wizard?' he said.

Menlow thought about it for a moment and then said, 'Good memories – some of them, but, no, I should not say that I would wish them back. Although I tried to do good as a wizard, good did not always come, but trouble often did. I am happier here as I am.'

The strange little old man smiled at him. 'Happier only means comparing one sort of happiness to another. It does not mean quite the same thing as being happy.'

'What are you saying? That I am not happy?'

'Bah!' The Traveling Merchant said, making a face. 'Happiness – that just *happens* or it doesn't. Anyway, I did not bring up the subject. Let's talk about something that means something.'

'What about you asking me if I missed being a wizard – does that mean something?' Menlow replied. He was not angry, but he decided that he was going to show that the Traveling Merchant was not going to talk circles around him this time.

The little old man laughed. 'It *does* mean something or I would not have brought it up. I was leading up to asking if you would be willing to sell the rest of your magical powers for this magic seed here.'

He held out in his hand a speck of a seed.

It took Menlow a moment to speak, and when he did, he wondered aloud why the old man was not satisfied with his magic staff that he should want the rest of his magic, too.

The other grinned and said, 'It's not a matter of my being satisfied. I did not want or even need your staff – and I do not want or need your magic either.' He poked the erstwhile wizard in the chest. 'It is a matter of what *you* need. You gave me the magic staff simply because it became too dangerous for you, and you needed to rebuild your cottage. But you really need something more. This seed will be the start of that something more. It now depends on whether you *want* it or not.'

'What will happen when it is planted?'

He frowned and shrugged. 'I don't know. I don't always. For instance, I didn't know what would happen when Jack planted the magic beans I sold him. But I always do know what is needed, and you need this seed just as much as Jack had needed those beans.'

'Why? It does not look special,' he said, while having a hard time even seeing it.

'Oh, but it is,' the old man replied. 'That much I do know, or I would not have seen it in my vision. It contains the most powerful magic of all, and therefore it is the very last. You know the prophecy, just as I do: "The last of all magic shall be the greatest, for it shall reawaken those who in magic sleep." It starts here, with this seed.'

Although it was the biggest decision of his long life, it only took a moment of consideration for the hermit to agree to make the trade. He added, 'Are there any precautions I need to take?'

'Yes. You must understand that you are only a steward to this seed. Your duty is to plant, water, and protect it. Its magic is not yours to take or use. Everything else will be taken care of in time.'

He paused and then added in an even more serious tone, 'But are you certain you want to do this? 'The trade may be the hardest or the easiest thing you ever did. It all depends on your reason for the trade.' The words, combined with the look and tone of his voice, nearly made Menlow change his mind. He seldom changed his mind and he decided that he wasn't going to start now.

'What good is my magic to me now? Besides, you have proven yourself trustworthy, and that is a rare thing in this world. Yes, I'll trade,' the hermit said adamantly.

Immediately the Traveling Merchant offered the seed as he held out his open palm. The instant that the hermit grasped it, he understood the reason for the other's consternation. While outwardly nothing happened, it felt like a fire bolt ripping through Menlow, threatening to consume him from the inside out. Thankfully, he passed out, but that was only because a man can only take so much pain. In fact, he nearly died from it.

• • •

Menlow concluded his story to Gopher: "Obviously I didn't die and I ended up planting the seed. It did not spring up all at once, but grew like any other carrot seed would grow. I watered it and kept it covered at night and watched it during most of the day. It never occurred to me that a gopher would find it and when it did – I mean, when you did, I thought that the magic was lost forever. I must admit that I wanted to kill you. I'm glad that you were quick enough or I would have. Then the magic would have been truly lost. When I saw you being chased by that bobcat, something told me to save you. It was no accident when you ate that carrot, Gopher. That you can talk and clean this cottage even in your sleep proves it."

Gopher did not feel the same way. He looked at the hermit, saw the trust and hope alight in his eyes, and felt the responsibility that came with them. Suddenly, being a humble creature, he wished that he was just a mere gopher.

"But how did I do it?"

The erstwhile wizard smiled but shrugged. "If you have magic – though there's no doubt – it will find its way. Be patient. You'll come to understand how to use it in time."

Yet Gopher could not help but try to summon the magic. He quickly discovered that he was not able to raise a cup by merely "willing" it nor could he make the fire flare up by picturing it in his mind. No matter what he tried or how hard, nothing happened, and Gopher felt certain that Menlow was mistaken. There must be another explanation, he thought but did not say anything, because he did not want to douse the hope that Menlow had placed in him. He practically sighed himself to sleep that night.

Perhaps it was his feelings of uncertainty that did not allow him to sleep so deeply, or perhaps it was because of the multitude of thoughts that Menlow's story had filled him with. Most likely, though, it was a little of both. At any rate, during the night he was roused from sleep by the faintest of sounds. He opened his eyes and what he saw made him think that he was dreaming.

Four little men, about six inches tall and dressed in brown trousers and vests and high-buttoned boots, were cleaning the cottage. One swept, or tried to, since another silently wrestled with him for the broom. The third, while holding in a laugh with one hand, danced quietly as he scattered sparkly dust with the other. Strangely, the dust reminded him of music, except it made no sounds but filled him with the same cheerful feelings that the songbirds gave him with their twills and warbles. The fourth little man seemed in deep thought, though with a perpetual grin, as he paced around the room, studying it with his chin cradled in the crook between thumb and finger. From time to time he would suddenly stop and use his other hand to point and something magical would happen, like the wood rearranging itself into a neat pile, or a flying cloth dusting a shelf, or dirty dishes being washed by a floating sponge over a bucket.

All of it was done without a sound, but then an accident happened. The broom, over which the two were wrestling, knocked over the bucket with a loud crash, splashing water everywhere. Immediately, the little fellow who was spreading the sparkly dust threw a handful over Menlow's bed, but he should have chosen Gopher's first, for the crash made the rodent realize that he wasn't dreaming. He sat up and the little men froze in surprise. By then, however, the fairy dust had reached him and he fell instantly into a deep sleep.

In the morning he awoke refreshed and happy, but then he saw the halfway tidied up cottage. This time the sight was more than merely familiar, but the hermit's face showed a mixture of drowsy happiness (no doubt from the fairy dust) and puzzlement.

"What happened?" Menlow said.

Gopher told him of what he had witnessed last night, which made the ex-wizard's mouth drop open. The rodent ended by saying, "I guess I don't have magic after all." He tried not to make it sound like a relief since the hermit seemed to have held such high hopes for him.

Menlow scratched his beard thoughtfully. "Dressed in brown – little men – cleaning the place, eh? No doubt about it, but they were Brownies. If they knew you saw them, then I'm afraid they won't be back – unless it's to make a mess of the place for revenge.

"Do you know the meaning of all this?" the hermit continued. "When you ate that carrot, you released its magic; some of it enabled you to talk, but the rest started the Awakening. That would explain the Brownies."

This time they made their own breakfast and Gopher actually enjoyed it, no longer feeling the burden of responsibility. Now he felt that he had a chance for a normal life. He did not notice that it was Menlow's turn to be too distracted to eat much.

Chapter Six

For the next five weeks life seemed to promise a sense of normalcy, just as Gopher had hoped. There were no more surprises waiting for them in the morning, which Menlow said was because whenever Brownies are discovered, they never return to the same place. Soon the incident was forgotten as the end of summer approached. For with it came the many chores and jobs that accompanied the changing of seasons. As soon as the harvesting of the summer produce ended, the planting of the autumn crop would have kept him busy enough without having also to do the hunting and fishing. Then there were the skinning and cleaning of the furs, the smoking of the meat, and the stockpiling of everything in the "cellar" (which was only a deep hole in the ground under the floorboards). Hardest of all the chores, though, was the felling of trees with its endless chopping and stacking of firewood.

It was Gopher's least favorite chore, but not because he could do nothing but watch; rather, it was because it consumed so much of Menlow's time, attention, and energy. Those evenings after a day of chopping proved even worse since Menlow often retired early to bed just when Gopher's pent-up energy made him restless and want to do something, even if it was just to talk.

What made up for those disappointing evenings, though, were the early mornings when they went fishing. This was Gopher's favorite chore, even if the only way he could help was to keep an eager eye on the pole for any fish tugging on the line. It was exciting, and a little funny, watching Menlow tugging furiously at a pole that seemed to have a mind of its own.

Yet what Gopher liked most was actually when they were not catching any fish at all, because that was when Menlow would tell his stories of long ago while the sleeping forest slowly came awake. Gopher would listen, but like one lost in another time and place. He'd be vaguely aware of the pale horizon as it gradually fulfilled the promise of sunrise by chasing away the blackness and finally culminating as the dazzling rounded edge of the sun peaked over the elms across the creek. In that brilliant moment the light would turn their leaves golden, making them sparkle like clusters of stars that the pale blue sky could not extinguish with the coming of day.

He was aware of these details because the stories always tinged the morning with the same sense of wonder that they inspired in Gopher. This was especially ironic since most of the stories often included the telling of the deeds of evil fairy creatures: Giants climbing down beanstalks to rob and bully villagers, dragons setting aflame with their breath all that could be burned, hobgoblins raiding the countryside, ogres haunting bridges to waylay travelers, changelings stealing children, boogey monsters terrorizing people, black elves seeking conquest, sea monsters sinking ships and destroying coastal towns, evil sorcerers placing curses and casting spells on the innocent and the weak. Yet, where evil was at its blackest, throughout the stories ran threads of hope, nobility, and goodness that were shown to be all that much more wonderful by the brave and good deeds of the elves, pixies, sprites, dwarfs, and humans who fought against the darkness. Those deeds were, indeed, like the morning sunrise banishing the night, and leaving Gopher often in rapturous thought on that bank.

When the fishing was done by mid-morning, however, the talk would often turn to more practical things (that is, when the ex-wizard was not chopping wood) as the day's work proceeded, like gardening or wood-working or working on the cottage. Although often filled with laughter and cheer, their talk did not have the same wonder and charm, being more down-to-earth, but it conveyed a sense of camaraderie that was satisfying.

His other favorite chore, which Gopher nearly liked as much as fishing, though not for the same reasons, was hunting. The stealth of going out into the woods while perched on Menlow's shoulder captured a sense of the adventure in the hermit's stories, though what he liked the most about it was that, more than any other chore, he actually felt useful. With his sensitive nose and animal instinct, he would whisper directions in Menlow's ear whenever he sensed an animal before it could even be seen. This was particularly helpful since the hermit was not a good tracker. Many deer and rabbits and birds were brought down by his arrows that would have gotten away if it hadn't been for Gopher's lead.

It was during one of these hunting trips, though, when his sense of normalcy was knocked out of whack – and made adventure seem not so appealing when it became all too real. It started when the rodent caught a scent that was both strange and familiar – strange in that it did not give a sense of it being either man or animal, and familiar as if somewhere he had come across it before. Gopher acted, though, as if it were any other animal that they would hunt.

"There's something around that tree with the large knot," he whispered, and then sometime later, when the prey's scent was still all that could be found, he said, "Down there, I think," indicating a grassy slope. At the bottom, he said with a certainty that his nose gave him, "It can't be far, just past where the stream runs over those rocks." But Gopher's nose was proved wrong; it –whatever it was – seemed to be always just a little farther on. For nearly half an hour the familiar but strange scent led them on, until Gopher's nose suddenly lost the trail. That was when they realized that they were thoroughly lost as well. They wandered through the woods, searching for familiar landmarks, but when they crossed a stream and later re-crossed it, they realized that they were going in circles.

"If I had my magic, we'd be sitting comfortably at home by now," Menlow sighed. "At least we can get a refill on water." He stooped down to fill his leather canteen. "Don't worry. We'll eventually make it back," Menlow added, though his voice lacked conviction.

The remark had surprised Gopher, for the hermit had never

spoken like that before, but he forgot about it when he realized just how dark it was getting. They trudged on while the dwindling light allowed it. Gopher realized that soon they would have to stop and begin again in the morning. He dreaded the thought of sleeping out in the forest, for he had grown accustomed to cottage-living. Then suddenly he smelled the scent again.

"Over there!" he said.

"It's too late to do more hunting," Menlow said irritably.

"But I think we should follow it," he urged.

"What makes you so sure we should?"

"Instinct," Gopher said, sounding more confident than he was. He did not say that it was the same scent, for he feared that Menlow would just believe it would lead them even farther astray like before. The rodent did not know why he did not believe it himself. An irrational feeling of hope, rather than reason, had persuaded him.

Menlow laughed. "What else can we lose? Very well then! One last effort!"

Following the scent proved to be as evasive as before, and this time it was even harder. The hermit was forced to go slower, though he still managed to stumble, especially when the moon and stars became their only sources of light. Yet he kept going, and soon Gopher realized that Menlow really held no hopes of finding their way home but was merely doing it out of friendship. It was just at that point of revelation, before he could appreciate it, when the scent suddenly dissipated. This time he felt worse, not because he felt like a fool, but because of letting Menlow down.

"I'm sorry –" he began.

Menlow suddenly exclaimed, "Look!"

Before them was the dark silhouette of their cottage.

Chapter Seven

Not surprisingly, the incident garnered more appreciation for the cottage and their settled way of life. Nothing wakes us up to appreciate what we have better than the fear of losing it. Gopher recognized that the cottage was more than just a place to live; it was a home. The chores and their meals, the stories – all were part of that home and, most importantly, were a part of him.

Gopher even discovered that he didn't mind when Menlow chopped wood anymore, though this was mainly due to another reason. The hermit's willingness to trust in Gopher's direction, despite his exhaustion and the fact that he had gotten them lost in the first place, now inspired the rodent to put aside his own feelings in consideration for Menlow's. He came to empathize with the hermit's chopping and thought about ways to ease it, such as by bringing him a wet cloth or (with more difficulty) a cup of water, but it proved more satisfying than just waiting for him to finish.

In doing so, he found new sources of enjoyment that had previously been unlooked for. When Menlow chopped wood, for instance, he began enjoying the beauties of the forest instead of just waiting for the hermit to be done. Most importantly, it led to a deepening in their friendship like never before. But it was not always beauty he was looking for. The ex-wizard had theorized the morning after getting lost that it had been a fairy, probably a pixie, who had led them astray.

"They like to get travelers either lost or found, though seldom both! It's a sign of the Awakening, I think."

This theory felt true and it got Gopher's imagination going even more than the stories did. So real, so immediately present, did the creatures seem that, with quick glances here and there throughout the day, he expected to catch the sight of one, especially when there was a scent in the air that he could not readily identify. He never did, but he felt a certainty that, given time, he would. Meanwhile, he was too contented with life in general to be disappointed; in fact, he had never felt happier.

A week later, however, something unsettled Gopher even more than getting lost had, and it happened in the most unlooked-for and unlikely way. In fact, it occurred early one morning while fishing. Menlow was leaning back against his favorite boulder, the one with a comfortably curve to it, with his pole loosely held in his hand as he told about how he bested a witch and her goblin minions. Gopher was sitting next to him, looking out as usual at the gradual turning of night to morn. All was perfect, especially since it was the first time that Menlow was telling about his own wizard adventures. When he told about two knights whom he rescued from an evil witch, Gopher interrupted.

"What's a knight?"

"They're men who have vowed to serve the king. They wear armor and live by a code of called chivalry – or honor."

"King? What is that?"

Menlow laughed. "Oh, they're just men who set themselves up as rulers over others. The civilized lands are riddled with kings and lords and nobles, wherever there are more people and more money to be made. Most of them today are pretenders, but not all of them have been in the past...," his eyes misted and his gaze became briefly distant until he shook himself and laughed again before resuming his storytelling. "Anyway, as I was saying, after I sent her goblins scurrying, I told their mistress, 'Your own foul deeds be upon your head!'"

Although Menlow continued with his tale, Gopher had stopped listening. It was not as much what he said but *how* he said it that triggered an unsettled feeling. The ex-wizard had deepened and projected his voice in a tone of authority so that he had sounded like someone else. It jarred Gopher with a thought of how little he really knew of Menlow. A conviction came over him that the hermit was holding back something in his past from him, and that hurt Gopher. Here he had been trying to consider the hermit's feelings and now he felt that he really didn't know them. He quickly rejected the thought by telling himself how silly he was being, that the past didn't matter as much as their friendship did.

Actually it was the idea of their friendship, however, that brought to light another discomfiting idea. It was that, with all of Menlow's years of life as a wizard, it was inevitable that he had saved and befriended many besides himself. How many had been as close to him as Gopher was? He did not know why this would bother him, but it did, even to the point that he wished that Menlow had never been a wizard.

It was the first time he had ever wished something out of jealousy, and for once he was glad when Menlow stopped talking about the old days. As the day progressed into a busy one, his feelings evaporated into the waning heat of the late season. By the evening he was perfectly content again with only a vague memory of discomfort. In fact, he even talked himself into believing that there really had been nothing to be upset about – never mind the fact that even the thought of fishing was now met with an unsettling twinge.

The feeling did not go away. Rather, the inner turmoil returned the following morning, but this time it was only the feeling itself that came to him, not the memory of its cause. He felt as if he could *almost* remember the reason. The harder he tried, the more evasive it became. Menlow must have noticed something in the way Gopher acted or looked, for he said, "What's wrong, Gopher? Did you have a bad dream?"

"Dream?" Gopher said in surprise. "I – I don't dream."

Even as he said it, though, the words felt false to him. He realized that he *did* dream, but the thing was that he could never remember them, and therefore had eventually forgotten that he ever did. (The closest he had ever gotten to remembering a dream had been the night when he saw the Brownies, but, of course, that didn't count since he had only *thought* that he had been dreaming at the time.) He was sure that they must usually be good dreams, because he would often wake feeling exuberant or joyful or playful. They also always left a vague notion that there were reasons behind those feelings. Usually he did not bother too much to find them out. This time, however, the same thing was happening, only the dream (if it had been a dream) left an inner turmoil that naturally got his attention, like a sharp pain in the finger that leads one to search for a splinter or bluster.

"You don't?" Menlow said. "I thought everybody dreams."

"Do you remember your dreams?" Gopher asked.

"Oh, some of them," Menlow said. "Most dreams are hard to remember, especially as the day goes on, but some dreams are more memorable, especially when something that is either wonderful or terrible happens in it."

"I must dream," Gopher said after a moment, "but why can't I remember any of them? Some of them *seem* wonderful. That is the feeling they give me in the morning, at least."

Menlow shrugged. "Don't let it worry you, Gopher. Memories come best when they are not forced. Anyway, most dreams are usually about something that happened to you, or something you felt."

That was it! Gopher remembered yesterday's jealousy and realized that was what he must have dreamed about. Relief came to him like sudden sunshine and a fresh breeze, but for a short time only. Soon he felt the same horrible cloud of anxiety return. It was then he discovered that understanding his dream (even if he couldn't remember it) did not change the feeling it caused simply because emotions weren't rational.

But once again the day's busyness lightened his mood and happy contentment soon returned, the kind which took the work out of work and made it more like "play with a purpose." While Gopher was sweeping and whistling through his long teeth, Menlow came in with an armful of vegetables from the garden. After setting them on the table, he announced something that swept in a whole new set of emotions.

"This will be the last from the garden for a while," he said, placing the baskets of vegetables on the table, "and our supplies are starting to dwindle. In a few weeks we'll need to go to the town to stock up for autumn."

The town.

The thought of going to where strangers lived and worked together in one place was a vague but perplexing one. Never having seen another human or habitation before, Gopher could not imagine what they would look like, except as copies of Menlow and the cottage. Of course, that could not be true. But it was not merely their differences that scared him; it was the *uncertainty* of what their differences might be like and how they would treat him. Everything here had become more or less predictable and, therefore, comfortable and welcoming – and certain. For him that meant safety.

The preparations, in addition to doing their regular chores, during the next few weeks provided a near-cure to his perplexity, though not to his uncertainty. The animal furs and skins, which would fetch the highest prices in the village, had to be cleaned and brushed; this gave Gopher plenty to do since the hermit had ingeniously fashioned a small knife and brush to fit his claws just for that purpose. Gopher also helped sniffing out various wild roots and plants for Menlow, who dried and ground them into herbs and spices, which were almost as valuable as the furs.

Yet what helped Gopher's anxieties the most was Menlow's reassurances and descriptions. At least Menlow gave him an *idea* of what to expect. One major source of perplexity was removed to some extent when Menlow assured him that the rodent would not actually meet anyone since he would be hidden in a bag slung over his back.

Because of the many things to consider and plan for, Menlow hardly spoke of the Age of Magic nor did he tell anymore of his own wizardry stories. Gopher occasionally felt a sting of guilt about being relieved because of this, for even jealousy, when not enflamed, has a conscience. Mostly he was too busy and... too happy to give it more than a passing thought.

Yes, he realized one day with surprise that he was happy about going, happy and eager as the day of their departure approached with only a spasm of perplexity every now and again. When the morning of departure dawned, Gopher suddenly and surprisingly felt hardly any dread or anxiety at all, only an eagerness to begin. He thought, with some satisfaction, that he had become much braver and more adventuresome than ever before. It did not occur to him that he might have felt differently if it hadn't been for Menlow's assurances and the knowledge that he had a bag to hide in.

"We should be back in five days," Menlow said as they set out. "It would be shorter, but I'll be carrying a much heavier load on the way home. We'll have to take the longer way around instead of over the ridge."

The idea of being gone for so long had not occurred to Gopher. Until then he had only considered where they were going to, not what they would be leaving behind or for how long. Having settled on Menlow's shoulder, he looked back at the retreating image of the cottage where it was set in the clearing with the garden. The modest building was both the most beautiful and painful sight he had ever seen, for he was already homesick for its comfort and security. He consoled himself with imagining how ecstatic he would feel five days from now when they returned; he could hardly wait. It would make the trip to the village worth it just for that, he thought. Yet he would never find out, because he was seeing the cottage for the last time.

Chapter Eight

Not knowing sometimes is better. This was one of those times, for Gopher was able to have an enjoyable day that was not diminished by knowing something he would have no control over anyway. To the rodent the trip to town did not seem to start out that much differently than their hunting trips, except that Menlow brought along things for trading rather than for hunting. He carried on his back a large pack, in which he stuffed twenty pelts of deer, rabbit, and fox, along with spices, herbs, and roots. This was the bag Gopher could hide in, because Menlow had left room in the opening at the top for Gopher to slip into if and when they came across somebody.

Soon, however, more differences between this trip and a hunting one became apparent. Menlow did not bother to step lightly nor did he whisper. They took the main path instead of following the trails left by wildlife. A rabbit ran out of some foliage past them without coming to harm since the erstwhile wizard had a walking staff instead of a bow or spear. As they ascended toward the heights, Menlow paused to admire the graceful bearing of a doe standing motionless on a steep slope to their left, its silhouette etched out against the soft blue sky, making it a perfect mark for a hunter.

Menlow said, "Choosing to spare life makes it all the more beautiful, don't you think so, Gopher?"

Having enjoyed the hunt so much, Gopher was surprised not only by the comment but also by the fact of how graceful and noble the doe did in fact appear. He realized that it came from seeing it for itself instead of as an object of prey.

In a clearing that was overshadowed by the ridgeline, they stopped to eat a lunch of dried rabbit meat with some berries that they had found along the way, all washed down with draughts from the water skin. It wasn't much, but food did not matter at the moment for the spirit of adventure had come upon him. Gopher had never been so far from the cottage. Looking up at the ridge that separated this valley from the one next over, he felt an eagerness to climb it. The erstwhile wizard seemed excited, too. He talked about the beautiful view from that height.

"It has always been my favorite part of the journey," he concluded, and so was their meal. Stretching, he shouldered the pack again, placed Gopher back on his shoulder, and took up his staff. "Now's the time to get secured, Gopher."

As part of the preparation for the trip, the hermit had sewn in two leather straps on the left shoulder of his robe and fastened their ends to a leather loop measured to snuggly fit Gopher's middle. After slipping it over that portion of his anatomy (he was too eager and happy to grumble about it being a bit *too* snug), Gopher was glad of it when Menlow began ascending the cliff face, for the slope proved to be every bit as steep and dangerous as he had been warned. The rodent would have fallen off many times. As it was, Gopher kept being tossed about until he finally learned to some degree to move in anticipation of Menlow's movements.

Eventually it came so naturally that it freed the rodent's attention enough so he could consider the topography. The rock face was uneven at best, and at worst it was sheer and slippery with smooth as well as gravelly spots, many of which, thankfully, the hermit avoided. He wondered aloud that a path could be discerned at all.

"It's more of a way than a path," Menlow explained breathlessly. "I look for landmarks to help guide me."

Whenever he stopped, though, it was more often to catch his

breath or wipe the sweat off his brow than to be checking for landmarks. Little wind stirred, and the sun beamed down from a clear blue sky, beating on their backs, as its heat and glare reflected in their faces from off the surface of the stone. It grew so warm, even for the rodent who wasn't doing any of the climbing, that he found it difficult to believe that autumn was just around the corner.

A raven suddenly cawed loudly overhead. Its noise was in sharp contrast to the quietness that he had failed to notice all day. The liveliness and busy activity of summer was coming to an end within the valley, but the same could not be said about what was happening in the sky. Birds were flying in several huge V patterns, heading in the same direction as if they, too, had a purpose that came in anticipation of the season change.

"Do the birds have a town to go to for supplies, too?" he asked.

Menlow paused in his footing and said, "They sense the change in the weather and are flying to warmer places. They'll be back by spring."

Even though Gopher could not see Menlow's face (it was upturned to the sky), he could somehow tell in his voice that he was grinning.

"Did I say something funny?"

"Oh, I – uh, was just imagining what a town of birds would look like."

"I don't even know what a town of *people* looks like," Gopher replied. This time Menlow really did laugh and he joined in, though he still didn't understand.

During all that climb, Gopher never thought to turn and look over the valley; that is, not until they reached the top – then what a view the rodent saw! He could never have imagined it, and Menlow's descriptive words had fallen short of the real thing. The wooded valley below where the cottage lay hidden was just one of many. The heights that separated the succeeding valleys undulated like rolling sea waves of forest in all directions, peaked occasionally with rocky bluffs that were topped by snow at their highest peaks. A silvery streak seemingly hung over a cliff to the north, which Menlow said was a waterfall that fed the very stream that they fished. Breathing in the cool, gentle breezes, he listened to the cawing of the birds and the rhythmic flapping of their wings as he watched their V pattern fade into the horizon.

Yet best of all the sights was the crowning dome of blue sky. It made him feel so small, but strangely he was unafraid. Perhaps it was because it was so big and beautiful that he didn't seem to matter. He felt like he could stay up here forever. Even Menlow was reluctant to leave. But after they had talked and rested awhile, watching the sun move towards the far horizon (and Gopher sometimes gazing at the waterfall, wondering why the water did not seem to move at all), the hermit groaned as he got up.

"Mustn't let moss grow under our feet," he said, "or, in my case, let rust stiffen my joints. We have a long climb down on the other side."

After the safety loop was fitted on him, Gopher said, "If we meet someone along the way, how will I get this off in time?"

"Oh, I doubt that," Menlow said, cheerfully. "The town is a long ways off still. Even if someone did see you, it'll give him a good laugh since they already think I'm addled in the head. That's what people think about hermits – and most of the time they'd be right!"

Gopher became reintroduced to fear when Menlow started down. It was not only steeper and slipperier than the other side, but the hermit had to take it climbing feet first, frequently hugging the cliff face as he felt his way down with his hands and feet. Sometimes he did not find any toeholds and all he could do was to lean into the rock face with his body and his hands scrambling to find any purchase to slow down their slide. Those were the scariest moments, but thankfully it didn't happen often and Menlow would only slide a few feet at most. Not surprisingly, Gopher was even more thankful for being strapped in. The short slides, the nearly constant small landslides of loose rock that Menlow inadvertently caused, and the tedious slowness that came from taking great pains to be careful, all began to blur together until it was hard for Gopher to remember when the descent had begun and to believe that it would ever end. The worst part, however, was that the prolonging of his fear began producing a numbing effect so that he started seeing himself as if from the outside, as if he were disembodied and floating about and feeling less and less attached to reality. It was a strange awareness and, in its own way, more terrifying than fear itself. It felt like he was losing himself.

Even when Menlow had at last reached the bottom, the numbed sensation persisted and Gopher did not realize their trek had ended, but then he heard a voice, which took him a moment to recognize as belonging to Menlow. Relief flooded in as did understanding at what his friend was saying.

"Gopher, are you okay? Gopher?" his friend was saying with consternation that was immediately replaced by relief when the rodent blinked.

"Are we... down yet?" Gopher said.

Menlow laughed, glancing at the cliff face behind. "That was a lot harder than I had hoped – or remembered. Phew!"

It was such an uncharacteristic expression for Menlow that it made Gopher laugh. In doing so the last of his numbing fear dissipated. Instead of being frightening, it was now a memory with the sting taken out, something to laugh about and to even treasure – until a thought, a horrifying thought, came to him.

"Do you have to come back this way?" Gopher asked.

"Oh, no! With all the supplies we'd be bringing back with us, we'll have to take the long and less steep route. Remember? I told you about that."

Gopher felt his breath return.

They rested and drank the rest of the water in the shadow of the cliff, their high spirits ebbing into a feeling of peaceful contentment and then gradually into a readiness to resume their journey. Menlow, however, groaned and stretched as he got to his feet just like he had done before their descent.

The woods looked the same to Gopher in this valley as they did in theirs, but there was a smell about it that made it vaguely different. It reminded him of.... of Menlow, but then he realized that this must be scent of people.

Strangers.

The scent, however, did not make the word so ominous, so

unfamiliar, anymore. Nevertheless, he was glad that Menlow did not put the loop around him again, for it would making slipping into the sack to hide impossible if they suddenly came across someone.

The sun was dipping halfway below the tree line by the time they found a small clearing. A streamlet trickled beside a patch of grass, upon which the waning light cast a soft ambience, while its slanting rays illuminated the leaves above in a refulgent display of gold and orange colors. That and the birds flying in their pattern overhead reminded Gopher of the changing season and the purpose of their own trip.

Gopher sunk his legs in the luxuriant, thick grass, while Menlow filled his water skin and then washed his scuffed hands. The hermit held them up and laughed. "You see these? They never got even a splinter or a blister before, but it's not so bad. I always felt that magic was *cheating*."

"I wish I had hands to scuff!" Gopher said, and then after a thoughtful moment added, "Do you think my speech is *cheating* then?"

"Because you are a gopher and gophers aren't suppose to talk, is that it?" Menlow said. "No cheating is taking the short cut, the easy way – there is no easy way for a gopher to talk. It just isn't done – except by magic."

"But it was an accident that I ate it," Gopher said.

"Accidents are not cheating, but I've ceased believing in accidents at all."

Gopher came to the trickling stream and gulped several mouthfuls of the icy cold water. Its exquisiteness traveled down his throat to the rest of his body, sending a shiver of delight through him.

"Why not?" he said breathlessly.

Menlow, now sitting on the grass, was going through his pack that held their food. He looked up. "About accidents?" he said. "Everything is too connected to each other, more complicated than you know; nothing *just* happens. If magic taught me anything, it taught me that; yet magic is only a small part of that invisible connection that everything has with each other. Everything lower depends on that which is higher, like plants depending on the sun. Likewise, the higher embellish some of itself to that which is lower, like the sun's reflection in that stream, making it sparkle."

After this they turned their attention and appetites to their dinner, which consisted of the remaining portions of dried meat and a few vegetables. Gopher felt ravenous and was hardly filled up when they finished their meal, such as it was. The day's trip and its mixture of excitement and fear seemed to have created a greater need for food, but at the same time it deepened the bond between them, just it had when they had gotten lost before. It reminded him that there was something much more satisfying than food; yet that bond made food, no matter how poor, a delight. They reminisced about their travels that day, laughing and at ease.

But it would not be for long. The human scent in the air, although still faint, was the slightest bit more distinct than it had been a moment before – yet it was enough for Gopher's instinct to kick in and take over. He darted across the grass and dove into the open mouth of the discarded pack.

"What are you –" began Menlow but then his instincts appeared to come alive, too, as he reached for his walking staff. It was just in time. A man in a blur of motion jumped over the stream and would have been on the hermit if the staff had not deflected his course. The attacker rolled on the grass, stopping near the pack and sprang up in a crouch. The look in his eyes, as they darted here and there, was like an animal that was both frightened and angry at the same time, the impression of which was increased by his disheveled hair, mud-streaked cheeks, and bleeding lip.

"Where is your demon from hell? I heard you – heard you both! I am not running anymore!"

Chapter Nine

Menlow, straightened up, lowering his staff, and replied, "Am I mistaken or aren't you Tobias the woodcutter? What has happened? Are you being chased?"

The other man, whose posture was still on the edge of either running or fighting, exclaimed, "Ha! As if you didn't know! You're the one doing it!"

Menlow chuckled. "It wasn't me whatever it is I'm supposed to have done. As for what you heard, hermits have a way of talking to themselves. Don't you remember me? You have known me since you were a child."

Tobias frowned. "Hermit? Are... are you Menlow? What are you doing here?"

"Just traveling to Kentfell for autumn supplies."

"But I heard two voices," the man persisted, though his posture had slightly relaxed. "Are the stories about you true then? That you are a wizard and a friend to ghosts?"

Again Menlow chuckled. "Stories about an old hermit like me? I guess that is to be expected. People do have imaginations, especially about those who keep to themselves and nobody knows much about. It seems I know those in Kentfell better than they do me.

"Tobias," he continued, "I promise that I am not a wizard and have not and will not play any tricks on you. Neither is any ghost, devil, nor imp my friend."

"Nobody is safe," the other man said, relaxing slightly more. "There is an evil goblin or something running about – the old stories about *them* are true!"

"I know they are," the hermit said. "I have been around a long time, like I said. Tell me what has happened to convince you that they are still true *now*."

The man sat down with slow, deliberate, and self-conscious movements as if forcing himself to be at ease but not yet totally convinced that he should be. "This morning I was plying my trade and a creature suddenly appeared in the shadows and threatened to cut me down with my own axe if I did not stop hacking away. Like a fool, I dropped my axe and fled. The creature has been shadowing my heels all day, laughing, throwing rocks, and making dreadful noises. I never got a good look at it, for it was always in the shadows and often in the trees. It was not alone either. There was another. I could hear them laughing and talking together sometimes. I did not let them get close enough for me to be able to hear what they were saying. At last I thought that I had finally lost them until I heard you... uh, talking and laughing, and I thought..."

"No wonder you thought what you did," Menlow said. "I don't blame you for your mistake. Fear has a way to easily mislead a man."

"This was not the first time something like this has happened," the woodcutter went on, "Such things have been going on around Kentfell these past few weeks. Some say it's a poltergeist or a kobold or a goblin. Whatever it is, it likes to scare people and play tricks, nasty tricks. I used to scoff before. Whatever it is, it seems to like woodcutters the least, since I am not the only one to fall prey to its mischief."

Gopher listened to all of this, not daring to peek out of the sack, though his fear slowly began draining away. In its place he found a growing dislike for the man, especially as Menlow began asking him about his family and the village, things Gopher only knew about secondhand or not at all. It made him feel excluded, especially when they laughed together – just like he had felt while listening to

Menlow's story that time, only this was worse because this exclusion was not caused by his imagination; it was real – so real and so painful that he curled up and quickly fell asleep, and not just because of exhaustion. It was the only way he could escape his feelings.

Sometime during the night Gopher woke up hazy and confused. Menlow's short beard was the first thing he could clearly see through the sack's opening, shining faintly in the moonlight. A leaf sticking to it like glue (or most likely sap) reminded Gopher all at once about their trip, the meeting with the woodcutter, and his own subsequent feelings. At the same time he realized that Menlow was whispering something to him. It took him a moment to decipher "Are you all right in there?" The hermit's genuine concern inflected in his voice suddenly pierced Gopher with shame at thinking that his friend would ever truly exclude him.

"I'm fine," Gopher whispered in reply, and added, "thanks."

He had wanted to say "I'm sorry," instead, but that would mean confessing his shame. Eventually he fell back to sleep, happier, though not as happy as he could wish to be, for he also felt troubled at how unfair he had been. It was like he was seeing a part of himself that he had never known before: untrusting and selfish. Before slipping off into sleep, he promised himself that he would be better and never jump to such wrong conclusions about his friend again.

Morning came much too soon. Gopher wanted to yawn and stretch but the bag was restrictive, but most importantly, he dared not. Tobias was up already and talking. After a quick breakfast (the hermit had slipped Gopher some wild berries), they started on their way to the village. For the rodent, the trip seemed endless since he could not see anything more than outlines and shadows through the thin cloth. It made distances difficult to judge, so that it often felt as if they were just walking in place.

Most of what he discerned was through hearing. The hermit and the woodcutter were talking probably as much as they had the night before, with the latter doing most of it as he rehashed his experiences. Now and again Menlow was able to glean more news of the village. Gopher was able to detect something in Menlow's tone that puzzled him at first. Then he realized that, although friendly, the hermit seemed to be a little stiff and distracted as if he weren't really listening. Gopher could not help but find pleasure in thinking the hermit never sounded like that whenever *they* talked. The pleasure did not last long, however, for it was supplanted by a growing misery that came from the perpetual swinging of the sack, the stuffy confinement amidst the furs, and his inability to see. Worst of all, though, was Tobias' incessant morose conversation. The rodent would have felt sorrier for his friend had his own uncomfortable condition not been so miserable as well.

It was at some indiscernible point in time, when Menlow had just managed to get a word in about stopping for lunch, that a new voice in the distance aroused Gopher from his numbed reverie. Before he could make it out, another voice joined in, and then another, which was followed by a fourth. They seemed to be coming from different places and to be crying out the same thing repeatedly.

"Those voices sound familiar," Tobias said. "I think they're saying... Adia – ah, yes, that's it. She's the mayor's daughter."

Menlow cried out, "Hello!"

A large beardless man met them in a clearing soon after, whom the woodsman identified as a storekeeper named Harrow. Following promptly behind was a stout fellow with a bushy beard in a vest that had seen cleaner days. He was introduced as Mayor Dryden. He would have been pleasant-faced if it had not been overshadowed by anxiety as indicated by the many furrowed lines around his eyes and forehead. Their many creases deepened when he saw them and his head dropped slightly with barely concealed disappointment. There was a strain in his voice.

"Tobias, what are you doing out here? And... aren't you Menlow?" the mayor said with a sudden smile that created more wrinkles, which ironically made him seem younger, for genuine smiles often do. "Perhaps you can help us find my daughter? I would be most grateful."

Harrow added for further clarification, "The whole town's all riled up. There've been reports of a haunting again last night and now the mayor's daughter has disappeared."

Dryden snapped instantly, "Rumors! That's all they are! I told you that. Just some kids playing pranks. We'll catch them yet. The point here is to find my daughter." Then he managed to compose himself again, but as one who was under great pressure. "Forgive me. I am just worried because she's never away this long. She probably got lost picking berries. It would be most kind if you could join in."

"Most certainly, Mayor Dryden," Menlow said.

"But, Mayor, they are not rumors!" Tobias exclaimed emphatically.

The mayor and Harrow looked at him in surprise.

"What do you mean?" Dryden replied.

The woodcutter then proceeded to tell his story. Even though he told it in a much calmer manner than when he had first related it to Menlow, the story visibly shook the mayor's poise. With the air of helpless agitation, the town leader looked about and wrung his hands.

"If that's so, Mayor," Harrow said, "we should have taken more men to search the forest!"

"No need," the woodcutter added, clasping his hands, though not helplessly like the mayor but with surprising complacency, as if he were saving some bit of good news for last. He continued, "I'd wager two days wages that I know how you can find your daughter."

All three men stared with open mouths. The mayor was the first to speak, with no reserve of pleasantness left. "Then tell me! This is no game! Where is she?"

"Oh, I don't know *myself*," Tobias replied, brightly. With the air of having all the time in the world, he added in a drawn-out fashion, "But Menlow's friend can sure tell a few tales, I'll bet. He's hiding in the sack. I heard Menlow talking to him twice last night. The second time they thought I was sleeping! They're the ones playing tricks on us – and now the jokes on them!" He laughed roughly.

"Really?" Dryden said, taking a step forward, with an eagerness that seemed strange to be coming from a father who is supposed to be desperate over his lost child.

Menlow's eyes suddenly took on a fierce light and his lips became set in a stern line as he raised himself up much taller and more imposing, at least in seeming, than he actually was. Yet when the mayor stepped back, Menlow seemed to deflate with a sigh and looked like himself again. The hermit swung the sack off his back and handed it to Dryden with it open for inspection.

"Go ahead. Take a look. Tobias is, of course, mistaken. I have nothing in my sack that is capable of doing such things," he said in a slightly raised voice.

Gopher recognized his danger of discovery even without Menlow's subtle warning, for he had been listening quite intently, but it did not matter. Fear had already gripped him so that he was curled up tightly in a ball amidst the furs.

The other two men gathered in close about as the mayor peered within. He frowned. Warily putting forth his hand to search by feel, the town leader gave a start.

"What is it? What's in there?" Harrow said, tugging his beard, while Tobias made a complacent sound in his throat, like "I told you so."

Dryden hesitated, his frown unchanged. He slowly removed his hand. It was empty. He said, "Furs... nothing but furs, though one of them still has a claw attached – that's what had startled me."

Harrow laughed and Tobias frowned.

"But I heard –" the woodcutter began before he was interrupted by a voice in the distance.

"I found her!"

Off they all went through the underbrush with excitement that even Menlow got caught up in. It resulted in Gopher being swung about more roughly than usual, but still comforted at not being found out, though he did not understand it. Soon and nearly simultaneously, they converged upon two other searchers in a thicket where one of them held an unconscious girl in his arms.

"What's wrong with her?" The mayor said frantically.

"I don't know. I found her like this, lying over there," said the man who held her.

The girl was wide eyed with a vacant stare in a face that was pale and sagging, like a ruin of a dying old woman in a twelve-year-old child's body.

Everybody stood frozen, except her father who, after a poignant whimper, put his mouth next to her ear, pleading in a whisper for her to wake up. He touched her cheeks, stroked her long brown hair, and brushed strands of it away from her unblinking brown eyes. No response, except for a soft rising of her chest.

Menlow said softly, "Perhaps if you speak to her as her father with authority. *Tell* her to wake up."

It was after several tries with Dryden increasingly becoming firmer, until his tone itself expressed the ardency of a father's love for his dying child, that her eyes finally blinked. They fluttered some more, and then they closed, only to open a moment later. She frowned as her eyes seemed to be focusing on her father's face. Strangely, at the same time, her face appeared to be subtly moving like shifting sand. Then it seemed to settle and it left her skin brightened with the return of vitality and youth, like the reversal of aging.

All the while her father was so worked up that he did not notice. He kept commanding her to awake until Harrow put a hand on his shoulder. The mayor jumped and then, in bated breath, fell abruptly silent. That's when they all heard her say in a small voice, "Father... I'm sorry."

The girl recovered quickly and was soon standing on her own, looking like a little girl again, though there was a certain sadness in her eyes that did not belong there in one so young, though it added sweetness to her already cherubic face. She never did say what she was sorry about, except for the bother she had caused. In regard to how she had gotten here, she said that she could only remember playing around her house yesterday morning and nothing else after that. In return, she and her father received many concerned looks, shaking heads, and clucking tongues, but they did not question her any further. Harrow muttered, "Another one of those tricks goin' round, I suppose."

The girl consumed some bread and water, which Harrow had brought along, before they headed back to town. The trees started noticeably to thin and the ground to level off as they approached the valley floor. By this time Adia was able to walk. Her father set her down and she held his hand for most of the way. More and more, she had begun to act – and look – like a child, the sadness fading from her face. In fact, soon a childish restlessness took over; she let go of her father's hand and caught up with the other four men, skipping and laughing as she pointed at the river ahead. From this angle it looked like a blue winding strip. On the other side of it, making a beautiful backdrop, were the wide park-like expanse of the Village Green and then beyond that was the town of Kentfell itself.

"Many tend to spoil her. Ever since her mother died," the mayor said quietly, "practically the whole village has tried to help me raise her, but half of them think that she can do no wrong, and almost all of them believe that I can do no right with her. I grant it that they give me some good advice, though, all in all, I wonder if it really has turned out for her good or for mine as her father –"

Dryden paused and put his hand on Menlow's shoulder to hold him back a step from the others. "But," he said, slowing a little more, "that's not what I want to speak to you about... I suppose it's none of my business. In fact, I did not say anything about it before in front of them because it really isn't any of their business either since I don't think it has anything to do with what's been going on around here, but I'm dying to know – it won't go any farther, I promise – but why do you travel with a live gopher in your sack?"

Chapter Ten

Menlow did not answer right away. For Gopher it seemed like forever. Finally the hermit said in a low voice, "He's a friend. Would you like to meet him – later?"

Dryden queried with a raised eyebrow, "Friend?"

"He is not responsible for whatever is going on–"

"I know," the mayor cut in and added mysteriously, "I had wished, though – wanted to believe it but..."

He fell into a morose silence, though it only lasted a few moments. They caught up to the others who were now waiting on the ferry on this side of the river. Adia's feet were dangling over the side. After cautioning her, he then acted and talked with the others as if nothing had been on his mind.

The trip over, both terrified and fascinated Gopher, mainly because, though he could see very little, he could hear, feel, and smell a lot that was new to him: the splashing and rolling of the waves, the quacking of ducks, the creaking of the ferry, and the fresh smell of the river that was accompanied by a slight mistiness that penetrated the sack. His terror, though, sprang not so much from the newness of his unseen surroundings but from the close proximity of the others. More than once he felt himself being bumped into and some of their voices were alarmingly close, sounding as if they were right next to his ear. It was all he could do to keep still and not draw attention to the sack.

Even the terror, though, did not take his mind off the ominous and impending "later" that Menlow had promised the mayor. In fact, the fear of his surroundings enhanced his dread for that moment to come. Each new sound and smell reminded him of what lay ahead. He had hoped to go to the village and back without discovery – and now he was going to be *introduced*!

When they crossed over, they were met by a crowd, the noise of which did not make him feel any better either. Besides Adia, it was the first time he heard women talking. Their high-pitched voices and the way they spoke (most seemed to him to be verbally climbing over one another) emphasized how alien it all was from his cottage-life. It made him desperately yearn for its quietness and simplicity.

Yet that was not to be all. A host of new sensations of the town assaulted him after they had crossed the Village Green, which was a broad expanse of grass and trees for picnics, games, and other community outings. Horsey smells, the clip-clopping of hoofs, and jangling of a harness preceded a creaking wagon, followed by more new voices and noises, such as a blacksmith's clanging hammer, a door slamming, feet shuffling, and a baby bawling. The noises started running into each other so much that Gopher quit trying to separate them. Simultaneously, a spectrum of fragrances found its way into the sack's dark interior, ranging from delicious (bread baking) to pleasant (perfume) to repulsive (sewage in an alley). He was glad of being hidden inside the sack. If only he did not have to leave it!

The deluge of fear that these sensations unleashed eventually proved too much for Gopher; he either passed out or had so inwardly retreated that it was as good as passing out. Thus, his fear gave him a sort of refuge from those very things that had inspired it. Even so, it did not last long.

Stopping in front of his house, Mayor Dryden thanked the search party and called for a council meeting that night to address the issue of the mysterious happenings going around. Some cheered at this, while others were skeptically silent. The women were not so easily dismissed, for they wanted to come in and tend to the "poor darling." Ever the politician, he succeeded by suggesting that they do so while he was at the meeting. His daughter sighed when they were gone far enough to be out of hearing distance.

"I don't feel like company tonight and being treated like a baby," she said with a wry face.

Her father nodded, patting his rotund midsection. "I quite understand," he said, "for on my part I don't feel like going to the meeting; sometimes we must do things to please others. Anyway, the women mean well," Then he looked on her with commiseration. "You have really been through it, my child. How about a hot bath? I'll get the maid to start it."

Adia's eyes flashed for a moment, opening up her mouth to say something but paused as if by some internal struggle. The fire suddenly went out of her, replaced with the bright and innocent submissiveness of a child.

"Yes, father," she said but then her eyes flickered inquisitively towards the hermit.

"Oh, he's staying for supper and to rest – which is what you need, too," Dryden said, smiling as they entered into the living room through the front door. Giving orders for a hot bath and an extra place to be set for supper, he sent Adia off with the maidservant and proceeded to give Menlow a tour of the house. It was probably the biggest and nicest in town, but he had a distracted air about him as one who had long become disillusioned by his own wealth, though he became wistful for a moment when they came into the Summer Room, the windows of which displayed an overgrown garden.

"My wife loved this room," he said, "but mostly the garden. She spent hours tending it. It was so beautiful." Yet his full attention returned, and his wistfulness dissipated completely, when they returned to the living room. He stood with his back to the unlit fireplace, facing Menlow.

"As a politician," he began, almost formally, "I have gained an instinct about people. I know that you're not a crazy hermit like some believe, but yet traveling with a gopher is... not common –

neither for you nor for the – err… rodent. I didn't even know they can be made into pets. Is he tame?"

"Quite, but not how you suppose. I promised to introduce him, but it will have to be our secret," Menlow said.

The mayor laughed. "Of course. I don't think anybody else would care about a pet gopher. As a mayor, it would be embarrassing to admit anyway that I had a gopher in my house as a guest, you know! Just don't let him loose in the garden – heaven knows that it's bad enough already!" He closed the doors that led to the rest of the house so that they were alone. "The maid will not enter without knocking first, and Adia is still taking her bath."

Menlow began, "It is different to have a gopher as a pet. As a rule, they don't make good ones, but this one is especially intelligent. You'll be amazed. I have trained him so well that he could do most anything *but talk*. He has kept this lonely hermit company and I could not bear to part with him on my journey to town. And the reason for the secrecy is that if others find out how clever he is, my privacy will be lost forever. I don't want to live the life of a showman and I'm sure that he would not care for being an exhibit."

Then Menlow swung the sack in front of him with a grunt and a sigh, for he had carried the heavy load on his shoulder all day. It was this swinging movement that brought Gopher back to his senses. He felt himself being lifted out with gentle hands, Menlow's hands, and the light from the curtained windows made him blink repeatedly as the hermit placed him on the floor. He sensed Dryden's presence before his eyes could focus on him.

Not having heard the hermit's subtle cue to remain speechless, fear prevented him from talking anyway as his eyes picked out the stranger. The sight also prevented him from doing any of the tricks that Menlow tried to get him to do, like sitting up and playing dead. In fact, he did not even respond to his friend's voice in the slightest. He could only stare at the mayor like a petrified prey would stare at a predator.

Menlow laughed self-consciously, stroking his beard. "Uh, it must be you. He's not used to strangers. It took me a long while to win his confidence," he told Dryden and added, "Now, Gopher, can you hear me?" He snapped his fingers in the rodent's face. "It's all right. He's a friend."

The mayor chuckled, patting his stomach. "It must the size of my girth that is intimidating!"

At last Gopher, sensing that expectations were being placed on him and realizing that nothing horrible had yet happened, made an effort of the will to inwardly shake himself out of his terrified stupor. He saw that Menlow was unafraid. This encouraged him and the hermit's words started to make sense once more. He nodded slowly and then stood up on his hind legs like he normally did. The mayor stopped chuckling.

"Hmmm... so straight, too" he said, clearly impressed.

Menlow then repeated his instructions: "Sit down, will you please? Thanks. And now play dead. Very good."

"Impressive. You talk to him as if he could really understand you."

"More than you think," Menlow said and then addressed the rodent, "Now climb up on my shoulder." He stooped halfway. Gopher leapt the rest of the way to land on his usual spot without hesitation. It was the closest place he had to home right now. Even as he perched there, he felt that that jump had somehow breached through much of his fear.

The mayor clapped. "Excellent! Anything else?"

"*You* tell him to do something."

Gopher inwardly froze, not believing his ears.

"Me? He doesn't know my voice."

"Try it."

Gopher wondered why his friend was doing this to him.

After a moment, a corner of Dryden's mouth curled into a half smile. "Okay." He looked around and then pointed at a small stack of firewood, "Pick up a stick and put it in the fireplace – that'll be a hard one!"

It felt strange doing something for someone else. Worst than just strange, it felt unnatural and it stirred up his animal instinct to resist. But for Menlow's sake (and with a word of encouragement from him), Gopher forced himself to obey. Jumping down after Menlow bent forward, he went to the stack and picked out a stick that was small enough for his paws to handle and then placed it on the grate in the cold hearth.

Mayor Dryden's eyes bulged in amazement, which at least gave some satisfaction to the rodent. Finally the man managed to say, "*Does* he understand words?"

"Like I said," Menlow said, "it is a secret just between us."

Just then, however, the secret was spread a little thinner as Adia came in through one of the doors. Drying her hair with a towel, she did not see Gopher at first. "Dad, I took a bath but do I have to take – oh!"

Suddenly her brown eyes seemed to become browner and larger and coming out of her head, but she recovered much faster than most adults would have. In other words, she acted like the twelve year old that she was who hadn't yet grown an aversion to rodents. Her eyes, no longer bugged out, were practically beaming as she squealed "It's a gopher!" and came rushing forward. All of this was done simultaneously.

To Gopher it was both like and unlike an attack. He felt no animosity from her or even a threat of danger in her face or voice, but her action was so sudden and intrusive that they instantly aroused his instincts. Yet, because it did not appear he was in any real danger, he did not flee as he probably ought to have but rather he reacted like any mature human might when facing a stressful situation. He held his ground and exclaimed, "Stop!"

Immediately he knew that he had spoken one word too many.

Chapter Eleven

The reaction from hearing a rodent speak was not immediate. In fact, it was so unexpected that it might have been ignored completely, thanks to the human ability of dismissing as impossible those things that do not fit into one's assumptions. Hence, almost immediately Dryden had convinced himself that the gopher had either screeched or that it had been uttered by someone passing by. His daughter, however, was too young to fool herself so easily. She heard what she heard, impossible or not, and the command brought her to a stop.

"I'm not going to hurt you," she said. As if that was proof enough, she started toward him again; at the same time her father chuckled nervously to Menlow and whispered, "She's always pretending, the dear thing."

Meanwhile, the rodent fled behind Menlow's legs. "Please. Don't. Will you please –stop?" he pleaded.

"What?"

It was all Dryden could say at the moment, while Menlow said in a kindly voice, "Adia, he is not used to strangers. His name is Gopher."

"Can I play with him?" Her brown eyes asked as much as her words did.

The hermit shrugged, stroking his scruffy chin. "He's not my pet. He only belongs to me as much as I belong to him. You see, we are friends. You may ask him to play, but I think you should just try getting to know each other first."

"Is – is this some trick?" Dryden said, awkwardly as if his tongue was stumbling to get the words out.

"No – no, it isn't," Gopher nervously replied as he bravely came out from behind Menlow.

"You do talk."

In the stunned silence that followed, Gopher edged closer to the hermit and whispered up to him (or thought he whispered), "Is he a king?"

This was greeted with unexpected laughter. Adia squealed, "A king!" Even Menlow grinned.

"No, he is a mayor," he said. "He was chosen by the leading men in the town, but they have the final say in things. Most everything is voted on. It is a sign, I believe, that the kings have seen their day. Now a king concerns himself mostly with lands that are rich in some sort of business. He's not interested in poor towns deep in the forests that are difficult to reach. One day kings may be more symbolic than having real power."

"That is true," Dryden said. "It is already now more a thing of the past – though I see that the past is not altogether gone. The stories are true, though I have never known one about a talking gopher." His tone and the glint in his eyes directed at the rodent invited comment and also exuded good will.

After that, it became easier. Gopher's nervousness faded as, for the rest of the afternoon, he found himself, and his story, the center of their attention. Menlow added some detail from time to time, though most of the time he grinned like a proud father. That and their open-eyed wonder and rapt attention made Gopher realize (and feel) that his story really was special. Better yet, he began to see that, although they were different from Menlow, they weren't *that* different, and that differences did not always mean danger.

But then suddenly his fear returned as if it had never left, all because of a gentle tapping at the door. Gopher disappeared in a blur under the sofa. The maid came in and announced that dinner would be served in a short time.

"Very good," Dryden said, casually. "But we'll have the dinner in here. Thank you."

The look of surprise and confusion on her face indicated that such a thing to be unusual, but, like a good servant, she quickly recomposed her countenance with serene acquiescence, which she reaffirmed with a nod of her head and a crisp, "As you say, sir."

The mayor chuckled when she closed the door behind him. "That'll make her wonder," he said. "I'm generally a man of habit."

Gopher came out from hiding. Even though relieved enough to laugh, he could not; his heart was beating too rapidly and most of his breath seemed to have left him, which he never quite got back before another tapping sounded at the door that preceded the arrival of their meal. In that short time, though, he had managed to conclude the entirety of his story – at least, up to the point when they had met the woodcutter last night.

Trays were brought in with plates of roasted fowl, taters, and greens. Gopher rejoined them once more after the maidservant had departed. He sat between the mayor and Menlow, with Adia in a wing chair opposite. It was during this meal that Dryden became noticeably quiet and almost distracted; however, this afforded his daughter the opportunity to talk at last and she took it with gusto: "What was it like living in tunnels? Do you miss it? Are there any others like you that can talk? What did the magic carrot taste like? Are you the one who got into my mommy's garden...?"

Gopher found some of the questions perhaps even more difficult to answer than it had been in telling his story, for they pried into his thoughts and feelings, which did not fit easily into something as concrete as words. For once the maidservant's return to pick up their dirty dishes was welcomed since he didn't have to describe the difference between the taste of the magic carrot and the experience he had after eating it. (His previous answer that "it tasted like any regular carrot but the feeling it gave was like warm sunlight after a cold night" had only confused her and left him quite unsatisfied that he had done the feeling any justice.)

Afterwards, Dryden sent his daughter to wash up – quickly adding when she looked longingly back, "You can come back as soon as you're done." Adia, nevertheless, left with a protruding lower lip and a pouting face to match it. Then the mayor revealed the reason for his thoughtful silence.

"Knowing her, she'll be right back, but I wanted to ask you something and I didn't want her to pressure you. You can say no, if you want to, and she'll never know." As he spoke, he looked at each of them, so that Gopher felt that he was being asked as well. It gave him a good feeling.

"What is it?" Menlow said with a trace of wariness.

"Will you be my guests for the next three nights? I'll – I'll be honest with you. Adia has been so... ah, sad and lonely since her mother has died – it's been four months since the sickness took her – but these past few weeks, Adia's... changed. She has been acting moody, sometimes happy, sometimes sad. I never know what to expect, and often there's something else... guilt and sudden tears. Sometimes I don't even think I know her. She'll disappear and then show up. This was the first time I had others look for her with me. I've been at my wits' end at what to do, but now you have come along and she's like herself again. Maybe with your company for the next few days she'll heal from her grief – it will do me some good, too, for Lydia was a dear wife... I'll make it worth your while in supplies for your trip back home. What do you say?"

Menlow stroked his scruffy chin and eyed the mayor for a moment, and then looked at Gopher.

"What you do say?" he asked.

"Okay," the rodent found himself saying, almost without realizing it.

"But what was your daughter doing last night in –" the hermit began but was interrupted with the girl's bouncy return. After her dad told her the news, she squealed with delight.

"Can they *live* here?"

"No, no, only three days at most. They may have to leave before that," her father said.

His words seemed, however, to go right past her – or rather she went right past them in her excitement. She got on her hands and knees and started talking to Gopher without pause: "Do you like to play? Do you like hide and seek? How high can you jump? Are you afraid of cats? Don't worry, we don't have one; we have a garden, uh," she hesitated with a vague troubled look, which immediately was cleared up as she went on, "but I'll show that to you later. Do you still dig up things in gardens? What's your favorite –?"

Her father harrumphed twice during this rapid fire of questions and comments, but to no effect. At last he bent down and laid a hand on her shoulder. "Now, now, you are being too much, my dear. Don't rush it all at once, and remember, he's a guest – not a pet or a toy – every bit as much as Menlow here is, so you need to treat him as one. Okay, dear?"

"Yes, Father," the girl said reluctantly but then to Gopher she smiled sweetly and said, "I am sorry. Will you be my guest?"

The news of their stay was also announced to the maid (omitting, of course, Gopher's presence). Under his breath, the mayor whispered to her, "The old man's good for the girl, like a grandpa." The maid nodded and smiled approvingly before going off to make up the guest room.

It was not long after this that Dryden excused himself, with some reluctance, to go to the town meeting. He enthusiastically brushed his beard with a cheerful mood, but there was something in his eyes that contradicted it. "I'd ask you to come along, Menlow, but you will need to make sure that Gopher is... uh, safe."

"He's safe!" Adia said with heat. "Why do you say that?" She added with her eyes becoming glossy with a threat of tears.

"Oh, dear, I wasn't talking about you!" He said quickly, drawing her to him. "I was talking about the town women. Remember I promised them that they could come and look after you while I'm gone. How would you like them to stumble upon our friend? With Menlow here he can help make sure that won't happen. That's all I meant, dear."

"Oh!" For a moment she sounded relieved but then she said, "Oh!" again in a more exasperated way. "Do they have to stay long?"

"Maybe they won't if they see a man around the house," her father said.

It proved, however, that, generally, Menlow went unheeded by the women who showed up as soon as the mayor had departed. When the hermit had been noticed, it was with an upturned nose from a couple of the richer ladies or with a flare of irritation by a few of the others who thought themselves more practical than men. The hermit took it all in good humor as he retreated to the guest room. He brought Gopher out of his pocket, in which he had been shoved at the last second when the chattering throng had arrived.

"Sorry," he said, "about the pocket – and everything else."

It was the first time they were left to themselves, and there was such wonderful freedom in the moment – to stretch, to not *have* to talk, to just be oneself – that Gopher had not realized how much he had missed it, almost as much as he missed the cottage. It also made him think about the three long days ahead. Menlow seemed to have felt the same thing.

"I didn't plan on us being guests here and having to entertain a girl... I hope you don't mind. Three days is not so bad." His voice, however, betrayed that he felt otherwise.

Gopher did mind; that is, until that moment. He had been sore at himself for agreeing to stay, but the concern in Menlow's voice and look made everything right. He sighed more in commiseration with his friend than for himself.

"We'll make it," he said.

For nearly two hours, they just stayed in the guest room, talking or just listening to the tittering of the ladies through the wall. Gopher peaked outside through cracks in the shuttered window, though it was too dark to see much. He also explored every nook and cranny in the room.

His commiseration even extended to Adia after the women had gone upon Dryden's return. At first, Gopher didn't recognize her because she was in different clothing – a dress, the first he had ever seen, bright and flowery – and her hair was combed back and put in a pony tail. Strangely, it was the fierce expression of joy on her face that provoked his pity, for he recognized in it the same exuberance of freedom that he had felt when finally alone with the hermit. He realized that there was more than one way to be a prisoner. When she shared a piece of sweet bread with him, with which the ladies had plied her, it made her even more endearing to him.

Endearing, though, still did not mean that he had a sudden and complete change of feelings; he still would rather have gone back home. With deep longing, he often found himself wondering how much longer they would have to stay. He was glad that, soon after the mayor's return, it was time to turn in. Menlow and Gopher were given the same guest room they had retreated to.

The worst of his longings, however, came that night while trying to sleep. The sounds of Menlow sleeping in the bed above him as well as the familiar smell and feel of his fur bedding, in which he lay, emphasized by contrast the fact that he wasn't home. Alone with his thoughts and feelings, despair grew and grew until, no matter what he told himself, a certainty came over him that he would never see the cottage again. It pierced through him much like a knife would, with sorrow that was just as sharp, but, unlike a physical infliction, he could only suffer. It would have lasted all night if the allure of sleep hadn't finally (and wonderfully) proved stronger.

Unexpectedly, the next day he woke feeling much better. The sunlight through the shutters and Menlow's cheerful greeting cast a different light on last night's despondency. At breakfast (again served in the living room) the new delight Gopher found in berry jam and toast helped soften his homesickness.

Much to his surprise, Adia herself taught him something to distract him and to speed the time along by filling it with laughter and fun. As simple and childish as it may sound, what proved to be a source of new joy and delightful distraction was nothing more than the playing of games, about which Menlow had always been too busy to give any thought.

At first Gopher thought it was a lot of silly nonsense, especially since their first game was hide-and-seek. Taking turns to hide from each other seemed pointless, but he went along just to humor the child. At Menlow's prompting, Gopher hid behind the rocking chair that he sat in while she counted. As the girl shouted, "Ready or not!"

and began her search, he found a slight stirring of emotion within him that was new. It was called "giddiness," though he didn't know the word. It, nonetheless, grew in his chest, as her searching drew her nearer – and then it exploded into laughter when she found him. He could not help himself.

"That was hard!" the girl exclaimed, giggling.

Soon he was counting and she was hiding – and then they were laughing again, much sooner because hiding places were scarce in her room for someone her size. They played a few more turns, and even when the excitement of the game itself had worn off, Gopher found that the delight on her smiling face, the twinkle in her eyes, and the merriment in her laughter prolonged the fun.

The next game they played, Do-As-I-Do, produced more laughs than excitement, but it lasted an even shorter time. One reason was that the rodent, given his size and body, could only physically do so much, although his quickness easily enabled him to keep up with her. The other reason was that she couldn't keep up with him when it was his turn. Soon they were huffing on the floor between laughs.

The next game was the silliest; it was the game of pretend. He played "house" by drinking non-existent tea and sitting around a table that was even slightly too small for him, eating invisible food and pretending to converse and laugh with dolls, while Adia spoke for them by changing her voice and moving them about as if they were alive.

Gopher was glad at least that Menlow was asleep during all of this. His snores were quite reassuring. After a while, though, when Gopher forgot his self-consciousness, he discovered that pretend was even better than the other games. It sparked his imagination and made him forget his own limitations. However, after an hour (it seemed like three), he wearied of maintaining the illusion and began yearning for real talk and real play with real people. Adia, on the other hand, seemed like she could go on and on pretending.

Then, as if with perfect timing, Menlow awoke with a snort and he rocked forward in the chair. Gopher had a sudden inspiration. He abruptly set down the small little cup, which fell over.

"Oh! You spilled your tea!" Adia scolded.

"Tell us one of your stories, please," Gopher said to the yawning hermit.

This was seconded with pleading from the girl, who had in the next moment forgotten their game of pretend. Menlow gave little resistance and after a little ruminating he began with one of Gopher's favorites, Jack and the magic beanstalk. Then he went on to tell other stories, many of which Gopher remembered hearing while fishing. For Adia, the stories evoked a look of enchanted rapture on her face that increased his own enjoyment, while Menlow rocked slowly as he spun the tales in such a dreamy voice that even he seemed swept into it.

Listening to stories, Gopher realized, was a lot like pretend, though it wasn't as much work, at least not for the listener. He could have listened for the rest of the morning but that was not meant to be.

When Menlow was telling about a little pauper boy being enticed by an evil goblin into all kinds of mischief, Adia sprang to her feet and exclaimed "But it's only a story!" Immediately she became self-conscious. Her face fell as she added, "I am sorry...I like happier stories."

"Not all can be happy, but you haven't heard the end of this one," Menlow said.

"No, thank you very much, but –but I'd like to do something else. Wouldn't you, Gopher?"

Again the timing proved perfect. Dryden came home for the midday meal. It was served by the maid this time in the Summer Room. With all the light coming in from the windowed doors that opened to the garden, the rodent felt exposed, but the mayor reassured him that nobody would see him and that the maid had gone out to acquire food for tonight's supper.

Afterwards, he and Menlow played a game that sounded silly since it was called the Fox and the Geese. It was a completely different kind of game that aroused Gopher's interest at once, for it was a game of strategy, rather than of the imagination. Gopher and Adia watched on either side of the table as they ate their own meal. The girl yawned a lot and soon became restless, especially after she finished eating, while Gopher took no notice, for he enjoyed watching and learning. Her father said, after her fifth yawn, "Oh, sweetie, why don't you stretch your legs and show him the garden?" Then to Menlow he said, "Don't worry. The garden's all shut in with the brick wall and the maid has also gone out for ingredients for tonight's supper. She won't be back for an hour at least."

"I have an idea!" Adia said, showing sudden energy. "Why don't we play the Fox and the Geese in my room, just Gopher and me?"

"Let us finish first, sweetie, okay?"

It struck the rodent that she was not acting like herself, but he forgot about it as they went back to their game. Yet soon he noticed that she stifled a yawn and that she was trying to appear to be interested. When Menlow won, she even cheered, but he suspected that it was merely because it was over. Then trotting off with the board under one arm and holding the game pieces, the girl led Gopher back to her room. He wondered at her sudden burst of energy and enthusiasm.

Even though he would rather play with the mayor or the hermit, Gopher still looked forward to trying his hand at it. They played it in her room, and he proved to be a natural, but the excitement wore off even before he had won three games in a row. Whether he was that good or Adia was that bad, it made little difference. Winning held little satisfaction when he had to look across at her sulky face. It occurred to him that she really hadn't wanted to play to begin with, but why she had acted that way in the first place puzzled him. Out of mere pity (and not because he really wanted to, for he was ready for a nap), he spurted out, "Why don't we play pretend with your dolls again?"

"If you want," she said, still without much change. She gathered her dolls and set them on chairs around the little table, putting the tiny teapot and cups and saucers on it. She did it all so mechanically that she might as well have been doing any unwanted duty.

Gopher was stumped. If pretending with her dolls didn't stir her interest, then something besides games must be on her mind.

"Too bad we can't have real tea," Gopher remarked just because he couldn't think of anything else to say.

"I tried. Made a mess and I got in trouble," she said flatly.

Gopher went on with the play, this time doing all the pretending himself without the girl's direction. She just sat there, barely watching. He was just about to give it all up when he got an idea. He spoke to the prince doll next to him: "Your highness, I like your clothes. Why don't you let me wear them?" He paused to glance at Adia. No spark of interest. He went on, "They *are* nice. Do you know it's not fair that you get to be prince... eh, what's that? Not talking to me? What would you do if I decided to be the prince instead?"

He at once began trying to strip the doll of its royal purple and gold clothing, but the best he could do was to remove the crown, for his claws struggled awkwardly with the robe. His fumbling knocked the doll off its chair and he let himself fall with it so that it looked like they were wrestling. This elicited the giggling from the girl that he had hoped for. He kept wrestling and added grunts of frustration and saying things like, "Now let go!" and "It's my turn. Let me be prince so I can tell you what to do for once!"

This drew even more laughter, but which stopped as she said, "He *is* the prince. He'll have your head if you don't leave him alone. You're just a beggar. I'll go get the clothes that you deserve!"

She removed some of the doll clothes from the castoffs that were piled under her bed, but she went through a number of them before she discovered that none of the trousers were baggy enough to hold Gopher's tail in. As she left "to get something to fix it," the rodent felt ridiculous. He stood there waiting with one foreleg stuffed through a scrunched up sleeve and the other somewhere lost in a mess of clothes, while a hood slid over his head and blocked half his eyesight, and the trousers sagged, because of his tail's obstruction.

Much to his alarm, she returned with a little knife; his alarm increasing as she whispered, "Now, don't say anything. I shouldn't have this, you know, but I'll be careful." Before he could protest (because he was still too surprised), she wielded the knife on the seat of his trousers and thankfully proved to be deft with it by safely poking a hole in it large enough for his tail to fit through. Then she adjusted the hood and the arm sleeves.

"Now what do you think?" She said, bringing a hand mirror in front of him.

Gopher was more than just shocked; he was utterly cast into a horror of astonishment, for he had never seen himself in a mirror before. Although he had caught his reflection in the shallows of the stream plenty of times, its clarity was nothing like this. Having been around Menlow and treated like an equal, he had always *felt* human to some degree, but this reflection – oh, so accurate and clear! – revealed that it was a lie. The ill-fitting clothes only made it an even greater farce, accentuating his claws where hands and feet should be. His head was the worst. Compared to humans, he was *ugly*! No matter what he felt or believed about himself, the reflection proved that he was no more than a gopher, and being able to talk put him in a category all by himself where he didn't belong to either his own kind or to Menlow's. For the first time he wished that he hadn't eaten that magic carrot.

As if to remove all doubt, it was just at that moment when he heard a gasp behind him. In her excitement, Adia had left the door partially open, and the maid, obviously thinking the room was vacant, had come in with some cleaning supplies. It was only the briefest of moments, but it was enough to see the shock and disgust in her eyes – and to set her off in a fit.

"A rat! A rat!"

Immediately, but awkwardly due to the doll clothes, he scurried across the floor and plunged under the bed and into a jumble of castoff toys, not thinking (until later) how it was the most appropriate place for him: just another castoff. The only thing he could think of at the time was to wonder desperately if the girl would be able to save his life, considering the uproar that seemed to pursue him no matter how far he burrowed down into the pile.

Chapter Twelve

The truth was that he was definitely not in eminent danger. The ruckus merely came from the falling cleaning supplies after the maid had thrown up her arms in fright – and the bed gave plenty of protection from any of them landing on him. After a long shriek, the maid found her voice once more (and forgot her place) as she demanded: "What is a RAT doing in here in dress-up clothes?"

Dryden and Menlow appeared in the doorway almost instantly.

"It's quite all right, Maggie," the mayor said, "if it's what I think you're upset about."

"All right?" the maid said, "Surely, you don't know, or you would be upset, too, if you knew that –"

"It's not a rat," the mayor said. "It's a gopher that Adia found in the garden and made a pet out of." He looked at his daughter. "I told you not to bring him into the house, dear."

"I – I'm sorry, father," she said. "We were just playing."

"Maggie, I'm sorry," Dryden said as he bent down to put a brush in a bucket that she had righted. "I was afraid something like this would happen. You know children and their strange pets!" He laughed, but it had no effect on the maid, except a curt nod. He added, "Please, keep this to yourself. It could be embarrassing, you know."

She left the room like an arrow, muttering to herself and shaking her head. The mayor and his daughter began picking up her cleaning supplies, while Menlow bent down to look under the bed.

"Are you all right under there, Gopher?"

"Yes," he said, coming out.

Menlow chuckled. "Now why didn't I think of that? Clothes!"

"You like it?" Adia said, proudly.

"Yes, indeed," the hermit said, looking at him from different angles.

In a way, the attention should have made Gopher even more self-conscious about being different, but it actually made him feel better, for Menlow's kindness and genuine friendship was even better than a mirror. It made him realize that what he felt about himself wasn't the only thing that mattered. Nonetheless, he couldn't get out of the doll clothes quick enough, despite their pleading.

Dryden, having finished picking up the supplies, said, "The maid will tell. I'm not so much worried about what they might say about *me*, but it will give them more reason to pry into our lives. You'd think that being mayor entitles a certain amount of respect!"

Menlow chuckled, this time with empathy. "Respect comes easy only when people are having everything their way. The problem is that you cannot please everybody at the same time."

The mayor looked at him with surprise, at which the hermit shrugged and said, "Us old hermits have too much time on our hands. We start philosophizing about everything."

Dryden chuckled and then sat down on the rocking chair, becoming serious again. "To solve the dilemma," he said, "or at least to make the town ladies happy to some degree..." he turned his attention to Adia. "Gopher should go back to the garden where he belongs – I mean, of course, where the ladies think he belongs."

"But –" the girl began. However, her father continued on:

"Adia, why don't you and Gopher play in the garden the rest of the day? It would definitely lessen the chance of Maggie running into him again. This evening you can both come back in around suppertime. You know that's when she never sets foot out of the kitchen."

Menlow shook his head. "There are too many predators out there. She won't be able to protect him."

"Ah, too true!" the mayor said. Tapping his chin, but only for a moment: He brightened and said, "There is a spot against the back fence with a bench under the Great Oak and some grass around a pond. We could all go there and you two can play nearby."

"But there's no grass there anymore, daddy," the girl said. "And the pond is green and slimy."

Dryden chuckled. "It's all the more reason to check it out. We can make plans to reclaim the garden from the jungle! Mom would be so – ah, so proud," he said with his voice catching. He went on more brightly, "At any rate, it will do us good to get out, and you won't have another chance to show him the garden since they'll be leaving tomorrow."

His daughter said nothing, but suddenly Gopher understood something: Adia had been avoiding the garden all along. She had changed the subject when it had been mentioned earlier, and she had decided to play the Fox and the Geese only after Dryden had suggested that she show him the garden. What he didn't understand was why. Gopher felt a sudden sick feeling in the pit of his stomach. Then he recognized that it wasn't sulkiness on her face but dread because it matched how he felt, though he was still at a loss to explain it.

. . .

"What a beautiful garden!" the hermit said as they stepped through the double doors from the Summer Room on to the back porch.

Although beautiful, it struck Gopher as more of a wilderness than a garden. It was so dense that it was hard to imagine that it was enclosed within walls. The bushes, vines, and trees all grew together with the reds, yellows, whites, and blues of the flowers mixing indiscriminately with the greens, yellows, and reds of the prolific vegetables, vines, and fruits. The only tamed portion of the garden was a brick pathway that weaved through it until it disappeared around yellow flower hedges. Besides the beautiful flowers and the appearance of vegetables, it was the only feature that gave it any sort of an impression of it being a garden.

"One would suppose that in the middle of the town there could not be such a place, do you think?" Dryden said.

"No, indeed..." murmured the hermit, "How are the flowers and fruit trees not totally taken over by the weeds and the vines?"

The mayor shrugged. "I don't know. I'd like to think that it is part of the influence my wife left on the garden..." His voice trailed off, and after a moment, he laughed self consciously and went on, "Since – since then, everything seems to grow so fast. Even the colors are brighter and the produce larger than I have seen in other gardens – though, I'm afraid that if you look closely, the weeds and vines are starting to take over at last."

The mayor continued speaking as they followed the path, but Gopher did not hear any of it He was looking for Adia who had gone skipping on ahead so buoyant that he wondered if he had been wrong about her reluctance. As they rounded a curve, he saw the wall that marked the back limits of the garden, though its boundary did not stop the ivy that climbed up and covered much of its grey bricks, nor did the wall hinder a huge leafy canopy of tree branches that disappeared over its top. Then he caught a glimpse of a huge oak tree. Even from that distance, what arrested his full attention was a dark gash in its bulging trunk. Suddenly Gopher's stomach fluttered, and his head felt slightly dizzy, and the air seemed as dense in his lungs as the wild growth of the garden around him.

It was only a glimpse. When they walked on, the foliage hid it from view. Immediately Gopher felt relief, so much so that it was easy for him to imagine that it all had been a fancy. He even let loose a laugh. Menlow had not caught the glimpse (or heard Gopher's laugh) since Dryden's conversation had dominated his attention. Gopher found that he was glad that the hermit had not seen the gash. For some reason he felt embarrassed about it.

Before he could think more upon it, they came to the bench set amidst a patch of grass and weeds that bordered a moss-covered pond. Adia was already there, having disappeared on ahead of them at some point. She was now jumping over the algae-infested water, laughing and giggling to herself. Had she really been afraid of the garden? There was certainly no sign of it now. She seemed like a different person, even.

"Let's play hide and seek again!" She said, landing on the patch. "It'll be more fun out here!"

Dryden chuckled. "Children can be so moody and get away with it."

"Mmm-mmm," came from Menlow's throat and then, looking at Gopher on his shoulder, he said, "Now remember to be careful, okay?"

Though he meant well, Menlow's caution pierced Gopher, for it reminded him of his own reflection, that he *was* different, and what was worse, that the hermit was aware of it, too.

"Oh, you needn't worry, Menlow," the mayor said, patting his stomach and smiling indulgently. "It's all fenced in and, odd as it may sound, I've never seen a snake, a wild cat, or even a hawk in the garden. Too far into town, I think."

They were the words Gopher needed to hear. Suddenly he found himself *wanting* to play hide-and-seek, though in truth what he really wanted was to show that he wasn't just some fragile, helpless rodent.

"I'll be all right," he asserted.

The hermit gave in with a smile, which was followed by a nod. "Go to it then," he said amiably.

"I'll count to ten, so you'd better hurry up and hide," Gopher said, feeling like a veteran at the game. He plunged his face in what he had thought was grass but was a coarse patch of weeds. He began counting aloud.

"No fair! Count to twenty!" said the child, whose voice was more playful than plaintive.

After reaching "20," he looked up and saw nothing but the garden with Menlow and the mayor on the bench. The hermit was laughing and saying, "He wrestled it almost right back into the water and, I believe, he still would have held on!" At once Gopher remembered the incident a few weeks ago about the fish that the rodent had determined to not let get away. They had laughed about it the rest of the day, partly because he hadn't been able to get the fish smell out of his fur.

Affection shone plainly on the hermit's face as he spoke, and it was that which made the rodent feel ashamed for having been irritated at Menlow a moment before. Suddenly hide-and-seek lost some of its appeal. Nevertheless, he went on to look for the girl whom he hadn't the heart to disappoint.

It was not until he found himself suddenly alone that he realized, walls or no walls, he was still small and vulnerable. A predator could be lurking in the depths of the mass of creeping vines on his left or in the shadows of the azalea bush on his right, and he wouldn't stand a chance against it. He could not fool himself any longer. He *needed* protection, whether he liked it or not.

And he needed to find Adia, so they could finish this game – the sooner, the better.

Despite his fears of those dark places, he searched the jumbled growths of vegetation and flowers, looked around trees, and gazed up in their lower branches where she might've climbed. He explored behind a wall of ivy, and then in ditches that were filled with brambles– everywhere, that is, until there was only one place left. It was then that he realized what he had been trying to avoid: the Great Oak (as he could not help but call it), the one he had caught a glimpse of, the one with the dark gash. It was silly, he told himself. After all, *what* was there to be afraid of? It was just a tree, wasn't it?

First, though, he sought the girl within the thick hedge of rose bushes that surrounded the tree. No matter how vibrantly beautiful it was, he could not help the impression that it was like a formidable wall of protection. To his disappointment he saw that its density and innumerable thorns would make hiding impossible, however. Then, as he circled the hedge, he saw the gap, and his disappointment turned to unexplainable dread.

It was the same gap that had allowed him to view the tree trunk in the first place. He now saw the Great Oak with the dark gash in its twisted trunk for the second time, and it drew him like inevitable doom. He slipped through the gap as one who really had no choice, though it did not mean he was not afraid. Silly or not, he was afraid and he could no longer convince himself that it was just an old tree.

He froze immediately. On the other side he saw the girl sitting on one of the tree's gnarled roots that protruded out of the ground like half-buried arthritic fingers. She was smiling at him and so was the smallish young woman, whom he almost didn't see, sitting in the mouth of the dark gash.

"And who is *this*?" The strange woman said. Her clothing, which looked like the tree, was what made her hard to spot. When she stepped down from the tree's opening, though, much to his surprise, he saw that they were not clothes at all, but herself. They gave the impression of bark, grass, leaves, and moss. Yet the only way to tell her gender, he realized, was by her feminine face, which was rather strange because it too appeared tree-like. Her almond-shaped eyes, set in a light brown face, looked like small knotholes while her perpetually upturned mouth was large enough for a squirrel to live in. Beside her feminine look, the feature that differed most from a tree was her hair. It was like long wispy grass that, although brown, was as alive and healthy as if it were green. It seemed to listlessly float about her in a continual breeze.

Adia introduced him, no longer smiling. "Gopher – is a friend of mine. He can talk, too," she added with a nervousness that Gopher understood. The strange woman's penetrating gaze made him fidgety, too, but when she suddenly smiled, he found that it also made him happy.

"A talking gopher – The Awakening from the Age of Magic has started indeed. I thought I was the first! You, too, shall be a friend of mine. I and my tree are called Maythenia. I am a hamadryad, a tree nymph, and this Great Oak belongs to me and I belong to it."

"I am not from that Age," Gopher said, "for I have not been able to talk until I ate a magic carrot."

"Oh! What news is this?" Maythenia said, "And what does it

mean? Magic carrots that make rodents talk? Are there anymore of them – of magic carrots, I mean, but what about talking rodents? No more? That's good – err, I mean that makes you special, doesn't it?"

"Thank you," Gopher said, though he wasn't sure if it was really a compliment.

"Anyway, let us not worry about such things," she went on as if he hadn't said anything, "unless such things mean fun for us. Are you fun?"

"Yes, I think so," the rodent replied slowly.

"Ah, but I bet you've never had as much fun as Adia and I have had. It is because we have a secret that we cannot share with anyone, even gophers. But we will let you share in our fun. First, though, you must close your eyes, Gopher. It will only be for a moment. I'll even give you a kiss."

As he did so, the touch of her kiss on his head, as well as an intoxicating woodsy smell, left him swooning and unable to open his eyes, even though he hadn't wanted to be left out of the secret.

"You may now open them," Maythenia said after a few, long moments. Her words seemed to release him.

Nothing seemed changed… except that there appeared a resemblance between the girl and hamadryad (who were now closer together) that he hadn't noticed before. The hamadryad and the girl laughed at the same time. He laughed, too, because otherwise he'd be an outsider.

•   •   •

Menlow interrupted the mayor the moment the sounds of their laughter reached them. "What is that?" he said.

Dryden laughed. "The sounds of playing! I think Gopher must have found Adia's hiding spot."

"But it sounds like someone else is laughing, too."

"Oh, I think *that* is just a strange bird. I hear it occasionally. Isn't it the silliest sound ever?"

Menlow replied, "I think not."

Without an "excuse me," he dashed off, but by the time he found, and passed through the gap in the rose hedge, the laughter had already stopped and Gopher and the girl had vanished. Neither could they be found anywhere else in the garden. By this time Dryden's concern had grown to even surpass the hermit's.

"Not again!" he wailed.

Chapter Thirteen

Their disappearance came about like this: While still laughing, Adia's mysterious friend climbed up the trunk and paused at a crook between branches, saying over her brown shoulder, "Catch me if you can!" With an answering laugh, Adia began to climb in pursuit but then she looked back at Gopher, her laughter momentarily broken by a look of irritation before scooping him up and putting him on her shoulder to take up the chase.

What happened afterwards was an incredible blur. As the girl followed, she scrambled up and along branches, jumped across gaps, and at times swung like a monkey from one branch to another. It was all done with the ease that one has in dreams. Strangest of all, despite all the twists and turns, ups and downs, that she took, Gopher had so little difficulty in staying on her shoulder that made it even more dreamlike.

Finally, having at some point crossed over the back wall, she dropped down into an alley. Maythenia, who was already on the ground, went cartwheeling down the lane as fast as any cart wheel could go. Adia gleefully pursued, and Gopher was also caught up in her frivolity. Somehow the girl was able to keep up without the cartwheels and he to remain on her shoulder without tumbling off.

Much happened next that quickly dampened his frivolity and that Gopher could hardly bring himself to believe. That was because he did not *want* to believe what was happening. For instance, the hamadryad, skipping along, paused at a back window, leaned in, and brought out a pail of walnuts. She swung the stolen container, giggling and looking back at Adia as if proud of her theft. At the head of the alley, Maythenia gave pause long enough to peer around the corner, and gave further pause before she tossed the pail's contents into the street. The walnuts scattered under the feet of some women, whom Gopher wondered might be the ones who were at the house last night. Delight shone in the girl's eyes, and her hand covered her giggles, as she watched the ladies frantically grabbing each other and anything else to keep from falling.

This trick was followed by an even nastier one a short time later when, having ascended on to the roofs, Maythenia dropped a cat on a young woman who was stepping out of her house. The lady's shrieks followed them as they continued dancing above, skipping from rooftop to rooftop. Some of the pranks Adia did herself, such as plugging up chimneys, throwing loose tiles, making frightening noises to a child taking a nap, crowing to get the dogs barking, and drenching the head of an old man with water from a bucket he had just set down. The girl also removed wagon bolts, loosened saddle straps, and she sneaked fish into a pair of boots. But it was the hamadryad that contrived and set forth into motion most of these tricks. The tree dryad and the girl were like a whirlwind of mischief.

At first Gopher questioned whether the tricks were all that funny, for laughing at someone else's distress had never occurred to him before. Yet because everything seemed so unreal, he convinced himself that it was either a dream or one of the dryad's enchantments. The latter seemed likelier, he thought, for that could be the "secret" that the fairy and the girl shared. Either way, it set his mind at ease and so that, after a while, he let himself get caught up in their merriness and in excited expectation at seeing what new pranks that they were going to do next. There was something appealing, enticing even, to be free to do anything one wanted to, especially since it wasn't real. It was like an adventure that continued as long as one chooses, doing whatever one chooses.

What gave him pause to reconsider, however, was a cross look from an old woman, whose path they briefly crossed. In truth, she did not see them for she was nearly blind, but her perpetual squinting was misunderstood, for it felt like an accusation to Gopher, whose conscience asserted itself, filling him with guilt. At once he knew that he was neither dreaming nor enchanted. As a result, he began wondering if those who had tripped on the walnuts or the woman with the cat dropped on her head had been hurt. He also imagined those in the houses choking on the smoke. He pictured expressions of fear, pain, and anger as the riders fell off their horses. *They* wouldn't be laughing, he knew.

The more he thought of the consequences and to consider how the victims might feel, the less funny the jokes became and the more something became increasingly clear to him. It was that even if it *was* all a dream, why would he think it funny anyway, especially when he wouldn't like it done to him? Real or not, he concluded that he had to stop it. What wasn't so clear, however, was the How.

The moment that he began to ask that, it was as if his eyes were opened and he noticed some strange things about his two companions. For one thing, the brightness of the hamadryad's greens and browns was diminished so much that the colors were now hard to distinguish from each other. Likewise, even Adia's appearance, too, seemed to lack in coloring. It was as if... as if they were *becoming* shadows. In fact, he realized that the shadows that they had been retreating into were actually their own. For another thing, he noticed just how close they always kept to each other. Wherever Maythenia went, no matter how quick, the girl was always able to keep behind, though sometimes the girl led the way and the hamadryad would laugh as if this was somehow funny in itself. Then it dawned on him all at once: The hamadryad was Adia's shadow. Or was it the other way round? Both, in fact, seemed part shadow, part real.

It was this realization that decided a course of action, which required no thought. In an impulse born out of equal parts fear and disgust, he jumped from Adia's shoulder just as she was climbing over a fence with the hamadryad ahead of her. Gopher, intending to head back in the direction they had just come, had thought that, with the fence between them, he could easily slip away. Beyond that, however, he had not bothered to think.

He landed on a crate that the girl had used to climb on. Just then Adia, now on the other side, called out, "Gopher! Where are you?" There was such concern in her voice that he immediately regretted his impulsive action, but then he felt just the opposite when the hamadryad's voice said, "Did the little one slip off? We must find him. It's dangerous for a fellow like him to be alone in a town."

It was strange how her voice made him feel, especially because she sounded even more concerned than the girl. Yet the concern was... different – not false, but different. Whereas Adia's concern was centered definitely on him, the hamadryad's seemed "off center." Maybe the clue was that she was expressing too much anxiety coming from someone whom he had just met. It raised the question: What was she *really* worried about?

A vague fear that the answer was "nothing good" rose up in him and it paralyzed him from running away. He managed to break free of its grip, though, as he heard Adia scrambling back up the other side. He slipped in a gap between the crate and the fence to find that the container was backless and empty. A perfect place to hide- or rather, the only place, he thought. It shook and creaked dangerously when the girl landed on it. She seemed too heavy to be part shadow.

"Oh, dear, how could you have lost him?" Maythenia said, accusingly.

"I don't know!" the mayor's daughter whined.

"Hush!" said the other. "Don't be such a little girl! Think! If he had *just* fallen off, we would have found him around here, right?"

"But he might have fallen off before and I didn't realize it."

"Wouldn't he have cried out? No, I'm afraid he jumped."

"Jumped? Why?"

"Perhaps our games were a bit too much for him. He got scared. I dare say that he's not used to so much fun... or perhaps he noticed something that gave away our secret and it was *that* which scared him."

"What do you mean?"

The hamadryad sighed. "That I have taken your shadow. You're used to it; he isn't. Perhaps if he realized that it is just for fun and that you haven't given your shadow to me permanently, he'd understand better."

"Let's find him," Adia said impatiently.

"No need," Maythenia said. "I already did. I said these things in case he wanted to change his mind. It's not too surprising – is it? – that being a shadow makes it easier to see shadowy things. He's hiding in the crate."

Gopher blinked when Adia removed the crate, despite the dimness of the light in the alley.

"I'm sorry, Gopher," the hamadryad said, "It's really all my fault that you are so scared." The hamadryad looked pale and dim in contrast to the girl, whose pouting lips and furrowed brow somehow seemed to give her more substance. Even though they did not make her look like her normal childishly happy self, the rodent decided that he liked her better this way rather than as a shadow. It was probably why it was easier for him to say what he wanted to say.

"I don't like the games you play. They hurt people and I don't think they're funny."

The shadowy dryad seemed to fade even further so that she was starting to blend with the dim surroundings. "You are right," she said, her voice seeming to come out from nowhere. "It's my fault, because I don't like people, I guess. They tend to cut down trees or approve of those who do. I guess that's why I like the two of you. Children and gophers are much more agreeable. Can you teach me how to have a *better* type of fun?"

"But how have you taken her shadow?" Gopher said.

"That is our secret, but –" Maythenia said, "it can be your secret, too. It will help you not be so afraid. You can show him, Adia."

The girl pulled out a large silver locket that was dangling from a chain around her neck and opened it. Inside was a thick sliver of wood that was so white that Gopher did not see it at first because it matched the silver interior, though, at a closer look, he saw that it glowed softly with an inner light.

The hamadryad said, "It is a sliver from the very heart of the Maythenia. Just as I am bonded to the tree, so I am to Adia but only when she holds the heart-sliver. It is a weaker bond, so I am only able to dwell in her shadow."

"Can Gopher get one, too?" Adia asked eagerly as she closed the locket.

"I cannot be two shadows at the same time," Maythenia lectured but then more softly, "Besides, there are only so many heart-slivers and it takes years to re-grow them. Since the life in one of them lasts for only so long, I shall have to go back to the tree soon. Shall we find something better to play at before my time is up?"

Adia pursed her lips for a moment. "How about some games in the woods? Only this time we won't play tricks on anyone or chase any woodcutters."

"What? Not even –" she stopped as the girl shook her head, and then sighed. "Okay. No tricks. On anyone."

It was not until they started moving again, with Gopher on the girl's shoulder, that he realized something that was so devastating that it made him feel sick. To put it simply, he realized that he had forgotten about Menlow. By now the hermit must be searching the garden, the house, and... the town. Now, however, it would be too late, for they would be in the woods. Yet what made him so sick was the fact that he had so easily forgotten Menlow. It was as if his friend hadn't really meant anything to Gopher.

In that moment he might have once more slipped from Adia's shoulder and defied the risks to go on back alone – to make things right, to be a better friend. It was tempting, but there was still a part of him that was afraid to get ran over, stepped on, or eaten by an animal. Besides, soon they'd be back, and then he'd apologize. Really there was no reason to believe otherwise. Obviously the girl had gone on many outings with Maythenia and had returned safely. Why not again? It was that internal argument that stayed him on the girl's shoulder as they slipped out of town and into the woods.

If he had thought that their mischievous excursion through the town had been exciting, this "traipsing" in the woods proved terrifying, especially at first. The hamadryad led the way, and just like at the Great Oak, they immediately climbed up the nearest tree and started swinging and jumping from branch to branch, but only much faster. The trees blurred by in greens and browns, mixed with shadows and light. Gopher would have felt even more amazed at the girl's abilities than before if death hadn't threatened to occur at any moment as they spanned the wavering and thin-branched treetops in a dizzying whirl. Yet he did not fall off and there was never a slip or a wrong step or a breaking of a limb. Each time, when death was impossibly averted at the last moment, the relief was so intense that it gave him a heightened sense of being alive, though terror would engulf him once more when he suddenly faced yet another seemingly lethal acrobatic feat. On and on they went, terror and relief playing his emotions back and forth. However, it was only when he realized that he wasn't going to die – that he could trust Adia and the hamadryad's judgment – that his screams no longer stemmed from terror but from the joy of the thrill. When not screaming, he was laughing whole-heartedly out of excitement for the next big "death-defying event."

At last they hopped down into a clearing. Adia was puffing loudly, while her shadow companion, not having lungs, kept up a steady stream of talk: "Did you see that sleeping owl we came upon? Ha! What a mighty hunter he is! We could've gone higher – did you see that one giant tree? –but it was too much. I didn't want Gopher to lose his voice! Nobody enjoys a forest like we can, eh? Gopher, what do you think now? Was that better? Innocent play is fun, too. Let's play chase when you get your breath, okay? Or how about hide and seek? I'll hide first. That will give you time to catch your breath before you try to catch me! Close your eyes to give me a chance, and I mean both of you!"

Gopher obeyed, hiding his face in Adia's hair. Somehow he sensed without having to use his eyes when the shadow had gone a distance. At the same time the rodent found that he could think a little more clearly, as if the distance away from her had been the reason.

Immediately with that gained clarity came the remembrance of Menlow, and a horrible wave of guilt swept over him. He had forgotten him again! Without opening his eyes (lest the hamadryad was watching from a distance), he whispered into Adia's ear: "We ought to go back. They'll be worried."

"I know," she whispered back and after a pause added in a strained voice that indicated inner conflict, "but just one game, please? And then I'll tell her that we've got to go, okay?"

The rodent sighed heavily. "Okay."

They soon started the "seeking part of the game – or rather Adia did, since Gopher still rode on her shoulder. Although the dense forest proved to be ideal for hiding, it soon became more of a game of chase. The hamadryad never seemed far away. Unnatural flitting of shadows here and there, which were accompanied by laughter and playful taunts, seemed so close but were far enough away to keep them in pursuit.

"Over here... oh, to your left... err, I mean my left. Ha! Ha! Oh, too slow, now I'm over this way... keep going, over the stump... here I am – no, over here! Fooled you, you went right past me and didn't know it...."

Maythenia went on in a steady flow while Adia followed deeper into the woods until it was impossible to tell one shadow from another, but the girl did not seem to mind. Even Gopher once again got caught up in the excitement of the play. At last Adia stumbled out of some bramble and into a clearing where the hamadryad stood quite evident in the sunlight. She was bending over, not from exhaustion, of course, but from laughing.

"I give up, I give up...! Now, it's your turn... Hey, why don't you make it hard on me? It's only fair since what I've put you through. What about this? You can *both* hide!"

Strange as it may seem, this sounded like a grand idea to Gopher. It did not occur to him that he would be *alone* in the woods where danger lurked, for he was swept into the ecstasy of fun, and that, by definition, was all that mattered at the time.

"Okay!" Adia said, "Now, close your eyes – but how are we to know they're closed? We can't see them."

Maythenia gaily replied, "That's right! Shadows have no eyelids! How grand! I never thought of that before!"

The tree spirit went on, "I'll hide in the knothole of that birch. I can't see out of it because it's not my tree... You hear that frog? I'll count up to twenty croaks. Better make that thirty, he's quite lively!"

The shadowy figure then funneled itself into the knothole of a tree set at the edge of the clearing, and just when she disappeared, her voice came out of it, like an echo: "Better hurry, ten croaks already!"

"You go that way, and I'll go this," Adia said in a whisper, stooping to let the rodent down.

"That way" for Gopher was towards the sound of the frog. As soon as he stepped out of the clearing and entered the underbrush, the croaking stopped. He thought, "Ha! How's Maythenia going to count now?" It was at that moment, however, that his thinking sharpened again – and again he remembered Menlow. "It is because of Maythenia," he realized. "She must have some kind of magic in her voice that makes me want to have fun when I shouldn't. I won't be fooled by it next time."

He was thinking all of this while traveling through the undergrowth, forgetful of the game until he heard Maythenia's voice call out from the clearing, "Scaring the frog away won't help you. Here I come anyway!"

Then Gopher had a sudden and strong urge to hide, though it did not stem from the spirit of hide-and-seek but from fear, for two ideas came into his head almost at the same time. The first was the sudden realization that the hamadryad did not actually like him – if the hamadryad was intruding into his friendship with Menlow, he wouldn't have liked her either, just like he hadn't liked Tobias – and, secondly, he had a suspicion about her intentions: She had wanted to get Gopher alone without Adia to interfere.

Noiselessly, he scurried through the undergrowth away from the clearing. He was going towards something that made a steady sound, but before he could reach it, a smiling voice sounded close behind: "Oh, Gopher, where are you? Just up ahead, I gather by your smell. You know everyone has their own particular smell of fear, especially gophers. What are you afraid of? Surely, you don't think I planned to get you alone like this? You don't think that I'm jealous of you being chums with Adia, do you? Oh, that's funny! Friends with a gopher! Ha!" she exclaimed and then her voice took on a sharp, quieter tone, "But girls are silly creatures, aren't they? She just might be silly enough to prefer you over me. I've never been one to take chances. Friends are hard to come by for dryads who only have their trees. So keep on running, running far away from here and make friends with your own kind!"

During all this speech, Gopher had been speeding through the forest in a zigzagging pattern, for the hamadryad's voice seemed to move about, blocking whichever way he chose. The most despairing part, however, was that the voice was never out of breath, whereas he was quickly running short of it. What would the fairy do to him when he could run no farther, he wondered?

He never found out.

The forest ended abruptly at a sheer cliff, but Gopher didn't see it. One moment he was running as fast as his four legs could manage over roots and boulders, down and then up gullies, through brambles, and around trees. Then in the next, he felt his body tumbling in mid-air, though Gopher only experienced it for the briefest of moments before he plunged into the icy-cold river fifteen feet below.

Sheer instinct saved him, for he did not have the presence of mind to think to swim. He swam because he had the will to survive and the natural talent for it. Despite the turbulence that knocked him against the rocks and spun him about so that he didn't know which way was up, he somehow managed to break through to the surface with gasping breath.

The first thing he saw was Adia's face peering over the cliff above. It was so contorted with distress that he did not recognize it; that is, not until he heard her voice, which was raised in a frantic pitch.

"Save him! Don't let him drown!"

Then Gopher heard another voice, which he recognized as belonging to Maythenia. It was nearly in his ear.

"Still alive?" she said with impressed amusement. "Don't get your hopes up. I'm only pretending to help, or she might never forgive me. Ha! Funny, though: if I really wanted to help you, I couldn't. After all, I'm only her shadow. What can I do?"

Her laughter was the last thing Gopher remembered hearing before the cold, rushing darkness took him.

Chapter Fourteen

Gopher awoke immensely happy, but at the same time it felt strange, out of place, to feel that way since he could not understand or remember what he should be so happy about. It was such a wonderful feeling, though, that it did not seem to matter. He didn't even bother to open his eyes and look about his immediate surroundings. Yet he could not keep from feeling that his back was encased in something cold and moist that was a contrast from the warmth on his face. A steady breeze ruffled his fur. These sensations roused him just enough to realize that he had been asleep and that the euphoric feeling must have come from one of those dreams that he could never remember. "Ah, it wasn't real, then – just a dream," he thought with some disappointment, though not enough to banish his happiness. He could just lie there forever...

Suddenly a splashing sound to his left roused him fully. Upon opening his eyes and seeing the river on his left and the forest just over the embankment on his right, he remembered all that had transpired. It wasn't until after he pried himself out of the hardening mud of the riverbank and looked out across the smoothly flowing river that he wondered how he had managed to survive.

Yet having survived was not enough to counter the desolation that came from realizing that he was alone and lost. His eyes brimmed with tears, for a strong certainty came over him that he would never see Menlow again – or hear his laughter, or listen to his stories, or ride on his shoulder. It pierced his heart and obliterated the blissful remnant feelings of his dreams. He could not imagine being happy ever again and regretted that he had not drowned.

He might have sat there crying until he died (which would not have been long for any rodent out in the open wild), if it wasn't for Menlow – or, rather, for the influence that the erstwhile wizard held over the rodent. Menlow had planted something in him that was fundamentally deeper than any lesson or lecture ever could. It was hope. Just picturing Menlow in his mind filled him with determination.

"I will find my way back!" he said aloud.

With extreme effort, he pried the rest of himself out of the mud encasement and quickly reached the shelter of a bush on top of the bank. Immediately he felt better, even more hopeful, as he brushed off the rest of the dried mud and checked for any damage. He determined that the soreness on his nose came from only a scratch and that the pain he felt throughout his body was nothing more than aches that could be expected from being battered by rocks in the river.

Next he took a careful stock of his surroundings as he tried to form an idea of what he ought to do. What he saw did little to inspire him. The river was broader and a little faster than he remembered it and the trees were mostly spruces and pines, types of which he had seen before. These indicated that the river had taken him downstream a lot farther than he had hoped. Just how far, he did not want to consider. On top of that, the sun was dipping towards the horizon, which meant very little time to travel. It also meant he would have to stay overnight in the forest. Alone.

He pushed the thought aside to keep despondency at bay. However long it would take, he knew that he had better start right away. With that determination freshly resolved, he left the protection of the bush and began following the river upstream. The bank quickly became rocky and steep, but he decided to avoid it as much as he could, for he knew by instinct that snakes loved rocks and water, perhaps as much as they loved rodents.

Yet the forest that skirted the bank provided even greater obstacles, such as thorn bushes so dense that even Gopher's small frame could not penetrate without getting scratched. Also there were felled trees, shrub-choked ravines, and boulders that he had to circumnavigate.

None of those mattered much when compared to the noises of forest life that began multiplying with the approach of sunset. The deepening shadows hid the sources of the rustling sounds that were in the undergrowth as well as in the leaves above, the hooting, the tittering, the fluttering of wings, and especially the noises that sounded like breathing and panting. They all aroused his deepest fears, which were nearly realized by the scent of a predator, a predator that could not be far away. It spurred him to do even more zigzagging and backtracking, though he managed to keep from panicking. He dodged from cover to cover, whether it was rock, bush, or low hanging branches; anything that would keep him hidden.

Then suddenly he stopped in terror when he realized that he could no longer hear the river. Its importance dawned on him: Menlow would be traveling downstream to look for him, and now they would miss each other. Even now, he thought despairingly, it might be too late.

Because of the darkness, he was too far away to attempt to go back. His only hope was that Menlow would also stop for the night somewhere upstream. In the morning the rodent would find his way back to the river and stay near it from now on. Predators or not, he decided that it would be worth the risk.

He did not go an inch farther that night, but curled up where he was, under the low branches of a pine tree, snuggling against its trunk as close as he could get. The wind softly blowing the branches overhead reminded Gopher of the cottage but it provided no peace but rather made him yearn for the peaceful and secure way of life that seemed so long ago, especially since the breeze created shifting moonlit shadows and soft stirrings that kept him vigilant. Finally he became so exhausted that he gave up caring and closed his eyes.

Even then sleep did not come right away. His mind wandered amidst memories so vivid that he seemed to be reliving them... crouching on the hermit's shoulder as his friend took aim at a deer at a stream, and then the sudden twang of the string's release and the blur of the arrow speeding towards its mark... of the fine meal of venison that they had that evening... of their laughing and talking around the crackling fire in the hearth afterwards... another time when Menlow had fought to catch a particularly resistant trout at the end of his line... of the stories on the bank as they watched the dark sky slowly brightening to a pale blue with the approach of morning... of Menlow, grunting and sweating, as he swung the axe and the wood splitting... of the hermit's exasperation at being burned while cooking over the fire... of his stooping figure and scruffy beard while digging around in the garden...

The memories filled him with a homesick yearning that broke his heart. He had never wanted anything so intensely. Then quite suddenly sleep took him, just like walking off an unexpected cliff.

He woke up late the next day startled by the cawing of a raven almost overhead. He must have had a wonderful dream because, upon waking, reality seemed to pale by comparison and the heartsickness from last night returned double. Even the golden beams of sunlight through the canopy of pine branches overhead that painted the forest in striking contrasts of dark and lights colors left him unfazed. He curled back into a ball, hoping to recapture the dream, whatever it was about, but the raven's persistent cawing made that impossible. Anyway, he pointed out, a dream certainly would not bring him closer to either finding Menlow or to returning to his old life at the cottage. What was a dream compared to that?

It was that thought which stirred him to life and to realize just how dangerously foolish it was to want something as insubstantial as a dream, no matter how wonderful it had been. He got up and faced the "ugly world." That was how he saw it, but he immediately countered it with the thought that he spoke out loud: "Today I'm going to see Menlow again!"

He set action to his words and began in the direction his

instinct told him was where the river lay. This world was really not so ugly after all, he thought, for he felt better already; unfortunately, as his appreciation and his hope grew, so did his impatience. It grew to the point that he forgot all caution. Instead of seeking cover, he trekked his way through the forest openly. In his determined, hopeful mind-set, the shortest way was the fastest and most direct way.

Crossing a grassy clearing, he came to a flat rocky ground that more than doubled the size of the meadow he had just left. He remembered it from last night because it had taken him a long time to circumnavigate it and had been one of the chief obstacles that had gotten him to veer far from the river. He failed to recall, however, the danger he had perceived at the time; rather, the sight of the flat, unobstructed ground spurred him into acting even more recklessly because he also remembered that the river had not been that much farther away.

He vaguely felt the heat on his feet or noticed the glare of the sun reflecting on the rocky ground. But then, more distinctly, he noticed when they were suddenly diminished. That's strange, he thought without slowing. Although he appreciated the relief, he didn't recall there being any clouds in the sky.

Perhaps it was that oddity or something else that made him look up – and then he suddenly froze in place, when the dark silhouette of the bird against the sun should have made him run faster. The falcon was diving straight for him, and in that brief moment he imagined feeling its talons piercing through his fur, burrowing deep into his body, and then lifting him off the ground. So vivid and horrifying was the picture in his mind that he realized that none of it had yet happened and that his eyes had been closed. When he opened them, the shadow was gone and the rock was as hot as ever, as if the swooping bird had been his imagination all along.

A voice spoke from behind him.

"Nothing now to worry about, little one – and I thought that *I* was always a little careless! Ha! I never saved a gopher before. Now don't ask me why I did it. Even I do not know that, but does it matter? I just go where the wind takes me! Ha! Ha!"

Gopher turned and saw not five feet behind him a small figure of a creature that could clearly not be mistaken for a human, or an animal either, which was evidenced by his intelligence that came not only from his words but also from the glint in his smiling green eyes that were the only round features amidst his rather sharp face, pointy ears and steeply sloping eyebrows. Even the corners of his mouth rose up so high and narrow as he smiled that the lower curved portion of his mouth appeared sharp like a "V." Most of his wispy green hair also pointed in the general upward direction. He wore a green dirt-smudged shirt and brown pants that were flecked with pine needles. All in all, he looked like a strange creature-like man who had crawled through the pine forest in the midst of a windstorm.

Gopher might have stared in astonishment, but he did not, for he felt towards the fairy (which undoubtedly he was) the same kind of familiarity that he had felt towards the brownies, the Great Oak, and the hamadryad. As in those cases, it made complete astonishment impossible, but in this instance there was something delightfully disarming about this creature.

All of this went through him in a moment, for then Gopher said, "Thank you – but what did you do – I mean, what happened to the...?"

The creature laughed and did a cartwheel without using his arms, landing in the same spot. "You were saved; that's what happened! But as to what I did to make that happen, I cannot take all the credit. Ha! Ha! Momentarily you shall see what I mean...." Then he just stood there, his eyes squinting as he peered into the horizon, but they suddenly brightened. "Ah, the other half of your rescuer has arrived – or shall I say returned?"

He put up his long thin-fingered hand and caught a flying green pointed hat, which he promptly placed on his head as his grin became pointier than ever.

"Of course, if I hadn't thought to throw my hat, I might have hurled a rock or did a number of things, but I didn't want to kill the poor hungry thing. I'm sure he'll find his breakfast soon enough, but at least it won't be you!"

"How did your hat save me?"

"By covering the bird's eyes and leading it away."

"How did –"

"By my magic, of course," the creature said, "though I had to give some of it away to make the hat do what it did. I could have easily changed myself into a hat and done the same thing but then you might have run away by the time I returned and, besides, I don't know how hard it would be to change back from being a hat! I've never been that before!"

Then he bowed in a complete change of attitude. "Excuse me. I forgot to present myself. I am a pixie, but I'd rather be called Farwyll. It means 'far traveler.'"

"I am called Gopher."

Farwyll winked. "Oh, I know that already. You see, I am the one who led you and the hermit on a merry chase, but it hadn't been merry for neither of you, was it?"

"What are you talking –" Gopher began, but then he remembered. He also realized why Farwyll had seemed familiar. It had been his scent that he had followed. "That had been you!"

The pixie's already rosy skin turned alarmingly red. He nodded. "Just a little fun that us pixies like to have. It was a weakness of mine – but now," he raised a wetted finger into the air, "the wind has got up and there's not much time for such foolery anymore. Will you forgive me for my prank?" He bowed and waited.

Waves of amazement and self-consciousness swept over the rodent. Even Menlow had never made him feel so important. He murmured, "Yes – uh, yes, of course."

In another abrupt change, Farwyll followed through with the bow, like he was falling forward, though the movement turned into another standing-still cartwheel. He righted himself and said, "In that case, would you care to let me lead you in the *right* direction– but don't misunderstand me. I do not lead at all. I only follow. Would you care then to follow along with me?"

"Follow what?"

"Why, the wind, of course! Ha! Ha! And it seems –" he put his forefinger in his mouth, pulled it out, and held it out before him before saying, "And it seems to be leading the same way you were going – was it the river? Good!"

Gopher laughed, and then the pixie led the way, skipping along and barely touching the ground with his bare, slender feet. Led by the wind, Gopher wondered? Not even the faintest breeze stirred the air, but that didn't matter. According to Menlow's stories, pixies were known for their nonsensical fun, but the good ones could be relied upon both for their faithfulness and their instinct in times of need.

They could also be relied upon for being unpredictable. Accordingly, it took them a little longer than it seemed necessary to reach the river. Farwyll sometimes zigzagged through the woods. Once they went in circles, and when Gopher mentioned it, it only inspired Farwyll to sing, "Around and around we go, wherever the wind does blow! Around the mountains or over them, if need be, we'd even swim through the sea!" This alarmed Gopher, of course, but he followed anyway, telling himself that at least they were going towards the river, in however roundabout fashion that the pixie was taking them.

His short four legs could barely keep up with the pixie's two longer ones. By the time they reached a steep embankment, he was so thoroughly winded and tired that he would have stumbled down it if pixie hadn't grabbed him by the tail.

"Not so fast there!" Farwyll exclaimed, and when he let go of Gopher's tail, he added, "Sorry about that. I've heard somewhere that rodents are sensitive about their tails, but there's no reason for letting someone fall just on account of their pride, right?"

The swift flowing, white churning river ran at the bottom of the slope. Gopher thought that it might have looked like that when he had first fallen into it, though he really hadn't seen it properly since he was more concerned about not drowning at the time. Nevertheless, the way back to the town felt close. He grew excited and impatient, even to the point that he began at once running in the upstream direction, despite his breathlessness. He was stopped by Farwyll's voice behind him.

"We ought to rest, my young little Gopher, oughtn't we? Rest and wait for the direction of the wind to lead us on. The temptation is to run ahead."

Grudgingly, Gopher turned back and followed the pixie down the embankment. The rodent drank, while Farwyll's idea of rest proved much different. He waded and splashed in the shallows, laughing and singing. His actions reminded him of Maythenia's, except the pixie seemed a contented type of fellow and was, therefore, an easy friend, while the hamadryad's thirst for fun made her a demanding one. A thought crossed his mind that they might come across her again, but in the pixie's company he could not bring himself to feel too concerned. Farwyll must have noticed Gopher's thoughtful looks.

"You look like you have been following a different wind, or you wouldn't be looking so worried," he said, sitting on the bank next to the rodent.

Gopher sighed. "I haven't been following any wind. I'm – I'm trying to find my friend..." He went on to tell his story, all the way to the part about being driven into the river by Maythenia, concluding, "And I know that Menlow must be worried! He probably thinks I drowned. Will you help me get back?"

"Ah, that..." the pixie said. "Of course, I'll help you but I can only do that by following the wind, so I can't guarantee that it would be in the direction of what you might expect– ah, wait a second..." Farwyll wetted his finger and held it up in the air. "The wind has shifted. We go..." he frowned and tested the air again, "Ah, the adventure truly begins. It is not upstream as we expected, but downstream. Will you come?"

"Has he already passed by?" Gopher said.

The pixie looked blank for a moment and then understanding broke on him: "Oh! Answers you want! Well, the wind does not talk to me, but the funny thing is that it is never, never wrong. Whatever way that it blows may not be the surest or the swiftest, but it is always the bestest."

"But will it lead to Menlow?"

"That I cannot say, my little Gopher."

"But I can't feel anything!" the rodent confessed.

"Oh, it's not *wind*!" Farwyll laughed. "I just call it that. Have you ever seen something out of the corner of your eye, but when you look for it, nothing's there? It's like that, only it's also like a distant song or twilight dance or soft laughter. To be plain, I don't know *what* it is, for if I try to pin it down, it would not be there. I can only let it lead me. In that way it's like the wind. You can never *really* see it."

"But why do you stick your finger out as if you're feeling for it?" Gopher remembered, with a pang of homesickness, Menlow doing just that once or twice while hunting.

"Ha! Ha! That's true. I do do that, don't I? Forgive me my silly habit! It means nothing. Ah! I sense the wind is getting a trifle stronger. I must be off." He looked hopefully at Gopher.

"But how can I know whether it's the bestest – I mean, the best way for me?"

"As to *knowing,* that is water too deep for me. I don't *know* much of anything at all, but I can be certain of one thing and it is that the wind won't lead me wrong." Then the pixie became serious, bent down, and looked Gopher right in his eyes. "Listen, little Gopher: Follow what you ought to follow but remember to stay honest. Never mix up your 'wants' with your 'oughts.'"

Gopher did not understand, but he felt some relief because he knew that the most sensible thing to do was to go upstream because that seemed the most likely direction Menlow would be coming from. He was just about to say that when something deep down rose up inside, a certainty that he should go with Farwyll, despite his sensible objection. He understood that *this* was what the pixie had meant. He made up his mind right then, even though it felt like entering into a gopher tunnel that was not his own.

"I'll go with you."

Instantly, Farwyll became his jovial self, letting out a "Hey! Hey!" and spun a cartwheel, though this time he did not do it staying in one place. He landed in the river. Then he spun some more in the opposite direction, going up the embankment. Gopher managed to barely keep up. By the time he reached the top, he felt as if he needed another rest; though, of course, the pixie was not winded in the least.

Somehow he managed to follow the pixie on his seemingly meandering paths in the forest with the river somewhere to their left. As they went, it seemed to get farther and farther away, until he could no longer hear its murmuring and soft splashes. Would Menlow have strayed so far in looking for him, he wondered?

Immediately a sharp jab of both horror and regret pierced him, which was as painful as if it had been a physical one, for he suddenly realized the truth of the pixie's words. The fairy wasn't even trying to find the hermit; all he cared about was following his stupid wind. Yet Gopher could not bring himself to turn around, because he knew something else: With all the crazy turns, the rodent could no longer even guess the way back. Only by holding on to the slim hope that Farwyll would somehow lead him to his friend was all that kept him following at all.

.   .   .

It was a little more than an hour later, however, when Menlow reached the bank. It was above the very spot where Gopher and the pixie had rested. He stopped, too, and looked down at the shallows and even glanced at the turned up ground where the pixie had done his cartwheels. In a sudden but brief display of anger, he pulled off his hat and crumbled it in his hands. Slowly his expression softened into resignation, as he shook his grey head. Wrinkles that creased his face in new places and his posture that was now stooped made him look older than ever.

"Gone... but why, after all this?" he murmured to himself. Putting his hat back on, he turned and went back the way he had come.

Chapter Fifteen

For the rest of the day, Gopher followed the dancing, meandering pixie deeper into the woods. The forest was so dense and wild that no human could have penetrated it without leaving some sign, which did not encourage Gopher in the least. And Farwyll's ever-so-cheerful mood with the accompaniment of his humming, singing, rhyming, and whistling only made him feel worse. They stopped occasionally to eat some berries, wild roots, and even some honey, but that didn't help since he didn't have much of an appetite.

At first he tried to ignore his feelings by telling himself that somehow, someway the pixie did know best and that he was better off now instead of being on his own; after all, didn't Farwyll prove it when he had rescued him from the falcon?

But words were not enough to hold back the mounting despair. At least trying to keep up with Farwyll diverted him from completely surrendering to it; that is, until the pixie's pace began wearying him. But just when he could not go on any longer, his traveling companion stopped.

"Something wrong, Gopher?" the pixie asked, his eyes rounder than ever with concern. He had stopped on a trail that only he could have detected in those thick woods. The song on his lips had paused, and his sharp v-shaped smile had frozen in place. His concern surprised the rodent, for he had thought that the pixie had nearly forgotten about him.

"I'm – just tired," the rodent said.

"You look sad."

"Oh, uh, I'm okay – now. I was just... feeling scared that I wasn't going to see Menlow again."

Farwyll made a wry face. "Fears, eh? Nasty things they can be! Best to keep them in their proper place by setting your nose to the wind and let *that* lead you! But for now let's have a proper rest."

The pixie's concern made Gopher self-conscious, but it also made him feel better about his companion. Although he still didn't have much of an appetite, he forced himself to eat some mushrooms and radishes, which surprisingly improved his spirits considerably. Consequently, he even found it easier to believe that following Farwyll had somehow been a good decision.

When they resumed, he began taking notice of his surroundings. The thick woods were stuffy and dark from the branches of the elms, oaks, and pines intertwining to create a canopy. Despite the dim light, there was still much to see to distract him. As gloomy as it was, he found that he actually preferred focusing on his surroundings rather than giving himself over to his feelings, which were, in their own way, so much darker.

The woods soon thinned out to show that it wasn't quite as late as Gopher had thought. The terrain leveled, making their way less circuitous. Gopher gradually felt a renewal of hope, though at first he could not understand why, for none of the surroundings were familiar, and his instinct told him that he was far, far away from the cottage – and Menlow. Passing through a meadow of tall yellow flowers, Gopher briefly viewed the unfamiliar sweep of green rolling foothills that stretched all the way to the misty outline of a far off mountain range. Still, he did not despair, though indeed he thought that he ought to. That was when he realized that his hope was not necessarily in finding Menlow but in the pixie himself. He was so sure-footed and confident in their direction – and joyous. At some point the pixie's jubilancy, instead of irritating him, had begun to be a source of strength, an anchor to keep him from his darkest fears. He had nothing else but Farwyll to pin his hope on.

Occasionally when he would lose sight of the pixie, his humming or singing would guide the rodent, while the joy he expressed in them would keep him from panicking.

But then Farwyll's joy seemed to falter. Dusk was approaching but had not yet turned to night. They had stopped to eat some berries from a bush in a clearing when the pixie jumped to his feet and tested the wind. A black cloud seemed to pass over his usual sunny countenance and his features appeared sharper.

"It's changed a bit, but not in direction. It feels sharper, colder – danger of some sort? We must keep to the wind more carefully."

Then suddenly he brightened like the sun breaking through and laughed, "Dear me! I'm sounding like a troll who thinks only of a bridge as a thing to hide under instead of going over! Ha! Ha! Perhaps the danger means we are closer!"

"Closer to *what*?" Gopher asked excitedly.

"Why, to whatever or wherever the wind is leading us, of course!" He laughed.

Despite his apparent carefree gaiety, the pixie led a more circuitous route than usual, while staying within the shelter and shadows of rocks and trees. Soon, as the sun began to descend over the horizon, their pace quickened because the slanting and lengthening shadows hid them easily. If it hadn't been for the darkness, however, both Farwyll and Gopher might have seen that a particular black shadow in front of them was not a large boulder at all. It let out a deep-throated roar as the remaining light caught the whites of its teeth and eyes.

"A bear!" the pixie exclaimed and he might have even sounded overjoyed by the discovery if he hadn't added quite seriously, "Now wait up for me, won't you?"

Farwyll proceeded immediately to yell out something that was a mix between a yodel and a piercing cat scream as the fairy leaped forward and upward, nearly clearing the top of the bear, but not quite. His left foot helped him make it the rest of the way as it used the animal's head as a springboard. He fled into the shadows behind the momentarily stupefied bear before it could gather enough wits to be angry. With a roar, the great beast spun around quicker than its bulk would seemingly allow, and it charged in the same direction.

Gopher held no fears for the pixie. In fact, he started laughing. The bear had no chance. This was the second time Farwyll had saved him!

He laughed some more, but not for long, because a smell suddenly startled him. It came drifting from his right, something savory that stirred his hunger, but, most importantly, it stirred his memory. It reminded him of...of stew – Menlow's stew. He sniffed deeply and detected... spices... chicken... carrots... potatoes... and – he stopped sniffing when he realized it wasn't just any stew. It *was* Menlow's. In an instant his imagination conjured up the whole picture of the hermit having traveled downriver in a tireless search, and then, as night approached, coming up with an idea of making a stew that Gopher would recognize and be drawn to. Of course!

He hesitated before following his nose, however. He didn't want to leave Farwyll behind, especially after all the pixie had done for him. It wasn't like Menlow was going anywhere. Together they could meet the hermit.

Three minutes later the pixie returned, skipping, but Gopher felt like he had grown old waiting for his friend. Farwyll was singing, "A bear, a bear, a great big black bear, running high, running low, hither here and hither there; oh, I am so glad I am not a bear!"

The rodent felt as if he matched the other's elated mood, if not his capability for expressing it by skipping and singing, but rather in an excited, joyful impatient jumping about. To make it nearly unbearable, however, the pixie did not seem to see him. He suddenly quieted down as his eyes scanned the woods and wetted his finger to hold it up for a moment to test the wind. He shook his head and then turned to address Gopher.

"That was fun. Now let us be off at once. This way!" he said and turned to resume their travel. Gopher was stupefied, for the direction the pixie picked was not in the direction of the stew.

"Wait – wait!" he stammered.

Farwyll froze in mid step and turned his head, giving him a

confused look.

"We shouldn't linger, Gopher."

"Don't you smell it? That is *Menlow's stew*! He is not far away."

"But that is not the way, my little friend! Let us be off."

Suddenly Gopher realized that he had been a fool to have placed so much confidence in the pixie or the wind that he followed, since he could not understand the one or feel the other. The rodent made his decision: If he could not feel the wind to follow, he could trust his nose.

"I must go to Menlow – and if you won't follow, well, farewell and thank you."

"Oh, I see, the stew," the other said, "but it may not be what you think. Why don't you –"

Anger came over him, setting his heart pounding so loud that he could no longer hear what the pixie was saying even if he had wanted to. He set off at once, feeling hurt and betrayed that Farwyll would deny him being reunited with his friend. What did the pixie know about friendship anyway? Let him have his wind to keep him company!

Darkness shrouded the woods, and Gopher found that following his nose did not keep him from running headlong into a log, slipping on some loose rocks, and falling into a ditch. He was not deterred, though he fought down panic when he realized that he could not smell the stew anymore. Crawling up the other side of the ditch, however, he picked up the scent and proceeded through the forest that, to him, was merely a morass of entanglements designed only to keep him from his friend and from returning to his old, happy life.

The savory aroma of meat, spices, and vegetables grew stronger, which was followed by the sound of voices. To Gopher it only meant that Menlow was nearby. He did not think beyond that or things might have turned out differently.

He burst through a hedge into the fire-lit clearing. The delicious smell of stew was heavy in the air and that to him confirmed that he had finally returned to his friend.

"Menlow!" he exclaimed.

What he saw on the other side would have alarmed him if he had not been blinded by what he wanted to see, which was more blinding than the tears in his eyes. A man, sitting in front of the fire, had a face that did not resemble Menlow in the least, especially with his bushy brown hair, the lack of wrinkles about the eyes, and the utter look of astonishment that made his eyes bug out and his jaw look frozen in the open position.

"Menlow, I've found you!" Gopher said.

He intended to jump into the man's arms, but he never made it. Somebody to his right, whom he had barely noticed until it was too late, scooped him up into darkness.

"Did you hear that? On my father's grave, it *talked*!" A voice said, which was not Menlow's; it was much deeper and rougher and younger sounding.

"A talking gopher?" Another voice replied, "Mmmm, what was it that it was saying? 'Minnow?'" This voice was as much different from the first as it was from the ex-wizard's; it held a higher tone than either.

Gopher barely heard the voices, but he did not understand the words at all, for his sudden terror had reduced him to a mere non-talking rodent as he frantically squirmed, twisted, and clawed at the interior of a sack that enfolded him in a darkness that seemed just as inescapable. The only reasoning left to him, which was not gopher-like, was the thought that he had made a grave mistake.

Chapter Sixteen

His non-talking condition did not last long, but long enough to have missed the conversation between his two captors and their repeated questions that they directed towards him. When he was calm enough to think and listen, the two men were in a heated argument.

"I *told* you that you shouldn't have shaken the bag," said the higher voiced one, but in his agitation it was a little deeper. "Gophers have soft heads. You see he quit moving around in there."

The other boomed, "Oh, I didn't rattle him anymore than I have any of the rabbits I've caught in our traps – and *they* lived! Don't tell me they're much different than this here rodent!"

"He's not moving," the first pointed out firmly, and then added, "and by the way some of them *did* die. What's the good if he is dead? Have you thought what this means? A talking gopher?"

"But he *isn't* dead!" the voice said rougher than before. "Look here. I'll show you –"

"Don't shake him up any more!"

"But if he's dead, what would be the point –"

Gopher had heard enough.

"I'm alive, I'm alive!" he exclaimed.

Their argument couldn't be blamed entirely for his irritation. He *had* been shaken a bit too much, and now the inside of his head throbbed so much so that it didn't leave room for fear – or for wise deliberation. He realized that, after the two men fell immediately silent, he should have played dead. If they had buried him, he might have been able to dig his way out, but now it was too late.

"See!" said the deep voiced man finally, but at the same time the other had decided to address Gopher.

"Hello there – ah, are you okay?"

"Yes," Gopher said, "but I would do much better if I wasn't in this bag!"

The two men chuckled, but it made Gopher even more irritated, which at least did feel better than being afraid. "Would you please let me out?"

"Wit *and* manners, too!"

"Let you out so you can run away?"

Gopher wanted to promise that he wouldn't, but that was a lie. He would run as soon and as fast as he was able. Something in him resisted an intentional lie, even to captors. It was because it would be his first one.

The man continued, "Look, we don't mean you any harm, little – err, fellow. If we did, you would be dead by now. Do you know *what* we do for a living? We're hunters. That means we kill little animals like you. Normally. Of course we won't kill a *talking* one. That makes you different – you're like us –"

"What? It's not like us –" began the other man, but the first man grunted loud enough to cut him off.

"– BUT we can't just let you go because... well, because you wouldn't get a chance to know us and us you!"

"I don't want to know you," Gopher said, realizing that it was a rude thing to say, but so was being held prisoner in a bag. "I just want to go home!"

"Where is your home?"

"In a cottage."

"You live with *someone*. You have a human friend?"

Gopher chose to remain silent. For some reason he did not like the idea of them knowing about Menlow.

The gruffer-voiced one said, "Who would let a gopher live –"

Again the other, the one with the higher voice, interrupted

sharply, "We would for one, that's who!" His tone softened and lowered as he spoke to Gopher. "Don't misunderstand my friend here. He's not used to talking gophers, that's all... His name is Loggins, and I am Wells. What is your name?"

"Gopher," he replied.

"No, I mean, what is your name? Not what you are," Wells said.

"That is my name."

"Oh – ah – are you hungry, Gopher?"

"Yes. Very," he said, "but do I have to eat in here? It's rather stuffy."

Wells chuckled once more, but cleared his throat. "Sorry. It just occurred to me that I never would have thought that I'd hear a gopher say something was stuffy – or anything at all, for that matter! I'd have thought that you were used to stuffy tunnels and all. But it is – confining, isn't it? We'll have to fix that. After all, I shouldn't like to be in a bag myself."

"But –" Loggins began before the other cut in.

"It's all right. Over here."

"Oh."

Gopher felt the swaying of the bag for a moment, and then heard a hard clanging sound. Suddenly the bag dropped, but it was only for a short distance. The sides of the sack lost tension and fell open. At once he realized his chance. He sprang forward before his eyes could adjust to the light – and hit something solid head on and toppled back. After blinking away the dizziness, he saw that now he was in an even bigger prison. It was a cage.

"It's really used for trapping and holding rabbits," Wells said, apologetically, "but the cage is for your own protection."

As Gopher eyes adjusted, he wondered how he could have mistaken any of the two men for Menlow. Wells was twice the size of the hermit, clean shaven and with long brown hair that was tied at the back in a pony tail. He stood next to the one called Loggins who was about a foot shorter and half as broad around. A short stubby beard partially hid a frown but did diminish the disapproval in his squinting brown eyes, which contrasted against the friendly glint in the larger man's blue eyes.

Wells also had a smile that was friendly, "Now about food... what about a potato? Ouch!" He dropped a slice that he had picked out of the simmering pot. Snatching it off the ground quickly, he juggled and blew on it until it was cool enough to pass it through the bars. Then he turned and retrieved a carrot, this time with a fork. He said over his shoulder, "Let me know when you've had enough – oh, not hungry anymore?" he added, seeing the potato untouched. "That's okay. I understand. I wouldn't be either if I was just put in a cage, and it was dawning on me that I wasn't where I wanted to be... but I think that you'll get used to us."

Well's show of consideration did little to improve Gopher's appetite or feelings, but then he remembered the pixie and felt suddenly hopeful. After all, if he had already saved him twice already, why not again? Gopher vividly imagined the pixie hiding somewhere nearby, waiting for his chance to free him. This hope eased his anxieties, and, in doing so, returned his appetite to him.

The potato tasted good, but that hardly mattered. What did was that he keep up his strength for escape should he need it.

"Ah, that's it! Feeling better already, eh? You are resilient. Eat up," Wells said, smiling. He placed the cage between them as they sat down to eat in front of the fire.

Its blaze got brighter after a while, but then Gopher realized that it was because the evening was getting darker. So many places for the pixie to hide, the rodent thought eagerly. Wells told him about themselves between mouthfuls and even long after they had finished eating. Not being particularly interested, there was much that Gopher had missed. What he did hear was something about killing a brown bear to save their own hides, but then his attention was finally grabbed when Wells added, "When we got to Kentfell and sold that skin for *twenty* gold coins, we considered hunting bears instead!"

"You mean that *you* were considering," Loggins said, breaking his sullen silence. "That bear swiped my leg before your arrows managed to bring it down! Don't ask me to make a living doing that again!"

"It would have been different if we had been more prepared by –"

"Kentfell?" Gopher interrupted. "That's where we just came from."

"Really? I thought that you said that you live in a cottage – is it a cottage that's in town or outside it?"

"No, we don't live anywhere near there. It's in another valley."

"Oh! I know the one, mostly rocky; with a large river, wasn't it?"

"No," Gopher said. "There's only a small stream and more trees than rocks."

Wells pursed his lips and shook his head as if he didn't recognize the description. "Small stream, eh? Not much good for fishing, I suppose."

"Oh, we caught a few. Menlow showed me –" Gopher stopped upon realizing that he had slipped up by telling them his friend's name. Worse than that, he was talking to them as if nothing was wrong. It scared him to think that he could become so careless.

"Menlow?" Wells said casually, one busy eyebrow raised. "That was the name you were saying, wasn't it?"

Gopher did not reply.

Loggins grunted, but, looking at Wells, he seemed to decide not to say anything.

The other raised his large frame up from the ground and sat down on a fallen log. "I guess you're tired, eh?"

"Will you let me go?" Gopher pleaded. He just couldn't make himself cooperate with them even if he was going to be rescued.

"Let you go?" Loggins said, almost angrily.

"Let you go?" Wells echoed, but his tone was amused. "Go where? To the cottage?" He paused and his face brightened, "Or Kentfell! So you're the culprit who was the cause of all that trouble going around there! We heard talk about it."

"I am not!"

"Hah!" Loggins exclaimed, to which Wells gave a dark look before turning back to Gopher with a smile.

"Excuse my rude partner. He doesn't seem to appreciate gophers like I do –well, talking gophers. You are special, you know."

"Will you?" Gopher repeated.

"Will we take you back there?" Wells said. "Mmm...Well, I'll be honest with you. We haven't made much money with our trapping and hunting lately (except for that bear, but I'll have to agree with Loggins that I wouldn't want to chance that again). But you! You could really help us out."

"What – what are you going to do to me?"

"*Do* to you?" Wells said with astonishment raising his narrow eyebrows. "Why, nothing at all, except feed and take care of you. In return, we would be beholden to you if you talk to... well, folks. They'll like talking to you, I think." He turned to Loggins who was scratching his beard and sitting on a stump. "What do you think?"

"Oh... I think that it's a grand idea," a slow smile spread on his face, the first one Gopher had seen. It didn't make him seem so rough.

"But why?" Gopher asked.

"Because you are like one of those magic stories come to life – and then people won't have to be afraid when they see what the stories are all about."

"Yeah!" Loggins said, his eyes fully lit, but they were staring off into space as if seeing something wonderful.

"I won't talk to them – or to you!" Gopher exclaimed. He remembered something Menlow had said about not wanting to make him into a "sideshow."

The gleam in Loggins' eyes disappeared as he stood up. His thick brow thickened, especially when his eyes narrowed and the corners of his mouth turned downward. Gopher thought that, although not as big as Wells, he was twice as dangerous.

Wells waved him aside as he pursed his lips. His brows were also furrowed, but his were not portending danger, only thoughtfulness. At last he spoke.

"That's fine. We can't make you talk and –" He cast a pointed look at his brooding partner before going on, "and we won't do anything to you either... but if you do go along with us and cooperate, I *promise* that when we make enough money, we'll help you look for your friend Menlow. The decision will be yours, of course."

"Why don't you let me go now? I am not going to do what you want."

Wells sighed. "Okay. I'll tell you what – and this is another promise – I'll put on only *one* show with you, and if you decide not to cooperate with us, if you don't talk, then after the show we will take you back to your friend. At least we will have made some money. Fair enough?"

"Hey, just a minute!" boomed Loggins.

"I made up my mind," Wells said firmly, facing his friend. "I said it and I *won't* take it back."

Something about the look in his eyes, his posture, and the tone in his voice made Gopher wonder if Loggins really was the more dangerous of the two. Wells turned back to Gopher, though, without a trace of danger.

"So what do you think? One show only and if you don't cooperate, we'll take you home," he said smiling.

"I won't," Gopher said.

"Okay, if that remains your decision, then I will stand by my promise. After the show, you'll go home. Even if Loggins doesn't go, I'll take you myself. It's my promise to you, okay?"

"Okay," Gopher said before he realized it. He was stunned. Wells had appeared dangerous just a few moments before, but now Gopher was finding himself wanting to trust him! He felt as if some battle had been lost. Then he remembered Farwyll and realized none of this would matter when the pixie rescued him... but what was taking him so long? Maybe he was waiting for his captors to fall asleep first. After all, he wasn't in any immediate danger.

"Good, good!" Wells replied, "Tomorrow we go to Clarin. Let's get ready for bed."

As the two men prepared to do that, a war of contradicting emotions of hope and impatience ensued that left Gopher in a quandary of how to act or what to do – or how he felt. Even the discomfort of the bottom cage's hardwood went unnoticed. Eventually the intensity of those feelings could not be kept up. He stopped thinking altogether and that was when he realized how uncomfortable he was. By that time, Wells and Loggins had already cleaned their dishes, added some wood to the fire, and covered themselves up in blankets for the night.

"Good night, Gopher," Wells said brightly.

"Good night," the rodent said and he really wished that it was going to be a good one – for himself, that is.

The men tossed about to get comfortable. It seemed like forever before he heard snoring and other sounds of sleeping from the two long mounds by the campfire. Hope ballooned in him even more... anytime now, he thought. The deepening of night and its increasing chill marked the slow passage of time. Then his own discomfort inspired an idea, a plan that he might use if necessary.

He peered into the darkness, just outside the flickering light; his hope so focused on detecting signs of rescue that sometimes he forgot to breathe for long stretches. Thrice Gopher detected movements in the shadows and more times than could be numbered he heard rustling in the underbrush or in the branches, but nothing happened. At last, he decided that the plan was necessary after all.

"Loggins," the rodent whispered. Although he would have preferred calling the other man, Loggins was the one closest to the cage so that he would not have to whisper too loudly. Both of them waking up might ruin everything.

"Loggins!" A little louder.

The man stirred, though he looked more like a moving mound of fur.

"Mmmm?"

"I'm uncomfortable. Do you have something that I could use? Please?"

"What?" The irritated voice came out from under the fur. His scowling bearded face appeared soon after.

Gopher repeated his request.

"Oh, all right, but don't try escaping on me," he said much too loudly, although his partner's snores continued uninterrupted.

When his captor opened the cage to shove in a rabbit pelt, Gopher did not move; he didn't even breathe. This would be the perfect moment for the pixie to come to the rescue. He was held in the vise of anticipation. How the pixie would manage it this time he did not know, but he knew that it would happen...

When Loggins shut the cage, its clang jolted Gopher with the fact (and the horror) that the pixie wasn't coming after all. The rodent's heart fell, but he tried to rally it by telling himself that Farwyll would still rescue him, maybe in the morning or when they were deeply asleep... yet he could not shake the certainty that the pixie would not return.

Farwyll probably held a grudge, he thought bitterly, but then he took it back because, at heart, he was an honest gopher to whom spite did not come naturally. The pixie was not capable of such a thing, he had to admit. It did not take long for him to realize the truth, however; that it was the "wind" that he followed which was to blame. It simply wasn't leading the fairy this way. With the passing of that last hope came the full crushing weight of what being alone and helpless meant. It was a weight for which the pelt could not provide any comfort.

Chapter Seventeen

By late afternoon of the next day, they came within sight of Clarin as the path they followed descended a rocky slope. Compared to Kentfell, twice as many buildings congregated together at the beginning of the rolling green foothills that stretched away from the forested mountain range. Many of the structures were twice as large as those in the other town and were bisected from each other by twice as many roads.

Wagons, horses, and people moved seemingly slowly along the thoroughfare, looking small but not insignificant – not to Gopher, at least. In strong discomfort, he realized that soon they would be in the midst of all that traffic, and no doubt probably be the center of their attention. Who wouldn't notice two straggly looking men carrying a stretcher piled high in two mounds of furs and supplies with a caged gopher set in between?

It was this discomforting revelation that brought him out of his reverie, which had begun when he had awakened that morning in a numbed state of mind. Nothing, except one thing, had been able to penetrate into his waking consciousness, which was that he still had not been rescued. It had become the fixed thing in his universe, the great Disappointment. All else – their simple breakfast of dried fruits, the breaking up of camp, the sparse conversations between the men, and their trek through the forest, stopping occasionally to eat – seemed to occur far away from him. This had not alarmed him because he simply did not care about anything; that is, not until he saw the town. What Wells said next was the first thing that Gopher really heard that whole day, and it helped ease his immediate discomfort, if only a little.

"Once we get out of these blasted woods, we'll find a place to settle down. I'll head to town in the morning to get what we need."

"Why can't I go instead?" Loggins said. He sounded irritable and out of breath.

"Because it'll be easier for me to carry the furs; we'll probably need to trade them all. Let's go over the list…"

Gopher tuned out again, but this time only to their conversation. He was keenly aware of the swaying and jostling of the stretcher as if these sensations were new to him. The town lay below them but became increasingly veiled by shadows in the fading daylight. It gave him the impression that they were going farther away from it instead of nearer, but Gopher was too sensible to entertain that this was so. Instead, the rodent imagined the pixie coming to free him sometime during the night– though he suspected that in this he was not being sensible at all. Why would Farwyll suddenly change his mind, if he had not done so already?

As shadows deepened, they came to the bottom of the slope and stopped at a ravine. It was full of gorse scrub and thorny bramble that successfully impeded their passage across, but only because it was dark and they were too tired to try to find a way through. They camped in the shelter of a boulder, while a wind continually rustled the underbrush on either side. The noise would have made listening for any sounds of the pixie pointless since Gopher already knew that it was pointless anyway. He would be rescued – or he wouldn't. Simple as that.

What he could not help but hear, though, was his captors making plans for their talking-gopher show over a cold dinner of cheese and venison. Thankfully, because words like "tent" and "profit" and "cost" did not mean anything to him, their talk did not fill him with dread and apprehension as it should have, but rather it put Gopher to sleep before he knew it.

It came, therefore, as a surprise that when he opened his eyes, it was already morning. The sun was already high up and warming the air, which was abuzz with flies. A bird atop the boulder chirped as if it had been awake for hours. Loggins was cleaning a pan over the smoldering campfire, the logs sizzling as the water from the canteen dribbled on them.

It was that sound which had stirred him, but then he wondered if it had really been the delicious smell of the two fried eggs on a platter inside his cage that had been the cause of his awakening instead. His ravenous stomach was responding to it in uncomfortable flips and gurgles. How could he sleep through that?

Loggins, seeming to have eyes in the back of his head, said, "He left them for you. Hurry up, so I can finish washing."

He said it as if giving him breakfast hadn't been his idea, which it, undoubtedly, wasn't. Gopher did not bother to ask where Wells had gone. He remembered enough of their plans to know that he was going into town in the morning. Although the thought put a damper on his appetite, the act of kindness by giving him the eggs (he wondered where Wells had gotten them) made Gopher also remember the man's promise. Would he keep his word to take him back to Kentfell if he didn't say a word during the show? For some reason he believed it. Perhaps it was because he had nothing else to hope for. At any rate, it revived his appetite and he found the eggs delicious, even if they were a little cold.

There was a long space of boredom after this: of watching the flies flying about in erratic patterns, the birds (now there were three of them) chattering on top of the boulder, and Loggins whittling on a stick. Gopher would never have considered any of this boring before, but there was something about being a captive audience that seemed to drain beauty and joy out of things.

Boredom notwithstanding, Wells' return came much too soon. It was heralded by his voice booming with excitement from beyond the boulder. He came with news that Gopher dreaded, though it was no less than he expected.

"Hey! I've found us a place!" He came up out of the ravine, huffing and brushing off the brambles, before continuing, "It's perfect. Outside of town – and I already spread the news. We've got to set up in a hurry, while the pot's stirred!"

"You traded all our furs? What'd you get?"

Wells raised his hands to emphasize their emptiness, but then he laughed. "You'll see – and, no, I didn't trade all our furs, but enough of them."

His excitement seemed to spread to Loggins. They quickly reloaded the stretcher like before, minus the furs; this time, however, strapping the cage, for which Gopher was soon to be thankful. The steep slope, brambles, and uneven ground on the other side of the boulder made crossing the ravine difficult and dangerous. Twice the stretcher almost flipped; once, when Wells tripped on something that was probably a rock, and the second time when Loggins stumbled into a hole that his partner, who was in the front, had evidently missed.

The worst, however, was going up the other side. It seemed to last forever and was so steep that he thought any moment all the things would slide right off the stretcher and into Loggins' face. Somehow it never happened. By the time they reached the top, his captors were out of breath, sweating, and muddy. They brushed off themselves as they inventoried their scratches and bruises.

"So where is it?" The smaller man said when he got his breath back.

"It's over here." Wells led the way through the remaining bramble.

The sight was anticlimactic, even for Gopher who had only seen a few wagons in Kentfell: A plain cart that was loaded with what looked like tarps, a small pile of furs, and a few other things, harnessed to a sorry looking old donkey.

"Sure, it doesn't look like much, but it's a fine tent, almost new," Wells said. "Anyway, if Gopher cooperates, after tonight we'll afford something nicer. Don't worry."

Loggins grunted, while Gopher felt irritated that Wells seemed to take it for granted that the rodent would cooperate.

The cage, along with everything else, was then placed in the back of the cart. The ride proved a great improvement, despite the monotonous creaking of the wheels and the donkey's clip-clopping.

It was definitely faster, but to Gopher that didn't mean better. It only meant that the show would start that much sooner. Not long after they had begun down the road, Loggins leaned back from the buckboard and threw one of the remaining furs over the cage, leaving the rodent in darkness.

"No sense in giving them a free show, eh?" He laughed, gruffly.

Gopher never got used to traveling blind, but now it threatened to terrify him, for it made him feel as if he were blindly rushing headlong into an even deeper darkness and, worse still, it left him as a prisoner to his own imagination. By comparison, the sack, in which he had hid previously, had given Gopher a sense of security. He realized that it was because he had trusted in the one who had carried it. As dismal as he felt, however, he felt tempted to doubt that Menlow even existed and that all those good memories had been nothing more than dreams.

Soon Gopher began hearing sounds of traffic to distract him: the clip-clopping, jangling, and creaking of other horses and wagons. Greetings and words also reached his ears, though they were too muffled for the rodent to understand. Later, when the cage shifted suddenly forward, followed by a momentary stillness, Gopher suspected at last the wagon had come to a stop. The unloading a moment later confirmed it. Lastly, he felt the cage being lifted. Loggins' voice addressed the rodent in the darkness.

"Don't worry. Wells will keep his promise, but, for your sake, I hope you cooperate."

Gopher did not know if that was an implied threat or... a warning, but, whatever it was, it had the opposite effect; it doubled his determination not to cooperate. They would *not* get a word out of him; then Wells would have to keep his promise. Surprisingly, he found that the man's words had also changed him in another way. As much as he had been dreading the show, they now stirred in him an impatience for it to begin. It was because Loggins had (no doubt unwittingly) renewed his hope.

His impatience made time drag in the darkness, but at least his hope restored a sense of reality. That was a good thing, too, because his imagination would have made horrendous things out of the strange noises that were going all about him. Being ignorant about, or at least unfamiliar with, many things in the world outside of the cottage, it was not surprising that he had no idea of what was going on. Whatever they were doing, he just wished that they would hurry and get it down.

Yet, having nothing else to do, he could not help but listen. An impression that something was being built or put together came upon Gopher when Wells said, "Put it here, Loggins... to the right in the shade... it's crooked... keep the sides even as we pull... if all the stakes are in the ground, why is there still a gap?" This kind of talk was volleyed back and forth between the two men for almost an hour when suddenly a stranger's voice interrupted them.

"What's going on here, sirs?"

Wells replied, "Greetings, fellow! Didn't see you come up. We're putting up a tent. Haven't you heard the news? No? Well, have you ever seen an animal talk?"

"A parrot once," the man replied.

"Well, this ain't no parrot –" Loggins said, which was followed by Wells cutting in with a showman's ringing voice.

"And he's a lot smarter than any bird. He makes up his own words. Guaranteed. Show starts an hour before dusk. A silver coin is all it will cost you to find what it's all about. Spread the news!"

The exhortation to "spread the news" proved hardly necessary, since the tent was situated on a hillock that could be seen from the town. Not surprisingly, but very happily (for his captors at least), curiosity seekers began stopping by soon after. Unlike the first man, they did not go away, but started slowly massing at the foot of the hill as the afternoon waned.

Gopher did not see any of this, of course, even when the fur was removed. It took a moment for his eyes to adjust to see that he was inside a structure unlike anything he had ever seen before. His cage was a few feet off the ground and was next to a pole that seemed to support a sagging cloth roof, which seemed of one cloth piece with the circular walls. His first impression was of being outside because those walls filtered in sunlight and sounds. His second was that of as a babbling brook nearby, until he recognized human voices.

These were those who had come to see him perform.

As if that wasn't intimidating enough, Loggins seemed to loom over him with his arms folded and frowning. No doubt he was nervous that Gopher wouldn't talk. On the other hand, Wells was peeping through a gap in the walls, eagerly rubbing his hands together. Then he turned and crouched to bring himself level with Gopher. A friendly smile lit his face that contrasted with his partner's frown.

"It won't be long now. Whatever you decide is up to you."

There was something smug about him, in the way he spoke and the way he looked that once more irritated Gopher, even to the point that he no longer felt intimidated. He clamped down his mouth tightly and turned his back on the man.

"I see," Wells said, sighing with resignation. "Well, if that is your decision, then we might as well get it over with."

Wells stepped out through an opening in the tent wall, leaving Gopher taken aback that the man had given up so easily. Had he misjudged him? Maybe Wells wasn't as confident as he had seemed. Whatever the reason, it did not, of course, deter him from his decision.

A few moments later Wells' voice addressed the crowd. His tone and words were much like what he had used towards the passerby earlier, only much longer – though Gopher realized that it was not long enough. He found himself so scared that he probably couldn't talk even if he had wanted to.

Yet when the first ten people finally began shoving and shouldering their way inside, his fear lessened somewhat now that he had something real to fear. All were men, except for a middle-aged woman whose face drew his attention. Her scowling, hateful face was perhaps the ugliest he had ever seen, and from it he felt an animosity that made his cage seem a refuge.

The others were not much better, however, their faces in general showing disgruntled cynicism, expressed in sneers and doubtful squints, though one young man wore a slanted smile with a twinkle in his eyes as if he saw everything as a joke. He moved to the front and was the first to address the gopher as he bent down to look him in the face.

"Well, well, a talking gopher, eh? Are there anymore like you out there?"

Somebody nudged him. "Oh, bother! You've got to be joshing! Talking to *that*?"

"I've seen plenty of the likes of 'im afore."

The young man straightened up and turned to address those around him. "You know what I think? I think that all gophers have always been able to talk. That's right. It's why they're so darn clever and hard to catch. One lets the other know when we're coming – but nobody must've told this one to scram!"

This remark resulted in a few guffaws, but not from the woman. Somehow her ugliness managed to increase with her deepening scowl. Her voice, something of a growl, matched it.

"I paid two days wages to hear a *talking* gopher, not one that just stares back at me. He's not any different from the thieving rascals in my cabbage patch!"

"How come it hasn't said anything?" said one of the men with a sneer. His remark was followed by other similar ones in the tent.

Loggins, whose his forehead was glistening, managed a scowl but incongruently said in a faltering voice, "Sp-speak, Gopher."

The rodent closed his eyes as if he was going to sleep.

"It ain't gonna talk because it can't!"

"Even if it could," said the young man, "what do you think it could tell us? Hey! Maybe it will confess to raiding Myrissa's cabbage patch!"

This did not elicit as many laughs as it did an angry murmur, which Wells, who standing on one side of the cage, managed to quell for the moment by raising his hands.

"I give you my word that this gopher can talk – we both give our word," he looked to Loggins for confirmation, who was now sweating so profusely that it was getting in his eyes so that he could no longer scowl properly. He continued, "But you see... well, he is a lot like us in a way. Put yourself in his place. If you were put in a cage to be showed off, what would *you* do?"

"Phooey!" exclaimed Myrissa. "You think you're clever, don't you? Making excuses is what you're doing! We're suckers enough giving you our money; do you think we'd fall for anymore of your lies? Well, I don't know about the lot of you, but I want my two coins back! That was the guarantee!"

"Now, now," clucked Wells, straightening to his full height and fixing a solemn, unshakeable look on his face. "I lived up to my word. You got to see a talking gopher. I never – NEVER – said that you would *hear* one. If he doesn't want to talk, I can't make him. I'm no wizard."

Then someone in the crowd exclaimed, "Ha! Of course you're not a wizard. That's the first true word you've said all night 'cause you're a liar and a cheat!"

"Paying just to see a gopher! We *are* a bunch of fools!"

"Sure, we were fools enough to pay," the woman said bitterly. "How can we complain about that? But don't you think that *everybody* pay?"

"Yeah!" said several of the men, while one of them went even farther by exclaiming, "Yeah, it's their turn to pay now!"

The small group of ten seemed like twenty as they crowded in on Wells and Loggins. Myrissa called out from somewhere in their midst, "Leave the gopher. I want to learn him not to eat my cabbages!"

Wells stood firm, while his partner pushed out at those nearest with a burst of bravado and exclaimed, "Now get out! You can't scare us! Just you try –"

At that moment someone did try. To be specific, a large man swung and connected with Loggins' eye. His captor toppled to the ground.

"Stop!" Gopher shouted in a loud, commanding voice that he didn't know he had.

Something in him had risen up which could not let him remain silent and see someone get hurt, no matter who it was. The moment he said it, though, he realized that this was the second time he had said one word too many. With an even deeper chagrin, he also realized that it had been the same word.

Chapter Eighteen

The show, which had nearly become a riot, made a complete turnaround with that single word. When the rodent had shouted "stop!" they really did, but that was only for a moment. Then the astonishment passed, or diminished enough for the show to really begin. In a wave of initial excitement, they pled, coaxed, urged him to say something more, until Gopher could take it no longer, which wasn't long since his determination had already been broken – and because no reason remained for him to be silent. Wells would not have to keep his promise.

"Will you go away – all of you – please!" the rodent said at last.

Wells came to his aid as he stepped forward. "You heard him! Stand back! Give him some room!"

Whereas a moment before they had been ready to rise up, now they obediently stepped back as yet another wave swept over them; this time it was of hushed astonishment. It did not last long, however. The young man, who had first spoken, broke the silence by saying under his breath "my, my, my." This drew a laugh and then more laughter, which was soon followed by questions, though not quite like before. Wells directed them to ask only one question at a time.

Gopher resigned himself to answering them, yet even as he spoke, he found that it was not so bad. The people hung on his every word with a gleam of delight in their eyes and a look of fixed amazement in their faces that made him feel embarrassed at first.

But then a growing sense of acceptance and worth came over him. In a way, it wasn't too different than his talks with Adia since the questions were similar. Some ranged from the expected and familiar "How did you learn to talk?" to the surprising "Are you really an enchanted prince put under a curse?" It was not this particular question itself that was so surprising, but rather it was because it had been Myrissa who had asked it. The question had come out suddenly as if it had been welling up inside. Everybody erupted in laughter, and it left her red in the face, but then she gave in and started laughing too. Even Gopher found it amusing (and flattering that she of all people should ask such a thing) – and noticed with considerable surprise to see how her laughter and smile had instantly transformed the ugliness of her face into something almost pretty.

Gopher was also just beginning to wonder why he had been dreading the show when Wells announced that the next group needed to have their turn. It was met with resistance all around, of complaints about it not being long enough, of pleadings for a few more minutes. Gopher himself was surprised to feel irritated at the interruption and even more surprised when he felt a touch of sadness as they filed out. Yet when a new group was rotated in, he did not feel dread any longer. His first word to them –this time it was "hello" – began the show all over again. The shock, the amazement, the wonder, the ensuing excitement and the stream of questions did not differ from the previous group (except nobody asked if he had been a prince). Then he felt the same reluctance and irritation when their turn was up.

The shows might have gone on all night with never-ending crowds, but in total there were four groups to hear Gopher talk. Each in their turn proved almost as astounded as the first group had been. Of course, word of mouth being confirmed by those coming out had lessened the degree of amazement, but not remarkably so. It seemed that everybody had to hear the rodent themselves to be completely convinced. Wells finally closed up the fourth showing much to the disappointment of those outside who were still waiting.

"The show begins again tomorrow night an hour before dusk!" Wells said, his voice ringing outside over the boos and other sounds of disappointment. He came into the tent, grinning and rubbing his hands together.

"Good job, Gopher! With paying crowds like these, we'll soon be set for life, and you can go back to your friend!"

"Yeah!" Loggins said, smiling.

Gopher took back what he thought about a smile diminishing someone's ugliness, at least in Loggins' case. His was too toothy in the middle and too sharp on the raised ends, giving the gleam in his black eyes a hungry look. While Gopher may have had reason to believe Wells would return him to his friend eventually, he held no such belief that Loggins would go along with it. He was glad that obviously he wasn't the boss.

After a late meal of bread and ale, his captors tallied the night's profit. The clanging of the coins kept Gopher from sleeping, even though he buried himself under the fur in a corner farthest away so that he could be alone with his self pity. At first their sounds did not bother him as much as the metallic clanging shut of the door to his cage had; that is, however, until he realized that money was the very reason for him being a prisoner. It was but for their love of those coins that he could not be reunited with his friend!

Helplessness turned his self-pity outward to become hate. That hate would have turned into rage if he had been more hot-tempered by nature, but fortunately he wasn't. Instead, its ferocity scared him. Realizing what he might be capable of if he only had the opportunity and means, and not liking the kind of person he would turn into, he willed himself to stop – or he tried to, but it was like trying to hold back a wave by leaning one's shoulder into it. The anger built up in him the more he resisted it. Desperately, he wondered what Menlow would do – and, in doing so, realized that the anger had diminished if only a little.

It was enough of a clue for Gopher to know what to do; up to this point, it was the only thing that helped. Like a man fleeing to refuge (or running from a wave instead of pushing against it), he fled from his anger by imagining... what? What Menlow would do?

147

That proved too hard to imagine, and the frustration in trying to only added fuel to his emotion... what would his friend tell him to do? Although Gopher didn't know *what* that advice would be, he could imagine the hermit's patient look on his face, his calm presence, and the warmth of friendship in his eyes... It felt as if Menlow's feelings, though imagined, were starting to flow into him, to ease his anger and to expose the hatred for the ugly thing that it was. Then, as he gained more control over himself, it occurred to him what Menlow would tell him to do – think.

Gopher began by reviewing the events of the past two days from the point of a view of a bystander, remembering details that his emotions had blinded him to before. Still, nothing occurred to him for escaping, and he was tempted to despair, but he knew that it would begin the whirlpool of emotions again. Instead he calmed himself and kept thinking, with the hope that something would eventually occur to him.

He relived the show in his mind, not that he believed that doing so would give him any ideas, but at the moment he could think of nothing else. Then something interesting occurred to him as such things do when unlooked for. He reflected that, in being forced to talk to strangers, he saw that they all shared something similar despite all their varied looks, dress, speech, and personalities. It had been more than their curiosity; it had been a look of child-like wonder in their eyes. For some it had lingered a while, but for others the wonder had turned into excitement. In a few others, though, he had seen a gleam in their eyes that had made him uneasy, like Loggins' smile. It had been as if they were thinking of something else – like the clanging of those coins. Yet it had been that initial wonder that they all shared in that fleeting moment that mattered. For in that same moment it had seemed that he could see through their eyes. Not that *he* felt wonderful in the least, but that he was catching something much, much greater than himself in their faces. It had made his captivity, at least for that moment, a trivial thing. Yet his practical side rose up and asked what good did it do him *now*?

This bothered him, until the answer suddenly occurred to him.

As long as people were amazed, they would spread word about a talking gopher – that word would eventually reach the hermit's ears! Hope blossomed seemingly in his breast. The way seemed suddenly clear: His best plan would be to cooperate with his captors and to make himself as endearing to the crowds as possible. With his mind settled, and his hate and anger calmed, he fell asleep at last despite the clanging coins and their drunken, loud partying that followed soon afterwards.

•   •   •

He woke up the next morning, seeing the shadow of a tree swaying lazily on the tent wall. Wells and Loggins, lying sprawled out at the foot of his pedestal with the money box between them, appeared to have fallen asleep while guarding it. A bird nearby chirped melodiously as the peaceful sounds of the town drifted up the hill.

Gopher, however, felt a stranger to the peaceful scene, as if he were seeing it from a distance. It was because something was troubling him, which would not allow the peacefulness to enter in. Was it because of another one of those strange dreams? He was not so sure. Usually he could *almost* remember if he had had a dream, but this morning, he didn't feel even close to remembering anything.

Whatever the cause of his unease, though, it was short-lived, because that was when he also remembered his resolve to put on "a good show." He acted upon it at once, for here was something definite he could act upon, here was something he could put his hope in. After all, being reunited with his friend was all that mattered, wasn't it? Not feelings and unremembered dreams.

"Good morning!"

He had to repeat it a number of times before they stirred. The response he finally got was not one he expected since Menlow was always an early and cheerful riser.

"Pipe down!" Loggins growled, holding his head, and even Wells rolled on his back and groaned with ill humor.

"Sorry," Gopher said, trying to make it sound like he really was.

He waited patiently for the men to rouse themselves, though even then their sour mood persisted longer than he expected, for he had never seen anyone with a hangover before. It wasn't until Loggins had gone to fetch breakfast that Wells began to revive his friendly self.

"Was a long day, but a good one. Too many of those, however –" he rubbed his temples, "and I'll be an old man before my time." He began to laugh but suddenly winced. "Yep, one too many," he murmured.

To Gopher's surprise, when Loggins returned, he brought breakfast (a pastry and some cream) that was only meant for the rodent. His captors left the tent and, from their sounds, they seemed to be taking in the fresh air as hungrily as he took to the fresh, warm scone. Sometime later they came back restored to better spirits. The rodent wondered if every morning would begin this way.

He sighed. How long would he have to keep up this facade? Maybe tonight Menlow would show up for the "performance" and then he could be himself again.

There is nothing like anticipation to make time seem to go slow, but for Gopher it was hardly a problem. So much was going on, especially after Wells came back from town with a wagonload of merchandise, for then began the work of unloading and decorating the tent's interior. A roll of red and gold carpet covered much of the patchy grass. They hung two colorfully patterned tapestries on either side of the entrance. Wells positioned a dressing screen a few feet behind the cage, which was in front of a copper bath tub that they both had to carry. Then Loggins brought in a silver gilded pedestal and a cage that matched it in style. After reassuring them that he wasn't going to make a run for it, Gopher kept his promise and transferred to his new "accommodations."

There was no temptation, actually, since he would not know where to go anyway and it was safer to pretend to cooperate while waiting for Menlow to come to his rescue. The inside bottom of his new cage was lined in soft blue upholstery. Something that seemed familiar lay in the center. It took Gopher a moment to recognize it to be a pair of pants and shirt. It reminded him of Adia's doll clothes and especially of how they had made him feel like a fraud. Now these clothes, just looking at them, made him feel like one even more.

"They're to go on a doll," Wells said, peering through bars, "but I think that, with a few alterations, they'd fit you."

"But – but, why?" stammered Gopher. His resolve to hide his feelings was quickly crumbling.

Wells said, "Why? Who wants to see *just* a gopher? A talking one that also wears clothes – now *that* would add to people's imagination and give you character."

Gopher, who had been on the point of refusing and showing his true self, realized that they were just as much a fraud. They were only nice to him for the sake of getting more of their rotten, clanging coins in their money box, so why should he feel bad about himself?

"True, but will it fit and not look ridiculous on me?" Gopher said.

Wells laughed. "Ah, a gopher with vanity!"

"I'll make it fit," Loggins said.

Gopher did not like the determination in his eyes or voice; that is, until he saw what the man had meant. With scissors, needle, and thread, Loggins revealed his skills of a tailor as he went to work on altering the doll clothes. Measuring and re-measuring, cutting and sewing, and trying on and taking off, he worked with a patience that was even more surprising than his skills, considering his usual grumpy and surly disposition.

It was during the tailoring that Gopher had been allowed out of his cage once again, and once again he had resisted the idea of trying to run away. At one point, when his captors both had their backs turned, he had thought about it, but even if he had wanted to, he had been too tired, what with putting on and taking off the clothes so many times.

It proved to be a good thing that he hadn't tried. At the time Loggins and Wells were repositioning the screen in front of the tub. The looks on their faces, when they turned around, became pleased ones. Gopher was pleased, too, for he realized that it had been a test. *They had expected him to run.* Earning their trust made him feel elated, but only because it added to his hope of eventually escaping.

After enduring a few more alterations, he then made a greater show of cooperation as he asked them to put him back into the cage so that he could take a nap. Yet he did not intend to sleep; he only wanted a reprieve so that he could be left alone to wait for the show to begin. He watched as Wells and Loggins changed into new outfits, for the wagonload of merchandise had also included a small stack of clothes. Behind the screen they took turns trying on their new clothes, all of which were as gaudy or flashy as their shiny walking sticks.

Those walking sticks might have added a sense of security (considering the near-riot last night) if he hadn't realized that they could also be used on Menlow if he should suddenly appear. By this time, however, a lethargic feeling caused by his inactivity made it impossible for him to get worked up about it, and before he knew it he was asleep.

Loggons woke him up a few hours later to try on his clothes. They turned out beautiful, which even Gopher in his sleep-fogged mind had to admit. The brown pants and tan shirt, with sleeves and legs cut perfectly for his short limbs and roomy enough in the back to hide his stubby tail, made him feel almost human. When asked if he wanted a mirror, however, he refused and was relieved when they did not press him.

He did not have time to dwell upon it, thankfully, because they began coaching him on his conversation and behavior, like saying "sir" or "my lady" and to sound happy and act willing to please, while expecting *them* to treat him respectfully. "Never let people think of you as their doormat," Wells said, "or that's how they'll treat you." They also taught him tricks, such as whistling through his two front teeth and doing cartwheels (which wasn't easy with the restrictiveness of his new clothes). Gopher did not have to pretend to be grateful or willing to learn, for he really was, since these things fit in with his plan.

So what might have been a long day of waiting turned into a

seemingly short one, especially since the crowd arrived early to assemble at the foot of the hill. Immediately, and unexpectedly, Gopher felt his stomach drop at the sound of their arrival. The security of the cage and the walking sticks were not enough to dispel a dread of natural fear. He thought that he had gotten over such feelings. At least, just like the rest of the day, he didn't have enough time for them to grow. Before he knew it, the first crowd of ten was ushered in, and, like before, the fear fell away when he saw the familiar wonder on faces, some of which were also familiar, having seen them from last night.

Tonight's performance, however, proved to be different – and not for the better. It was due to those returning patrons. Some of them acted as if they were the "experts" about talking gophers. They guffawed at the newcomers' look of wonder and "helped" Gopher in telling his story and answering questions. Others had been drinking and were loud and vulgar. For them, the novelty of hearing a rodent talk and seeing him do tricks had worn off, so they acted as if they were part of the show. The worst for him were their insults and demeaning jokes, such as "I really gopher you!" and "I saw your cousin slinking around in the cellar the other day. Boy, is he a rat!"

During it all, he talked and sang (when he could be heard); smiled and laughed at their jokes; did back flips, head stands, whistled and danced to their clapping. Fortunately, there were some groups who came in that hadn't seen him before, and their wonder and amazement was, especially by comparison, refreshing.

Something happened that night, though, that made all the other nuisances seem trivial by comparison. It came during the fourth performance. Gopher was telling how, after surviving the river, he was found and taken in by these two kind men. (He thought it safer if he never mentioned the pixie on the off chance he might still be rescued by him.) For once the men and women were listening quietly, gathered in front of the cage, when there was a cough from the back. Something so sickly and pathetic about it made everyone turn and it even distracted Gopher from his story. It was followed by a soft voice that conveyed a sweet sadness in its tone. It made the rodent forget about his story altogether.

"Excuse me... I, uh, I was hoping that I could see better – if you would be so kind? Thank you."

A way was made through the small crowd for a child, whose soulful blue eyes in an innocent face contrasted endearingly to the rest of his ragamuffin appearance. There was such innocence in that look that it made Gopher realize the hate that he held in his heart toward his captors. His deception to cooperate with them suddenly seemed disgusting to him.

He was not the only one to be affected. There were more than a few sympathetic clucking of tongues and sad sighs. Yet when the child, who could not have been more than eight years old, saw Gopher, his face and eyes seemed to literally light up, which, in turn, seemed to light Gopher up, too.

"Hi," the boy said.

It wasn't meant to be funny but everybody laughed, and so did Gopher. It suddenly occurred to the rodent that there was something vaguely familiar about the child. Had he seen him last night? Or in Kentfell? Those would be the only times he could have met him. The familiarity troubled him, though he did not know why... like how he had felt this morning. During these thoughts, he realized that the child was waiting for a reply from him, and so was everybody else.

"Hi," Gopher replied at last.

The child's smile, which would have been toothy if not for two missing front ones, broadened in response.

"Gee, I never talked to a gopher before!"

More laughter.

"Can I play with you?" he asked.

"I – I can't. This cage..." Gopher's voice trailed off. It was painful to deny the child.

Wells cleared his throat. "Uh, maybe just for a minute. The ladies and gentlemen here might enjoy watching."

As he bent down to unlatch the cage's door, everybody, for some reason, watched with bated breath, but then Loggins said in a gruff voice, "That'll be an extra ten silver coins for the privilege, young 'un."

There came a collective gasp of amazement. Strangest of all, Loggins looked just as amazed. He also looked pale and his posture rigidly stiff.

The child blinked and his smile faded and the corners of his mouth turned downwards. "I don't even have one silver coin," he said sweetly. "I just wanted to play with him."

Loggins did not look amazed anymore but his mouth was contorted into an odd frown and his thick brows were scrunched as if he were in pain. Gopher thought how greedy he must be that he could be so hard-hearted, though clearly he was struggling with himself. Nevertheless, the man just stood there, ramrod straight and said nothing. Wells was speechless for once.

"Here, I have a coin – if you must insist!" said a woman in the crowd.

"And I have two!" said a man.

"I got a silver coin," said an old man.

But no more were forthcoming, everybody else saying that they had spent all they had just to see the show. The child looked at Loggins expectantly, as if to say "Isn't that enough?" But the short, stout man did not move and his frown seemed to be even more contorted, as if the internal struggle had escalated. Then the boy tapped Wells with a pleading look, who then turned to his partner.

"Oh, Loggins, it wouldn't hurt –" his partner, uncharacteristically, started to plea, when the other cut him off.

"No!"

The word, while not shouted, had such finality that it made everyone jump, including Wells and Gopher – everybody, that is, except the child. In a moment the boy's sweetness changed to ferocity that made the former seemed to have been impossible. His face became so scrunched up and his eyes so narrowed that, instead of a sweet little boy, he looked like an imp, a very angry imp.

"Give him to me!"

Loggins, even paler than before, looked as if he would give in, his body shivering, but still somehow he managed to remain standing and unyielding as he glared with that strange frown on his face at the child. It was Wells who recovered first, though his shock was replaced with unusual timidity.

"Uh, I don't think so. Where – uh, where are your parents?"

The boy did not answer, except his frown deepened, his hands tightened into fists, and his body began shaking. The trembling increased, and those around him stepped back with worried looks. Even the women who appeared motherly shied away as they gasped and their eyes widened in horror. It was then that the child started changing in more than just facial expressions and behavior, for his entire body began to transmutate into a blackened, misshapen... resemblance of a child... no, not really a resemblance, but like a poor imitation of a child. It had coarse hair all over its body that looked like it was *supposed* to be clothes. His eyes were no longer soulful or even human, being too big and far apart with a quality of darkness that expressed a lifeless emptiness. It began to scream, and the sound of it, so harsh and piercing, from a mouth with no teeth but a single sharp one, did not come from a child's throat either.

Pandemonium ensued amongst the townsfolk: yells and cries accompanied the shoving and the mad rush to escape. Thankfully they were a small enough group to flee quickly through the opening without tearing down the tent itself. At the same time the creature charged the cage, lowering its head like a ram. Gopher closed his eyes, but when nothing happened, he opened them to find that his would-be attacker had disappeared. Instead, it had left an odd odor in the air. At first it smelled sweet and lovely but as it lingered, the odor became rotten and repugnant, like that of something dead. Somehow that, too, seemed vaguely familiar – and troubling.

Chapter Nineteen

"But I didn't say *anything*!" Loggins said. "I couldn't!"

It was the same evening. The three were alone in the tent.

"What do you mean?" Wells said.

"I went all stiff-like... I felt trapped inside myself and couldn't get out. Somebody else said all that – but with my voice! It was the strangest thing..."

Wells rubbed his chin thoughtfully but then shook his head and shrugged. "Almost as strange as that – what was that... child-monster?"

"A changeling," Gopher said. He was as surprised at his reply as his captors appeared to be, for his memory had come unexpectedly. He quickly added defensively, "My friend told me about them once... 'The changeling woos people with its magic, mostly children, to capture them and take on their likeness because they hate their own ugly looks.'"

"But why would they want to capture a gopher?" Loggins said.

"Yes, it was clearly after you," Wells said, "but whatever the reason for choosing you, Gopher, I'd say that you are definitely better off with us." He said it as if they were doing him a favor.

Loggins cleared his throat.

"I don't know *what* to make of it," the man said, "but you can follow a trail by reading the signs as well as I can. I'd say everything points to the fact that he'd be better with someone else."

Wells spun around to face him.

"What? Do you mean the hermit? I thought that you didn't want –"

"Of course not," Loggins said. "After all, how much could *he* pay us? No. I mean someone wealthy, with lots of gold lying around. How about a king? Or a lord? There're plenty to choose from, but I'd say choose the nearest. The sooner we get rid of him the better. I don't want *that* to happen again."

The idea visibly stopped Wells almost completely as if he had been frozen in place, but it was only for a moment. He slowly shook his head like one coming to life. He chuckled, "I have to hand it to you, Loggins. Fear does teach lessons, doesn't it? It is a brilliant idea, but, no, I cannot do it."

"Why?" the other said angrily.

"Simply because I gave my word to Gopher. I promised him that when we've made enough, we would return him to his friend. And that is that! Tomorrow we'll head for another town." He then turned to Gopher.

"Don't let this worry you. You've been through enough already than to let this unsettle you."

Gopher wasn't upset, not about what Wells and Loggins talked about at least. He could not imagine his life could be worse with a king or lord, but the implication about the changeling coming back had set him to thinking. The evil creature who stole others to take on their appearance reminded him of the hamadryad who also, in a similar way, sought to live through Adia. He wondered if all evil lived off of the good and the innocent. The thought was a diverting one, for it kept him from thinking about what really upset him.

They didn't bother to count the money that night. After a while, he wished that they had because that would have been something else to divert his attention. Soon they turned down the lamp, with Wells taking the first watch just in case the creature came back. Leaning his back against the center pole and bringing his long legs up to rest his elbows on his knees, the man became so still and quiet that he became part of the ensuing silence, which gradually made all the more peaceful by the chirping of crickets and the whispering of the breeze that shivered the tent and rustled through the branches of the tree. It was so serene that it contrasted against the restless, uncomfortable truth that Gopher wanted to avoid thinking about.

Even so, it soon proved impossible to resist. First, the rodent's thoughts slowly began drifting towards the less painful truths. What he had said about the changeling had surprised him just as much as it had his captors. How had he remembered so suddenly and with such certainty? Why did the creature seem so familiar?

This led him to even more uncomfortable questions. Were Wells and Loggins now being nice because they suspected that there was more to the rodent than his ability to speak? Did they suspect that somehow he was to blame for tonight? Undoubtedly, it was why Loggins had wanted to get rid of him so readily? Yet it was not how *they* felt that bothered him. The more painful truth was that he had felt something in common with the changeling, especially when it had changed to its true horrid appearance. That was what bothered him.

He sighed, expelling his breath as if to expel the last of his reluctance to admit the truth. As he did so, a weight seemed to lift from him; he felt as if he could breathe again. In fact, a short burst of relieved laughter escaped from his throat without being able to help himself.

And then he laughed again, even harder, but for a far different reason, because now relief had brought clarity of thought. He saw, all in a moment, just how ridiculous it was to think that he was anything like that creature or that he was somehow to blame for the incident. How could he be? It didn't even make sense. And how – or why – could he even think so to begin with?

He laughed some more, mostly at himself, but he didn't mind; he was so relieved. He had been trying to suppress something about himself that wasn't even true. The more he had tried to suppress it, to hold it down, to hide from it, the truer it seemed. Guilt, whether real or imagined, proved to have been, in its way, a worse kind of prison than this cage.

Then he became aware of Wells stirring about.

"What's so funny?" he said, his voice thick as if he might have fallen asleep on his watch.

"Nothing really," Gopher said. "Good night."

Not long afterwards he drifted to sleep with the contentment of someone who had been set free, while his captors were ironically bound to their duty of keeping watch.

●   ●   ●

Gopher awoke the next morning without being able to relive the taste of freedom from last night, for he awoke to the hustle and bustle of moving. The tent was already down and a heavy morning mist met him with an invigorating coolness. The same mist prevented him from seeing the village down the slope, though he heard sounds that reminded him of Kentfell – which, n turn, reminded him of Menlow – Ah! The ache of missing his friend ran right through him like a sword.

At the same time Wells was chuckling and saying, "I'm glad of this here fog. After last night we might not be too popular. We'll be gone before they know it."

"After what happened," Loggins said, "this fog gives me a different sort of chills, if you know what I mean. What if that changeling comes back? We won't see it coming."

As much as his hope depended on the show staying in one spot as word spread of a talking gopher, Gopher could not help but be glad they were moving on. Although it was mostly for the same reason as his captors, the thought of another night of performing was too much for him. Just a short break was all he needed – and, of course, distance from that changeling. Anyway, he told himself that once Menlow got word of the show, distance wouldn't stop him from coming.

When they set out, the mist was still so thick that, except for a slight raise in temperature, the sun was evidenced only by a milky glow in the east. The mule pulled on its harness to move the loaded wagon, causing the wheels to creak and to jostle the load noisily. The sounds from the town were drowned out, and, except for the bumps in the dirt road, the wagon seemed to stay in the same spot in that unvarying mist. For a long time Gopher imagined that the town remained not far behind them.

Gopher's cage had been set between the two men instead of in the back of the wagon. He wondered if it might be because they feared the changeling would return and snatch him away. Still, he appreciated that it was a less bumpy of a ride on the buckboard and that it had a better view, what there was of it, since they didn't cover the cage.

Neither did they try to hide him when they encountered two men on foot. One of them looked familiar.

"Where you heading to in a hurry?" asked the familiar one.

Gopher could almost hear an accusation in his words; it was as if he were acting like Wells and Loggins were thieves – as if they had no business leaving the area. The rodent's heart sunk, for it occurred to him that, if not Menlow or Farwyll, any would-be rescuer might very well be like one of these – or like that changeling.

"Is that *him*?" said the companion. "I didn't get to see the show, but I still don't believe he can talk. Let me hear, will you?"

"He can talk," asserted the first man. "I didn't go traipsing up to your place yesterday to lie to you. I heard the gopher talk myself."

"I'm sorry but we don't give free shows," Wells said amiably.

"My money is as good as it was the other night," said the first man sharply.

"Of course it is," Wells said, "but the truth is that he is a little tired after last night; we all are. Our next show will be in Sorell. It's not too far and it'll be worth the trip. And if you show up early, I promise to give you a private interview, just the two of you. Have a good day, sirs." He shook the reins to get the mule going again.

"Tired, eh?" persisted the first man. "Is it true what I heard in town about what happened last night? Most people are 'tired' too – if that means *scared*!" He laughed harshly.

"That's it!" Loggins growled. "Now get out of here!"

"No, wait," the man said, not intimidated. "I brought my friend all the way here for the show. We ain't going all the way to Sorell to see it when we have the gopher here right now. Just because you're scared and want to –"

"Just go away and leave us alone!" Gopher said suddenly. "I mean it – or you'll be sorry!"

Gopher was too swept up in the sharp emotions of irritation and impatience to recognize his own forcefulness in his words, though it surprised everyone else. Wells was once again the first to recover from being surprised.

"Now, that's your free show, my fellows. Good day."

The two seemed to disappear into the fog with their mouths open and astonishment frozen on their faces as the wagon pulled away. After a few moments of silence (not including the creaking wheels, the jangling of the shifting load, and the plodding hoofs), Wells chuckled and looked down into the cage.

"Well done, Gopher. They *were* annoying, weren't they? Generally speaking, threatening the customer is not good business, but in their case... it was the only kind that they deserved."

"Hopefully word won't spread ahead of us because of it."

"Now how could it, Logs? It definitely couldn't reach any faster than us in this blasted fog!"

Gopher had slept only intermittently as they proceeded, though he had wanted to sleep more. The effect of his outburst towards those two disagreeable men had been satisfying, thrilling even, at first, but as the wagon had trudged along, a depression had come over him. It was a depression that came from feeling like he was changing into something he didn't like, but the incident, and the depression, was pushed from his thoughts as the mist evaporated along the way, gradually revealing the unfamiliar sights of the foothills. That's when he wanted to sleep the most, but, unlike the numbing depression, the swelling pain of loneliness would not let him, for it was not about him anymore. All he could think of was Menlow – and all he could feel were the pain of separation and the deep ache of loneliness.

Their arrival at Sorell, nonetheless, proved to have been anticipated despite what Wells had said. By the time they reached the outskirts of the town, the sun was less than two hours from dipping behind the hazy horizon in the west. It had been a long journey. The mist had faded as they had slowly traversed up and down the grey foot hills that turned slowly to green. Then they made up more speed and distance in the bottomlands where the monotony of brown and green fields was broken by herds of cattle and sheep and the occasional farmhouse and barn. The forested mountain range began to fade behind like that fog and like a distant memory. They stopped only for a late lunch by a stream and another time when a wheel had gotten stuck in a rut.

Gopher saw none of it. The pain of his loneliness had numbed him after the long, monotonous hours of hearing the plodding of the mule's hoofs and creaks of the wheel and wagon. One can only feel so much pain for so long. But when at last the strange buildings and streets of Sorell appeared in the distance, against the backdrop of a broad river, the wound was reopened. It was not until then that he realized that the monotony of the journey had become a constant in his life for that short of time and, in so doing, had given him a portion of familiarity, however small. Now that the journey was over, the reality of his strange surroundings hit him, leaving him bereft of even that.

Almost as soon as the town came into view, the tired donkey was reined in to stop the wagon in a wide clearing. His captors, jumping off, unpacked their things in the wagon as quick as they could. The sun, now a burning crescent, was dipping beyond the black horizon of low hills. It propelled Wells to work as hard as Loggins for once, though he still managed to shout orders at the same time.

They made good time, but, in the midst of assembling the tent, a ruckus of voices interrupted Wells' tirade and heralded the coming of a crowd, their figures becoming distinct in the last remaining slanting rays. They were dressed colorfully with scarves, caps, and sashes.

A short man, in a red and gold garment and with a long moustache, said merrily, "Hullo there, you the ones with the talking rodent! When's the show?"

This request was echoed among the rest.

Wells replied at last, "How did the word about the show reach you already? We have just arrived."

The first man replied, rubbing an end of his moustaches between his fingers, "Word did not reach us; rather, we reached it. We are gypsies, and we range far and wide, for our freedom beckons us never to set roots but to be like the wind, traveling as fast and free! We came upon a little boy who told us all about a captive gopher who wants to be set free of two free men whose desires makes them captive. Is this not true?"

"It is too late for a show tonight," Wells said, "but tomorrow I promise you –"

"Psaw! Tomorrow's too late for tonight's satisfaction. Why be constrained by the lack of light? We shall make a fire as you finish setting up!"

"But we are tired. Tomorrow –"

"Tomorrow, tomorrow, tomorrow!" The gypsy said, laughing. "There is no such thing until it comes. We have only now, for now is the only time there is.

"Besides," he continued, "you are only tired because you settle to easy for what does not satisfy, while we are strengthened by seeking that which does. It is the purpose of our freedom. Hear, hear?"

"Hear, hear!" confirmed the other gypsies.

Before Wells, or Loggins, could say anything, the fellows in the colorful garb set to finding wood in the nearby copse of trees and dragging branches and pieces of wood into one pile near the wagon. The gypsies moved as if they were dancing like children at play, but they were more efficient than most adults. Somebody lit the pile and in moments a crackling fire blazed forth, the brightness of which made the approaching dusk seemed darker by comparison.

It sickened Gopher to watch, for the sight of them that the flames made possible confirmed something he had felt when they had arrived. It felt like he knew them with that same sense of familiarity, in which a part of him thrilled at their frivolity and delighted in the chagrin it caused his captors. It was as if he shared their feelings. Another part of him was instinctively repulsed by them, a part that did not want to share anything with them.

The gypsy who had spoken to them turned from dancing and laughing in front of the blaze with a sudden change in countenance.

"Enough of this!" he cried, clapping his hands. The others settled down at once, though some grumbled. "We didn't come here for fires and dancing." He turned towards Wells and Loggins who still stood amidst the tent that was still unassembled on the ground. "What is this? You have not started?"

"Like I said," Wells said, resuming the same patient tone as before as if nothing was unusual, "we are tired. Thank you for the fire. Because of it we will charge you only half price– tomorrow night," he added firmly but not unfriendly.

The gypsies stood still with complacent smirks on their faces. One of them, a young man with squinting eyes and a red bandana, suddenly laughed and practically sang, "Half price? Half price, full price, double the price! We don't care!"

The first gypsy chuckled and turned to Wells. "You see, price does not matter to us. Money is only good for what one buys with it. Is that the gopher on the wagon? Let him speak and if we are satisfied that he is satisfied, we will give whatever price that would satisfy you, though that may be impossible since you don't know the word 'enough!'"

Loggins spoke up, "We get paid up front."

"Okay, okay, whatever!" the gypsy said. He crossed his arms with a smirk. "If you want it now, then we *shall* get our satisfaction first."

His smirk became a full-blown smile – and then some, as the corners of his mouth rose higher and higher, revealing teeth that weren't white teeth but silver and gold. They sparkled in the flickering firelight – and then the teeth seemed to multiply and multiply until they were falling out of his mouth. As they chinked to the ground, they became silver and gold coins. This was joined by other chinking sounds, coming from the other gypsies whose mouths, too, were overflowing with coins.

After the last coin dropped, the first gypsy cried out, "Yuck!

Now I know why it's called filthy lucre!" He laughed at his own joke and so did the other gypsies, while the two men watched dumbfounded.

The gypsy went on, "Don't imagine that even this will be enough to satisfy you. It's why we spit it out. At least *we* could never develop a taste for it, because once you do, it develops a taste for you. Ironic, isn't it!"

"What –what do you mean?" Loggins said, trying unsuccessfully to sound unimpressed.

The gypsy replied, "I'm glad you asked. Shall we demonstrate? It's so much better than a lecture!"

The gypsies snapped their fingers, though one danced a two-step jig and another clapped his hands. Nothing seemed to happen, except after a moment the gypsies appeared shorter... and then it became apparent that they became slighter both in body and face as if they were shrinking... into something less than human – and definitely not as friendly.

Then something else changed. The piles of coins at the feet of each gypsy began to shift and separate into a single shimmering layer, carpeting the ground in large gold and silver patches that shimmered in the fire light as Wells and Loggins stepped away from the semi-raised tent and skirted the coins to stand with their backs against the wagon and the cage. By this time, the shimmering had increased, for coins had righted themselves and began to spin on their edges, rotating faster, faster until their blur truly resembled golden and silvery carpets that seemed alive. Then, just as the spinning became so fast that they did not seem to move at all, the coins disappeared. But what happened was that they spun themselves so fast they tunneled themselves into the ground.

The gypsy chief exclaimed, "And now for the harvest!" and gave out a lingering laugh before he, and the rest of the gypsies vanished.

"What does this mean?" Wells breathed when all was quiet once more. This was immediately answered by what happened next.

Loggins cried out, "Hey! Something's got me!" He began stamping and pulling and striking at something around his legs.

"What do you mean?" Wells said but then he exclaimed, "Ouch! What in the –!" as he, too, followed his partner's example.

That was when the firelight caught the golden and silvery whipping vines and thorny stems that were sprouting up from a thick, undulating carpet of moss. The stems grasped anything or anyone within reach. The donkey hee-hawed and stamped about to escape them, though unable to move much because it was still harnessed to the wagon, which the vines held in a writhing coil. The vehicle rocked back and forth, causing the cage to slide along the buckboard.

"This is a gypsy curse! Let's get away!" Wells said.

"How can I? It's got me. Oh! I'm going under! Help!"

Only half of Loggins showed, while the rest had already been sucked down into a thrashing bed of golden and silvery moss. He flailed his arms about and managed to grasp a shiny limb, but that proved to be his undoing for that branch quickly intertwined around both wrists. He gave one last scream before he was completely pulled under. Wells, who was wrestling with a thick vine, let out a shriek of rage and terror at seeing his partner's fate and doubled his effort to escape.

Gopher never saw if he was successful or not. The cage was suddenly lifted from the buckboard, the movement jolting the rodent about. A strand of silvery ivy, he discovered when he had righted himself, had wrapped itself around the bars like a silver snake, and now other strands, some golden, had intertwined the rest of the cage. Then the cage door opened and Gopher felt something grab him about the middle. It pulled him out and he saw the cage behind him sink into the gold and silver ground.

"Now don't fret yourself, my little friend, about all this nonsense," said a familiar voice; Gopher saw that it was Farwyll who was holding him. "Shall we be on our way?"

The pixie practically skipped through the evil undergrowth,

completely untouched. When they had gone far enough so that the campfire was little more than a pin-prick of flickering yellow light amidst the dusky grey countryside, the pixie clucked his tongue and shook his head sadly as he looked over his shoulder.

"Maybe something good will come out of that back there," he said, hopefully.

Chapter Twenty

Without speaking any more (but with plenty of merry humming that no longer irritated Gopher), they traveled some time through the rapidly deepening shadows, the pixie moving as sure-footedly and quickly as he would in broad daylight. For Gopher it made for an exhilarating ride in the dark where the silhouettes of the elms and pines stood out against a starry expanse of deep blue that was almost black. He spotted the half moon low in the sky when they crossed a stream that softly swished and gurgled.

Those sounds could have been ominous, but with Farwyll's presence Gopher could not feel afraid. A frightening moment occurred, however, when the pixie began climbing almost straight up the face of a rocky slope. Nearly halfway up, the pixie's footing set loose a small but rapidly growing avalanche. The rodent felt sure they were falling with it until he realized that Farwyll was still going up despite the cascade of stones passing all around them. Somehow he was able to dodge most of them, though a few smaller ones hit them both. Instead of grunting with pain, the fairy laughed as if they tickled. When they reached the top, the pixie paused for the first time, testing the air with his wetted finger. Gopher had not realized that he had missed the gesture until now.

"Oh, 'tis time to rest 'til the wind blows best!" the pixie rhymed brightly, as he abruptly settled down under a tree, whose thick branches swept low enough overhead to make a shelter and with a matting of pine needles underneath to make it cozy. It was not long after this that Farwyll began to chuckle as he lay there as peaceful as if he had been relaxing all day.

"What is it?" Gopher said, but he could hardly bring himself to really care, for the bed of needles was so soft and comfortable. In fact, as his body relaxed, it even felt luxurious. Until now he had not realized just how exhausted he was.

The pixie's voice sounded in the near total darkness beside him, "I was just remembering what happened to our friends back there... I do not mean to make light of their misfortune, but I cannot see that it was really such a misfortune. I walked right through a thrashing branch and did not feel it. I suspect it was nothing more than a magical deception. Still, I should not laugh. It was real enough to them."

"Why was it real for them and not for you?"

"I suppose it is their greed that gave substance to that illusion. For me I could barely even see those vines, but I saw those who made them," he said with a shudder. "Few things bother me as much as those who think themselves superior and set themselves to teaching lessons to their inferiors."

"But who are they?"

"Fairies, but I've forgotten their name. Sleep now," the fairy urged, "We'll have plenty to talk about in the morning."

Gopher did not need any further coaxing. Those were the last words he heard and the last of anything intelligible to pass through his brain.

He awoke with the dawning light, hearing the pixie's musical humming nearby. As he listened, Farwyll sounded at times as if he would burst out into a full-fledged song. Gopher could almost convince himself that nothing had changed, that they had never been separated, but then, as he gazed at the low-hanging pine limbs over him, he thought about how he had gotten there and all that had passed before.

Yes, he thought, a lot had changed, and so had the pixie. Gopher had noticed the difference in him almost immediately last night. The pixie was almost twice as big as when he had last seen him, but he had been so preoccupied with the thrill of being freed by his friend that he hadn't thought about it. (Ah, the thought that he would never see Wells or Loggins again still made him giddy!) He now decided to ask the pixie about it.

Farwyll was playing around a campfire. That, at least, was Gopher's immediate impression. He was actually cooking. With one hand he was flipping something in a shiny pan over the flames, and with the other he was poking at the fire with an equally shiny poker, all done with a bouncy exuberance of a child. Seeing the rodent, Farwyll added to that impression by singing, "Stir the fire and flip the eggs, whistle a tune and add some sage; that is the way to greet the morn, that is the way to start anew!"

"Very good!" Gopher laughed. "Good morning, Where did you get the pan?" the rodent added, forgetting for the moment his question.

"And the poker, too?" the pixie asked. "And the plates?"

"What plates?" the rodent said.

"You'll see...These are done, I think, if you like over-easy. And now for those plates."

As soon as he set the poker down on a rock, its silvery metal started coalescing as if it were melting. Then the ends began drawing in towards the center of the bar where it expanded uniformly outwards, flattening and rounding its edges, until it was a perfect silver plate.

Farwyll slid two eggs on to it and then placed the pan on another rock and it, too, underwent the same transformation into another silver plate. Two other eggs remained on it.

"Careful, magic may change their shapes, but they'll still be too hot to handle," Farwyll said.

"Did you make them out of the air?"

"Even the most powerful magic can't make something out of nothing, my little friend," the pixie said. "These are some of the silver coins I picked up last night, but the eggs came from a nest far up in this tree."

When the plates had cooled down enough and they began to eat, Gopher remembered to ask his first question.

"Have you grown since I last seen you?"

"True," the pixie replied, "I grew a good two inches or so that night– but I'm not bragging."

Suddenly Gopher was no longer hungry. How could he have forgotten his disappointment in the pixie for not coming to his rescue sooner?

"Was it a good choice, leaving me behind in a cage?" he said bitterly.

Farwyll noticed it, for his facial features sharpened even more as he winced.

"Of course, it was, but following the wind is not always the most pleasant choice. The hard choices always make you grow – or shrink, if you choose unwisely."

Gopher could not contain himself: "How could leaving me in a cage be wise?"

"How? Seldom do I know the *how*, much less the *why* of things... Did they treat you okay?" he went on, "Did you eat, get a place to sleep, keep some kind of company?" To his credit, he sounded concerned, but Gopher did not want to believe it.

"I was in a *cage*!"

"Hmmm... Sounds like they protected you, at least –even though they might not have meant it that way," Farwyll mused.

"You sound just like them! That's what they said!"

"Ha! Really?" he said it as if it were an amusing coincidence.

Gopher forced himself to change the topic: "So why did you decide to rescue me this time?"

"Oh, that! The wind led me to do it."

Of course. The wind. Gopher should have seen that coming.

The pixie continued, "By the way, I rescued you one other time before that when you were in the cage. I am not bragging, but you ought to know that it wasn't that stout fellow – Loggins, was it? – who stopped that changeling from walking off with you the other night. That was my voice you heard."

"You were there?"

"Right behind the screen and next to the tub," he said. "By the way, you weren't the only one I rescued that night. The child, who the changeling had kidnapped, got his appearance back – and his freedom. (You see, changelings lose their power when they don't get their way.) The boy – the real one – should be back safe at home with his parents, I should think.

"But now," he continued, "is the time to put out the fire and get going before the hawk comes back and misses her eggs."

After stamping out the flames, Farwyll did something new that proved just how much he had grown: he placed Gopher on his shoulder as they set out. It, of course, reminded him of Menlow, but not painfully, since sudden hope had overwhelmed his bitter feelings.

They proceeded past the pine tree into the beginning of a dense forest where the shadows deepened and the birds chattered noisily overhead. As if inspired by their singing, Farwyll took up humming the same merry tune that he had left off last night.

The rodent was surprised to realize that the pixie's course did not meander like before. His route lay in almost a straight line, despite the obstacles that the woods presented. The pixie passed practically untouched through thorny hedges, climbed over boulders that looked insurmountable, and easily skipped across a wide ravine. Seldom did he test for the wind, too; his stride seemed to be longer and his pace faster than his usual lackadaisical manner. Gopher felt sure that they were nearing their destination, and he asked the question that he should've asked a long time ago. (At least it seemed a long time since he had been rescued.)

"Where are we going?"

"No jumping to conclusions," Farwyll cautioned merrily. "I *think* I know, but if I'm wrong, it's best that at least only one of us is disappointed. Anyway, we shall see in a moment: The wind is most definite in its direction. There's no mistaking it and *that* is usually a good sign that we're coming to the end of the journey. Of course, that usually means it's the beginning of another."

Gopher was too happy to let himself be annoyed by his answer. As agile as a monkey, Farwyll began scrambling up the largest and sheerest boulder yet, somehow finding purchases for foot- and hand-holds where ascent seemed impossible. The rodent shifted all his attention to holding on by grasping the fairy's neck. It seemed likely that the sharp points of Gopher's claws would cause pain, but the pixie's whistling did not let up or change one merry note. The pixie said at one point, "I do my best whistling at these times, you know? Then the steepness is not so steep!" Gopher heard some birds chirping nearby that sounded like the pixie's tune.

When Farwyll finally crested the stone face, he stopped, for on the other side was a sheer drop, overlooking a broad expanse of green land, whose flatness was interrupted here and there by occasional gently sloping hills. Immediately below lay a winding black ribbon of a river. So awed by the panorama, the rodent did not see the man sitting in the shadow of a young oak tree to their right until he spoke.

"Gopher, you are long overdue, but you are welcome all the same! I am he whom they call the Traveling Merchant. Greetings and well done, Farwyll!"

Chapter Twenty-One

The Traveling Merchant sprang up and bowed so spritely that it did not seem that he was the little old man that he was. His youthfulness stemmed also from his perpetual smile, though it was framed by a thick bushy gray beard. The twinkle in his eyes made him look as if he found joy everywhere. His merry voice and his easy manner added to that impression. As if to accentuate his youthfulness with hints of careless frivolity, he wore a dirty brown vest that might once have been red over a faded blue shirt and dark pants that bordered on black, except in torn places where the white of his legs showed through. High boots covered in dried mud reached halfway up his shins. All in all, he looked as if he had just got through playing in the dirt. In contrast, his gray-haired head was topped by a tasseled floppy cap that was definitely red and obviously the nicest, newest, and cleanest piece of clothing he wore.

The cap fell off when the Merchant bowed. It landed just on the ledge, but instead of picking it up, he held up an acorn with an expression of child-like triumph.

"Ah, here it is, just as I dreamed!" he exclaimed.

"Why? It's just an acorn." Gopher could not help asking. There was something about the old man that made him so easy to speak to.

The Merchant's smile broadened. "What I dream is always important. I had dreamed of my hat falling off right next to the

175

acorn right after meeting you. That's how I knew it was the right one."

"Does that acorn have magic, like the carrot seed?" Gopher asked.

The old man shook his head, saw the tasseled cap on the ground, and replaced it back on his head before replying: "No, that carrot seed was the last of the old magic. It is also the greatest that ever was in the world. I thought Menlow would have told you. Anyway, this acorn –" he held it out on his open palm, "– is just an acorn, but that doesn't mean it isn't special. It has its purpose and whatever it is, it is not for me but for the one who buys it.

"You must be hungry," he went on, changing the subject as he slipped the acorn into a pocket in his vest. "I have some dried beef that I have been saving up for this very moment – though I did not dream of it. Will you be staying, too, Farwyll?"

The pixie clapped his hands and sang, "Not a breeze stirs me, and so with you I'll stay until it leads me another way!"

"Excellent! Perhaps the three of us will travel together! Let's find some shelter to make our lunch more comfortable. Brrrr – this wind's cold. I must be getting old!"

The Merchant led them along the cliff edge to their left. A stiff breeze that foretold the coming of winter steadily pressed them from that side. Soon the old man chose a path away from the ridgeline and into the shade of tall, leafy elms where they stopped in a pleasant grassy clearing.

"A perfect place for a rest, and, it is tempting, to stay the night here, but, alas," the Traveling Merchant said as they sat down, "this acorn presses me to go on."

"How does it press you since it's just an acorn, sir," said Gopher, climbing down from the pixie's shoulder.

"The dream of it does, not the thing itself, for in my dream I had felt compelled to bring the acorn to the one for whom it is meant – though, as yet, I don't know who that person is. To delay is to tempt myself to keeping the thing for myself. It had been especially tempting to keep that magic carrot seed, for it took me days to find the right person to give it to."

"You mean, to Menlow?"

"Yes, but that was only because it was to go through him to you. That's what confused me, because I dreamed of you, not the hermit, to receive the carrot."

"But how did you know that I would get it?"

"I didn't *know*. I had to use a little bit of common sense and a little bit of faith. You see, I knew that a gopher who couldn't talk would never have something to trade, much less understand anything about the whole matter. Secondly, I knew that the hermit's magic had done him great harm and that he might, as a result, be willing to trade. I had to trust that you would come along at the right time."

The Merchant broke off pieces of the jerky into three parts and passed them around, along with some raisins, nuts, and carrots from a pouch that he kept under his belt.

As the rodent chewed his portion, he asked, "What if you were wrong? What if he hadn't been the right person for the magic seed – and I wasn't the one who was suppose to eat the carrot?"

He shrugged, "I do the best I can, but up to this point in my long life, it had been the hardest choice I made... but (at last!) here we are together. That's proof enough for me. There's no mistake in that... Here, I have a water skin. Drink up. "

"Will you take me back to Menlow?" It was what he should have asked already, but the surprise meeting had distracted him.

The Traveling Merchant winked while vainly straightening his already wrinkled vest.

"I was wondering when you would get to that! Rest assured, I will in due time. I know because last night I had dreamed it."

"You have? Of Menlow and me? What –"

The old man raised a hand. "Hold on there, Gopher. I just saw the two of you together again. The dream told me no more, but also no less. It's enough to know that it will come to pass one way or another."

"Is that all?"

"You don't understand. My dreams often are fuzzy with only bits that I can make out. Sometimes I can make out more and more of it

177

as I follow where the dream leads me. Another thing the dream told me is that you should come with me a little longer. There is much for you to learn still."

"Menlow has taught me a lot already," Gopher said rather sharply, for he felt a stinging criticism implied in the Merchant's statement. Besides, he didn't want to learn; for that only meant delay, when all he wanted was to go home.

"Ah! He has, he has!" beamed the old man, holding out his hands in surrender. "To be sure, but it isn't nearly enough. You see, the more you learn, the more you also learn how much you *don't* know."

Ever since their meeting something had been troubling Gopher, and it was the Traveling Merchant's answer that brought it now to the forefront of his thinking. It was that nothing about the old man lived up to the picture that Menlow had seemed to paint about him. For one thing, the old man's continual joyfulness seemed out of touch with reality, much like Farwyll's. For another thing, apart from the cheerfulness and mismatched dirty and worn clothing, the Merchant seemed... well, plain. It wasn't that he was ugly, but never had the rodent seen someone look so ordinary and *un-special*. Still, there was no denying the magic carrot, so all the other stories were probably true as well, which undoubtedly they were since Menlow was no liar.

As soon as they started on their way again, Gopher rather reluctantly agreed to ride on the Merchant's shoulder. Because the old man was roughly the same height and apparent age as the hermit, Gopher kept forgetting that he wasn't Menlow, and each reminder came as a painful jolt. At least he was cheerful and nice – and a definite improvement on Wells and Loggins. Oh, he was glad to be away from them!

Even while thinking that, however, his attention was drawn to the familiarity of a small deformed pine tree, a moss-covered flattened rock, and a thorny hedge that, by the many sounds within, contained a bird's nest. It was those sounds that clicked his memory and made him recognize the same route the pixie and he had taken hours earlier, only now they were going back.

The old man's reply, when Gopher pointed this out, did not

help: "Oh? This is the way you came? Some may call it a coincidence, but I don't believe in those just as grownups don't believe in fairy tales."

What the pixie said did not help either: "The way back? Ha! Ha! The wind can lead anywhere and everywhere but never truly back, just as one moment can never be the same as the one it follows! Ah, just hear me talk so! What do I know?"

"You know more than most, my friend," the Traveling Merchant said.

Something had been troubling Gopher, something about the way they were going. Now the pixie's words shed light on it.

"You're right, Farwyll," the rodent said. "This couldn't be the same way. It's not as steep."

The Traveling Merchant chuckled and said, "It is the same way – same but different; that is, it is different when you're with me, just as there's a difference between following the wind and a dream. Can you imagine what it would be like to follow something Real? All the steep places made smooth, the dark turned to light, and the rain of sorrow become mists of delight! Oh, what a day that will be like!" He lapsed into a happy, contemplative silence.

After a while, the old man roused himself and said, "Are you worried, Gopher, that what happened last night might happen again? Don't. You're with us this time!"

"And not in a cage!" added the pixie with a grin as he trotted alongside.

They fell back into a thoughtful and contented silence for the rest of the journey, if the pixie's humming could be called silent. Going downhill most of the time, they moved quickly, the old man as sure-footed as the pixie beside him – except for one time when he seemed to trip. He would have stumbled headfirst down the steep slope if Farwyll hadn't grabbed onto his breeches. At the same time, the Merchant, with surprisingly quick and gentle hands, snatched Gopher as he flew forward in mid-air.

"Sorry about that," he said to Gopher, straightening up, and then to the pixie, "Thanks. I'll have to be more careful to keep my feet in this world as I follow my dreams." And with that, they continued on, but this time the Merchant was humming the same merry tune the pixie was. The old man seemed *glad* that he had nearly stumbled headlong!

Soon after that they saw a town in the distance by a river that the old man identified as Sorell, which Gopher did not recognize from this angle and from having only seen it once.

"Look!" the pixie said, pointing to a clearing overlooking the village. "That's where I rescued you yesterday!"

It took a moment for what the fairy was saying to sink in, because what Gopher was seeing was nothing like what he remembered. The clearing was now a bare patch of dirt with no indication of any kind of scuffle – let alone no sign of any vines, whether gold or silver or even green. There were wagon and horse tracks, however, and a burned out campfire.

"So it really was all... an illusion?"

"Of course!" Farwyll said merrily.

"But I felt the vines touch me."

"Do you mean that touch can't be an illusion, too?" the old man said. "The real difference between an illusion and reality is that one can stand the test of time and the other can't. It probably wasn't long before your captors realized that they weren't really strangled or buried alive, though I hope neither one will forget how they felt about their money when it was happening to them!"

"Do you know what were they – those who made the – err, illusions?" he asked the Merchant.

"Sounds like they were the rapiscan," the Traveling Merchant said.

"The rapiscan!" exclaimed the pixie. "That's it!"

The old man went on, "They are free-loving imps who often look like gypsies – or perhaps gypsies look like them. Anyway, they use illusion to play tricks, but *they* wouldn't call them tricks – oh no! – 'lessons' is what they claim to be teaching. They think that they are all teachers, but, mind you, never try to give them a lesson! That's when they'd *really* set out to teach you!"

"Why do they do it?" Gopher asked.

"It's because they hold humans in contempt since we get

attached to things so easily and so often. Freedom is all that matters to them."

"Doesn't it?"

The old man shook his head. "Oh, no! To make freedom all that matters does not answer the next question, 'freedom to do *what*?' Everybody has a different answer to that question, and many of those would be in conflict with each other. Arguments would arise, and cheating, and stealing, and fighting, and on and on. Where's the freedom in those things? You see, the freedom they had loved in the beginning would be lost along the way because they have forgotten that true freedom is about love."

"It's a poor joke and not funny," commented the pixie.

They went on in silence for a while, but then Gopher had a sudden thought and shuddered on the old man's shoulder.

"What is it, little fellow?"

"What if they're still somewhere around here – Wells and Loggins?" Gopher said.

The old man ran his fingers through his bushy beard as they continued on. "You don't have to worry about that. I suspect that even if they were in town, they wouldn't even notice you. It's why I suggested you ride on my shoulder. Anyone who might make trouble won't even see you."

"Why? Is it magic?" Gopher asked.

The Merchant shrugged. "Some may call it magic, I suppose. I don't give it much thought what to call it. As long as I am following my dreams I am barely noticeable to any, except to those with whom I make a trade. I rode a cow through town once – yes, it was Jack's cow, for which I had traded those magic beans – and nobody gave me the slightest notice.

"Now for the pixie here," the old man continued, "that's a different story; he'll have to make himself scarce – unless he can climb on my other shoulder."

Farwyll grinned, "A pixie on one shoulder and a rodent on the other, who can't fail to notice that?"

The old man thought that this was funny and was laughing when the next moment Farwyll dove into a bush. Almost simultaneously, sounds of horse and cart reached them. The Traveling Merchant sidestepped off the road as a man, woman, and child passed in a loaded wagon, heading away from town. The child was wailing loudly, and her parents appeared so anxious and stressed that they did not even notice her screams. The heaping pile and the speed at which the husband was urging the horse gave the impression that they were fleeing from something. They did not glance in their direction, though the wife looked back with a pale, worried face as if afraid they were being followed, which augmented that impression.

"Yes," the Traveling Merchant mused, "I'm sure the town has changed since yesterday."

Gopher held no doubts but that he was right when they later walked into town. Farwyll had not reappeared, but, as the Traveling Merchant strolled down the main street, Gopher wondered if anybody would have noticed the fairy anyway. Chaos reigned as people ran here and there, some carrying buckets and dousing a fire inside a blacksmith's, while others were engaged in fighting amidst each other or carrying things that they were either looting or packing up in the process of flight. A few were trying to maintain a sense of order, but their yelling and waving of their arms only added to the pandemonium. They were also drowned out mostly by some of the women, who tended to be the most vocal and wild-eyed, their voices shrill and their words desperate: "What shall we do? The world's gone mad! Hurry up! We've got to go NOW! They may come back! Oh, if only we had been farmers! I never trusted the river! Imagine fish doing *that*!" Many of the children were wailing, some because they were being dragged by their parents, while others because they were being spanked.

"It appears," the Traveling Merchant murmured, "that the rapiscan had taught their lessons sometime earlier today."

He crossed the main street, deftly avoiding a bickering old couple who were coming out of a building as they were going in. The elderly man seemed convinced that the trouble was over, while his wife was not. Perhaps to convince him otherwise, she was swinging something that struck him and which nearly had hit the

Traveling Merchant, too.

"AAAH! That hurt, woman! If you want us to leave, knocking me out won't help! And it won't change what happened. It wasn't me who bewitched our horses to turn on us, you know!"

"You make it sound as if *I* did!" she exclaimed, "I never could stand those beasts..." The sounds of their quarrel blended in with the rest of the commotion outside.

Even when the old Merchant told him that he was perfectly safe, it took a real effort for Gopher to loosen his grip on his collar. "Don't worry," he went on, "I don't suspect we'll be here long."

The room stretched far back with two rows of long tables and benches denoting it as an eating establishment. The fishy and baked bread aromas confirmed it, further evidenced by the half-eaten food, most of which had been spilt on the tables and floor. Bowls, plates, and cups were scattered all about; that is, those that hadn't been broken. While the mess emphasized the emptiness of the room, the crackling fire in the large hearth seemed to testify to a gaiety that was now lost, for it conjured up a picture of jovial families laughing, singing, and dancing together in front of it.

"What happened here?" Gopher whispered.

"When it comes to illusions, the ironic thing is that anything could have happened and nothing at all. The fear and panic that they cause are real enough, though," the man said.

Whimpering came from the far end of the room where some of the benches lay in a jumble. Gopher jumped down from the Merchant's shoulder as his companion moved a couple of smashed benches out of the way. A little girl crawled out, who could not have been older than eight. Her face was red from crying but a dab of blood made the end of her nose even redder. She was carrying a torn-up doll, which also had some of her smeared blood because she had been hugging it to her face. The Traveling Merchant, clucking his tongue in concern, bent down and in a grandfatherly gesture wiped her nose with a handkerchief from his vest pocket.

"What happened, little one?"

"My dolly, sir. She... she..."

"Did she try to hurt you?"

Guiltily, she shook her head, "She bossed me like I was her toy- she made me mad and... and I did this to her," she held up the doll to show the torn arm and leg, "but then – it was only my doll again. I'm going to fix her and tell her I'm sorry!"

"How did you get your bloody nose?"

"It happens when I – I cry so hard," she said, tears beginning to flow down her freckled cheeks and her nose beginning to be redden again. "I was meaner than she was to me!"

"Don't cry, my dear. It will make you feel worse," he said, dabbing at her nose with a handkerchief from his pocket. "Look, you have already done more harm to yourself than you could do to your doll. *She* can't bleed."

"I can't help it," she muttered, tearfully.

"I know how you can feel better."

"How?" she sniffed.

"By letting me have your doll to take care of. I will give you something that will give you more joy than she ever did," he said. Reaching into his vest pocket, he pulled out the acorn and held it out in his open palm.

Her eyes widened. "Is it magic, like in that story of Jack and the beanstalk?"

He shook his head. "No, but it's special. I had a vision of it growing into a great oak, reaching high to the sky, beautiful and majestic. Birds will nest in its branches, and people's hearts will swell at its sight, but it can only do that if you plant it."

He lapsed into a silence that was made meaningful by the patient and kindly look on his face.

The girl looked at her doll and then the acorn. Then she saw Gopher next to the Merchant.

"Who's he?" she said.

"Oh, he's my friend, and he can tell you if you should trade your doll."

The girl's stare made Gopher so nervous that all he could do was nod his head, but it was enough. A moment passed, and then slowly she lifted her stuffed doll.

"Take care of her, okay?"

Before leaving the eating establishment, carrying the doll, the Traveling Merchant paused before the hearth. Suddenly he bent down and reached in with his hand at the far end where the fire no longer burned and plucked out a small piece of coal. Carefully, then, he stuffed it into the doll's chest through the rip in its shoulder.

"Yes, yes, that'll do it," he said, pleased with himself. After wiping his blackened hand on his dirty vest, he proceeded on.

Chapter Twenty-Two

"I thought you said that you didn't know what would become of the acorn?" Gopher asked as they returned to the rowdy street. He was back on the Traveling Merchant's shoulder. Worry about being noticed no longer crossed his mind.

"I didn't."

"So you made it all up when you told her about the acorn becoming a beautiful oak tree?"

The old man chuckled. "Of course not. Remember when I nearly took that tumble along the way? Sometimes revelations can come at the most unexpected times!"

"Why didn't you say anything about it?" Gopher said before he realized his sharp tone, but there was something so *approachable* about the Merchant that the rodent found it hard to hold his tongue or soften his tone. He wondered if it had something to do with that quality which made the Merchant so easily taken for granted to the point of being invisible.

"Say what? That in my vision, besides an acorn, I now recognized a beer hall and a bloody-nosed doll, too?" the Merchant replied good-naturedly. He added, "When I saw the little girl holding that very doll, then I knew she was the one to make the trade! At the same time I had another vision."

"About what?"

"About the little girl; she was all grown up and beautiful. There was delight in her smile and gentleness in her eyes as she gazed up at a majestic oak tree – *the* oak tree, the one that would grow from the acorn. (In visions one often knows things without knowing how.) It also struck me that the secret of the oak tree's majesty was the same as her own, and that the two were in a way bound together."

The Merchant stopped talking because of the loud raucous of people gathered around two men fighting. Skirting the edge of the crowd, they reached the edge of town when Gopher took up their conversation again.

"But what *is* the tree's secret?"

"Oh, its majesty is the tree's secret."

"I don't understand. How can it be a secret when everyone can see it?"

"That's because its majesty is only a secret to the tree itself. You see, the tree isn't aware of the very qualities that everybody else admires in it. If it could be made aware of them, the tree would cease from taking in so much of the sunshine or the nutrients and water from the earth. It would be looking inward, instead of outward to those things that make the tree beautiful, strong, and majestic. Because of that, its beauty would start fading.

"You see, the girl needs to discover that secret herself," he continued, "because her plain appearance has made her self-conscious. In making that trade, the doll for the acorn, she will take care of that tree because she will always remember how much it had cost her. And by attending to something else besides herself, her natural beauty will come out, not only in appearance but in her character as well. Or at least that's the gist of what I saw in my dream."

As they left the last of the town's outlying buildings behind, they came to a well at the edge of some white cypresses. A three foot high wall of brick tightly encircled it with a small shingled roof. Although Gopher could remember those particular trees around it, he could not recall the well, try as hard as he could. He couldn't have missed noticing it on their way into town. In fact, the red bricks looked new and clean with the mortar still wet between, and the wooden shingles appeared un-weathered and freshly cut. His attention was thus drawn to it when Farwyll came strolling from around its other side.

"How do you like it?" he said. "It made for a bit of fun while I was waiting."

"We weren't gone that long," the Traveling Merchant said, clearly impressed, and then added with a questioning eyebrow, "Magic sure helps, doesn't it?"

Farwyll seemed a bit embarrassed. "Well, I didn't do it *just* for fun. I don't use magic that way – at least, not anymore... I figured that when things have settled down and they quit fighting and destroying things, this might come in handy, especially when they won't trust the river for a while."

The Traveling Merchant pursed his lips and nodded. "We might put it to our own use first."

After they all had gotten a drink from it, using a bucket and rope that the pixie's magic had also furnished, they also filled up the water skin. The Traveling Merchant then turned to Farwyll.

"I've been thinking. This well... if they see it all built up brand new like it is now and they can't figure who did it..." he trailed off.

The pixie laughed and completed the other's thought, "They wouldn't come to trust it either, would they? Not after all that's happened."

"Most probable, most probable," the other replied, scratching his beard. "That is the problem with not being able to depend on anything, you become afraid of everything – even the best of intentions. It'd be better if they discover this source of water on their own, don't you think?"

"Right you are," the pixie said and snapping his fingers, the bricks crumbled and the wood shingles, bucket, rope, and posts practically exploded in all directions (though not a splinter or a speck touched the three of them). In the next moment only the hole remained.

"Looks like it was just for a bit of fun, after all," the fairy said brightly.

"At least they won't have to dig for the water now," the Merchant said, "but I think we should cover the hole up. We don't want anyone discovering it by falling into it. That could also be another useful thing for your magic to do."

After the pixie magically piled some of the scattered boards over the hole, they started off into the woods and the pixie whistled as happily and contented as ever. Suddenly Gopher was struck with a certain amount of envy. If only he could be as happy when things don't turn out the way he wanted them to! This thought, however, did not distract him for more than a moment when he noticed the Merchant still carrying the doll.

"What about that? Did you have a dream–?" Gopher stopped himself when he realized that he was starting to be abrupt again. He decided at that moment that he did not like being that way. The Merchant who, despite the disappointment the rodent felt towards him, deserved more polite consideration.

"About what? Oh, this?" The old man said, having been drawn out of his thoughts. He held up the girl's doll. "Yes. It was another vision. It was of me stuffing a piece of coal inside it – so that was what I did. Don't ask me more because that's all I know. For now, at least."

After passing through the copse of trees, they made their way through a lonely countryside that was largely flat. Every so often they came on a dell or a hillock or a copse of trees that briefly changed the shape of the landscape. Except for the Merchant's feet thud-thud-thudding on the hard, barren ground and the pixie's humming, it was an oppressively quiet countryside with the occasional bird chirps and the flapping of wings to make it seem even more desolate. The grey, overcast clouds seemed to match the mood. Although he was no longer in a cage, the dull, vast loneliness made Gopher feel like he was just in a larger one somehow.

Then something happened that made him forget about being in a large cage or being bored, but that didn't mean he was glad about it. It was because the pixie unexpectedly announced "I'll see you sooner or later – I hope!" and abruptly disappeared behind some hedges with his laugh still in the air. Gopher blinked in surprise, while the Merchant only laughed and muttered, "I suppose it was the wind."

Less than an hour later, when Gopher had stopped worrying about their friend's welfare and started grousing how undependable the pixie was, they came upon a dell. At the bottom of it bubbled a spring that watered a small grassy patch hedged in by a dozen white aspens. Nearby the pixie was roasting a hare over a campfire. He greeted them with "Right on time!"

"Good spot. We'll camp here while there's still plenty of daylight. My eyes aren't what they used to be." the Traveling Merchant said without surprise, though with pleasure in his voice, as if he had half-expected to see the pixie at that very moment. The rodent was surprised, however, and pleased. The sight of his friend made him forget about his grousing, but the smell of the roasting meat that awakened his rumbling stomach also helped.

Gopher found out what the Traveling Merchant meant about the daylight after eating their delicious supper, which also included some roasted mushrooms that they had found earlier along the way. The old man, sitting with his back against a tree in the full sunlight of the afternoon, started stitching up the doll with a needle and thread. He still had to do a lot of squinting.

Now was the time that the rodent had been dreading without actually realizing it, for now was the time of inactivity, when he had nothing to do but think – and feel. Even the cozy setting with the bubbling spring, the crackling fire, and cool shadowy canopy of the trees did not distract Gopher from the deep set anguish of his heart. Actually they made him feel worse because he felt like he ought to be happy, but their campsite and their company only reminded him of how much he missed Menlow.

At least there was this in which he found some comfort: It was that his disappointment in the Traveling Merchant had lessened to some degree. The acorn and the little girl provided enough proof that perhaps the man wasn't merely a dream follower or just plain crazy. Ironically, in the middle of thinking this, the Traveling Merchant looked up from his stitching with a satisfied smile and said, as if in triumph, "That's all done!"

The pixie, who was dragging a large branch twice as large as himself towards the fire, dropped it to have a look. He scratched his head.

"Funny why children like pretend things over the real ones."

"You're confusing children with adults!" the old Merchant laughed. "Children pretend so that they can handle the real thing later. It's *because* the little girl likes the idea of babies that makes it fun for her play with her doll."

"But what fun is there with a piece of coal inside of it?" Gopher asked, coming up to have a look, too.

The old Merchant shrugged.

"It doesn't look like it has a piece of coal inside, does it? It resembles how a lot of people are... By the way, my little friend, the same holds true for you: No one can tell from looking what great magic you have inside that is trying to get out."

More than anything else, this revelation succeeded in distracting him completely from his sorrow. It seemed long ago when Menlow and he had dismissed, once and for all, the possibility of him having such a thing.

"What do you mean? What magic?"

"I mean, of course, the magic that was in the carrot and is now in you, the magic that changed you so that you can talk and think like a human."

"Oh, that," Gopher said, disappointed. "It doesn't do anything else. I tried."

"How do you know? If I give you a tool and you don't know what it's used for, would you say that the tool was broken or no good? Of course not! You have to understand what the tool is for and how to use it. Let me ask you this: How are your dreams?"

Suddenly, and for no understandable reason, Gopher felt both ashamed and infringed upon. He had never told anyone but Menlow that he could not remember his dreams, and now here was this old man, whom he hardly knew, seemingly able to look into his inmost being.

"Why? What do they have to do with my magic?"

The old man stood up and stretched, and then he went over to gaze into the fire before speaking. "Consider magic. Think of it as a type of fire that is inside of you," he said without turning, "and your dreams are like its smoke because they come from inside of you too. Now, smoke tells you a little of what fire is like because it carries some of its heat and, despite the stinging in the eyes, you may still be able to see some of its flames and embers beyond its dense cloud. In the same way, your dreams may provide a clue to help you understand what the magic is about or what it's trying to tell you – like my visions do. What are your dreams like?"

"I – I don't know," Gopher admitted. "I can't remember them. I only know that I have them."

"Ah. That is significant. Then your dreams *are* like smoke. They're keeping you from understanding your magic."

"But why can't I remember them?"

He shrugged. "Perhaps you are not ready to. The best thing is to be patient and stay hopeful. Don't try to remember them, but if and when you do, try not to jump to any conclusions too quickly. A small amount of knowledge is a dangerous temptation to those who are too hasty."

The pixie bobbed his head up and down. "Dangerous like jumping ahead of the wind," he said.

"Do as I do," the old man continued, "follow what you have been given – and then you will often come to know more."

Gopher felt better after that, for now he had something to think about instead. Because of this, however, it took him longer than usual to fall asleep. The next morning he awoke, half hoping to remember at least *something* of his dreams, but (alas!) he could remember nothing of them. They were as vague as ever. Then he recalled the Merchant's admonition to not even try; to let them come.

Yet something had changed. He felt it, and, as the day wore on and they traveled through the bleak countryside, he became more aware of what it was. A certainty had been imparted to him by the knowledge that he possessed magic and by the new hope of understanding it in time, a certainty that grew until it exceeded mere hope. It was an expectation that something great was "just around the corner" waiting for him to discover it. That it included reuniting with Menlow he had no doubt. So certain was he that, even as much as he wanted to discover whatever it was, he didn't *have* to rush it; The revelation would come, and somehow he would also see Menlow again. These were as much of a fact in his mind as that the sun was in the sky, and through such acceptance he found a new freedom, a freedom from hoping, wishing, wanting – not that he didn't still want to see the hermit again or to plumb the mysterious depth of his magic, but they could not torment him.

It also brought about another change. The old man seemed much less disappointing and even Farwyll made him laugh as the fairy splashed about in a stream, chasing after a fish for their lunch. They ended up eating crawdads instead.

They discovered signs of civilization by mid-afternoon as they came upon a road that was both broadened and hardened by traffic. Woods gave way increasingly to green cultivated fields on either side and were dotted by occasional huts, cottages, and barns.

It seemed a vacant world, until a groan stopped them in their tracks, though it sent the pixie off so quickly that he seemed to vanish into air. The sound came from a ditch and, more particularly, they found that it came from a man. He lay sprawled in the ditch in tattered, muddied clothing that made him hard to see, though his unwashed smell was more easily discernible.

He looked up when the Merchant greeted him. Something in his worn and wrinkled face hinted that he was not as old as he looked, except for his brown eyes. They looked old and... empty, vacant, as if they might belong to a blind man, though the moment they came nearer, he looked them over like one assessing an opportunity. A smile spread on his face as he held out a filthy hand: "Can ye take pity on a poor man? A coin or two will do."

"You are poor, that much is true," replied the Merchant, "but pity is something you don't need, and not even three coins will help you. But this will do, if you will make a trade with me."

He held out the ragged, blood-smeared doll.

A moment passed and then a light seemed to come into the bedraggled man's eyes. It was as if he was actually seeing for the first time.

"What is this?" He said, raising himself partway. "Did Maris send you? Do you know her?" There was something in his voice that seemed alien to his whole demeanor and appearance. Gopher realized that it was hope that had, in a sense, given his sight back.

"I don't know her nor did she send me."

"But how? It looks just like her. Her nose was always red, too. I used to call her 'my doll'; she made them for a living, but you had to have known that! Why did she send you? Why don't you say?"

"No, she did not," the old man said firmly but kindly. "I am merely a traveling merchant who trades in the most unusual items. That's because every person is unusual. This doll is meant for you, perhaps because it happens to resemble her. There are no coincidences."

"I don't follow," the man said, his emotion dulled momentarily by confusion.

The Merchant laughed softly. "Let's just say that this doll is *meant* for you and only you. I will make a trade for it, because that is what I do."

"Why should I want a doll just because it looks like the woman who left me? So she could torment me more with its resemblance?" the stranger said.

"No, not to torment you," the old man replied, "Rather, this doll can be the beginning of a new life for you. See? Already you are filled with new hope. You feel it, don't you? This is no trick, for all I want in exchange for this doll is your wineskin and your promise to swear off drinking spirits forever. What has that done for you anyway but land you in that ditch?"

The man looked down at the wineskin. He replied at last, "How do I know that you're not playing a trick on me? I'm not just a drunken fool," his voice cracked as if even he was not convinced of what he was saying.

"Ever hear of a talking gopher? He will tell you about another one of my trades. It was how he was gifted with speech."

Much to the man's surprise, which seemed to sober him, Gopher briefly told his story. By his open-mouthed stare, the rodent wondered if he heard a word he was saying, but by the end of it, the drunken fellow crawled out of the ditch and looked closely at the doll still in the Merchant's hand.

"Is there magic in the doll, too?"

The old man shook his head with a patient smile. "No, but there *is* something inside of it: A lump of coal. I believe that is what you think of her heart after she broke yours. Isn't that true?"

The man went wide-eyed. "That was exactly what I was thinking – that she had a heart of coal –before I saw you," he breathed. Without needing further proof, the trade was then made along with his solemn oath.

The Traveling Merchant said, "Remember this, my dear man: Diamonds are made from coal. Go back to her and through your patience and understanding, a diamond is what she'll become – also, I'd give her the doll as a gift, if I were you." Then he added with a grin, "Though I'd take out the coal first. She might not understand like we do."

The man left walking toward the town, staring down at his new purchase with a new light in his eyes and even a spring in his step. Even though still dirty and disheveled, Gopher could hardly believe the change in him.

They started off again, but not in the same direction, when the pixie reappeared. He was even more joyous and bouncier than ever, for he admitted to having eavesdropped on them. Gopher felt the same jubilancy. Never before had he felt someone else's happiness as if it were his own. A deep, rich satisfaction filled him, so that he joined in pixie's humming, while the Merchant whistled a merry tune. Nobody said anything, since words weren't needed. In fact, they would have only gotten in the way.

That night they made camp on top of a low hill with the firelight casting long flickering shadows from the trees around their clearing as they ate a late dinner of fowl that Farwyll had caught and roasted. The draughts from the wineskin weren't bad either. As Gopher settled down to sleep in a scarf that the Traveling Merchant had wadded into a comfortable heap, he reflected that he never felt happier since having been separated from the hermit.

The feeling made it easy for him to slip peacefully into slumber.

That night he had a dream that for once did not evaporate from his memory upon waking. In fact, every detail of it stayed with him, which he would never forget. However, it wasn't a cause for celebration. It was because he had dreamt of Menlow on his deathbed.

Chapter Twenty-Three

He had more than one dream that night, and fortunately none had been as bad as the one with the ex-wizard. In the first dream, he saw the river in which he had nearly drowned. Instead of reliving the horrible experience, however, the dark, rushing body of water evoked a rapturous emotion that he hadn't felt since he had eaten the magic carrot. He saw the river as if it were almost alive. He sensed and thrilled at the life that thrived in its black depths and whose dance was made marvelous by the river's powerful current that was both mysterious and wonderful. The river's surface was broken intermittently with splashing fish, but as he watched, he saw that they were not only larger than fish but they also had hands, fins, faces and smooth scaly shapes that were all covered in silvery green skin.

Naiads.

Gopher remembered the name of the fresh water nymphs that Menlow had told him about. It was surprising that they looked just as he imagined that they would. Perhaps because of that, they seemed familiar to him... but *how* were they familiar? In the next moment he had his answer. One of the naiads was holding a small limp creature above the water. It came as a shock when he recognized himself. It was at this point when he realized that the dream was not a dream at all, but what had happened to him after he had fallen into the river and nearly drowned. The naiad had held him up very carefully as if he had been something more important than just a soaked, limp figure of a rodent. He felt a rush of gratitude towards his deliverers, and he remembered that was how he had felt upon waking on the bank, only then his gratitude had centered on just being alive.

He was just thinking about this when the scene changed from the river to a rocky bluff. The view overlooked a patchwork of green and grey lowland hills and a skyline mottled with ominously dark clouds. As desolate as the setting was, the sounds that the wind made, blowing in sharp gusts and whistling through the crevices and moaning in the hollow places of the bluff, sent a thrill of delight and a longing for high adventure through Gopher. It reminded him of the time when the lure of the beautiful and the unknown had first lured him out of his tunnels.

At that moment, a small figure emerged from a cave in the bluff, jumping and dancing and cartwheeling. The motions themselves cued the rodent instantly to his identity without needing to see Farwyll's face. Gopher also knew he was witnessing the very act of the pixie awakening from the Age of Magic. The rodent wanted to go with him, to dance, to run, and to cartwheel – if only he could! Alas! He could only view the scene like someone who was looking from a great distance, while at the same time seeing it so vividly.

But when the pixie had disappeared, skipping down a steep ravine, the dream changed again: He saw the brownies inside the cottage, busy cleaning, straightening, and cooking, while Menlow and he were asleep. The joy of working was intermixed so satisfyingly and so thoroughly with the joy of playing that it was impossible to separate the one from the other – and impossible to resist from entering into, even by a spectator like himself. He laughed and laughed until he cried...

He blinked open his watery eyes to see... nothing. Blackness. It was more than just an absence of light, however, that troubled him. The darkness was accompanied by knowledge that he was losing something he loved. He did not know how he knew; he just did, and the idea of its loss scared him and made him desperate. It was how Gopher had felt when Menlow had been talking to Tobias the woodcutter or when the hermit had talked about his old wizardry days.

Then he heard something in the darkness above. It was crying, coming from a girl, who should be filled with life and joy and freedom, but was instead pierced with a vulnerable sorrow. Then Gopher saw that there was a figure in the darkness with him as it crept upwards where the girl was. Somehow he sensed the figure thinking that if only it could reach her, befriend her, it could live through her, appreciate what she couldn't and, best of all, be free of the darkness, free of the sense of loss and the desperation that it imparted. The selfishness of the thought shocked him deeply. That was when he realized to whom it belonged. Maythenia!

Then the dream without warning changed, and so did his thoughts and feelings. He saw a group of children playing on a knoll that overlooked a town on one side and a forest on the other. Their play irritated him. Unlike Maythenia, he did not want what they had – their fun, their laughter, their smiles only provoked him because they reminded him of his emptiness and misery. Their smiles and laughter merely pierced him with envy.

Yet when he saw one particular child with the most innocent and sweetest appearance, a child whose face showed sensitivity and was full of compassion, he forgot about the others and what they were doing. The boy stood out alone, much like himself, and at once he decided that it was time for a change. He was tired of this current body. It never *really* fit him. He called out from the shadows in a voice magically directed so that only the little boy could hear. As the child drew near, Gopher recognized him. The changeling!

Or was it?

With a shock of repulsion, he realized that he was seeing the real child – before he had been abducted by the very one whose thoughts he was now sharing.

The next dream abruptly followed, which was about the rapiscans whom he recognized right away. By contrast, it was a pleasant dream with their jolly traipsing freely about, though they were also full of disdain for humans and especially for their folly over such things as money, houses, and anything they deemed as having worth in and of itself. Yet then he remembered Menlow and began yearning for the confines of the cottage and the comforting security of his friend's warm presence.

That's when the scene changed. At first it brought great joy because he saw Menlow. His friend was wandering through the forest with the river to his left; as he came nearer, Gopher saw that he was in great sorrow, stooped over like a feeble old man searching for something that he had no hope of finding. Gopher's yells went unheard as Menlow continued to approach. If only the rodent could move, could be heard, could be seen!

Then the hermit abruptly stopped when a soft glow appeared. It silhouetted the trees with a luminescence that was faint but beautiful enough to promise even more exquisiteness if one could get closer. Also from the light emanated a faint harmony that inspired dreams of rapture with a promise of their fulfillment if he would but follow. The rodent, watching as his friend turned towards it, found himself yearning to go towards that light, too. Soon Menlow's figure began to blend into the trees until he was lost in the glow beyond, and Gopher felt a twinge of envy.

Envy turned to shock, however, when the dream suddenly changed and he saw Menlow lying in the bed at the mayor's house. He was smiling contentedly, perhaps even rapturously like one lost in a wonderful dream. Yet it was a look of happiness that did not match the rest of his pale, sunken face– a face of someone who was dying and did not know it. At one point the hermit stirred and in a brief opening of his eyelid, Gopher saw a soft iridescent glow instead of his friend's brown iris. A certainty came to him that the hermit was lost within himself.

•   •   •

He had had many other dreams after this – dreams that seemed much more dreamlike and vague. That was because they were of other fairies, other places, none of which were familiar to his memory, though ironically they still *felt* familiar. Yet it was, of course, the dream with Menlow that mattered to him when he woke up the next morning.

"Do you think it's true?" Gopher asked.

He had told the Merchant and pixie his dream of the hermit over a breakfast that had been waiting for him, but which he was too worked up to eat. He hadn't told about the other dreams. Perhaps it was because they made him feel uncomfortable to talk about, as if the Merchant and the pixie might look at him differently. He wasn't sure why he should feel that way, but he concluded that they weren't important, anyway.

The old man smiled. Poking the fire with a stick, he shrugged at last, "Who am I to say? What do *you* think?"

"I – I think so, but I don't want it to be true," Gopher replied.

"Ah!" interposed Farwyll. "That's an argument that is in its favor for being true!"

The Merchant nodded, contemplating the fire for a moment. "I believe that what you saw was true. Menlow is, or will be, on his deathbed. But the question is, after all this time why did you start remembering your dreams *now*? Maybe... you weren't ready before. Going through what you did – falling into the river, wandering lost, being captured. Enduring all of that changes a person like nothing else can, whether for good or bad. Or it could be that when you finally believed that you had magic without trying to use it, something in you stopped holding it back. Maybe this is just the beginning of something bigger."

Gopher said, impatiently, "It doesn't really matter why, and I don't care about anything bigger. What matters is that, if Menlow is dying, then we have to go to him – right now!"

The Merchant straightened up and looked at the rodent next to him with such calm directness that Gopher would have found his own rashness embarrassing if his concern for Menlow hadn't been all consuming.

The old man then said, "I cannot fault you for wanting to help your friend. But do you even know *how* you can help him?"

"No, but maybe if I'm there, I can talk to him or – or do something..." Gopher said, struggling to maintain his patience to think clearly, but, failing, he exclaimed, "Oh I don't know! I just *have* to get there. Don't you just follow what clues your dreams give you? You never know exactly what you're going to do either! What's so different between you and me?"

The Merchant looked at him with a pitying look, and replied at last, "Because my dreams have proven to be trustworthy time and again. They are *meant* to be followed, but you don't even know what yours are meant for yet. Trust in my dreams for a while longer, Gopher, and maybe you'll understand your own in time.

"Speaking of which," he continued, "I, too, had a dream last night with you in it. We were selling this very wineskin at a shepherding village that I believe is not far from here. That is where we should go. I would not have dreamed such a thing if it was not important that you were with me. It's why you should wait a little longer. Will you?"

"But how will that help Menlow?"

The pixie spoke up. "Such a question is like trying to see the wind instead of letting it lead you. You go nowhere and get no answers."

"Farwyll's right," the Traveling Merchant said. "I want to help Menlow, too, and I believe we will, but it can only be at the right time."

"But what other time will there be? He's dying! If we wait any longer, it may be too late... If he can only hear my voice, he'd wake up." As he said it, a certainty of its truthfulness sprang up. It was that which suddenly persuaded him. He looked at the old man and then at the pixie, but not with hesitancy; he was trying to imprint the scene on his mind, for he had made a decision.

"Whether you help me or not, I have to go to him. You may not trust in my dreams, but I do," he said with a finality he had never felt before.

"Will you not wait a little while? It may make all the difference," the old man said. He was not pleading but there was such earnestness in the narrowing of his eyes and the firm set on his mouth that it tested Gopher on the seriousness of his choice.

"Thank you so much for helping me," the rodent's voice shook, but not his decision – at least not much. He went on more firmly,

"I'm sorry, but I have got to go."

"You are decided then," the Merchant said resignedly. "Your motives are good. I quite understand. So how are you going to get there?"

"I don't know... I'll just follow the wind, I guess," Gopher said, quoting the pixie.

"But you are not like the pixie –" began the old man.

"But I am," Farwyll interrupted. He stuck his finger in his mouth, pulled it out, and held it up. "Mmmm... there are crosswinds here and it seems that I've a choice to make... I shall go with you, Gopher."

Chapter Twenty-Four

Even more surprising than Farwyll's offer was the Traveling Merchant's response. He nodded and was silent for a thoughtful moment, but then suddenly his heavy face suddenly lit up with a smile. "If you feel like you must go, then I could entrust you with no one better! Shall we finish our breakfast before parting ways?"

Despite the urgent tug in his heart to go at once, the pleasant surprises of the pixie's offer and the old man's acceptance improved his appetite. Anyway, he knew it would be unwise to travel on an empty stomach, especially when there was food available.

Another surprise for that morning was that it turned out to be an unforgettable meal. It wasn't because of the food, for by now the eggs were cold. It was the knowledge of parting ways that made the real difference, for it gave special value to each other's company. Odd, Gopher thought, that he should have felt that way since they did not talk much and there seemed a tinge of sadness in the air, but yet he felt a genuine sense of camaraderie amongst them that needed no words or laughter. It was such a strong sense that it alone might have persuaded him to change his mind had not his love for Menlow been just as genuine.

With Gopher on his shoulder, the pixie set out soon after, since the Traveling Merchant insisted on doing the washing up himself.

"You've got a long ways to go and longer if the weather doesn't hold out. Now off – and we shall meet again!"

Without anymore than that for a goodbye, Farwyll followed the stream that issued from the spring. As soon as they rounded a bend, the Traveling Merchant was out of their sight. Gopher felt a momentary regret, but it could not overcome his excitement. The pixie seemed to share it as he fairly jogged along in a determined, though elated, pace. But then again he was almost always excited, just as he was always humming or whistling or skipping about.

The dale, in which they had spent the night, proved to be the first of a series of steep-sided gorges as they followed the brook. Some of the gorges were so rocky from landslides that they came up nearly level with the countryside, but the water managed to trickle through and around the boulders to find the next gorge. Others were either filled with thickets or were so steep-walled that it forced the pixie to wade in the stream.

By noon they came upon a meadow of tall grasses and wildflowers, stirring in a soft breeze, while the billowy clouds added a brief touch of a chill. Gopher's fur bristling on his back signaled the approach of a storm, but overall the weather was still nearly perfect. The pixie stopped suddenly and slapped his forehead – nearly hitting Gopher on his shoulder.

"Oops, sorry about that... I forgot we're not following the stream! It just happens to be going the same way. At least I think it is..." he tested the wind and nodded, "for now anyway."

As pleasant as their journey started and as accommodating and friendly as his traveling companion was, yet inwardly Gopher felt a dark sinking feeling that he was making a mistake. Flying to Menlow's side now seemed like an impulsive thing to do. Staying with the Traveling Merchant might have been a wiser course of action. After all, the old man knew about magical dreams and seemed to have a knack at doing the right things despite all appearances... if only Gopher had listened to him and had been patient.

Yet at least he found comfort in the fact that the pixie did not seem to act as if he were making a mistake; he traveled in such high spirits and with such certainty in direction and footing. After all, the wind had never led the fairy astray before and was even now leading them. At one point, however, a doubt suddenly arose. He kept it to himself until they were safely over a particularly steep ridge.

"Farwyll, how do you know that the wind is bringing us to Menlow? You said you never know where it leads."

"I don't. But I know the lay of the land and the wind is leading us in the general direction of Kentfell. Anyway, like I said before, the wind changed at the very moment that you made your decision – AND it was in the direction you wanted to go. That might mean something, don't you think?"

He drew hope in the pixie's words, enough so that he could shove his doubt aside and focus on the journey itself. An hour later the walls of another gorge, along which they had been traveling, widened and the vegetation thinned until they gained a view beyond, of rolling foothills and the not-so-distant wooded mountain range – all of which stirred up the rodent's instinct that assured him as much as any definite landmark could that they were headed in the right direction. Gopher grew dizzy with excitement. His regrets were instantly dispelled. But then remembering Menlow dying on the bed dampened his excitement and reminded him that their trip wasn't just about returning.

When they stopped for a rest at a patch of heather next to the stream, Gopher hurried through the midday meal, like one getting an unpleasant task over with, doing so at the pixie's urging. Farwyll, however, only nibbled on the heather, since he wasn't hungry, having eaten mushrooms, roots, and flowers along the way. He immediately resumed their journey as if he, too, felt just as impatient. More likely it was because the wind was a little chillier and the clouds dark and heavy looking.

Before they had gone much farther, the storm was nearly upon them. A freezing gust blew right through him, and then another, followed by the stinging pelts of the first rain drops. He shivered, and so did the branches around them.

"It's going to be fierce!" he exclaimed.

"Yes, indeed!" Farwyll exclaimed happily, unaffected by the cold winds or the rain. "I love storms. They mix things up so!"

"Isn't that a bad thing?" Gopher yelled.

"Only if you hold on to the things that get mixed up!"

"I mean, isn't it a bad thing to *travel* in?"

The pixie laughed. "Uncomfortable is not the same as bad!"

"But how do you know what is bad?"

"It is bad when we *shouldn't* travel...!" He checked the wind (which seemed a ridiculous thing to do in that tumult) and added cheerfully, "But only uncomfortable when we must. The wind leads that way... don't worry! Just hold on!"

The rain started pelting them steadily, as they crossed a narrow ridge with crumbling sides. Even then the pixie did not show any signs of seeking shelter. An intense wind, funneling up the rocky chute, would have swept him away if Farwyll's hand hadn't held him in place. The fairy laughed as he ran with a sureness of foot that was a miracle upon the loose, treacherous ground. Upon reaching the semi-shelter of some trees, the wind died down and the storm decided on a new tactic as the rain now fell in full earnestness, almost like a river in the sky being let loose, blurring their gray surroundings.

Farwyll's spirits were not conquered, though, nor was he seemingly blinded by the grayness. He did not hesitate in his direction or slip in his footing as he set out again into the full face of the storm. In fact, he now was positively singing in the nearly deafening deluge, though Gopher could not make out the words, and, as he ran, it seemed as if he were also dancing. Later Gopher wondered how long he could have kept that up if they hadn't had found another shelter soon afterwards.

It was a crevice in a steep rock face that was not quite deep enough to be called a cave but went far enough in to give them a dry place that blocked out the wind, though the chill itself could not be quite so easily eluded. Gopher's fur was drenched, making the coldness cling ever that much closer. Not having any blankets, the pixie made him curl up next to him and was humming a soft melody that reminded him faintly of Menlow's singing at night. It was that act of friendship, which gave the rodent a different kind of warmth that helped him to fall asleep despite the chill.

That was when he had another dream that he would not forget.

The rushing, splattering sounds of the downpour seemed to have merged into the dream, though in it there was no downpour but the roar of a waterfall. It cascaded down a cliff, disappearing into a mist-enshrouded valley. Gopher stood on the sheer precipice where the water began its fall only a few yards to his right. The icy winds that emanated from the valley below gave him the shivers, but it was the waterfall that drew his attention and held it – so much water, urgently rushing by and then plunging. Its power, unstoppable power, stemmed from that urgency.

How long he stood there watching it he did not know. As the steady rush slowly numbed his amazement, he began wondering where the water might be going. Following its downward plunge with his gaze, he tried to penetrate the mist. He realized, as he did so, that it was indeed a mist and not a fog, a mist that was a product of the plunging of the waterfall on rocks below. From it, also, issued a mighty and steady roar.

The mist caught and held his attention, just as the waterfall had, but for a different reason than that of power and urgency. Gray at the wispy fringes that lay at the foot of the valley wall, the vaporous cloud became denser and darker farther in, until it became as black and solid as a coal pit. It was an uncomfortable darkness that reminded him of the gash in Maythenia's oak tree. Empty and cold as death.

His eyes shied away from it as they returned to gaze at the wispy borders where the misty veil would occasionally lift teasingly, to reveal fleeting sights. He caught glimpses of a river from its silvery sheen or its white rapids here and there, and then he saw trees... boulders... and then something moving, something indefinable but terrible in that way it seemed to slink about. He saw it for only the briefest of moments, but the mist could not hide its piercing wail that suddenly reached his ears, which was even more terrible. Somehow there was an accusation in it that aroused in Gopher a crushing weight of guilt. He wanted to flee, just like how a criminal would, even though he did not know what he was being accused of. Yet his body, as well as his eyes, was held in a vise of guilt, from which flight or denial was pointless.

Then his emotions found a focus when a dark crouching figure separated from the mist and began crawling up the rock wall, scaling impossible vertical slopes, and sometimes jumping from ledge to ledge. He knew at once that it was not only coming towards him, it was also coming *for* him, the Accuser! It paused in its ascent to howl that plaintive, mournful cry that filled him unbearably with crippling shame.

The creature caught him in its grasp much quicker than he anticipated. It shook him and yelled in his face, though there was something different in its high-pitched voice – it had lost its accusatory tone, and because of it, he felt free to move again. He struggled against the creature, but that was when he woke up and saw Farwyll over him with his brows so scrunched up that his eyes, instead of looking bulbous, were slits – piercing slits that could see into Gopher's heart. Even the pixie knew, the rodent thought, still caught in the madness of dream. He resumed his struggling, although he knew it was in vain.

"It's all right... all right," the pixie was saying, soothingly. "It's only me. Don't worry. You just had a dream."

•　　•　　•

They were sitting around the campfire sometime later. The ominous look of the storm clouds had been reduced to a blanket of gray that occasionally drizzled the ground in front of their shelter. At its western fringe, however, the sun was thinly hidden by a layered section of clouds that cast a burnished bronze along the edge of the horizon. Some golden shafts of light escaped to highlight the greens and yellows of the rolling hills. It was a vivid contrast from the slate grey overhead. By comparison, Farwyll's fair mood, however, did not contrast so beautifully against Gopher's, for it only made him feel worse.

They were having pheasant, which the pixie had caught and had been roasting over the crackling, hissing fire, when Gopher had had his nightmare. The meat, however, had been over the fire a little too long, which even Gopher, with his sharp teeth, found difficult to bite into.

Farwyll had not asked what the dream had been about, and for that Gopher was grateful. The dream disturbed him, much like how his previous dreams always did upon waking. The difference, of course, was now he could remember it, but that did not comfort him; neither would talking about it. In the same way that someone who has a fresh, open sore, he was not ready to talk about it. It was still too painful. Anyway, what good would it do? Something was wrong, deeply wrong, and no amount of words would change that.

It was not until after their meal that Gopher realized how uncharacteristically solemn, Farwyll was being – and how much he had shut himself off from his friend, how selfish he was being, and how it was actually making him feel worse. So he told the pixie about the dream and found that he had been wrong. Putting into words how guilty the creature's cry made him feel began eroding the strength of that emotion. What Farwyll said in reply helped, too.

"It sounds like it was a banshee. I once met one, you know..." he shivered before going on: "Its wail – I'll never forget it... All the bad things in my life, the deaths, the partings, all the regrets and losses, went through me in a single moment. It was the last thing I heard and felt, for that wail was what cast me into the Great Sleep. It's a dangerous thing to listen to a banshee's mournful cry. At least maybe this dream was just a dream and nothing more."

The pixie's remark reminded Gopher about his other dreams that he had failed to mention to the Traveling Merchant. So was that what he had been feeling guilty about? Perhaps talking about them would make him feel better. He took a deep breath and said, "I think it was real somehow... I didn't tell about this before because I didn't think they were important, but I had other dreams last night, too..."

Watching the dwindling of the fire, Gopher related each dream as he remembered them and how they had made him feel –and, yes, it had been a little uncomfortable for some reason, but soon talking about them, along with the accompanying sound of the rain's soft drizzle, proved soothing. Slowly he felt the shame and anguish that the wail had created release their hold on him until the dream was remembered as something vaguely unpleasant. When the rodent was finished, he felt glad that he had done it.

After a moment of quiet, Farwyll said, "You saw my Awakening. That was it exactly. Why did you not speak about these other dreams before? Oh! Menlow! That was what was important to you, but these other dreams may be, too, in some way. They are like the Traveling Merchant's visions, only different in some way that is beyond me. Let's not worry about it, and trust that all will be made clear in due time. For now we need sleep."

For the first time that Gopher had known him the pixie yawned. Farwyll laughed as if he was also surprised, but without apology the pixie wished him a good night. Gopher wanted to keep him engaged in more conversation, and, while he was thinking of something else to talk about, his companion began snoring.

Even though he felt so much better, the rodent did not want to go to sleep, since that might lead to more dreaming, and he was still very much afraid of that. What would he dream of next? A fire-breathing dragon or some hideous creature that held more evil power over him than an accusatory wail? It might, however, turn out to be something good, like the pixie or the water sprites or the brownies, but how could he know beforehand? How could he ever go to sleep again with any sense of certainty? If only he did not have the magic, then life would be so much simpler! Accordingly, he determined to stay awake, but at some point, when his eyes could no longer remain open and his thoughts began to meander, sleep stole him away without warning.

Chapter Twenty-Five

Gopher did not dream. He awoke feeling revitalized. Gazing at the low rock ceiling above, he followed with his eyes its contours all the way to the edge, and then to the sky. Its soft blue was patchily laden with fluffy grey cumulus clouds, some with touches of pink and others edged with gold. Rain still scented the air. Then a noise caused the rodent to level his gaze and he saw the pixie skipping up the slope. He was humming to himself and somehow managing to carry five eggs in one hand (was he juggling them?), while dragging a couple of sodden sticks in the other.

The scene made Gopher sigh with a contentment that thought no further than what his eyes could see or what his nose could smell. However, that changed in the next moment when Farwyll saw that he was awake.

The pixie's smile was like the morning sun, welcoming and soft. "Good morning," he said, "and it is good, isn't it? Especially after a storm. I think that's what I like about storms – when they're over." Then he added as if in afterthought, "How would you like it if we made it to Kentfell today?"

The question shattered his contentment as it aroused one word instantly in his mind – and all the memories and feelings attached to it – *Menlow*. What kind of friend was Gopher that he should be so happy while the erstwhile wizard could be dead already? Now there was no denying that the guilt and shame that the banshee had aroused in him was deserved. Yet no matter how poor a friend he was, it did not matter in comparison to Menlow's welfare.

Even so, Gopher did not let his urgency supersede his manners, because Farwyll had been so generous and giving and helpful, despite also being unpredictable and frustrating. The rodent replied with restrained eagerness, "Today? Do you really think so?"

"Oh, we can be there sometime in the afternoon, if the wind blows us a direct course," the pixie said, almost casually. He bent down and clapped. A sudden flame shot from his hands downwards to land on the sodden wood, which responded after a moment with a slight puff of smoke. He had to clap two more times before the wood began to blaze of its own accord.

This was almost too much. "Shouldn't we be going?" Gopher said, though still restrained.

"There's no hurry. The wind hasn't got up yet. That means wait, be patient."

"But you said you knew the way, didn't you? And Menlow may need us," Gopher said. He felt himself losing the battle for patience.

"The need should never lead; it may drive a person, but it is a poor guide. I never go without being led by the wind," the pixie said, shaking his head. "And I never rush when the wind does not, for that is almost as bad. Timing is everything. When the wind lulls, I lull, and when it blows, well, so do I!" He laughed, and then added, "But we should be thankful now's not the time to rush. I'm famished and, if the sounds of your rumbling stomach are any kind of proof, so are you."

It was true: Gopher was hungry, but he did not want to eat. He did so anyway to humor Farwyll, but when he had finished two eggs, he felt better, though he hardly noticed simply because it didn't matter to him. He only cared about Menlow and the sooner they left the better, though he kept telling himself that perhaps because the wind wasn't blowing meant that Menlow was doing okay.

At long last (though it was less than three quarters of an hour later), they set out. Safely ensconced on the fairy's shoulder, Gopher viewed the landscape for something familiar but failed to see anything definite, though he did not doubt Farwyll's assurance. Forests that had the same types of trees and foliage tend to blend together, he knew, for he had seen enough of them. It wasn't until they stopped on top of a low ridge to make a snack of mushrooms and berries that the pixie pointed out something definitely familiar. In the distance through a gap in the tree line lay a stretch of water, which the fairy said was the spot where they had refreshed themselves on the first day that they had met.

"But we have a lot farther to go," Gopher said.

"Not at all!" the pixie laughed. "The town's only a couple of hours upstream, and if we were birds, less than half of that!"

The news dropped like a stone in the pit of Gopher's stomach. "You mean that I was that close? How come you didn't take me there instead?" Of course, Gopher knew the answer the moment he had asked the question.

"Because the wind was taking us somewhere else!"

Suddenly he felt bitterness like one feels after being played a nasty trick. He had been so close that day and then to be blindly, trustingly led away! So much could have been avoided: being lost in a forest, living in fear of predators, and ending up in a cage to be used by those who only saw him as a means towards profit. Even more important than any of that, Menlow would not have fallen in an evil enchantment. What had all those trials been for anyway? Here he was, making a long trek back to his friend's side, from which he should never have been wrongfully taken.

As they started off again, Gopher consoled himself that they did not have much farther to go. Soon he wouldn't have to worry about being led by something as unreliable as the pixie's so-called wind anymore. He was thinking this, coincidentally, when the pixie took a direction away from the river. Gopher knew it was pointless to say anything, even when Farwyll seemingly doubled back a couple of times (though the sameness of the forest made it difficult to tell). He was sure that they went in the wrong direction twice. The first time it turned out that they were only skirting an open rocky slope, which reminded him of the spot where the falcon had swooped down on him before. The other time he had no idea why until he smelled some predator in the air behind them, perhaps a wolf.

The only thing he knew, which made the delays bearable, was his faith in the pixie. Somehow they would end up in Kentfell. That was assurance enough, but it irked him that, even in these last few miles, he was still being blindly led about. He wondered how the pixie could stand living with such uncertainty and without any clear sense of what to expect. He felt bad about feeling this way, but his growing excitement made it impossible to resist.

His longing for certainty came to include a roof over his head and a fire to ward off the chill when a damp mist rose out of the ground almost at the same time that the sky turned gray and ugly. When it started to rain again, he would have even settled for a gopher hole, though he had sworn months ago never to return to one.

Then his irritation was supplanted by fear when suddenly he heard voices so clear that he expected to see the men in front of him – and they him. The pixie stopped perfectly still without humming or shifting about, as they both listened.

"But, Clifton, 'tis not fittin' to be leavin' at this time," bawled one.

"Won't be fittin' *any* time! You, young 'uns, never learn 'cause you don't 'ave enough history in your years! Every man's for hisself!"

The first one replied, "Learn? Ha! Learn what? About fairy tales? I'd a thought that you'd 'ave enough years not to be taken into believin' those!"

The fellow named Clifton retorted gruffly, "I ne'er said that I was, but I ain't fool enough to think that *nothing's* happening. Bad things are stirrin'. Those pranks 'ad turned sour, and then there is that hermit stumbling out of the forest with his eyes a-glazed and an empty smile on his mug. More than just odd, they're portents; that's what they are. Nope, Kentfell isn't the only village to live in, so I'm a-going. Now what 'bout *you*? Why're you goin'?"

To which the other answered, "You know that my ma's laid up sick and that I'm headed for Clarin where there's medicine!"

"And you, of all people, know *why* she's laid up. She blamed the mayor's daughter and she got the hex put on her 'cause of it!"

"Ha! That's sheer mummery! The mayor's enemies made it up. Now *they're* the ones behind all of this! Mark my words. Dryden's daughter has naught to do with them tricks. 'Aven't you noticed that she's more affected than anyone by what's been going on in the town? I've ne'ver seen a child who 'ad been so happy take such a morose turn!"

"Ah! That's proof of her guilty conscience! Like as not, though," the other man said, "it's just another trick to pull the wool over our eyes. Her kindness and tears – bah! I'm done with all her tricks!"

They continued to argue long after their words, if not their tone, could be discerned. When enough distance and forest were put between them, Farwyll started forward and breached through a line of trees. On the other side was a hard-beaten roadway but the men were not in sight. The pixie took to the right, the direction from which the fellows had come.

"I'll stick to your side a little further," Farwyll said, "but, don't worry, I won't be far away."

The thought that the pixie would not remain with him throughout the entire trip hit him like a thunderclap. His guilt for being irritated at him returned all at once when he realized how much he depended on him.

"Why – why can't I hide with you?"

"To begin with, I won't be able to hide. I'll have to *change* to get anywhere near the town. Pixies are shape-changers; I can be a bird or a fly or even leaves in a breeze. Shape changing is the most dangerous of all magic, though, because I could forget who I am. If I forget, then how can I change back? "

He shivered and was quiet for a long time. Gopher got the impression that such a thing happening would be the pixie's worst nightmare. Yet it was the rodent's worst nightmare to be left on his own.

"But what should I do when you, ah, change?"

"Do what you did before you met me – just be more careful of swooping hawks and going over open places, okay?" he said with a wink. "At least this time you know where you're going. Besides, you don't have to worry; like I said, I won't be far away."

The afternoon grew a trifle shade warmer, the rain having stopped shortly after they had reached the road. The dark clouds lightened and moved on, being replaced by thick, cumulous ones; while some of them flattened out into striations so that the pale blue sky and sun could peek through from time to time.

The wind picked up slightly but with an edge of chill added to it. Except for his nose, ears, and short stubby tail, Gopher's fur kept him warm enough, especially since the pixie's head and shoulder provided extra heat. With his slow acceptance of the fact that they may soon be traveling separately but not altogether apart, the rodent came to identify the pixie's body warmth with his friendship, which he had taken for granted until now.

The idea of parting also awakened an appreciation of his surroundings. It was like grasping a moment that was about to slip away. He realized that it was as if the joy that sprang from their honest-to-goodness friendship was spreading itself outwards, becoming deeper and more delightful as it encompassed and painted everything with a richer glow. He delighted in the autumn beauty of the gold, red, and orange leaves in the branches overhead. Even the breeze that flowed through the leaves in a peaceful whisper invigorated him and made him feel that he could face whatever might lie ahead. A bird added to the tranquility and to Gopher's inner delight by singing sweetly on one of the limbs that stretched across the roadway. Far off the clunk-clunk sound of someone chopping wood vividly reminded him of Menlow hacking at a stubborn block of wood. He smiled at the memory with only a slight stinging to his eyes, which came not from poignant longing but from an appreciation of having been part of it.

Something rose up in him that resisted such feelings, however. He recognized it at once as the same guilt from this morning. After all, he thought, shouldn't he be feeling worried? Was he so uncaring about Menlow, so selfish, that he could be enjoying himself?

Yet he could not believe that he was. Menlow was still foremost in his mind and heart, while he felt a joy that went beyond any trouble or worry, which could not be touched by any darkness of feeling or thought. It reminded him very strongly of that Wondrous

Feeling that had come from the magic carrot and had seemingly spread outward to his surroundings, but this time it seemed to be working in reverse: The joy of friendship was leading towards that Wondrous Feeling or perhaps to something even greater, in which even friendship was only one spoke in its wheel. It was something that spoke whispers of reassurance, though strangely without words because they went straight to his heart.

That wonderful moment, indeed, slipped away, and quite abruptly, when sounds of someone approaching reached them, but it was so wonderful that it left a lasting impression. Even the intrusion of the voices and the clip-clopping ahead did not altogether unsettle him. And when Farwyll set him promptly down with a reassuring wink and vanished, he was not supremely bothered by it, though he knew that he had to act promptly if he did not want to be found by whoever was approaching. While wondering if the pixie had become that bird that tittered about the edge of a puddle, or that moth that flitted near the ditch, he jumped over the former and landed in the latter, which proved muddier and deep enough to hide in.

He peered carefully over the edge, waiting. Neither the bird nor the moth was anywhere to be seen.

Chapter Twenty-Six

A slumped-over old fellow on a mule that seemed just as downcast appeared. He had seemed so lost in his troubled thoughts that Gopher doubted that he would have noticed the pixie. The rodent didn't even wait until he was out of sight to start back on the road.

By late afternoon, with a dipping sun passing its golden rays over the buildings and making the river beyond them shiver like a shiny snake, Gopher at last came in sight of the eastern edge of the town. It had taken him much longer than Farwyll had led him to expect, but that wasn't the pixie's fault since Gopher's way had been hampered along the way. Despite the rain's return and subsequent downpour, there had been many on the road. At least the rain was enough of a distraction that nobody took any notice of him when he wasn't quick to hide, except for a frightening moment when a child threw rocks at him.

The pixie, not surprisingly, had remained absent; no doubt retaining whatever shape he had initially taken on as a disguise. After a while Gopher had quit guessing where his friend may be, or what he might look like. He had become too excited to think about that, not when he felt that he was getting closer. He had even hardly noticed the rain any more than he had noticed the wild thumping of his heart, while expecting at any moment to peer beyond the thinning trees to see the buildings of Kentfell.

Now that he saw them the town's intimidating size made the

moment anticlimactic, for it gave him enough pause to keep him from letting his excitement cause him to thoughtlessly dash forward. With further contemplation, he decided that, despite the rain, he would most likely be seen, what with so many people about. In much anguish that comes from repressed excitement, he hid in a hollow tree stump near the roadway to wait for cover of night.

An hour later (that felt like ten) he set out. The sun was dipping over the mountain ridge behind a screen of thin clouds, bathing the cloudy sky a purplish blue with a layer of cumulous cloud that were tinged with reddish grey, while casting the countryside with long shadows. He took a deep breath, felt the cold air enter in, and then he let it out, as if dispelling the all-pervasive image of the dying hermit that had been tormenting him during his wait.

Skirting the road on its right side, he scurried on four feet like any other rodent and used what cover the bramble, ditches, and rocks could afford, though the gathering shadows, deepened even more by the canopy of thick clouds, provided more than enough to keep his movements undetected. He went along cautiously, nonetheless, sniffing the air and scanning high and low for any signs of danger. He didn't know if Farwyll would, or even could, protect him within the limits of human habitation, but that wasn't the real point for his stealth and deliberate pace. Being seen would mean delay, and, after traveling so far and waiting for so long for night to fall, delay seemed worse to him than death itself.

The homes, shops, and businesses loomed ahead in lengthening shadows. Although he would have preferred taking one of the side roads, the main one was the most direct route, and which, incidentally, had turned out to be the very one he had been on all along; going off it to find another would have taken too long and involved more risk. Unfortunately, the road was very broad and had very few hiding places as he approached town.

He took more risks than he should have along the way, but a sense of vulnerability inspired in him a fear that gave him only two choices: either let it paralyze him or ignore it – and the only way to do that was to keep moving, whether or not it was safe.

At last he felt a modicum of security upon reaching the first of the outlying buildings, for it was empty and dark. It cast a shadow on its east side that was even darker. He peered out of it and what comfort he had taken in his progress faded when he saw that many of the townspeople still lingered outside in the damp weather. Some were packing up to leave town with others trying to talk them out of it. Most were banded together and seemed to roam the streets with torches. He knew what they were looking for, but it might just as well have been for him, for he was sure to be caught if he didn't turn back now.

He didn't even consider doing that. In the next moment, he left the shadow and proceeded in furtive spurts, scurrying forward to whatever hiding places he could find, while avoiding crowds and lighted buildings. First he hid behind a box, which a breeze suddenly whooshed away; and then he scurried behind a rock barely big enough for cover, which he then traded for the shadows of a darkened alcove. After that, there was a broad expanse of road without any hiding places to be seen. He set out across it anyway.

That was when he thought he had been spotted by someone who shouted and stomped his way. He immediately dove into a mud puddle, which was deeper than it looked. When nothing happened to him, he cautiously raised his head up and saw a man's broad figure disappear into a building.

Unlike other rodents, he had learned to dislike mud, but this time he preferred it because it would help him to blend in to his surroundings, though he didn't wallow long in the puddle since it lay in the middle of the road.

Avoiding people proved impossible at this point, but he discovered that, with the mud making him hard to see and the busyness of the people in their packing or the fervency of those arguing with them, he stood a chance of getting through. Even those who went about their business were too busily engaged in their own affairs or else too hunkered in their cloaks and hoods to notice a gopher.

Still, Gopher knew that this was no real safety. One glance, one wrong step, and all would be lost. If only he had waited longer, he thought, the townspeople would have been mostly tucked away in their homes and he could have reached the mayor's house with less risk. He decided to correct that mistake when he finally reached a darkened alleyway and found a barrel that would be the perfect place to hide behind and wait. The spot proved even better than he had expected, for the ground behind the barrel was dry, and the niche between the rounded barrel and the wall gave him a sense of security and was enclosed enough to hold in some of his warmth.

It wasn't long before he realized that he wasn't the only one who had thought it an ideal hiding place. While starting to clean himself from the mud, a pair of glistening eyes appeared not more than a foot in front of him, strangely floating in the darkness. They blinked and they even seemed to make a sniffing sound. He was wondering how floating eyes could do that, when another pair joined the first, followed by yet another, then by a rapidly increasing number of them. At the same time they started coming closer – close enough for him to catch their rat scent that was so strong that he wondered that he had not smelt it before.

What surprised him was that revulsion, instead of fear, was his immediate dominant feeling. Never before had he felt so unlike a rodent than he did now, for it was not until he saw the similarity between their furry bodies and his own that he truly appreciated the real difference between them. In contrast, their rodent attributes that they had in common with him made him cringe, almost as much as the fear did. Both feelings, however, urged him equally towards flight – except that a perfect hiding place also makes a perfect trap.

Perhaps they scented these feelings (or perhaps rats just hated gophers), but, whatever the reason, they began showing animosity; first, one snapped at him, and then another. Then all at once they started surging forward. Gopher found himself clawing, snapping, and hissing back like any other rodent fighting for his life, with no hope but only a driving animal instinct to survive at any cost.

This was met by an uproar of hissing, scurrying, and general pandemonium. Bodies rushed into him, pushing him against the barrel and threatening to suffocate him in their thick fur. All at once, however, both Gopher's teeth and claws found nothing but air to gnash and claw at. He opened his eyes and saw that the cause of the sudden disturbance was not more rats coming into the fray, but rather a large cat that had jumped into their midst. The feline spun about in a whirl of paws that lashed out lightning fast, with yowls and hissing. Twice Gopher nearly got swiped. He backed further into the niche between the barrel and the wall. It was not long before the cat had cleared the place of all the rats when Gopher realized that he was just as trapped as before. The cat loomed over him with its unblinking diamond-shaped eyes fastened on him.

Just then a gruff man's voice said, "What's going on back there?"

At the same time Gopher felt the barrel shift behind him. Instantly he planned that, as soon as a gap between the wall and the barrel became wide enough, he would make his escape. As what often happens with even the best of plans, though, his imagination did not quite turn out to match what really happened. When he passed through the gap, and then between the legs of the man, it was not because of his own speed or ingenuity. Instead, it had been because of the cat, for it had snatched him up in its sharp-toothed jaws and was shooting off in a blur that nearly tripped the man and caused another person to yell out in surprise.

In regards to another escape attempt, he felt little hope to even imagining one. The feline's jaws were clamped down hard on the back of his neck and in the right spot between his shoulder blades that immobilized Gopher, like a mother cat carrying her kitten. In this case, however, he didn't feel that the cat had any motherly intentions. It whipped him about so quickly that it made everything a blur. Gopher caught glimpses of people, around whom the cat dodged and darted. At one point he definitely recognized a pair of grasping hands reaching down, but they only received a sharp swat. Someone yelped, which caused others to follow up with laughter.

Then a woman said, "That's no fiend! Only a cat with a gopher! Ha! Let the tom have it!"

Their way went unhindered after that. Shortly later, the people and the muddy street were gone and so was the remaining light – or so he thought until his eyes adjusted to the faintest light from a crescent moon. They were in a darkened alley. Alone with the cat and helpless, Gopher imagined that death would be his only escape. He hoped, at least, that it would be quick and painless.

The cat didn't stop to finish him off, however, as it passed through the alley. This might have increased his hope if the feline hadn't been loudly purring. He could even feel its uneven vibrations from its throat, vaguely remembering that the cat had been purring all along, even while dodging through the crowd. The cat wasn't hungry; it was playful, he realized. That was worse because that meant the gopher would be its toy to play with until he died.

The tomcat reached a lighted house and went around to the side alley, a portion of which was lighted by an open window. The creature leapt up to the windowsill and, after a pause, jumped down inside, while the light dazzled Gopher's dark-adapted eyes. It was not until he had been released from the cat's jaws and felt himself dropping down onto something soft that his sight began to come into focus. Even then, he still had a hard time believing what he was seeing. Menlow was right in front of him, lying in bed just like how Gopher had dreamed it.

Chapter Twenty-Seven

The cat was gone, but Gopher did not notice. It wouldn't be until later when he would realize that its purring had really sounded like the humming of a tune, the familiarity of which would then lead him to the not-too-surprising conclusion that the cat had been Farwyll and that he had rescued him for the fourth time! At the moment, however, Menlow was all that mattered.

If anyone was watching, it would have seemed that Gopher was staring at his friend for the longest time, but for him time was irrelevant, which was one of those things that happen when one is shocked. The hermit looked more than just older; he looked different to the point of nearly being unrecognizable. Even the dream hadn't been adequate enough to prepare him for that, proving that, despite its vividness, the vision was not equal to its reality –and it was its reality that had a finality that floored him.

Menlow's face looked drawn with age, just like in Gopher's dream, except up close it looked more than just age. His eyes were pinched as if in pain with a thousand accompanying wrinkles. The clamminess and pallor of his skin gave it a waxen appearance, and the hollow check bones, in particular, were shockingly incompatible with his beatific smile, the peaceful rising and falling of his chest, and his languid repose of perfect relaxation. The covers, tucked snuggly beneath his chin, were held there by bony fingers. He would have looked like a child peacefully sleeping without a care in the world if the harsh, frightening truth was not so obvious. At least, he didn't seem to be in any pain, but the thought was not comforting. In fact, it was the smile itself that scared him the most. How could he look so happy, yet be so gaunt and dying?

Gopher did not have an answer, but there was another more pressing, and important, question, which had just occurred to him simply because he had not gotten that far in his thinking. But, upon seeing Menlow appearing so blissfully ignorant of his deteriorating condition, the question was blatantly obvious: What could he do about it? It seemed preposterous to think that the hermit would awake by merely hearing his voice.

He decided to try anyway.

He began by calling out his friend's name in a whisper and then in a coaxing voice that he steadily raised until he realized that he was yelling. He stopped to take a few breathes, but then he decided to try a different approach: conversation. Gopher gently urged him to wake, warning him that he was dying, and how much he was needed. He also talked about some of the times they had together in the cottage and even recounted some of the ex-wizard's old tales.

As the ex-wizard continued to lay there unresponsive, Gopher experienced how literal the term "heartbreak" was. He would have broken out in a flood of tears, if the mayor hadn't come in and gave such a whoop of joy and delight that his grief was instantly lessened.

"Gopher! Oh! Oh! I never thought I'd be seeing you again! How'd you survive the river? How'd you get here?"

The rodent felt so welcomed that he felt happy and at ease, but that was only for a moment. Menlow's breath – a long, happy sigh – reminded Gopher. He also sighed, but it wasn't a happy one.

"I haven't done any good. He won't wake," Gopher said. "I don't think he can even hear me." He was surprised that he was able to get that out without bursting into tears.

"But you've come back just when we were giving up hope!" the mayor said. "That must mean something!" As he glanced over at Menlow, however, his face fell, as if he, too, realized the ridiculousness of expecting him to just wake up.

"I heard you calling him," he said softly, "but I thought it was another one of those tricks that have been going on around here."

An awkward silence followed, in which Gopher felt not only helpless but foolish for even having hoped that his return would change everything. A dreaded certainty (and regret) came over him once again that he should have stayed with the Traveling Merchant a little longer. Maybe he would've learned something about his magic to make it of more use. His thoughts would have turned darker if Dryden hadn't suddenly clapped.

"Why, of course! I know where you can do some good – Adia! She needs some cheering up ever since you fell into the river! I'll get her."

After a brief interval, while Gopher looked helplessly upon his unconscious friend, Dryden returned with his face as pale as his nightshirt.

"I'm afraid it's one of *those* nights again."

"Is she – is she like *that*?" the rodent said. What had given it away was that Dryden had looked at Menlow right when he had said it. Gopher's heart sunk.

At once the mayor denied it, "No, no! She'll wake in the morning like she always does," but then added, "but it just scares me that she *might* not wake up. How can I not worry when...?" he could not finish.

He needed little urging to show Gopher into Adia's room. Dryden gently carried him with both hands, though the rodent could feel a slight tremble and tenseness in the mayor's grip. He soon saw the reason why when he was placed on her bedside table. Like Menlow, her countenance gave her such a different look about her that Gopher did not recognize her at first, except in sharp contrast to the hermit. Her down-turned mouth suggested deep sorrow while her furrowed brow between her raised eyebrows seemed to show fear, even horror.

"Honey, wake up!" her father pleaded and then turned to Gopher. "She will but only in her own time, and it seems to be getting longer and longer for her to – to find her way out. Even when she's awake... the look in her eyes... the way she... it seems like, deep down, she is still... lost."

Then Gopher jumped on to the bed and spoke into her ear as he had done to Menlow: "Wake up! It's me! Gopher. I'm back. I'm okay!"

Nothing happened, just like with Menlow. Gopher rebelled against the same encroaching helplessness and blurted out the same thing but this time with much more fervency, from the part in him where anger and frustration dwelt.

Still nothing.

He gave it one more try, whispering with an earnestness that would have been a scream if his voice had been up to it. It did not take long for him to realize that it was pointless. He finally collapsed next to the girl. He was more than tired, he felt empty. Maybe if he just went to sleep, one of his dreams would provide a clue. Closing his eyes, he let exhaustion flow over him.

That's when something happened. It could not be detected outwardly, but Gopher felt an inner connection the very moment he stopped trying. Surprisingly, he felt that all his efforts had actually been preventing it from happening. Slowly and increasingly he felt a darkness drawing him into itself until suddenly the black engulfed him. He was trapped. Worse still, it was not a vacant blackness. Rather, it was filled with a storm of whispering voices full of anger, spite, rage, and bitterness, with the underlying feelings of self-pity and heartbroken sorrow.

Instinctively he could feel the girl's presence in the midst of this darkness. The hushed voices, he realized, were directed at her. He could not imagine what *that* must feel like. The darkness was so oppressively thick with them that it was as if the whispers themselves were the darkness. He yelled, attempting to pierce through.

"Adia! Adia! I'm here! I'm not drowned!"

The whispers stopped immediately, and another voice, Adia's, said "Gopher?" in a disbelieving tone.

"Yes! Where are you? I'm over here," he said, although he didn't know where "here" was.

"Oh, Gopher! You're not drowned? I'm so sorry!" said the girl's

228

voice, much closer.

Then, as suddenly as he was drawn into the darkness, he was thrust out of it. He opened his eyes to find the girl wakening as well. She gazed at Gopher for only a moment, like one whose vision is coming into focus, and then she came instantly to life as she picked him up and held him close to her face. That change from sorrow and horror to a look of pure joy and delight was one of his happiest moments – but then he also became filled with a wonderful hope. Now he knew how he could wake Menlow, too.

As excited and impatient as he felt to get on with it, he reluctantly agreed to eat and rest a bit. After all, he was starved and tired and he still didn't know how long it would take. It was not long before he was glad that he did. The food and rest made a difference in him – and so did their talk, which they had while he ate on the kitchen table with the others seated around.

Even just seeing their familiar faces was just as revitalizing. Gopher talked briefly about all that happened to him. It was during this that he realized that the pixie had been his feline rescuer, but did not say too much about it. By their puzzled and amazed reactions, he realized that it was too much to tell in a few words. Yet it was enough to raise their spirits with a sense of purpose and destiny, since what they afterwards shared with him was far from good news. The pranks around town had indeed gotten nastier. A cat's tail had been set on fire and a dozen boats were sunk overnight, to name a few.

Only Adia was the one who said very little, but there was such a look of happiness mixed with hope on her face that words weren't needed. Gopher got the impression that she had not felt like this for a long time. How often had the tumultuous darkness of her sleep been tormenting her? He might have pondered this longer if he hadn't been so impatient.

Then, as their meal was completed, a look came over their faces that showed that he wasn't the only one too excited to wait any longer. They quickly and almost wordlessly gathered at the side of Menlow's bed. Adia solemnly placed Gopher next to his friend as if performing a devout ritual.

The rodent felt a sudden reluctance that stemmed from a thought that he might fail, but in gazing into the gaunt, yet happy, face of his friend he found that he was able to push the thought aside and get right to it without really knowing what exactly needed to be done. He started by doing what he knew to do; that is, what he did with Adia: Closing his eyes and relaxing, he reached out in his mind: "Menlow, it's me, Gopher." Nothing happened, but that was okay. He let go of even expecting anything to happen. It would happen, or it wouldn't. It was as simple as that. He just let the feelings of affection towards his friend flow over him, forgetting all else, even himself.

The connection came suddenly, much easier, but this time neither darkness nor a storm of emotions enveloped him. Instead he stepped into a green meadow with the sun overhead and a cool breeze that was sweet with the sweet fragrance of flowers. He found himself calling out Menlow's name when someone whispered on his left.

"Shhh! Don't you think someone your size should practice a little more caution –"

"Menlow!" Gopher exclaimed.

Chapter Twenty-Eight

"Hush!" Menlow hissed, kneeling down in the tall grasses next to Gopher.

About twenty feet away to their left slept a dragon under the branches of an elm tree. It stirred its green scaly body and swung its head around to nestle on top of his sharp claws, thankfully without opening its large hooded eyes, while wisps of smoke issued from its long, fanged snout.

The ex-wizard sighed in relief and said in a whisper, "Not that you're really in danger but why court it? Umm, let's go over there. He has sharp ears."

Gopher followed him to the trees that lined the meadow opposite the dragon. They were well out of view of the great lizard when Menlow stopped and began where he had left off: "You needn't worry. I would not let a single spark singe your fur, but hungry dragons make things complicated. He doesn't appreciate a talking gopher anymore than he does a non-talking one; they taste all the same to him," He laughed, but upon seeing Gopher's lack of response, he sobered. "Forgive me, my little friend. Us non-gophers can be quite insensitive."

Gopher's lack of response did not come from being offended – in fact, he barely heard what Menlow said – but from being perplexed. It was the change in the hermit that bewildered him. The man looked years younger with only touches of gray in his brown hair that framed his face much more thickly than before. His beard of the same grayish brown was also fuller, longer, and was pointy, which would have made him look older except that around his eyes there were fewer wrinkles. Yet the biggest difference was neither in his age nor even in his appearance but in his manner. Strangely he seemed like a different person – yet also the same. Right now he decided that it didn't matter.

"Menlow, you need to wake up," Gopher began, but immediately he felt awkward saying it. It was almost as if – as if he was embarrassed, like someone who had said something silly. Of course, he knew that Menlow was dreaming, that all of this was not real – but yet it all felt so solid and, most of all, so peaceful and beautiful that to contradict it as being unreal seemed to fly in the face of good taste. In short, he felt as if he were being rude. What Menlow said in reply, however, disturbed him even more.

"Interesting," the hermit mused. "Why do you keep calling me this – Menlow? Do you mistake me for another? Is there another wizard that looks like me? Is he the one who gave you the gift of speech? That would explain why you speak so familiar to me – but, believe me, you have the wrong man – or wizard."

His friend's words would have broken his heart anew if he had pondered them rather than forcing himself to remain focused on what needed to be done, which was to convince the hermit.

"But you don't understand! You're – ah, you're under a spell and I came – I came to bring you out of it."

The words had the ring of idiocy in his own ears. He felt it was also reflected in the ex-wizard's reply as he leaned forward to be nearly level with him.

"A spell? And *you* came to bring me out of it?" He did not laugh at him but his smile was so broad and his eyes so twinkling that it was practically the same thing. "I have saved many a small creature in my time – and that's been a long, long time – but never has one come to try to save me! What is this spell that I'm supposed to be under? And if I am, that means you are, too, doesn't it? Doesn't that also mean that you need as much saving as I do?"

Gopher suppressed the anger Menlow's words provoked

because his friendship meant more to him than anything else. Instead the emotion fueled his determination.

"Don't you remember me? You are the one who gave me the magic to talk. You took me in and we lived in a cottage. You are a hermit, but you were once a wizard."

The old man's smile faded as he bent lower, looking into Gopher's eyes. He shook his head and pulled thoughtfully at his beard. (The gesture looked familiar, Gopher thought. Didn't he do that before, although there had been less of his beard to pull? It was getting hard to remember.) The hermit spoke at last, shaking his head.

"Yes, I remember something of what you say, but I'm afraid that you are mistaken, my friend, in thinking that what you remember was real."

"What do you mean?"

"Oh, don't worry. It is a natural mistake since you don't understand the nature of enchantments. It's easy to make, especially for all those newly awake like yourself. You see, *this* is the Awakening."

"What?" Gopher said staggered.

Menlow laughed, "Look around you! This is real. Can't you just feel it? What you remember was an enchanted dream. It was real in its own way, but, compared to this, it was only a faded reflection of the real thing. I had decided long ago that it was not worth retaining in my memory. Whatever I had called myself to you, my real name is Merlin. I did not tell you then, because I thought that I had left it behind me. But I had not. I was and still am both magician and counselor to a great king whose name is Arthur Pendragon. Alas! He is still asleep! Even now it is hard to talk about, for his death had stung me to my heart. That's why when his body had been taken to the Isle of Avalon, I had put my name and reputation behind me – but now that I have awakened, I have taken them up again! You see, my little friend, I have come back into my own at last! All that is left is for King Arthur's return to save the land from a great evil. It had been prophesized by none other than myself!"

The earnestness in his appearance and speech were just as

convincing as the surroundings. Together they ushered in confusion. Maybe, just maybe, this is real, Gopher thought. After all, could dreams convey the sweet aroma of flowers or the woodsy scent of the elm or the coolness of a breeze or the subtle warmth of the sun? Still, hadn't he felt these things also in that other place?

Or had he?

Even now the memories of the cottage and the river and the pixie and the cage... all of it was growing vague, dreamlike, even nightmarish, in contrast to the vivid beauty of his surroundings that delighted and pressed upon his senses. He wasn't so sure what was real now and did not know what to say.

As if Menlow – no, Merlin – could read his thoughts and emotions, he said, "A meadow and a dragon are all that you have seen so far. They are but weak proofs of what I say. Let me show you the realm – then *you* tell me what is real!"

Instead of placing the rodent on his shoulder, his friend snapped his fingers and raised both hands from his sides. As he did so, Gopher felt the air sweep under him, not like a wind but rather like an invisible cushion being slid in place. After that, he felt no additional lift, even though he found himself level with the hermit's shoulders. At the same time he saw, to even greater amazement, that they were both above the treetops and looking down on the meadow. He knew he ought to feel afraid, but somehow he felt secure and excited, when a realization dawned on him.

"Menlow, you have your magic back!" Gopher exclaimed.

The hermit smiled patiently. "Menlow still, is it? You can't help yourself, but did you really think that I had no magic? I who am the greatest of all wizards? It is no boast but the mere truth, by the way," he added.

"Oh, sorry," Gopher said and was once again thrown into confusion. If this is real, he thought, then why am I still acting and bringing up things from the *other place* as if they were? With the help of the invigorating wind in hiss face as they flew, he concluded that it might be because he had been so long under the spell.

While the wind blowing in his face and through his fur were undeniable sensations, the panorama that stretched from horizon to horizon had the opposite effect of persuading him of their reality, for it looked too perfect. The forested snowcapped mountains that stretched out until they were blue-misted outlines, the cascading triple falls directly below, and the foam-churning river winding through a mysterious green wooded valley – all seemed like a wonderful, impossible dream.

So enthralled was he that he found that he could care less if it was impossible – or even if it was an enchanted lie – as they began descending into that valley. Thick, green copses of oaks and elms, dotting the steep grey walls on either side, reached out as if to be the first to greet them. The trees became denser and the air warmer with their strong woodsy fragrance as the valley narrowed upon their descent. A peaceful roar reached them from below, growing stronger every moment, while a hawk encircled them above in majestic flight. The bird then landed somewhere in the trees as they themselves alighted on a rocky knoll at the foot of the triple falls. The roar was that of its waters pounding on the rocks, from which a mist emanated and added to the coolness of the shadows.

"You've seen only a little of the King's realm so far," Merlin said. "There are the green foothills and the sweeping lowlands, the great rivers and the vast ocean. Even more majestic are the dwellings of elves, for the beauty of excellence is their craft. The dwarves live in the darkness of the caves and deep places where light is treasured and captured in their gems and precious metals. As for the sprites, their places are truly castles in the air!

"As long as you're with me, you'd be welcomed in any of them. The dwarfs and dragons may not be so accepting, at least not readily, but they aren't a bad lot. The dwarfs tend to look upon others with a sense of competition, and the dragons care mostly for those things that have an appearance of value or beauty. The elves, on the other hand, have the wisdom and skills to bring out the hidden beauties and treasures in things, just like the dwarfs, except for the elves it is more of a playful dance or game than a competition.

"Speaking of elves," he went on, "I want you to meet some of them. They're wood elves who have invited me to one of their many parties. They should be along any moment."

They "floated" down from the boulder and seated themselves on a patch of clover, upon which Merlin, notwithstanding his age, sat down quite easily, folding his limbs until he was sitting cross legged. This surprised the rodent, until he realized that he was again thinking of the "old Menlow" in his dream. He laughed quietly at himself and was glad that he hadn't said anything.

By the time the wood elves arrived, the sky shone pale blue through the gap between the valley walls with golden fringed clouds, indicating the approach of dusk; correspondingly, the breeze began to be noticeably crisp but not uncomfortably so. Even in the dimming light under the canopy of trees, he could see the merry troop approach, but that was because of the flaming torches that they carried. Except for their pointed ears, they appeared almost human from afar.

But he let those thoughts loose, and even forgot about the time of day and its temperature, when he heard their singing. It was this that set them apart from humans, he decided, for no human voice could sing so beautifully or hit such notes. Then suddenly their singing swept him up. Although he did not understand their language, the music itself filled him with a mix of rising and descending emotions like one gets caught in a delightful wave. More feeling than actual melody, he could never quite remember a single note afterwards. Sometimes it was deeply happy and at other times sweetly sad; at one point, it swiftly changed into a lively tune, making him want to dance and sing nonsense; and at another moment, the music mellowed out into a peaceful melody, stirring a deep longing within him that the music itself seemed to partially fill. Where one emotion left off and the other came in, Gopher was not sure, wondering if somehow they really came at the same time, and it was merely his deciphering of them that made the emotions seem to follow each other. Yet one thing he was sure of was that, surprisingly, they stirred up in him a strong wistfulness for that "other world," which he called a dream.

"Enough!" cried Merlin, suddenly standing up. He startled

Gopher but not the elves. They cheered and clapped, as if they had expected the interruption. "Sing a lively song instead!"

The next song was definitely lively. Whatever the elfish words meant, the tune was the kind that had a catchy beat and would stick with you long afterwards and would cause you sleeplessness as it replayed over and over in your head. The emotions that it aroused did not remind him of another time and place. In fact, it made him feel like he could do anything and as if that "other place" really didn't matter at all. He had all he needed here. When Merlin picked up Gopher and placed him on his shoulder like old times (though now he danced like a young man), Gopher was so swept up that not once was he reminded of the old Menlow – or Farwyll or the Traveling Merchant, upon whose shoulders he had also ridden. He didn't even notice that Merlin and he headed a parade through the woods.

The song seemed to go on and on as they danced on and on, through the forest, and then up the steep green-covered slope on the side of the waterfalls; their voices somehow drowning out the booming below. When they reached the top where the broad river began its plunge, their merry procession came to an end, though Gopher felt like they had just started singing and dancing.

Before them, on a broad flat rock, which split the coursing water into two cataracts, was a large table with heaping piles of food from roasted ducks and stuffed turkeys to fruits and vegetables, the likes he had never seen before. Not until then did he realize how hungry he was – so hungry that he didn't question why he hadn't seen it upon first descending into the valley.

Everybody finding a chair or a stool around the table in a jubilant throng, they began eating at once. All the while, it seemed that the music never stopped, but Gopher, being so hungry, did not realize that nobody was singing until he was nearly done with a second plate (he had never eaten so much before – it seemed as if he could eat forever without getting full). As he wondered where the music was coming from, he finally discerned it to be the sounds of the waterfall. It was as if its rushing streams had picked up where the elves had left off, the roar having been replaced by that same merry tune, except that it was now more sweeping and powerful. Was it the elves' magic that did it or Merlin's? It didn't matter. Gopher was so jubilant that even the fact that everybody and everything was a blur of colors, movements, and noises didn't bother him; even the taste of the food increasingly became kind of a blur, but he was so far from worrying what was real and what wasn't, that he didn't even stop to wonder if any of it tasted good anymore.

Then the music suddenly stopped, and so did everybody's gorging and frolicking about. For Gopher, and perhaps for the rest of them, it felt like getting the wind knocked out of him. Everything came into focus once more as a figure in a black robe approached. He jumped across one of the branching streams and landed on the knoll. His action was light and graceful in marked contrast to his somber presence. A cowl shadowed much of his face, except for the gleaming whites of his eyes and for his tight, compressed lips and strong jaw line. There was a neat little goatee on the end of his chin that seemed incongruent. For some reason it made Gopher think that maybe the man wasn't always so stern. Perhaps at other times he might prove better company, but right now he was nothing more than an intruder on their fun.

The man stopped before Merlin who, like the others, had been drinking and feasting and laughing a moment before. Gopher was close enough to detect the wizard letting out a sigh that might have been weariness or dread. His expression did not bear it out, though, for he greeted him with a smile and a merry voice (though not so merry as before).

"Welcome as always, Belthur! I take it by your demeanor that it is not the good news of the King's awakening that you bring!"

"You are right. No such good tidings," the man replied, "though ill tidings may be for the good to those who practice wisdom. I come from the southern part to spread the news that the Blight is yet growing. It has crossed over the Blue River and has left it murky instead of blue. It will not be long before it poisons these fair forests and makes a blight of your songs and feasts."

"But what is to be done?"

"You are a steward of the land," Belthur replied, "and a steward does not act as if a threat does not exist."

"I know! I know!" Merlin exclaimed. "But it will do no *good*. It is the only thing that my magic cannot prevail against. Anyway, King Arthur will come and rescue us all. Then all shall be fulfilled, the great evil averted. You know that!"

"Do I? And do you?" Belthur replied softly. "Perhaps it is the Blight that keeps the King from returning. Even if it isn't, as steward, it is your job to do what you can."

This caused a stir amongst the elves and even Gopher felt an uncomfortable shiver. The sorcerer sighed impatiently.

"You've said that before. If the Blight needs to be removed for the King to return, then show me how to do it."

"Like you, I don't know how it is to be done, but at least you can stay true to your word."

"What do you mean?"

"Bring your friend here to see the Blight," the man said with more than just a glance at Gopher; his piercing eyes made the rodent feel as if the fellow knew him. "Did you not say that you would show him the realm to convince him how real it was? Reality includes the good and the bad. Show it to your friend. Keep your promise."

"But what does that have to do with anything?"

The other man shrugged. "Nothing and maybe everything. Do what you know you should do. That is every man's duty."

Merlin sighed with resignation. "All right. I'll do it, but I don't know how that will help anything at all."

"Often the knowing comes with the doing, my friend. Farewell!"

After the mysterious herald had departed, the music and feasting resumed, this time with more vigor. Even the plunging of the waterfall seemed to be louder than usual. Yet Merlin just sat there. He took a few bites, but then he pushed his plate away. He clapped his hands, signaling another stop to their festivities.

"No time like the present," he said, stroking his beard, and then added wryly, "Or, as Belthur would probably say, 'there's no time but the present.' Let's go, my little friend, and you will see what there is to be seen," and then to the elves, he enjoined for them to carry on, saying: "If we let it take our merriness now, the Blight will have already won! Now do your part in fighting it! Sing! Dance! Laugh!"

Merlin snapped his fingers and raised his arms like before, and the merry feast somehow became merrier, almost a frenzy of merriment, as the hermit and Gopher rose into the air. The elves hooted, cart-wheeled, back-flipped, sang, laughed, and applauded as, higher and higher, the two ascended into the evening sky where the stars began to appear.

The party grew dim rapidly below as if darkness was swallowing them up, their sounds also becoming fainter until all Gopher could hear was the wind in his ears. In the gathering gloom, the valley could no longer be distinguished from the other ones. By this time they were already flying, presumably to the south. Despite what they were going to see, Gopher was so lulled by the peaceful shadows below and the twinkling beauty above that it was some time before he remembered his question.

"Who was that?"

"Who? Oh, Belthur? He is the Watcher of the Realm. It is said that he was born with the land, like the fairy; yet he is a man, though no one is sure even of that. He monitors the realm's borders as well as the dangers that arise within it.

"Once," Merlin continued, wistfully, "he stopped six giants from trampling on a whole tribe of dwarfs. They weren't evil giants; they just had poor eyesight for any who were smaller than themselves."

"How did he stop them?"

"He sang them a song about how big and strong giants are. It caught their attention, because their regard that they hold for themselves matches their size. By the time they managed to screw their eyes so they could see who was singing it, the dwarves had already removed themselves from underfoot."

He went on to tell of other times Belthur had prevented disasters: of a flood, of a great fire, of a misunderstanding that might have led to war between the elves and dwarves, and even of a feast that had been so festive that it had gotten out of hand. Often the Watcher would alert Merlin of the disaster, who, in turn, used his magic to avert it. Gopher was prepared to listen to his stories all night, as there was nothing much to see but a starry field above and a blanket of thick shadow below.

Suddenly, though, they came upon the Blight, and Gopher did not need to see it; he felt it. It was like a strange aching chill that threatened to numb him from the inside out. It made him feel restless, even panicky so that he had to fight the urge to ask Merlin to take him far away. They descended almost as rapidly as if they were falling out of the sky, and he wondered if the Blight weakened Merlin's magic. They even landed rather roughly.

"We must not stay long, but there is no need to, anyway. There's not much to see." Merlin's voice was calm and reasonable sounding, but Gopher wondered if he really felt the same fear, the same sense of panic that could barely be restrained.

A glow lit up from the wizard's open palm, a small blue fiery ball. He tossed it into the air and the ball broke out into hundreds of tiny blue pinpricks of light that spread everywhere like baby fireflies, barely illuminating the forest around them in the softest blue light. There was not really anything more to see than what Gopher had instinctively known to be true: everything was dead. The branches were barren, the trees looked like they were dying, and the earth looked as hard and dead as stone. There was not a blade of grass or heather, nothing alive but tangles of sticks and thorns, like the dried up bones of a forest.

"The light will not last long here," Merlin said. "The Blight will quickly drain it as it does all magic and life. It is why we must not tarry, for it will do the same to us. I don't understand why the Watcher wants me to see this again or what he expects me to do about it. It's always the same, only worse – I can't stand it here. Let us go!"

The desperate urgency in Merlin's voice was not necessary to persuade Gopher, but something made him hesitate, something in the man's frown and furrowed brow that reminded him of... what? It was important. Where had he seen it before? He searched his memory.

Then it came to him: it had been in that "other place" when that troubled look had occasionally supplanted Merlin's enchanted blissful sleep. Merlin? No, it had been... Menlow! The vividness of the recollection lasted for only a moment, but it was enough to break the spell. Instantly he knew what was real – and remembered why he was there.

"Menlow, wait," Gopher said (it felt good to call him that again). "You need to wake up. This is all a lie. I came, like I said, to wake you before it is too late. You don't know it but you are dying. That's what I think that this Blight is. I have the Magic of Awakening," he added, his words seeming to come out of a mouth without thought. Instantly, though, he knew that it was true.

"You? A gopher?" Merlin laughed. "Who do you think woke you up? In fact, I woke all the fairies and dragons and giants!"

"If *you* have the Magic of Awakening, how did you wake yourself up?"

Menlow scratched his beard, his eyes looking elsewhere as if he were deep in thought. At last he sighed patiently, "I remember now... I woke myself up by following the light in the forest by the river. That's how I broke the spell."

"You mean, that was how you came under a spell," asGopher said.

"What? Do you think that I would fall into an enchantment so easily? You think me a fool and you so much wiser – you, a gopher?"

The wizard's words sparked a sudden anger in Gopher, though he managed to keep it out of his voice (or at least he thought he did): "Of course not, but nobody here is awake at all, just like you. I cast myself into your dream with my magic to bring you back. Please –"

"Bring me back?" he said with an uncharacteristic sneer, "To what – to a place where I had no magic, where there is evil and pain and poverty? Even if this is a dream, it is better than *that* place."

"But is this Blight better?" Gopher asked, but it was more of an exclamation, a shout really – a shout that he had never used before. The depth of his frustration surprised him, but letting it explode out of him was exhilarating with a sense of power and relief.

It had another effect, though this time it was upon Merlin, causing his mocking sneer to soften, followed by a sad pursing of his lips and a shaking of his head.

"I am sorry. It's my fault. I shouldn't have brought you here. The Blight makes us think and do things that we never would otherwise. Let us go before something worse happens."

He snapped his fingers and they arose from the ground, though at first rather shakily. The farther they flew into the night sky and away from the Blight (Gopher could feel it fading behind), the smoother they flew and the better Gopher felt. Yet another part in him was feeling worse. They landed near a stream where the blue ball of light, much bigger and brighter, now reappeared in Merlin's palm and showed that indeed they were back in a healthy forest – leaves, grass, and all with no inner coldness, no creeping death.

The first thing Merlin did upon alighting was to go to the stream and cup some water in his hand to give to Gopher. Even as thirsty as he was, he declined it.

"It's all right, my little friend," Merlin said. "A little drink will make you feel better and forget. The Blight puts us all in a bad mood."

"But I don't want to forget while I'm *here* when this is not even real. I would just fall under the same spell that you are under. There is no hope if you don't wake."

"There is! King Arthur will come. It is he who will rescue the land from the Blight. So you see that we mustn't lose hope! We just have to stay positive and wait."

"But it's not –" Gopher began, but he was stopped by the steadfast conviction that showed in the wizard's eyes. No argument, no amount of persuasion would be of any use, he realized, and the realization pierced his heart with a pain that stemmed from caring so much while feeling so helpless.

He closed his eyes tightly, wishing the pain away, wishing everything away. When he opened them again, he saw Merlin's face almost right up against his own. The wizard's eyes were closed and there were more wrinkles around it than he expected. Gopher looked around, saw that he was back in the bedroom with Adia asleep in the chair next to the bed, and wished that he had been wrong about what was real.

Chapter Twenty-Nine

Gopher's awakening did much in raising Adia's spirits as well as her father's, who appeared soon after, but it had the opposite effect on his own because his friend still lay there enchanted; in fact, he looked even worse, and Gopher felt just as helpless about it as he did before, perhaps more. The smile seemed less blissful and perhaps even forced, and his face looked older, with more lines and wispier hair. Perhaps it was because Gopher had gotten used to seeing the younger version of the hermit – how he had looked when he had been called Merlin. However, it was now impossible to look at him and think that he had once been a great sorcerer. Despondency threatened to rise up when it occurred to Gopher that the visit into his dream, and their argument, might have sped up his dying. He had only made things worse.

Even if that were so, what really upset Gopher was more than just Menlow's condition. It was the change in his personality and attitude, as if the pursuit of his own desires had altered him into someone almost unrecognizable.

Of course, the rodent kept all of this to himself. He did not want to spoil their celebration, for he had been under the enchantment so long that they had feared he had been permanently ensnared as well. Now that he showed that he could enter and return from Menlow's enchanted sleep it gave them new hope.

It was not their fault that they believed this. As he had related to them what had happened, he did not indicate his helplessness. Above all, he did not express that he had no idea how he was going to persuade Menlow to wake up. To them, it was a done deal, for he had told them also about his magic, which explained how he was able to enter and leave Menlow's dream and which, to their thinking, also explained how the hermit would eventually be saved. Gopher would just have to try harder next time, they so much as said with the implication that he had not tried hard enough the first time. Gopher inwardly sighed as they ate a hearty breakfast that Adia made herself. If only it could be that easy, he thought, forcing himself to concentrate on the hot cereal.

It did not help that he was exhausted, for even though he had been in an enchanted sleep, it had been a very active one. With a nice long nap he would feel better and, perhaps, as a result he might think up a new approach that might convince Menlow to wake up. He did not blame Menlow for his reluctance; after all, except for the Blight, who wouldn't choose that world over this? One thing, for certain, he would never go back to the Blight again, not after the effect it had on him. Next time, if there was going to be a next time, he might just inadvertently push his friend all the way to his death.

Gopher didn't need to announce his intention to rest, for his weariness was readily evident by his frequent yawns and his increasing sluggishness. Dryden, laughed, and took up the rodent's empty bowl.

"Your old bed is still made up – no use worrying about Menlow until you're rested." Then to Adia, the mayor said, "Why don't you fetch it, so he can sleep in your room? And you'd better fetch yourself some sleep, too, young lady; you've stayed up all night."

When she stepped out of the room, the mayor said with a grin, "You know she's never killed a gopher since she met you. She was afraid one of them might be you, but the strange thing is that almost every morning there would be a dead one at our doorstep, under our beds, or on our windowsills – like some cat leaving surprise presents of dead rodents! It tormented her. The fact that none of them were you did not seem to give her any comfort. It even gave me an eerie feeling that I could not explain, what with all that's been going on in town. I am sure relieved you're back!"

Gopher had more than just an idea of who was behind all of this, and it sent a shiver down to the roots of his fur. Before he could think of how to pose the question without raising any suspicions of how much he knew, Adia came back into the dining room to say that his bed was ready.

Dryden left them after good nights were said and Gopher was tucked in next to Adia's bed. It was a moment that he had been both hoping for and dreading. He wanted to know what had been going on with Adia and the hamadryad, but there was a fear behind her eyes that seeped into him. The news, he instinctively knew, would not be good.

"Who has been killing gophers?" he said, trying to sound casual.

He was right. Adia's face scrunched up with instant emotion and her words poured forth in a torrent of sorrow.

"She has!" the girl whispered. "She does it to torture me. When you fell into the river, I threw away the heart-sliver... but, Gopher, I'm afraid that if she finds out you're back..."

"But how? I thought she needs your shadow? What can she do without it?"

Adia sucked in her lips for a moment, her eyes bulging with fear. At last she whispered, "Somehow she... she is free and – and doing all kinds of mean and nasty tricks... She visits me in my dreams – they're horrible!" The girl sobbed.

"I know," Gopher said gently, remembering her dream, from which he had rescued her, of how those accusing whispers had affected him.

His heartfelt concern reassured her to go on. "I feel her and I'm afraid that she feels me, too, like she's still a part of me. She may already know that you've returned – when you came into my dream."

Gopher said, after a moment's pause to gather himself so that he could sound chipper than he really felt, "Well then, I will just have to wake Menlow up as soon as possible! Then you won't have to worry. I think Menlow will know how to handle her! You see he really was a wizard, the greatest that ever lived."

Gopher realized the moment he said it that he had broken his promise to keep Menlow's past a secret. Up to this point he had managed to keep it. He had not told what the hermit had been in his enchantment, except as the Steward of the Realm.

The girl's jaw dropped. "Is he really?"

Gopher cleared his throat. "Uh, you keep that a secret, okay? He was a wizard, but not anymore, though he still knows a lot about magic. He will help us – once he's awake."

At least Adia did not detect the lack of confidence in his voice, for waking the ex-wizard up was a done deal in her mind. Being reassured, she soon fell asleep. As her breathing deepened and steadied, he worried. She would probably tell her father, despite her promise of secrecy, and then they would expect great magical and wondrous things. They would not be the only ones disappointed, however. It was painful to think how Menlow would feel when he found out that his secret was out. Yet even if she kept her promise, it was bad enough that Gopher had broken his.

Somehow he fell asleep, which, considering his feelings, proved just how exhausted he was. It was a deep unbroken sleep that he would have called perfect, since absolutely no dreams visited him, but the thing about not having dreams was that there is no gauge to measure time. It seemed but a moment before he was being jostled awake. The jostling wouldn't stop, and when he came fully to his senses, which took longer to do coming from a deep sleep, he wished indeed that he was having a dream. That was because he was inside the familiar cage, and, even worse, Well's face was smiling at him through its bars. It was nothing short of his worst nightmare come true.

"Good to see you again, Gopher," Wells said. The friendly glint was in his eyes, but there seemed to be something else, something new that Gopher did not like. The man had changed since the rodent had last seen him. Had it been the rapiscan, or had something else happened to him?

Gopher's astonishment and horror constricted his throat. He looked around and, upon seeing the empty rumpled bed, his concern for the girl trumped all other emotions.

"Where is she?" he rasped.

"My new partner is, uh – entertaining her. It seems like their old friends, and they have a lot of catching up to do."

"Let me go!" Gopher exclaimed.

"I didn't let you go last time. Why would I start now? You know what? I'll let them decide."

"Let me go!" the rodent repeated. He was so worked up that he didn't realize that the man was taking him out of the room.

Wells replied, "Now, now, why would I do that? So you can go about playing your pranks some more? What are you going to do next, huh? Burn down the town? I think not! Your days of mischief are over!"

"It *looks* like a gopher," a stranger's voice said.

It wasn't until then that Gopher realized that he had been moved to the front room where there were nine other men with familiar looks of amazement and suspicion on their faces. He was on display once again.

"Sure he looks like a gopher," Wells addressed the speaker, "but do gophers talk? Don't be fooled, councilmen! It is a pixie! I saw it roaming the streets last night in its true shape and I followed it here like I told you. I peeked in and saw it change into this shape so nobody would suspect. You see, pixies can change shapes and sizes and they have powerful magic, but you don't have to be afraid any longer – not of this pixie at least. When they are caged, so is their magic. This one won't hurt you in this... but it may not be the end of your troubles, I fear, gentlemen."

"What do you mean?" said one, whose eyes were narrowed suspiciously.

Wells replied, "I mean – where is the girl? Isn't she supposed to be friends with this – err, pixie? Perhaps she has other fairy friends to whom she has fled for help."

"Maybe we should kill it," put in another. "That's what it deserves after it flooded my wife's garden and turned my roof moldy! It even sealed my door shut so that I had to get out through the window! Don't laugh! Think of the other things it has done that was *not* funny: sinking our boats, damaging the town's goods, setting that miller's shed on fire, punching holes in all the water buckets. Killing it would teach the other ones, if there are any more, not to fool with us."

"But I didn't do those things!" Gopher cried. "It was a hamadryad! She did them –"

"Ah! That proves it!" Wells said, "There *are* others! And think, my dear fellows! If the pixie is friends with her, maybe it is with the other fairies, too. Might they not take revenge on the entire town if he is killed?"

He paused and then raised a finger as if under sudden inspiration. "Wait a moment. If I take this – pixie – with me away from here, maybe the others will follow. Then they'll be my problem, and not yours."

The one with the narrowed eyes replied slowly: "How come you're so helpful and willing to take on so much for us? You've just been in town for over a week and haven't even opened up your trading goods store yet. We don't even know you."

Wells did not bat an eye but replied, "True, I've only been here for a short time, but I admit that I have a selfish angle. You see, my helpfulness is really the businessman in me talking. When I saw that pixie turn into a gopher and heard it talk, I got the idea people might pay to see a pixie even if he did look like a gopher. I'll have to take my chances about any other fairies coming after me…. Mmm…. I might even use him as bait. What if I captured the whole lot of them? With my experience of hunting and trapping, I am the man to do it, and it'll solve your problem and put money in my pocket. We all could win!"

"Don't listen to him! He's lying!" Gopher exclaimed, but it was too late. Their attention was divided between Wells' slick proposal and the ensuing arguments. He tried several times to get himself heard, but then he became distracted when he heard them including the fate of Adia and her father in their arguments. Wells interrupted them.

"Really, sirs, it's none of my business, but what is there to worry about? She's just a girl. What can she do by herself? I am sure that this pixie and the rest of them put her up to it. Anyhow, that is your concern – or actually it is her father's, isn't it? He's still your mayor, despite what's happened here today (which, of course, is perfectly understandable and justified since you acted for the good of the town)."

This statement did not seem to settle anything but rather stirred up new arguments about whether or not the mayor should be removed, if the whole family should be sent out of the village, or if charges should be laid at his door to recoup for the losses caused by Adia and her friends. Gopher made out that a couple of them were willing to give the mayor a chance; while three agreed that since now they had proof, charges should be made; but the rest urged that ousting the entire family would solve the problem and that it should be done immediately before Adia could make any more trouble. Yet in the end it was decided that it should be voted on by the entire township. One of the more important leaders (if his waist-length beard and sober poise were any indications) added: "After all, it was with the town's consent that enabled us to enter here and affect this creature's capture in the first place."

Gopher did not understand what was meant by this statement until he was taken outside. The entire town seemed to be assembled in front of the house and to be bickering with each other, which stopped immediately when the group filed out the door. The bickering was replaced by silence, until Wells promptly announced while holding up the cage, "Here is the culprit!"

This was met with looks of disdain and skepticism, along with guffaws and snorts, from the young to the old, the poor to the rich, the wise to the simpleton, all except for the youngest of the crowd who evidently hadn't been so troubled by the pranks.

"So *this* is what has been causing all of the hubbub?" said a woman.

"Bah! A gopher can't do what it did to me!" exclaimed the raspy voice of an old man.

"You are right about that. There's been more than just digging holes in gardens," said a younger sounding man.

"You *are* right!" exclaimed a man. "He didn't do any of it! He's innocent!"

It was the sound of his voice, more than what he said that made Gopher look up, because he recognized it as belonging to the mayor. He then saw that the town people were tightly surrounding him, like one held prisoner. Dryden tried to pull away.

"He is my daughter's pet and nothing more. You have no right –"

"Nothing more?" said one of the councilmen next to Gopher's cage. "Nothing more? That's preposterous. Who would make a gopher into a pet, and, besides, since when did your daughter make friends with a *talking* gopher? That's right, people. We all heard him ourselves! And if a gopher can talk, I would bet (if I were a betting man) that he can do a lot more than dig up gardens!"

This resulted in a commotion that the councilman probably had not counted on. At first it was only raised voices, but soon Gopher found himself in the midst of a throng, of which he was not only the center but also the target of the townspeople. More people than just Wells were holding on to cage now. Other hands tugged at it this way and that, along with faces peering in and saying things like "Now talk!" and "Why don't you say something?" and "Gimme! I'll make him sing!" Then a booming voice that was even more powerful than Mayor Dryden's settled them all down instantly like water on fire.

"STOP! EVERYONE! THIS GOPHER IS NOT TO BLAME!"

Those around the cage parted and Gopher saw the approach of a dark-browed man. It wasn't until he faced the cage (though he was staring malevolently at Wells all the while) that the rodent recognized the man to be Loggins. He was unshaven and unkempt with clothes that, if the smell was any indication, had not been washed for a long time, but it was his blazing eyes, the sternness in his face, and his powerful bearing that drew everyone's attention, including Gopher's. His indignation made his stout frame appear twice as big.

"Listen!" he said, his voice now somewhat lowered, though still booming. His stare remained fixed on Wells who met it with a stone-face. "Me and this man here used to be partners and we captured this gopher once before. He *can* talk and we used to make money going from town to town showing him off, but he played no tricks on anyone, unless you call escaping from us a trick. We came to recapture him because we knew he has a friend here, a hermit named Menlow. But I changed my mind about the whole set up. You see, my partner had also changed – and in ways that I didn't like – ever since he climbed over the mayor's garden wall. He had found something other than a talking gopher: one of those fairy creatures. It was she who played all those tricks on you with my partner's help. I know because I followed them one time, but the fairy caught me and she gave me a thrashing I'll never forget. I ran away and have been hiding ever since, but I'm not afraid anymore! The gopher doesn't deserve this!"

Then a voice spoke that Gopher thought came from Wells, though it sounded different, like a hoarse whisper.

"It is only because you forgot the lesson I taught you. Looks like school's back in session!" it hissed.

With shrill cackling, Wells leaped on Loggins and began pummeling him. But then Gopher saw that Wells had not moved at all; rather, it was his shadow that was all over Loggins: hitting, kicking, biting, hair-pulling, and scratching so fast that it seemed to be all happening at the same time. Wells just stood there and was laughing, while Loggins tried to fight back. The shadowy hamadryad was so fast in her strikes that Loggins ended up hitting himself almost as much as she was.

It might have been funny but the reality of seeing a shadow beating up a huge flesh-and-bone man proved very disconcerting to the townsfolk. In shrieks and cries that blended in with Loggins, many of them fled. But when the man fell to the ground and began rolling about while kicking, clawing, and screaming, some of the younger in the crowd snickered, though even they gave a wider berth to the strange fight. It was at this time that Wells took a few more steps back and brought the cage up to eye-level.

"Now we'll be off," he whispered, "but you'd better be quiet or I'll shake this cage until it hurts."

To show what he meant he gave it a little jolt, which flung Gopher painfully against the iron bars. Instead of intimidating the rodent, however, it actually provoked him so that he forgot his fear.

"Where are you taking me?" he demanded.

Wells did not answer him as he carried the cage back into the mayor's house. For a fleeting moment, Gopher had a thought that Wells was taking him to where Menlow lay, but the man sped on through and so came to the garden. His captor finally answered Gopher's question when the screams and shouts and scuffling were far enough away.

"Just a detour. Up and over and then through some back alleys and we'll be free. Oh, and speaking of freedom, I'll just toss this back in. Don't need Maythenia anymore." He pulled out a sliver of wood from a pocket interior – a heart-sliver – and snickered. "She was quite helpful and fun, but now unnecessary."

Hurrying through the overgrown garden and then past the surrounding hedge, they reached the Great Oak Tree. It looked unchanged in outward appearance: its twisted branches spread out in all directions from its dying, twisted trunk where the jagged slit seemed as large and dark and fatal as it did before.

Yet now, because of the dream, Gopher understood that its darkness was part of the tree itself – part of the hamadryad herself. It issued from the hollow-spot where Maythenia had taken the heart-slivers, leaving an ever-growing vacuum. In an instant, Gopher understood the hamadryad's lonely desperation that made her basically abandon her tree to latch on to a little girl, through whom she could be free and enjoy life again; how she had hated anyone who stood between them, particularly Gopher; and how her feelings of being betrayed by Adia now propelled her to increasingly hateful and bitter acts towards her and everyone else. Even Wells had been part of her campaign of hate and retribution that now went beyond mere tricks. She had been using him just as much as he had been using her.

Part of him knew he ought to feel afraid of that darkness, but the greater part – the part where his hatred for his captor was prompted by his desperate concern for the mayor's daughter – connected with the tree's hatred, one fueling the other.

Then suddenly, as he felt a connection to the tree, Gopher saw Adia in his mind so vividly that it was like seeing her with his eyes.

She was being held captive underground within a tangle of the Oak Tree's roots, which were serving as both bars and manacles. Her fear seemed as tangible to him as the cold darkness around her. Her lips barely moved, but the moaning in her throat exuded terror and misery that the tree's void was sapping into. This terror and misery were Maythenia's revenge.

With revulsion he sought to pull away from his oneness with the tree. Although he understood the bitterness the tree fairy felt, cruelty towards someone whom she once called friend was unforgivably despicable. It was that which convinced Gopher of her underlying selfishness, which had once masked itself as friendship. He hated her as much as Wells who had pretended friendship in his quest for riches and fame. Their selfishness had made his life miserable.

Suddenly he saw in his mind another mental picture. From the depths of the earth, farther than even the roots of the tree could reach, creatures emerged – twenty five goblins. As distasteful as they were, he experienced their feelings as if they were his own. Hate and rage coursed through them, born from a long lifetime of living in darkness and harsh edges and uncertain footing where self-pity grew into hatred for others who had it better than themselves.

Squinting red eyes gleamed with those feelings along with hard, cruel smiles that revealed pointed sharp teeth. They climbed upward with amazing speed through the darkness upon broad feet and with strong, gnarled hands that, when not climbing or digging, sought only to destroy. Their hate seemed to reach out to him. In fact, as the goblins drew closer, their hate did not so much as try to draw him to their purpose as it did to merge with his own hate and emblazon it to the point that he forgot to be disgusted or even alarmed at their approach; that is, until he saw some of them reach the girl's cage of tree roots and felt their deadly intentions.

"No!" Gopher screamed aloud.

All that he had seen and felt leading up to this moment had hardly taken any time at all. In fact, Wells was just then throwing the heart-sliver into the tree's opening, At the same time one of the goblins emerged from the tree's dark maw and caught it in his teeth. It then smiled a sharp toothy grin that emphasized the hate in its eyes.

Wells screamed, dropped the cage, and fled. The evil creature uttered a guttural cry and gave chase, its arms and legs scrambling like a disjointed but very fast horse.

For a moment Gopher felt the goblin's pleasure and thrill, hoping that the man would suffer just as much as he deserved, but then he remembered Adia – and realized his guilt. For it was then that it occurred to him that he had somehow summoned them, and because of them, Adia was endangered even worse than if she had been left merely to Maythenia's devices. At least then there might be hope for her since the hamadryad was capable of some semblance of friendship no matter how selfish she might be. With the goblins there was nothing but irrational anger and hate – which he also felt was directed towards him when a dozen of them emerged from the tree's gash and surrounded his cage.

Chapter Thirty

In a way, it was Adia who saved him from the goblins. Yet actually – or more directly – it was Gopher's magic that came to his aid. That wouldn't have occurred, however, if his concern for the girl hadn't triggered it into action. This was how it happened:

While being surrounded by goblins that had no other thought than what they might do to him (some were in favor of eating him, others of setting him on fire and then kicking him around for sport), the rodent in contrast did not think of them at all. In his mind he saw two goblins prying at the roots that imprisoned Adia who cried and writhed about helplessly. Instead of being hateful towards her would-be assailants or feeling the same fear that she was experiencing, something else reached out to Gopher that was far stronger than either emotion. It was pity. He didn't know where it came from, but it made him capable of wishing that he could be in her place. Thus, neither hate nor fear had any hold over him.

At that very moment he felt a connection was made and immediately saw in his mind ten dwarves in armor wielding axes climbing from the depths, just as the goblins had done. He felt in them an iron-clad determination, even to the point of sacrificing their lives, if need be, to rid the world of these goblins.

Not being stealthy creatures, their approach was heard by the goblins around the girl's cage. As a result, the foul creatures attacked first, but they were no match for the dwarves' axes and daggers or the unwavering courage that wielded them in a deadly counter attack. The goblins were slain almost as quickly and easily as the same blades sliced through the tree roots to free Adia. With relief he saw the girl being carried up to the surface, though rather clumsily, by one of her rescuers. By this time, the rest of the dwarves had also become Gopher's rescuers as they had catapulted themselves out of the tree trunk and fell upon the remaining goblins. The latter bounded over the walls in flight as the dwarves pursued with their axes raised over their heads and a triumphant cry of "Aiii!"

Gopher yearned to go with them, though it was not for the thrill of the chase but for something that was more satisfying than any thrill could ever be. In this case, it was justice, not hate or vengeance, but seeing that the right thing was done. Fortunately, though, Gopher was being thwarted this satisfaction by being confined in the cage, for it was likely that, given his size and lack of fighting abilities, more harm would come to him than good.

The sounds of sniffling distracted him and drew his gaze over to the foot of the great Oak where the little girl lay hunkered, her shoulders shaking.

"Adia!" Gopher cried out. It took him three times to get her attention. Her bedraggled, tear-glistened face lit up when she saw him, a look that lit up his insides as well.

"Gopher!" the girl exclaimed.

With nervous excitement, she removed the peg and opened the cage door. Their joyous reunion was but for a moment, when consternation sharpened her features.

"Where's my father?"

Her concern provoked his own, especially since he realized the mayor's danger with so many goblins running about.

"He's on the street," Gopher said, and added with more hope than he felt, "But the dwarves will protect him."

He knew, though, there would not be enough dwarves to handle them all. But what could he do? The question provoked an immediate answer as if it had always been there waiting for him to discover it. He *could* help, for now he knew how!

Meanwhile, the girl responded as impulsively as any loving and brave daughter would whose parent was in danger. She started out at once with Gopher still in her grasp, though momentarily forgotten.

"No, wait!" Gopher said in a voice of authority that surprised even him. It seemed to do the same to her, for she immediately stopped, though her face was scrunched up with a nervous tension that seemed ready to make her bolt anyway.

"We have to do something!" she said.

"I will. Give me just a moment to use my magic. I know how to use it now. It's how the dwarves saved you."

The rodent tried not to let her anxiety distract him as he gathered his thoughts and feelings. The attempt was made harder because her hands, which still held him, reflected her perplexed state of mind. In other words, her fingers were unconsciously squeezing and pressing him. He didn't tell her to let him down because he was afraid that she might go rushing off.

Desperately, he forced the awareness of his surroundings – and the discomfort that Adia's hands caused – to the back of his thoughts and reached out with his concern for the mayor, but at once he knew that it was no good. He didn't feel towards Dryden the way he felt about his daughter. What could he do now?

Then he had an idea. He began focusing on goodness, nobility, joy, sweetness, light, and courage... anything that was good, for that would call the kind of fairy that would come to their rescue – and Dryden's. Yet even as he tried, it occurred to him just how difficult, even impossible, it was to fathom these virtues in his imagination. The effort of imagining them had the opposite intended effect, making them elusive, vague, and even illusionary.

Another idea came to him. He would think of things that were good, noble and courageous to inspire such feelings. He imagined goodness as a radiant, white light... nobility as a high mountain with lofty peaks...courage as a towering oak enduring the thrashing of a thunderstorm...

"Gopher, is it working?" Adia interrupted with impatience in her voice.

"Yes," he lied. The images in his imagination did not evoke those virtues that he intended, just pictures that inspired hardly any feelings at all. "Just wait a little more..."

He closed his eyes and tried painting more pictures in his mind – a sunset, an eagle soaring, a powerful waterfall – but nothing happened. Feeling hopeless, he tried a third time, feeling despairing, confused, and wearied. What *were* goodness, honor, and courage but ideas and notions? When he really stopped to think, they seemed so vague and unreal, like a fog that grew thicker the more he tried to decipher their substance. Were they even real?

Suddenly, however, a connection was made, but, much to his dismay, he saw in his mind what he had connected to; a thick grey fog where right and wrong, reality and illusions, were mixed and confused. It was, in fact, the same mist from which the banshee had emerged. He felt this in his heart to be true – and he felt beyond the fog's wispy fringes to its dark center where it was even scarier than the feelings that the banshee had stirred in him. At once he pushed the image out of his mind, but he knew it was too late. When he opened his eyes, Adia was staring him in the face with eyes that reflected an inner struggle between anxiety and expectancy. Even the pressure that her fingers were exerting was preferable to that fog.

"I – I did it. Let's go," Gopher said, trying to sound more positive than he felt. Really he hoped that he hadn't done it at all; hoped that it had just been a dream and that he had not changed anything.

Adia, still carrying him, rushed through the garden, neatly but thoughtlessly avoiding every root, hedge, mound, and low-lying branch. When they passed through the house, Gopher thought to suggest that they should check on Menlow first but he did not get the chance. The noises that were coming from the street propelled her that much faster as much as it repelled him. Shrieks of terror, battle cries, metal clanging, feet scuffling, and voices raised in anger and terror, all made Gopher inwardly cringe in fear.

The girl anxiously muttering her father's name did not make him feel any better, either, because there was another reason, besides danger, why Gopher did not want to go out there. When

Adia brought him out the front door, his fear was confirmed. The connection had not been a dream. The town seemed to have disappeared. In its place a swirling wall of fog faced them. It seemed impenetrable at first but then he glimpsed dark, grey, and white blotches of vague shapes flitting about here and there. They and the sounds that issued forth betokened life, but Gopher knew that even the soupy miasma was, in a strangely twisted way, alive in itself; he could sense it, just like he could with the goblins and the dwarves underground. However, there was nothing vivid or solid about the fog that he could see in his mind. It was a living death, in which its life was sustained by spreading confusion and disorder. It was alive like a disease was alive.

As he stared at the blotches, some of them would start to become visible as they drew near, but the next moment they would fade into indistinct shapes and shadows in the fog as they receded. Sometimes he would see a resemblance of a face or a hand or a limb, sometimes human, at other times animal, and often it looked like some fantastical creature from the Age of Magic. His magic gave him no more certainty than his eyes did. In fact, the more he tried to discern the images, whether through his eyes or magic, the less sure he became that they were anything more than his imagination making shapes out of the wreathing, shifting fog.

Then he heard voices that were not so indefinite, human voices which had not come with the fog but were victims of it. He thought of Dryden and the villagers. So did Adia.

"Father! Are you there?"

"Is that you, Adia?" replied a woman's voice.

"Yes! Where's my father?"

"Don't talk to her!" exclaimed a man. "It's a trick! She brought on this blasted fog like everything else!"

"Ha! Why should I trust you?" the woman's responded harshly.

"I did not bring this –" began Adia, when she was interrupted.

"Adia? Is that you?" The voice was frightened and sounded far away, but there was no doubt even to Gopher in its familiarity.

"Father!"

The girl started towards the fog, much to Gopher's terror. Its tendrils at the wispy edges looked like hands beckoning them to enter, but his terror kept him from warning her before it was too late: They plunged in – and in that very moment they were lost. Going forward had no practical meaning as they could see nothing but gray and feel nothing but a numbing cold that made feeling their way around impossible.

"Where are you, Father?" Adia's voice called out, but if she hadn't still been holding him, Gopher would have had trouble telling where *her* voice was coming from.

At some point (for time itself seemed confused) they ran into a living mass of gray, which was the only color seemingly allowed by the mist. Terrified shrieks resulted in the collision and simultaneously exploded in a number of directions. The next moment, except for their trailing cries, it was as if the mass had never been. Even so, their sounds quickly blended in with the rest of the cacophony that was part of the confusing, blinding vapor. Had they been some of the townspeople huddled together, he wondered? Then Adia confirmed it.

"I saw Harrow and Tobias... one ran that way and the other went over there... no, that way... oh, why did they have to run?" the girl wailed.

The names Harrow and Tobias sounded familiar to Gopher... Yes, he remembered. Harrow had been the one who had found Adia unconscious in the forest, and Tobias had been the woodcutter... It occurred to him why they had screamed and run away.

"They probably think we're monsters, too," Gopher said. "It's so easy to jump to conclusions in this stuff."

Then a voice sounded so muted that it was impossible to tell how close or far it was. "Is that you, Adia? It's me, your father. I'm over here."

Here, however, sounded as likely to be coming from the left as it did from the right, or even from front or behind.

"Where?"

"Here," he repeated uselessly, but then added, "You stay put. There're things in the fog that are evil. I'll try to come to you. I think I can tell where you are."

Staying put, however, became impossible when an ogre seemingly materialized in front of them. Broad-shouldered and tall, its body was shaped like a large muscular man, but it had the head of a boar – a boar, that is, that wore an iron helmet which matched the rest of its spiky armor. In its presence, Gopher felt its insatiable hunger for violence, such as he had felt when the vines had attacked his captors, or when the changeling had been unmasked, or more recently by the goblins. This malevolence was immediately demonstrated as the creature fell upon them with a snarl, but its attack was cut short when another large figure knocked it to the side. Surprisingly, though, instead of a fight ensuing, the ogre fled, yelping like a whipped puppy, the sounds of which quickly diminished as if swallowed by the mist. There was no doubt in Gopher's mind that its hunger for violence only included attacking those who did not put up a fight.

Their rescuer then turned and loomed over them for a moment as if considering their fate. He was larger than the ogre by at least a foot both in height and width. It had one eye in the center of its forehead over a broad flat nose and an almost human mouth. It wore no armor probably because its leathery skin, covered in thick furry patches, needed none. Despite its abhorrent appearance and size, Gopher did not feel as afraid of it as he did of the ogre. Perhaps it was because the Cyclops had rescued them, even though that may not have been its intention. Whatever Gopher's feelings were, it became quickly evident that they were not shared by Adia.

She screamed "Dad!" as she fled blindly into the fog with Gopher still in her hands. Although she had gotten far enough to get out of sight of the Cyclops, it was not enough to get away from its pursuit. The one-eyed creature seemed to materialize out of the fog in front of them (or she had inadvertently run in a circle) and the beast snatched her up in its huge hand. At the same time she dropped Gopher on to the ground. Even as small as he was, though, the monster's other hand scooped him right up, his fingers closing over him just tight enough to cage him in his palm. The creature then began running through the mist with speed and sureness of step as if the fog were no hindrance at all.

The Cyclops skidded to a stop when four knights barred his way, their armor glistening brightly in contrast to the surrounding grayness. Gopher felt hope rise up at the sight of them. Now these, and not the fog, were the kind of help that he had meant to summon when he had focused on nobility, courage, fortitude, and strength.

Two of the knights swung their broadsword at the Cyclops, while another wielded a battle axe with deadly intent. Yet, despite their quick moves, the creature proved amazingly quick for its huge size, neatly avoiding their attacks with sidesteps and ducking at the appropriate moments, but it was the fourth knight who proved the most difficult. He neither wielded a sword nor an axe, but instead he came charging and grabbed the Cyclops around its torso with his gauntleted arms. Gopher was surprised to see that his captor did nothing about it, that it could have easily sidestepped his lunge; rather, it was focused on avoiding the axe and swords of the other knights who took up the fight again. The fourth knight's metal-shod feet dragged and skidded with his armor clanking as the Cyclops spun this way and that, ducking and swaying, all as easily as if the creature did not have any additional weight around its middle, though that quickly changed.

With all that moving about, the knight's armor began shaking apart, piece by piece, while still clinging to the monster... until his protective covering had completely fallen away. What remained was not a man but a living skeleton. His bones now were doing all the rattling, but somehow remained intact.

Even more surprising was that the other two knights forgot about fighting the Cyclops and began to laugh at their disrobed fellow. It was that mockery which "unmanned" the skeleton-knight the most, for it suddenly realized its exposed condition and let go of the Cyclops to crouch down and begin gathering its scattered pieces of armor. Then, to Gopher's increased amazement and disgust, the other knights began to attack their peer, spanking him with the broad side of their swords, kicking his armor pieces about, and taunting him with such phrases like "I've got a bone to pick with you!" and "Ah, you're not one of us! You don't have the guts!"

With a furious roar the one-eyed beast swung a leg in a wide half circle and swept the knights aside so that they went rattling quite noisily into the fog, while leaving their skeletal comrade alone. Gopher wondered what was beneath *their* armor, but never saw, because the Cyclops continued on his way.

The grey fog enveloped them once again, though it seemed but a few steps when the Cyclops stopped for a second time. Before them a large group of hags and imps and gargoyles were huddled together. A familiar slinking creature dominated them with its accusatory wailing as it quickly moved this way and that to keep them massed together in a fearful heap.

It was the banshee. Its wails broke Gopher's heart anew with demands for more pity than could be given, somehow conveying in its shriek an unbearable weight that made him feel both worthless and guilty. It was Adia's sobbing that drew the banshee's attention. With a shrill cry, the piteous creature sprang directly at the Cyclops, like a charging bull.

Instead of attacking back, however, the one-eyed monster stepped to the side just before the moment of collision. The banshee passed by in a blur, and the creature rolled, righted itself, let out a mournful and angry yowl, and rounded back. When it sprang again, however, its flight was arrested suddenly in midair as if it had struck an invisible wall when the Cyclops roared, though it was not a roar of anger but of fearless challenge.

The one-eyed giant strode forward, bringing its head low to meet the banshee face to face… and then it started snickering. The Cyclops' shoulders began to shake, and its mouth grinned, showing teeth that were surprisingly human-like, as the monster's snickering turned to laugher.

At the same time, the banshee's wail faded to a whimper, as the levity of his opponent seemed to leave it bereft of its power not only to accuse but also to physically attack. Then the creature sunk even closer to the ground and slinked pathetically away.

When the Cyclops turned back, the hags and imps were now surrounded by shadowy, ominous beings whose hollow moans –

like wind echoing through the deep regions of a cavern – sent a foreboding shiver down Gopher's spine. Their pathetic, repulsive captives shrieked and writhed about in a frenzy of terror, clinging together in mass.

One of the ominous beings – a slope-backed, black-robed figure with an insidious grin on a skeletal face – broke off from the others and started gliding directly towards the Cyclops. Its hollow moaning changed into a high-pitched shrieking of a gale wind. A wave of fear that could almost be physically felt like the thickness of the grey fog preceded it. At the phantom's approach, Gopher tried to bite into his captor's hand to escape, though the skin was too thick. Adia kicked, scratched, and thrashed about in its other hand. The Cyclops, however, did not seem to notice either of them in the least, nor did it show to be in the least intimidated by the advancing phantom. In fact, it came forward in an almost relaxed posture with noises coming out of its throat that did not sound hostile or even defensive.

For a moment the Cyclops and the phantom stopped within arm's length, facing each other. Then, after an exchange of moans and guttural sounds, Gopher was simply and suddenly handed over. As much as he was surprised, it was not enough of a shock to prevent him from reacting like any other gopher by darting out as soon as the creature opened its hand – only to be immediately caught... by nothing at all... It seemed like he was floating, though it was hard to tell because of all the pressing, thick grayness. He could not feel the ground and when he tried to move, he seemed to be staying in one spot.

Then he felt the phantom's deathly cold breath on him as it moaned. Gopher got the distinct impression that the specter was trying to tell him something, but then cackles, shrieks, and screeches erupted to his right from the huddled creatures. The remaining phantoms were gliding towards them from three sides, so that their captives fled in terror towards the only way open to them. Soon the sight, though not the sound, of both the foul creatures and their ghostly herders disappeared into the swirling mist. That was when he realized that the Cyclops had gone with them – as well as Adia.

"NO!" he cried.

The phantom moaned sorrowfully in his ear, which might have plunged him into the very depths of despair if he hadn't been there already. Adia was gone, Farwyll had deserted him, and Menlow was beyond reach. All hope of joy had been extinguished. Nothing mattered, all had lost value to him, and he ceased to care.

That was why he was unaware of the fog starting to dissipate; nor did he realize that the moaning began to change, to form together into sounds that became more and more distinct. Even when they had become words, he did not hear them; that is, not until a sharp pain shot through him.

"Sorry about that," the Traveling Merchant was saying, "but sometimes pain is the only thing that'll get one's attention."

That was when Gopher saw that they were no longer in the fog. The barrier of mist was behind them, and they were facing the mayor's house. He also saw that it was the Traveling Merchant who held him, and not a phantom. The funny old man chuckled.

"They'll be safely out on the other side of the fog soon. Nasty stuff!"

"Who...?" Gopher asked dumbly. He wanted to think that nothing made sense anymore, but he knew that wasn't true; somehow it was *he* who hadn't been making sense.

"Who? Oh, do you mean the townspeople?" the Traveling Merchant replied, then added, "Though they probably didn't look like themselves to you, I suppose. And don't worry, the girl and her father, of course, are with them, too. Farwyll will make sure of it (oh, he was the Cyclops, for there was no trick of the fog about his appearance). I also sent two dwarfs to seek out any stragglers, just in case."

As the old man talked, and the fog retreated from his thinking, Gopher began to remember that the hags and imps had actually resembled the townspeople. As for the Cyclops, even though it retained its appearance in his memory, Gopher now recognized the creature, through the familiarity that came through his magic, to have been Farwyll.

It was while he was gleaning these facts from his "foggy" memory that the Traveling Merchant carried Gopher to the door of the mayor's house.

Chapter Thirty-One

The Traveling Merchant bent down and placed the rodent on the doorstep. He did not straighten up but looked Gopher almost levelly face to face.

"A lot has happened since we parted ways," the old man said, "Too much to tell, and too wonderful. It was a vision, a revelation, against which all my other visions and dreams pale by comparison. It was as if they all led up to it, for it was to be my last – and greatest."

"Why?"

"It's because I don't need them anymore. The visions were just glimpses. Now I see much more clearly, though still not clearly enough. The revelation had started a change in me – but that may not be quite right. 'Started a completion in me' fits better. If only you had been there..." he trailed off wistfully but after a moment he shook his head and continued, "But you are here now and *now* is what matters. It is your turn. I know because in that last vision I also saw this very moment. I saw you standing here and going in. Alone. What is in there is for you.

"But," he continued, putting a finger up for emphasis, "the importance of what I have to tell you is enormous. Now, listen: in truth you will *not* be alone. Remember that, believe it, hold on to it. No matter how you feel, someone will be with you, someone who will give you strength when you have none left, if you but ask. Don't worry that you do not understand now, just trust what I'm telling you."

"But who will it be?"

"He is the One who lingers near an honest answer, a kind deed, a friendly pat on the back, and, above all, a trusting heart. But you will find that trusting is harder than dying, but only at first. I do not say these things to alarm you, but alarm you they must, for you need to know that the price is high."

"What about Menlow?"

"I can't promise anything, because nothing is mine to promise. For any chance to help him you must do this first, however. Now go, if you will, and remember what I told you."

Wordlessly, Gopher went trembling forward only a few inches, for he found that fear had clamped his throat and stiffened his limbs. The Traveling Merchant smiled, patted him lightly on his furry back for encouragement, and opened the door a few inches. Wide enough to pass through, but too wide for how he felt at that moment. Fixing his determination to help his dying friend, the rodent quickly slipped in before he could think better of it.

The moment that Gopher crossed the threshold, he knew that the Traveling Merchant's words, no matter how much they had meant to encourage and warn him, had not been enough to prepare him for what assailed him. Such intense heat and light made him more aware of being mere flesh and bone – with highly combustible fur – than he had ever been before. The source of his extreme discomfort was a fierce blaze in the fireplace, which had been darkened and cold only a short while ago (though it now seemed ages). It burned so blindingly bright that he could not look at it; in fact, the entire room was lit up like the inside of a furnace. The light itself felt as if it even pierced through his tightly-shut eyelids.

It was only by his magic that enabled him to see. The room was completely barren of furniture as if even their ashes had been burned up, which was not surprising considering the intense heat. What surprised him was that he had not been burned up the very moment he had entered and that the house itself had not gone up in flames. Every instinct for survival screamed for him to flee.

He nearly succumbed to the urge to escape, but then the impossibility of his situation occurred to him. He *was* bearing the heat and light and even able to think while every bit of his fur felt as if it were about to burst into flame. It was all impossible, unless the Traveling Merchant was right. However, he did not particularly *feel* protected.

Even so, the argument to flee was still stronger because for the life of him he could not fathom any reason for having to go through this cursed heat. What would be the point of getting burned up, after all? How would that help Menlow?

From where he was, there was no other way to reach the hermit's room, unless... he was to go back outside and around to the window – and why not, he suddenly realized? Outside and through the window instead of going through a literal furnace – it made irrefutable sense, while *this* was plain ludicrous and unnecessary! Anyway, what kind of protector would let him suffer this much?

Then he remembered something else the Traveling Merchant had said: Trusting was harder than death. Of that he knew without a doubt, because he was experiencing it just by staying where he was and denying himself the urge to escape. He realized that actually he was doing all of this just because of only those few words that the Traveling Merchant had said. How did he really know there was an invisible Protector?

Yet somehow he still lived; he still had the will power to resist, and because of it and his trusting nature, he forced himself to move forward. The floor felt like hot coals, though he did not analyze how his paws could endure it, not without giving it all up at once. The burning did not stop there, however. He took a deep breath to steady himself before going on, only to find that the air scolded his lungs, and the burning did not stop there either. His entire body, inside and out, now felt like it was on fire... but miraculously he found the will and strength to hold on, if only barely. Yet he felt himself slipping.

A hardened determination rose up in him after realizing that he'd fail if he hesitated any longer. He literally pushed beyond the pain by crawling forward, somehow ignoring the demands that the searing pain made on his body, on his mind.

He managed only a few inches, though, when he found that his body would not, or could not, go any further against that seemingly solid wall of burning pain. He felt his determination collapse, but that did not give any relief to the unceasing, inescapable, and unconquerable heat. It was of no use. He could not move, either forward or back, could not escape now even if he chose to... that was the end of it. All the pain and the heat had been for nothing, except to drain him of energy and even the will to live.

Somehow it did not drain him of the power of thought, however. If someone was indeed protecting him, what good was that? No amount of thinking would be able to see him through this. Hadn't the Traveling Merchant said that he would receive enough strength to go on? Had it all been a lie and a twisted nasty joke to get him to go as far as he could in this heat just to be tormented along the way and to burn up in the end? Knowing the Traveling Merchant as he did, he could not accept that – would not accept it no matter how bad the burning seemed to be screaming it.

Then it suddenly occurred to the rodent: If someone *was* there, why not ask him for more strength? After all, isn't that what the Traveling Merchant had also said for him to do? In fact, he realized that he had been doing all of this as if he *were* alone, or as if the other person did not really care, which was not that much different than being alone. Either way, he realized that he had not been fully trusting. Considering his situation, he had no other choice, unless it was to let himself be burned up, which in itself was becoming surprisingly tempting since death itself would be a relief. He shut his mind to that thought immediately. Menlow needed him.

"Help – me," the rodent squeaked out to his invisible Protector, hoping that he would be heard. He did not know if that was possible because he could barely hear himself, but it was all he could manage.

He then found that he could move an inch, even though the wall of heat pushed against him as much as ever, if not more.

Encouraged by even this small progress, he continued to plead in his tiny voice, "Let – me – make – it – please – please." Slowly, as he squeaked out each word, he somehow dragged himself forward some more. The burning increased to the point that the thought of burning up to end the pain was now an unrelenting desire like a man in a desert craving water. More than ever, though, he desperately tried not to give in as he focused on his words, saying, "I can't – make it by myself – the pain – take it away!"

Almost immediately the burning sensation changed. He still felt its intensity but its pain had wonderfully diminished. It was wonderful for two reasons: firstly, in the exquisite relief from the overwhelming pain, and secondly, from knowing, really knowing, that he had been heard.

Once more he started forward. With each step the pain diminished dramatically as a growing sensation replaced it. Surprisingly, it became just as exquisite as the pain had been, but only wonderfully so. Just as a child recognizes the warmth in a smile, he recognized the feeling instantly as Love: It was an acceptance, full and whole-hearted like he had never known it. Yet it was a love that was unbearable because it was so pure, so strong and, so intense that it made him aware of his un-loveliness. Why was he being loved? The banshee had been right. How could this be since he was worthless, selfish, guilty, and, in the truest sense, unlovable? Oh, what a lie! What a contradiction!

Suddenly a voice – not one that he heard with his ears – said, *"Is it a lie that clothes cover nakedness? Let it cover yours. It was bought at a price that you could not pay."*

And through that voice emerged a clearness of insight that was his answer: Because his Protector, out of His own choice, had simply chosen to love him. There could be no other reason since he did not deserve it.

The insight did not stop there. Sudden understanding into the nature of Gopher's magic dawned on him. He saw that his magic was intertwined with the intentions and desires of his heart. It explained much of his dreams, because they, too, came from his heart and were, thusly, connected to his magic. It also explained how both good and bad fairies had awakened from their spell-bound sleep simply by responding to that which was in his heart since it corresponded to what was in theirs.

And now, as his understanding grew, so likewise the enchanted fog was beginning to lift in the village, enabling his magic to show him what the evil creatures were doing. It was too much for his small brain to take in all at once, but he saw it all in a general way: They tore down fences, scattered paving stones that made up paths, trampled the orderly rows of gardens, uprooted bushes and even trees, swarmed over buildings, broke windows, threw shingles, set buildings on fire. He felt in them the gluttonous thrill of gorging oneself at a meal without the satisfaction, driven by the urge for more, more, more. Fortunately, their evil traits that they shared did not mean that they would be unified in their actions. It would have made their violence far more destructive. Instead, they fought themselves as much as they delighted in the destruction of all that was meaningful.

They disgusted him, but only because he disgusted himself, for his own hatred, guilt, fears, jealousy, and selfishness would have eventually driven him to do the same sort of things had he been given the means and opportunity to do so. In short, they were merely the proof of his own evil heart. If he hated anyone, it should be himself, and because of it he threw himself down and surrendered himself to Love, offering no resistance, no excuse for his own un-loveliness.

Then, suddenly a wonderful peace swept over and covered every part of him. It was that *covering*, he knew. Suddenly, however, there was a part of him that rose up in response with a wild urge to reject it, but not because it was a lie; rather, because, as a gift, he had not earned it, that he was a mere charity case, a thing to be pitied and looked down upon. He'd rather die than to be –

Suddenly he felt love recede from him and even the heat and the light began to lessen, to become bearable. He opened his eyes and saw that the fire was indeed fading in the hearth. A triumphant thought came to him: He had won through and become his own person! But then it was countered by that other voice that challenged him gently, quietly.

"Did you really win? Are you truly free?"

At once he knew the answer, for in that moment of rejecting the love, his magic had lashed out (he could not see it, only somehow knew that it was happening) to awaken even more evil fairies to ravage this ill-fated town. He knew then that love was not a tyranny. If rejected, it would recede because that was what real love does, but what he was seeing now proved that the emptiness left behind in love's wake would bring real tyranny indeed.

"No! I'm sorry!" he cried out before any more creatures could be awakened.

Immediately the light and heat – and love – smote him, but this time, these sensations were those of an embrace, and he realized that was what they had been all along, only he had been too unfit to recognize it. In fact, it was the embrace of his Protector. In that embrace, he recognized the same joy he had felt after eating the magic carrot. This time, however, that joy entered and starting to change him from the inside out: To enlarge and reshape him, which is to say that it was painful, but in a way it was wonderful because, by enduring the heat, he had learned to cast himself before the Embracer and, in doing so, he discovered that joy was greater than pain. The more he let himself be embraced, to be accepted, the more he understood what the change was about. He was being transformed from a gopher into a man, a real man, so that the covering, which he had not deserved at first, was now fully his, just as he both fully owned and belonged to his Embracer.

Yet it proved to be only a momentary vision of what was to be, for in the next moment he was a gopher again. In fact, all of it had been a vision. The hearth was cold, the living room was furnished as it always was, and he felt not a trace of the heat. He was not disappointed, for he was still filled with the same love and the hope that the vision had given him. He was also filled with understanding about what was to be done next, though not about what to do after that. Each moment must be handled when it came.

While hearing the battling and destruction going on outside, he stayed where he was and closed his eyes again, calmly reaching out with love towards Menlow. This time he did not have to enter into his friend's enchanted dream to the extent that he could be ensnared again. The love and joy flowing in and through him could not be displaced by something as insubstantial as a dream, and, because of it, they enabled him to view the dream as such.

In it he saw Menlow feasting in a wide clearing in the forest with a myriad of elves, dwarves, and even goblins. They were all singing and dancing and eating. Only the hermit was sitting quietly in their midst with a pleased smile on his face and a rested composure, indications of having accomplished a great achievement. Gopher knew at once that they were celebrating a recent peace alliance among these separate races of fairies. They were in the act of drinking a toast to the wizard for bringing this about when they all froze, instantly transformed into a picture of abject horror and dismay. They were staring at Gopher, he realized, and even the great wizard, his friend, looked surprised and even shocked. The rodent did not let any of their reactions bother him, not even the hermit's. Instead he reached farther out to his friend in love.

It was then that someone in their midst cried out, "The Blight has come at last!"

After that, they ceased being a picture and, like a sudden storm, they cast themselves in an uproar and turmoil as they climbed all over each other to flee from him, screaming in horror and madness. Only Menlow remained still and calm, having risen from his seat of honor. His countenance, though, was pale and his frame, strong and healthy a moment before, now appeared crippled.

It was then that Gopher understood what the Blight was about, that it had been like the heat and light of the fire. The Blight was his love – only it wasn't really his love at all, but an extension of that greater love. Either way, though, it meant the end of his friend's enchanted world, for Gopher could not love the hermit and let him continue as he was, dying without knowing it, at least not without trying to save him. But he also suddenly knew that his friend could not be forced to be saved if he did not want it. The act of trying to save him would kill him if he held on to that which was unreal.

Gopher stopped reaching out, for this knowledge that the hermit might die as a result of his action was unbearably painful. He asked his Embracer, his Lord, whose presence he was always in, for strength, just like he did before.

The answer came immediately. A greater love, which did not come from himself at all, swept over his friend. Although Gopher could not see it, he felt confident that the same covering was also being laid upon the hermit. He saw the evidence of it as Menlow's expression of excruciating pain fade into a mix of surprise and fear... followed by confusion and uncertainty... and then gradually by a look of surrender, beautiful surrender. He was letting himself be accepted. Gopher felt like he was watching what he had gone through himself – and he left the dream as easily as one walks out of a room...

It was but a few moments later when Menlow appeared in the doorway, fully awake. The rodent had been waiting for him, expectant and patient, despite the tumult from outside.

"Is... is that you, Gopher?"

The hermit with his wispy beard wore wrinkled bedclothes that were seemingly draped over a gaunt and frail framework of bones, but his smile was lit with an exuberance of life and health and joy. The hermit moved with an unexpected sprightliness as he rushed forward and scooped Gopher up in an embrace.

"Forgive this old fool. I was trapped by my own selfishness! Oh, important wizard that I am! Ha! Now I am free to be the friend you deserve!"

The rodent was so astounded and touched by the hermit's admission and humility that he was speechless. He had always felt accepted by Menlow since the time he had come to live at the cottage, but until now he had never realized that that acceptance had been based on him being a gopher. Now he felt accepted as someone equal. It was like a weight was removed or a freedom given, either of which he had not known until that moment.

Before anymore could be said, however, a dragon blew its breath on the front of the house, setting it afire, while the floorboards rattled and the walls shook under the pounding steps of a giant, whose ankles could be seen through the flames in the window. As if that wasn't enough, gargoyles and goblins came in attacking from the rear.

Chapter Thirty-Two

Fortunately, the gargoyles and goblins were too caught up in fighting amongst themselves and destroying the house to immediately notice Menlow and Gopher. Jumping on to his friend's shoulder (without being able to relish the fact), the hermit slipped back into the bedroom and then quickly out the window. Fortunately, too, that side of the house had not caught on fire yet and happened to be situated opposite to the giant, so that the house was in between, cutting them off from his view.

That appeared to be the end of their luck, however, for they did not slip unnoticed by the dragon. The green-and-gold scaled beast had just maneuvered itself to roast that side of the house with its breath.

"Ah!" the dragon said, which sounded like a cross between a cat purring and a restrained roar, "Little ones to toast! Are you screamers? I shall have the pleasure of finding out, unless –" he winked his green lizard eye conspiratorially, "– unless you have a treasure map or something of value to redeem your lives with. No? Oh, well."

The dragon's arrogance and greed proved to be its undoing, for its speech had given enough delay to attract the giant's attention. It was a good thing that, like most giants, he was not the curious type to see whom the dragon was addressing. He cared only about literally throwing his weight around –or, in this case, anything else that could make the same point. As the dragon inhaled deeply to summon a fiery blast, the giant plucked a small tree as if it had only been a weed and then hurled it as the evil lizard blew out a great flame. Not only did the tree catch the full brunt of the blast, enveloping it instantly in a ball of flame, but its momentum drove the flaming tree down the still-bellowing mouth of the dragon. The lizard itself then erupted into an even greater ball of fire since its breath, once it had been let loose, had nowhere else to go. The giant roared in laughter that rivaled the frenzied cry of the dragon as it rolled madly on the ground to extinguish itself.

Menlow, still carrying Gopher, fled towards the rear of the house when four hairy man-shaped creatures appeared from around the corner of the garden wall. They stood no higher than five year old children, but their hairiness, their devilish grinning faces with their tufted pointed ears set them apart from anything human. The rodent knew at once, for his magic told him, that they were hobgoblins and that they preyed on the weak and the helpless, since, separately, they tended to be cowards and pathetic. (He recognized those traits in himself as well, remembering how he had relished watching the changeling attacking Wells and Loggins and wishing he could have joined in since there would be little chance of *him* getting hurt.)

The hobgoblins leaped upon them with cries of delight in a unified strike. At the same time, however, the Cyclops leapt down from the garden wall with a hoarse-sounding roar, one foot pinning a hobgoblin upon landing while his massive hands plucked the other two in mid-air. The fourth he just glared at with his one eye in the center of his horned forehead. It was enough to turn the vicious creature into a pathetic one. It shrieked as it cowered into a hairy ball. Snarling, the Cyclops kicked it and then flung both of its fellow creatures after it. The hobgoblin underfoot was let loose and went bawling after the other three as they fled back the same way they had come. It was all done with an amazing gracefulness that proved just how expert they were at retreating.

The Cyclops turned to Menlow, scowling, his eye fixed on them unwaveringly, and his leathery skin and fur patched shoulders heaving up and down as if fury was pent up in his chest. Gopher felt Menlow tense and ready to also fly, which did not surprise him. The fierce look of the beast made him feel uncertain and intimidated, too. Gopher remembered what the pixie had told him about shape-shifting, how one can lose himself. Had Farwyll gone too far?

He forced himself to laugh, though, and said, "Don't worry! It's only Farwyll. He's my – my friend. He's a pixie," he said and then addressed the monster cheerily, "This is the fourth time you came to my rescue, isn't it? Or is it the fifth? The sixth? I'm losing counting!"

He laughed again but it sounded even more forced. The Cyclops took a step forward and loomed menacingly with his breathing rapidly building towards explosion. Gopher made himself go on, though it was stemmed more from rising apprehension than courage.

"Now, then, Farwyll... ah, thank you. I – again thank you – deeply... ah..." then fear suddenly did a reversal, or, rather, he did a reversal on it as he faced it – and the Cyclops.

"Isn't that just about enough? Be yourself, will you, Farwyll! It's me – and you – well, you're you, and quit pretending otherwise!"

Then the Cyclops, who had started to ball his powerful hands into fists, froze... a look of uncertainty came into his eye as he blinked rapidly. Then a shimmering arose around the creature like a summer heat wave, increasingly blurring the massive creature – which by this time began writhing about – until it could hardly be seen, though its cries of great torment could be heard. Slowly they diminished as did the shimmering. When the air finally cleared, the Cyclops had disappeared altogether. In its place, looking so small by comparison as to be hardly noticeable, lay the pixie on the ground.

"Farwyll!" Gopher cried.

Menlow rushed forward and bent down. The pixie raised its head and weakly smiled, "Gopher... "

"Welcome back, and thank you," the hermit said.

"Sorry... nearly lost myself that time, the meaner the creature, the harder to... remember oneself. But if you will carry me for a bit, sir, I'll be all right." Then raising a trembling hand, he stuck his finger in his mouth and pulled it out to test the wind. "Just start that way, same as those hobgoblins – or had I dreamed them? All fuzzy..." His head fell back and his eyes closed with a tired but happy look about his face.

With a raised eyebrow, Menlow turned his head to look questioningly at Gopher who had climbed up on to his shoulder. The rodent answered, "The wind is his guide –" but stopped short of any more explanation when understanding registered in Menlow's smile, reminding Gopher that Menlow had many more years of experience with magic and the ways of fairies than he did. Instead of making him feel jealous, though, it added an appreciation and respect for the ex-wizard that he had never felt before.

Menlow set off at once around the corner of the garden wall, carrying the pixie. As they went, the fairy began to recover, raising his head more and making comments, like how it felt good to be his own weak little self again, but most importantly he would add further directions by testing the wind ever so often.

Little did Gopher know but they were traveling much of the same back alleys he had done with the hamadryad and Adia. Much had changed since then. Some of the thatched roofs were ablaze, and not a few of the buildings and walls were destroyed, some of them having been torn down brick by brick; the alleys and side streets were strewn with the rubble. Thanks to Farwyll's guidance, they managed to avoid being discovered by ducking into hiding places or taking quick detours into dark empty alleys. With all the sounds of destruction around them, it seemed that they were doing the impossible, though there were many close calls: once with three looting orcs, another time with two gremlins wrestling with a hobgoblin, and when three trolls unknowingly almost toppled a wall on them. Even closer than that was when a ghoul whisked right through them, but it kept going, for Gopher sensed that it could not find enough fear in them to be of any use.

The closest call, though, was with a nearly dozen dark elves. They suddenly appeared out of one of those dark alleys. Recognizable by their black leather and ferociously dark looks, they were dancing and whooping and hollering, while the ex-wizard crowded into the shadows as much as he could. But they were blind to all else except to their own delight of the destruction and chaos all around them. Somehow they managed to go unnoticed, and when a straggling dark elf bumped into Menlow, he merely looked with contempt at the three huddled together in the corner and thought that they were too pathetic to care much about. Even Farwyll started breathing easier again after the evil fairies had moved on.

It seemed that Farwyll's wind was heading them straight towards where the danger was the thickest, judging by the ever increasing sounds of battle – of metal clashing, shrieks of pain and terror, battle cries, furious shouts, and inhuman roaring. The most disquieting of all sounds, however, were the occasional booms that shook the ground and wobbled the walls, fences, and buildings along both sides of the alleyway. Soon they would come out in the open where there would be no place left to hide, but Gopher was not afraid. Instead, he was eager to fight, which came from too much hiding. The joy of self-sacrifice sprung up anew. If only he was bigger and able to do something – if only the vision of himself as a man would come true, then he would have hands that could wield a sword and long legs to take him into the battle!

According to his expectations, the passage, along which they had been traversing, suddenly opened up. Before them a grassy expanse sloped down to the river, the Village Green. It was hard to believe that it was often used for picnics and other get-togethers, for now it was a scene of battle and chaos. A host of evil fairies and monsters that were spread out in every direction surrounded a small band of elves, dwarves, and other noble magical creatures. Even in the air, dragons swooped down with tongues of flame sweeping over them as boulders flew in their direction, tossed by giants. Although the besieged group was a short distance from the river, the water was no way of escape for them. The boats were ablaze on the river. In its current could also be seen sprites, mermaids, merman, water nymphs, and naiads fighting each other with rocks, nets, and even burning timbers from the ships.

With his magic, Gopher hardly had to use his eyes to know all of this was happening, though it was the act of seeing that brought it to the front of his consciousness. He also knew that although the good fairies fought more skillfully and more united than their opponents, that they were hopelessly outnumbered whether on land or in the river.

Yet what his magic didn't give him was a clue about how the three of them were going to help the beleaguered defenders. The hermit was an old man without any magic, and Farwyll, though now able to stand on his own, was still haggard, which his forced smile only emphasized all the more. However, Gopher's immediate attention suddenly shifted from themselves when one of the four giants turned towards them.

Chapter Thirty-Three

The giant did not see them, because he was too busily engaged, like his other companions, in picking up boulders, which he did as easily as a child pulling daisies. His delight was not so innocent, though, for he threw it with a cruel laugh and an even crueler intention, just like the other three. Fortunately, the sight of the flying stones, many of which were as big as houses, proved more disquieting than their impact was – at least for the beleaguered host of good fairies. Ironically, it was because of them that the good fairies appeared to hold on for the moment. That was because they were thrown rather carelessly and most of the boulders ended up crushing some of the evil horde. Nonetheless, Gopher felt the moment was slipping away from being in their favor, because a boulder would soon hit its mark.

Farwyll tugged on Menlow's robe. "Sir, if you'd be quick and follow my lead and stop when I stop, I think that we will make it. And it would help if you would stay low and let Gopher ride on my shoulder so you won't have to worry about him slipping off."

The transfer was made wordlessly and the pixie set off at once; the erstwhile wizard, crouching, followed close behind. Quickly they ran to a boulder that had not yet been picked up, pausing in its shadow before hurrying across the open, rocky expanse to the next boulder. Farwyll, however, barely seemed to notice the giants and was more focused on checking the wind before they made each move. He did not even seem to be discomfited by the fact that, after their fourth boulder, there was seemingly nothing more to hide behind between them and the mass of evil fairies that were now uncomfortably close. After sticking his wetted thumb in the air for the third time, he nodded to himself and left their hiding spot to rush out into the open. Menlow followed without hesitation. Even though Gopher had no fear of falling off the pixie's shoulder, he wished that he had something to hold on to as if that would make him feel safer.

Not more than twenty feet along the broken and treacherous slope, the pixie fell unexpectedly into darkness. Gopher nearly screamed but the sudden stop drove out the air in his lungs. Behind came a soft thudding and in the darkness he could hear Menlow's breathing – and then feel it on his furry back. It, and the darkness, made him feel safe for the moment.

"Where are we?" Gopher whispered after regaining his breath.

"Where a boulder had been a moment before," Farwyll replied. He did not need to whisper because of the tumultuous noise of fighting, bellowing, and thudding crashes going on above them.

The rodent did not have the opportunity to enjoy their relatively safe position for very long. The wind apparently led them on, and into an even more perilous situation. In fact, he nearly fell off the pixie's shoulder from sheer fright when Farwyll leapt out of the hole and chose their course towards a giant, whose back was turned. Thankfully, he was raising an extra large boulder over his head at the time, for that made his legs bowlegged and easier to pass between, but then, to his even greater horror, they plunged immediately into the evil throng.

Gopher quickly discovered, however, that they were safer here than at the feet of the giants. It's not because they blended in with the goblins, dark elves, hobgoblins, gargoyles, brownies (not all were good, after all), rapiscans, changelings, and other malicious creatures of fairy; in fact, Gopher could not help but feel as if they stood out. Rather, it was because there seemed to be more fighting going on between their evil factions than against the good fairies. Of course, they had to do some ducking and dodging to avoid getting involved, though the problem often resolved itself, such as when a troll, who was lunging at them, was thwarted by an ogre who was swinging its club just as carelessly as how the giants threw the boulders. The impact hit the troll so hard that it sent the creature flying.

Whether the troll had recognized them as not belonging to their evil throng or just saw them as someone else to attack, the three did not linger to consider. Shortly after that, however, their luck ran out. A band of dark elves pointed their spears and swords at them, shouting something in their language, which drew the attention of those around them. It might have spelled a quick end to their lives if the evil fairies had not, all at once, scrambled over each other, tearing, kicking, striking, and stabbing to be the first to reach them.

During this delay came their salvation. Surprisingly, it came through a shower of shiny rocks. One hit Gopher on the head, which the pixie nimbly caught and held it up laughing.

"A diamond!"

They were not all diamonds, however. Silver, gold, and other precious gems fell like rain, and it took their assailants as long as it did the pixie to realize what they were. Menlow, Gopher, and the pixie were forgotten as they began fighting and looting each other. Of course, not all evil fairies were so enamored by such things, but those were generally the jealous, miserable types who joined in the fray anyway just so they could diminish the joy they (erroneously) believed that their greedy compatriots were experiencing. Although it was only a brief reprieve, it provided just enough of a delay which enabled them to slip past under their very noses to easily reach the battle line, over which they crossed unmolested and unnoticed, before the fighting could resume.

Those in the besieged camp, without slowing in their jabs and thrusts, immediately recognized and greeted them as friends instead of foes. A faun was even able to point them in a certain direction. Although they didn't know where they were supposed to go or why, it soon became apparent when the leader of the good fairies came in sight. That he was their leader there could be no mistake. He was a gray-haired man whose stalwart countenance seemed impervious to defeat and who expertly wielded a sword, going here and there like a young man, yet giving orders and encouragement all in the same breath that betokened the wisdom of his gray hair. He was the kind of leader whose presence inspired confidence, courage, and sacrifice.

Then the leader saw them, and instantly his face lit up with a joy that seemed odd in the midst of battle. Almost as instantly, and with amazement, Gopher recognized him to be the Traveling Merchant. How could he have ever thought him a funny looking little old man? Had he ever *really* seen him before? It was as if a veil had been lifted.

They met him in the middle of a small circle of dwarves and elves that were either wounded or resting.

"Welcome, Merlin, Gopher, and Farwyll! And just in time!" he said, "How did you like the 'weather' I sent your way?'"

"All those gems and coins that rained down on us – you did that?" Menlow said and laughed. "It reminds me of my old days!"

The pixie laughed. "Now that's the second time I've seen a real use for treasure!"

"But where'd it all come from?" Gopher asked.

"Oh, not all of the rapiscan are on the other side... There's the fellow over there who supplied the treasures..." He pointed to a gypsy-looking man whom Gopher remembered.

The Traveling Merchant went on, "But enough about that. This fight of ours is a good one, but – alas! – we are losing. It is reassuring, is it not, Merlin, that you have already won the battle that matters? And you, too, Gopher! I can see the change in you and it proves that one gopher does not necessarily look like another!"

He laughed, but then continued in a more serious tone, "That doesn't mean *this* battle isn't of great import, though. All of this land, and even beyond it, is in great danger of being overrun if our foes are not stopped today. It will bring about the Age of Dark Magic."

"What can we do?" Gopher said.

"We fight. A pixie is handy when changed into a fighting creature, but not now for you, eh, Farwyll? I can see that you are still tired, and a tired pixie is likely to forget who he really is, but no matter we will do what we can."

"I will change anyway!" the pixie exclaimed. "Who cares if I forget who I am? It won't matter anyway if we lose!"

He said it in such fierce determination that it surprised and saddened Gopher to see how desperate their strait really must be that the normally lighthearted fairy should speak so.

"Really?" The Traveling Merchant looked at Farwyll sternly. "Is the wind leading you to believe that *your* sacrifice will save the day – or are you just puffing up your own sails?"

There was such authority in his voice that it, too, surprised Gopher; but, instead of being saddened, it made him realize for some reason that winning wasn't everything, though he could not understand why, given the situation.

It seemed to have a similar effect on the pixie, for his "sails" seemed to deflate as he hung his head low, which the Merchant raised with his hand. He said gently, "But you are strong enough to fight as yourself, are you not? Besides, changing won't win this battle, even if we had a hundred pixies that turned into dragons or giants."

"Then how can we win?" the rodent said.

In answer, the Traveling Merchant turned towards Menlow and said, "Merlin, didn't you prophecy once that King Arthur will return one day to save the land from a great evil? That is our hope that will keep us strong in our fight – and hope that today is the day!"

"But what about me?" Gopher said. "How can I help? I can't hold a sword or shoot a bow."

"Oh, you have the most important part of all," the Merchant replied and, taking him from the pixie's shoulder to place him up on a limb of a tree (one of the surviving few on the Village Green), he added, "You are to remain here and stay hopeful when there may be no hope left. I mean it. We don't want you unintentionally waking up anymore evil creatures. Those that feed on despair are some of the evilest. Just remember what happened in the mayor's house and know that the vision is just as true now as it was then no matter what you may feel.

"Now then," he continued as he turned to the hermit, "I have called you Merlin three times, for you are not Menlow or a retiring hermit anymore. The old magic has at last lost its hold on you and our trade is finally complete. Now you can start being who you truly are. Besides, magic won't win this battle. What is needed is the King's return, but at least two leaders, if working together, are twice as good as no king at all! Here's an extra sword; it is no Excalibur, though."

"Good enough. Let us start!" Merlin said.

Then they entered the fray. The pixie, gaining a short sword from somewhere, disappeared immediately into the throng. Yet even with all the clanging, yells, and other noises of fighting, Gopher could occasionally hear Farwyll singing as if he were happier than ever, while the Merchant and Merlin went about shouting encouragement, giving direction, and slashing and parrying with their swords whenever a foe broke through.

The fighting was fierce, yet, strangely, Gopher felt a sense of exultation growing in him – or rather rubbing off on him, for it came from the good fairies that fought with such exuberance that he could not tell, except with his eyes, that that they were slowly being forced back and tightening their circle ever so slowly. Actually, it made losing seem not to matter so much, for the exultation was like the throbbing joyful pulse of self-sacrifice, with which he had awakened the dwarves from the Great Oak, but it was even more than that. It was an exultation of unity where each would gladly die for the other, and not just for an ideal like justice.

Immediately the magic opened up a picture in his mind. He saw another emergence from the Great Oak. This time it was much greater, for it rent the gash in the tree trunk wide open and shook the ground even more than the pounding feet of the giants. Instead of dwarves coming forth, a centaur emerged, a noble creature that was half man and half horse. A burst from his horn, resounding in a high jubilant note, proved even greater than the noble creature's emergence, for its vibrations pierced both air and earth.

Even from here, it silenced both friend and foe alike and momentarily ceased all fighting. Then, as the horn fell silent, the ground continued to vibrate, but, instead of fading, it became increasingly stronger until it sounded like a rumbling. The entire tree suddenly split in two as centaur upon centaur galloped up out of the earth and leaped effortlessly over the garden wall. (At the same time, Gopher sensed the hamadryad, Maythenia, being mortally stricken.) As terror swept through the evil horde, the small army of centaurs appeared at the top of the Village Green. Their enemies nearest them panicked and sought to escape their thundering hooves and the sweeping strokes of their swords. Almost too easily the centaurs cleared a way through the chaotic mass and crossed over the battle line to join them.

Their sudden and majestic, yet fearsome, appearance and the terrified response by their foes renewed the besieged fairies in their fighting and raised their spirits to the point of merriment. They laughed and sang out as they resumed their jabbing and parrying their way to retaking lost ground. Quickly Merlin, the Traveling Merchant, and the centaurs planned and organized separate contingents of elves, dwarfs, brownies. One contingent, headed by Merlin who rode on the back of one of the centaurs, broke through the enemy's line in a brief fierce foray, making their foes angry enough to draw a number of them back across the battle lines when Merlin retreated; then they were cut off from the rest and were easily overcome. Immediately, another centaur blew his horn with the Traveling Merchant astride who did the same thing, leading another foray at a different location along the battle line with the same strategy of drawing in enough of the enemy. The next contingent, led by an elf, met similar success. Merlin reentered the fray, followed with a band of relatively fresh fighters of satyrs and dryads.

For Gopher the sight of the courageous feats and sweeping victories struck a high and noble feeling in him. No wonder the evil fairies cringed, he thought! Who could stand against such nobility and strength? He relished equally both the anticipated victory on one side as well as the inevitable and deserved doom on the other.

But then a doubt pierced him when he remembered the prophecy that only the return of King Arthur would bring triumph.

Yet doubt found no lasting foothold in him. Under the intoxicating inspiration that the nobility of the centaurs stirred within him, it added another inspiration that was even greater. It occurred to him that these good fairies, with all of their courage and nobility and goodness, had been awakened because of what was inside of *him*. Although his magic was the key, so to speak, what had opened the door to such greatness was what had been in his heart. Therefore, if he could awaken such noble creatures as the centaurs, why not awaken King Arthur as well? It was such a great thought that he knew that a gopher like himself should be ashamed of even considering it, but wasn't that what his magic was for, to awaken those from the Age of Magic? Had he not been chosen to possess that magic, after all?

Without allowing any further thought that might argue against it, he began at once. He did not bother about trying to summon King Arthur; his magic would take care of that. All he had to do was believe, fully and without doubt, that it would happen. Accordingly, he let his magic work through him and flow out of him, embracing it fully, letting its exultation become ecstatically dizzying where the impossible seemed possible and where all his former troubles and stresses became mere trifles. Even this battle seemed unimportant in comparison to the greatness of his magic.

The magic summoned the king much quicker and easier than he had anticipated. At once, a picture came into his mind as a great shout rent the air and cut through all other noise. Once again, the fighting ceased, but this time there was no rejoicing on the part of the good fairies, just astonishment that registered on their faces as well as on their enemies.

Out of the darkest shadows at the fringe of the forest south of the town, the king emerged in a stride that matched his huge size. He wore a crown and armor that appeared all black until the rays of the lowering sunset hit them. Then they shone like beautiful jewels the next moment. Its brilliance drew all eyes to him, and held them there. In fact, everything about him drew one's attention and seemed to capture one's breath. His bearing was upright like an immovable pillar of awesome strength that made the evil fairies give way.

Gopher wished that he could have been happier to see the king than he was, for something in the king's appearance disturbed him. The impassive look on his noble brow and piercing fiery but cold eyes stirred within Gopher conflicting desires of wanting his notice while also fearing it.

Then something unexpected happened. The king unsheathed his sword and, pointing it in their direction, he shouted only one word "FIGHT!" which, in his fearsome voice, was enough to command obedience.

This time it was the evil horde to laugh and sing out as the battle immediately resumed, but now they no longer fought each other. Even the giants cared enough to start aiming and the dragons began to sweep over the besieged camp of good fairies with flames spouting out of their nostrils down below instead of at each other.

Chapter Thirty-Four

"What has happened, Gopher? Who is this?" Merlin asked him, suddenly appearing below the branch.

Gopher opened his mouth, though he doubted that anything was going to come out of it, because he didn't know the answer. He did know, however, that the man was neither King Arthur nor was he on their side. Gopher also knew that it was his fault for awakening him in the first place. He didn't even get to say that because just then one of the centaurs arrived and supplied the answer in a voice like rushing waters.

"He is one of the wizard-kings of old."

Merlin said softly, "A Nephillim from the First Age of Magic." The hermit had told Gopher about that First Age, which had also been called the Great Age, where the proud and powerful evil Nephillim had ruled all humankind as self-appointed kings. Yet when the Great Flood had wiped them out, it had ushered in the Second Age when the elves, dwarves, dragons, and the rest of the fairy creatures were born out of the earth.

"Now that one of the evil kings has awakened," Merlin continued, "the Great Age may yet pick up where it left off."

Whether intended or not, Gopher immediately felt the sting of an accusation in that statement.

"I didn't *mean* to," the rodent began.

The Traveling Merchant came up to them and exclaimed, "Look

there!" He pointed his sword upwards at a large black misshapen blotch in the fading blue sky. For the briefest moment, when Gopher saw that it was rapidly getting larger, he had a wild notion that night was trying to overtake the fading day before its appointment time.

Merlin shouted, "Boulder!"

A mad scramble followed. Nobody could get out of each other's way quick enough. Gopher fell out of the tree to land on someone's back, and then to be tossed about to find himself on someone's rather pointy helmet. He did not feel it, though, for that was right before the boulder blacked out the sky directly above. At the same time all movement around him stopped in anticipation of the impact... but a moment later he found that he wasn't crushed. The boulder was suspended in the air no more than ten feet overhead.

The large stone wavered for a moment and then it lifted, so that, not being so close up, Gopher could see a giant bent nearly double under the weight of it. A prolonged grunt and a grimace evidenced the terrific struggle as the giant raised the rock over his head. Then, at his full height, about thirty feet, the giant gave a great roar and threw it into the crowd of evil fairies. Their unity broke immediately as they sought to escape, and the good fairies took advantage of the moment for an offensive thrust with the centaurs blowing their horns and the giant joining in to press the fight even further into the enemy's territory.

Gopher knew from a familiar feeling that the giant was really Farwyll. Hope and gratitude swelled up within him and even brought a tear. Yet, like waves breaking on rocks, these emotions shattered when the wizard-king's booming voice exclaimed above the din of battle.

"JOIN ME!"

There was something so majestic, so commanding, so compelling that, if it had been directed at him, Gopher knew that he would have felt irresistibly drawn to obey. Although Gopher held no doubts that the pixie was made of far more sterner stuff, he was not surprised when the giant paused from swatting at a dragon.

"BRAVE, GOOD GIANT! PLEDGE YOURSELF TO ME!"

The giant scratched his huge head and his face became contorted with conflicting emotions. Gopher knew what was happening. Farwyll was slowly and inevitably being won over by the wizard king, and in the process forgetting (and losing) himself. It broke Gopher's heart, and suddenly nothing else, not the battle or even himself, mattered at that moment.

"Take me! I'll go!" Gopher cried out.

His cry, from the small throat of a rodent, was lost in the noise around him, yet the cry unleashed his magic. Immediately he felt that a connection was made – and even the giant knew it, for the connection had been with Farwyll – the pixie that was still alive in the giant. The hulking figure turned back and looked right at Gopher, even as small as he was in the midst of the tumult. He shook his head as if to clear its thoughts. Slowly, almost reluctantly, it took a step towards the rodent; its grimace deepened as if it was under another heavy weight. Then the air simmered around the giant like heat waves off of a road. The blurring thickened, increasing until even the ground shook. The giant began to blend into a mass of colors, but even they began to diminish as the shimmering intensified. All at once, however, the air became clear again, and the giant was gone.

Moments later, as the fighting resumed, a centaur lifted Gopher from a dwarf's helmet and carried him to Merlin and the Traveling Merchant. Another centaur was next to them, holding the limp body of the pixie.

"Farwyll!" Gopher exclaimed.

The pixie still breathed, but only slightly.

Merlin held up his hand in assurance. "He'll be all right."

The hermit's words registered just enough for him to realize that the pixie wasn't going to die, but beyond that fact he really heard nothing at all. It gave him some relief, but what he saw reflected in the pixie's face tempered that feeling: the deep hurt, the crushed spirit, the brokenness made him seem almost as unrecognizable as when he had been the giant. The wizard king would have kept him that way forever, Gopher knew, if the bedrock of the pixie's character had not been of genuine faithfulness, for it was that faithfulness which had connected with Gopher's magic and had saved him – not the magic by itself. That had been his mistake which had awakened the Nephillim

"He must rest. He's done his part," Merlin said.

Once the rodent and the unconscious pixie were ensconced in a crook of the tree, Merlin, the Traveling Merchant, and the two centaurs joined back in the fighting. They did not try their previous maneuvers, for it was quite evident that their foes, under the uniting direction of their king, would not be taken in again. Instead the evil creatures pressed on all sides at once with such intensity that it was obvious that they intended to bring the battle to a quick end.

Yet it did not turn out to be so easily done, not with the centaurs, Merlin and the Traveling Merchant opposing them. Gopher would have felt inspired by the acts of bravery and fighting prowess that had they both shown and inspired among those who fought alongside – that is, if that had been all he could see. His magic, however, enabled him to see more than he wanted to, and what he saw made these victories seem almost trivial. Yet that wasn't all: Gopher could feel the evil king's determination and knew that defeat was inevitable.

Suddenly his sense of helplessness, coupled by the presence of the still unconscious Farwyll, stirred anger in him so deep, so full of hatred, that another connection was made simultaneously. Without thought (for there is no room for thought in anger) he gave himself over to it, letting the magic do the rest as it poured through him like a river of such power that he marveled and quavered at its fearsome and powerful passage – until something happened that jarred him to realize that he was about to become overwhelmed by his own magic. Immediately his survival instinct shut off the flow.

Blinking rapidly and feeling suddenly very vulnerable after experiencing such power, he looked from the tree's perch to see what it was that had jarred him, that even now was deeply troubling him. When he saw it, he could not – did not want to – believe his eyes.

Merlin's limp body was lying across the back of a centaur. As the creature carried his friend away from the battle line, a dragon swooped overhead and would have spewed flames on him if thirty or so elves hadn't let fly a thick volley of arrows. Even so, Gopher felt a different intensity from the enemy that arrows could not avert or no amount of fighting could assuage; it was their wrath that was fueled by their unreasoning hatred.

He realized then that his own hatred had made its connection to the foe, and to no one else. It had been his fury and hate that, through his magic, had fueled them on, even more than the wizard king could. Thus, Merlin's injury (Oh, please, don't be dead!) was truly his fault; and not only that, but also the fighting and chaos, the death and destruction. The wizard king and the evil fairies had awakened only because his own heart, sharing the same evil that was in theirs, had stirred them from their enchanted sleep by his magic. That he had somehow managed to awaken the noble and good fairies seemed like a total fluke, but, even so, they were clearly not enough in numbers or strength to win.

The blame felt so horrible and crushing that it sickened and overpowered him. In fact, he would have succumbed and died of a broken heart right there had not a thought suddenly came to him. It was really a vivid remembrance of the fire in the mayor's house and of the invisible covering that had more than just protected him from its unbearable ferocity; it had enabled him to embrace it for what it was – pure love and goodness. It had only been unbearable because of those things which were in him that were unloving, mean-spirited, cruel, and selfish – things he could not change at all by himself, things in him that needed to be covered.

Like he did once before, he cried out, "Help me!"

This time, however, nothing happened. Actually it was worse than nothing. Gopher's words seemed to come back to him, sounding flat in his own ears as if they had hit a brick wall. At once a doubt came to him that his Protector had used the vision to trick him, and now, when Gopher had needed Him most, an even crueler trick of complete abandonment was being played on him. As if in response to his unspoken accusation, a thought came to him that was not his own.

"Is not my covering enough?"

Immediately he felt the awful but wonderful sting of truth, for there was love and hurt in that rebuke. He opened his eyes and saw the enemy still bearing down on them and felt their relentless hatred. Nothing seemed changed; they were still losing, good creatures of magic dying, and it was entirely his fault. He could not deny any of it, but now he remembered something that he had learned in the mayor's living room: It wasn't about losing or winning or even about his own guilt. By making those things the center of his focus, he had been rejecting the covering he had already been given, the victory that had already been won. By doing so, he had also been rejecting the One who had given it to him, the One who accepted and loved him. He made a choice right then to trust – to simply and completely trust, despite the unstoppable frenzy of the enemy before his eyes. Even when he saw the still and broken body of Merlin at the foot of the tree, Gopher still trusted, waited, hoped beyond all reason, and, when he could no longer bear to look, he closed his eyes but he kept trusting.

Then something happened the next moment that could not be put into words, except to describe it as something like a "change in the air." He wasn't the only one who felt it. Fighting stopped all at once, both on the land and in the river; even the flames on the ships died and the dragons, one moment swooping in the air, were grounded in the next. The giants dropped their boulders without realizing it, not even reacting when some of the great stones landed on their feet. All faces turned expectantly upriver, some with the expectancy of a hope turning into great joy at any moment, while others were gripped in dread and horror of the guilty who are about to be caught and punished.

A man in armor appeared, standing on the bow of a skiff that was bobbing along in the water at almost a leisurely pace. Gopher knew that his magic had not awakened the man, not only because he had failed to foresee his coming but also because he did not feel a connection to him. In fact, he felt an urge to be disappointed, for the figure contrasted almost pathetically against the stature and fearsome presence of the Nephillim king, but Gopher had learned not to trust his own judgment, so he waited, quiet and hopeful, and so did the rest of the noble fairies.

Their enemies were much more eager to jump to their own conclusions. They walloped and hooted and howled and roared and made all those noises that were appropriate to feeling both great relief and great contempt. The dragons took to the air instantly with mighty heaves from their scaled wings, fire blasting from their mouths. As one body, with the wizard king in the forefront, they turned all their attentions and energy to meet this single person to destroy him. Gopher felt the intensity of their hate and wondered that not one of them questioned why they would all feel like that towards a seemingly unimportant individual.

The skiff reached the shore on this side of the river and the armored man stepped off so casually that Gopher wondered if he was aware of the enemy rushing towards him from both land and downriver. By the time he took three steps they reached him as monsters with tentacles and long limbs emerged from the river's surface and dragged the skiff under as if to cut off his escape.

Then the man unsheathed his sword as they swarmed over him.

Light exploded from its blade, sending the mass of them flying back in all directions so that they looked like a ripple effect of a boulder tossed in water. Even from a distance Gopher felt the explosion, though he was not sure if it was its force or the light's intensity that struck him – but it also strangely drew his whole being.

Then he recognized the light as being the Fire in the mayor's house, or else it was very much like it, for it conveyed to his heart a power of love and goodness. That he could recognize it as such proved that the same invisible covering still protected him; there was no other explanation, for he did not deserve such love nor was he able to withstand the penetration of such goodness. Even then he could barely lift his head.

His magic, though, enabled him to discern the majority of the enemy fleeing in all directions, while some were falling where they were as if struck dead all at once. The wizard king shrieked like a coward, and then he... disappeared, completely as if he never existed. Only one dragon plummeted to the ground, while the others flew like a streak of darkness so fast that... they, too, disappeared into nothingness. Was that right? They certainly had no place to hide, for the sky had not yet darkened enough for that. Then he noticed that three giants turned away from the sword's piercing light to step into darkness, which the light then swallowed up, so that no traces of them were left, while the one remaining fell like mountains crumbling into rubble. He saw this on a smaller scale when the others subsequently disappeared after turning to flee. Suddenly, he understood what was happening: Those who fled were disappearing into their own shadows.

But why? What could darkness offer but blindness? As he watched, sorrow pierced him, stinging his eyes with tears. It was because he realized that it was not the darkness they were choosing but it was the love that they were rejecting; a love so pure that it showed them how unlovable they were by comparison, which was intolerable to their pride and twisted self-love that they clung to so needlessly, so pitifully.

Gopher felt pity for them, though not enough to follow them in hopes of changing their minds. That would mean rejecting the light itself. Instead, he received it into himself, and, in doing so, he started crying anew, this time not for those who vanished, but in the joy from which they had so tragically fled.

Not all had fled, however, but a number of them had immediately fallen dead. It was to these that King Arthur moved nimbly from one to another, his blazing sword piercing each in turn – as if their death was not enough.

That was only Gopher's initial impression. As he watched, instead of being acts of violence, the King's sword thrusts looked... right... and, as strange as it sounded, even beautiful. In fact, Gopher got the impression that he was dancing to music that the rodent could almost, but not quite, hear. It was like that sense of familiarity that he had when he could only vaguely recall his dreams.

However, as the king continued on, piercing his downed foes, Gopher got so caught up in delight at the flow and rhythm of his movements that he slowly began to hear the music itself – so slowly that he did not know when it happened. The king's dancing did flow with it, in fact, and very beautifully, too – but, oh, the joy and beauty and wonder that the music conveyed far exceeded it! It was as if the king's dance – and any dance or song or sunset or beautiful face– were only attempts to capture echoes of that music. It seemed to him that he had heard the glorious harmony all of his life but never *really* heard it. Then a remembrance corrected him. He had known it before, but he had not recognized it as music, until now. It had been that Wondrous Feeling.

Ironically, sometime after the evil fairies had been pierced by that wondrously fearsome sword, Gopher began noticing movement. First they started to jerk about, then to move, and finally to show definite signs of life – and something even more definite than that: joy. Some sat up and began singing, some to cry in joy or whoop in delight. The giant sat up and blubbered forth a river, though it did not look ridiculous; it just looked *right*, as if his enormous size was given to him just so that his tears of joy would be able to water dry land. Similarly, the dragon, still grounded after plummeting to earth, began to sing in time with that wondrous tune in the air; its voice, so piercingly beautiful and powerful, fitted the great lizard even more than fire ever did. The song went something like this:

sRejoice! The time is here, even now,
When the clouds from the sky forsake!
Sing! For the morning light will endow
Light to those who will dare to wake!

Then they came to their feet (or claws or hoofs), and the dance no longer belonged to the king himself but to those whom he had pierced, the number of which continued to increase as the slaying and simultaneously remaking of the evil fairies went on and on. Gopher watched it all happening in a rapture of joy that took no account of time. Therefore, it seemed to take no time at all when the king and the throng of revelers stopped at the edge of the camp of the good fairies – though they were all good now.

One thing Gopher did notice – besides the king, the dance, and the ever increasing number of re-born dancers – was that the circle of (former) defenders had not stirred ever since the king had unsheathed his sword. The rodent concluded, almost with more interest than with alarm, that they had been in fact slain by its light. Yet, considering what had been happening with the ones the king had slain with his sword, Gopher could not bring himself to be overly concerned. On the contrary, he was overly excited with expectancy, because, if the evil fairies had been so transformed, what would happen to those who were already on the side of the good?

In this, his expectancy was not disappointed. The king, however, did not pierce the good fairies but rather laid the flat of his glowing blade on each one of them as he would in knighting a squire. At once the fairy would rise utterly changed, completed in ways that could not be guessed at. Even the centaurs, as high and fierce in honor and strength as they had been before, proved to have been only a shadow of what they were now, yet with a kindness and joyfulness that did not glory in their own high and noble traits but in that of others. This could be seen by their dancing in self-abandonment with those around them. Their joy even equaled that of the satyrs' in gaiety, though the latter played music on their flutes that brought out beautiful strains and notes in the airy tune that he hadn't noticed until now.

The "knighting" went on and on, with time at a seeming standstill, as the dance reached closer towards the center where the tree was. The elves and dwarves and fauns and naiads and dryads and brownies and rapiscan – all of them arose at the touch of that blade, and they quickly joined in the music in their own special way: some to dance, some to sing, some to laugh, some to play instruments, and some to just beam a countenance like the sun. In fact, like the satyr's fluting, he realized that each of their music-making (or celebrating) seemed to reveal more of that wonderful, unearthly tune. Or, he wondered, was it rather all part of the tune, that there was no real separation between their dancing and the music?

The thought made Gopher realize something more: He could not tell the "enemy" from the others. Perhaps it was because their differences had been severed, so to speak, by that sword. Yet at the same time they were all different from each other; it was a good difference, a good individuality, that was unconscious of itself – or if there was a consciousness of it, it just didn't seem to matter to them. The difference lay in the fact that they were more themselves, made more complete by the action of love.

Now Gopher, who had been so merry at the sight and by the music, suddenly realized that he also had been unconscious of something about himself. He felt himself getting weaker by the moment as if dying. He wondered at it, but not with distress. It was because he knew that, while the light of the sword was too wonderful for his rodent body, it would be better to die this way than to vanish into his own shadow.

So he waited to see what would happen, but to say that he was being patient would not be accurate, for the word implies perhaps a hint of impatience to be reckoned with, which Gopher did not feel at all. Rather, he felt a growing expectancy that in itself proved satisfying. When the king finally stopped before him and looked as if he was about to "knight" the rodent, Gopher's thought was not primarily for himself.

"My king, wait, please," he muttered, wishing that he could bow. Instead he could only nod his head differentially. "I am your servant, but Merlin here is wounded and so is this pixie. Both have suffered because of my own fault and yet have given me so much, even though I am but a gopher. 'Knight' them first, if you would, your Majesty."

King Arthur smiled and it made Gopher remember and be ashamed of his initial disappointment when he saw the king on the river. Here was a king among men, of noble bearing, someone whose strength in his word and character was mirrored in his clear and piercing eyes. He said in a lordly, yet kindly, voice, "Ah, by your own words and countenance I see that you have been 'knighted' already and by One even greater. He does not measure by appearances – or sizes! Arise, Gopher! And Merlin, my old friend and counselor, feel upon your body my sword Excalibur! You, too, Farwyll, the faithful wind-follower!"

At the king's word, strength and vitality were restored to them all. Gopher jumped down from the tree into Merlin's receiving hands. He looked thirty years younger, like he had in his enchanted sleep but even better for there was no selfishness in that face. The pixie, fully restored and larger than before, leaped down alongside them.

There was a joyfully subdued light in all of their eyes as they immediately bowed.

"King Arthur, my friend," Merlin said, "I am honored that –"

"No, no!" the king interrupted, "Get up and do not bow to me, none of you! I am not a king anymore, for I have neither kingdom nor honor that belongs to me. We are fellow servants," he looked at the rodent, "and Gopher, here, is our equal." He nodded his gray head and waved Excalibur over him, adding, "Because of your deeds may your own kind be transplanted to find peace and safety for many years in a land far over the waters that is yet unspoiled."

"Arthur," said a voice that belonged to the Traveling Merchant. He was standing by the tree behind them, looking ageless. There was a glint in his eyes that reminded Gopher of the fire that exuded from Excalibur. "Welcome back, but not for long, is it? Not for you or for any of us. We have all outgrown this world."

"Fyodor the Gift Giver!" Arthur exclaimed. "Thank you for visiting my dreams as I waited for this very day!"

"Indeed, it was my pleasure and those visits gave me time to rest, too! But now," Fyodor, the Traveling Merchant, continued, "there is one last trade to be made, though it is not to be through me."

"You mean Excalibur?" the king said, "It was never mine to begin with."

"True. Nothing really is."

"Do I give it back in the same manner as was done in the old days – by breaking it?" Arthur added, "Yet isn't it unbreakable?"

"By you or me, but not by the One who fashioned it."

Arthur laughed. "Why delay any longer?" He raised the fiery sword over his head with both hands. Raising his face to the sky, he exclaimed, "It is Yours! Do with it as You will, my King and Master!"

That, indeed, was all that was needed.

The blade shattered with a culmination of its light in an explosion, which, had it not been for the covering, would have decimated them all. As it was, it shook the earth with a roar that even shook the air and reverberated through the sky. It felled the tree behind them.

Then utter silence as the brilliance suddenly went out. That was when Gopher realized that it was late at night. As his eyes adjusted to the stars and the sliver of moonlight overhead, a hush of expectation lay over the crowd that Gopher also felt, an expectation like before but this time it was for something even greater, something so great that he felt his heart quiver with both fear and promised exultation.

"Gopher," Merlin whispered, "I have a feeling that you won't need to be riding on my shoulder anymore, but neither of us will miss it – or the cottage."

Farwyll added excitedly but quietly with awe, "And now I know where the wind has been leading: Into the center of itself, but now we go even farther in."

Then it happened, the true Awakening, and it far exceeded any possible expectations of those born of earth, whether of magical origin or not. It didn't come through magic or by joyful music or even in a brilliant light. It simply came about when they saw the rightful King, face to face. It is true that no one could see Him and live – and neither did they survive, not as their old selves at least. In that moment of seeing His face, instead of being unmade, they were all remade as they gladly shed that which was more symbol than substance. But their deaths was not death at all, but real life crowding out the old, so that they could be what the King had intended them to be from the very beginning.

Arthur, who had thrown off his armor and cast down his crown, received another far greater on his head, sparkling with brilliant gems that were set in gold. He was also given white clothes that were even more magnificent.

Gopher, too, was bestowed a crown and new apparel, though only after experiencing the fulfillment of the vision, of being transformed into the kind of man that had been growing in his heart ever since he ate that carrot.

The pixie's crown of green and gold leaves fitted his noble head. His face was now handsome, but there was still mirth in his striking countenance.

Merlin, instead of a crown, held a long scepter, topped by a glowing ruby with his new name on it that only he and the King knew. His face was ageless and beautiful; his eyes, full of compassion and wisdom.

Fyodor the Traveling Merchant, who threw himself down since he had nothing else to throw, was lifted up and embraced by the King Himself – which was the longing of all their hearts, which is often mistaken for lesser things.

In the same way, the entire host cast off the lesser to receive the greater, which was given in an unimaginable abundance that flowed from a heart full of irrepressible love. To try to use words to describe more than that or to tell what happened next is impossible, except to say that they received the fulfillment of their longing and had outgrown this world to receive a greater one, just as children will outgrow their toys and nurseries. Beyond this, even the most accurate description, if such was even possible, would only be misunderstood by our minds that have not yet been perfected by that glory.

The End

Purchase other Black Rose Writing titles at <u>www.blackrosewriting.com/books</u>
and use promo code PRINT to receive a 20% discount.

CPSIA information can be obtained
at www.ICGtesting.com
Printed in the USA
FSOW04n0710160916
25088FS